Sherlock Holmes
and the
Crowned Heads of Europe

By
John H. Watson, M.D.

Edited by
Thomas A. Turley

Illustrated by
Marcia Wilson

MX Publishing
2021

Paperback ISBN
ePub ISBN
PDF ISBN

Published by MX Publishing
335 Princess Park Manor, Royal Drive,
London, N11 3GX
www.mxpublishing.co.uk

Cover design by Brian Belanger

For my Mom

Catherine Coen Turley

(1929-2017)

Who introduced me to Sherlock Holmes

When I was a little older

Contents

Preface and Acknowledgments

By Thomas A. Turley

It is fitting that the last of these four stories, all written near the end of Dr. Watson's life, quotes Sir Edward Grey's prophetic words on the evening of August 3, 1914. Just as Grey feared, the lamps of the Europe he had known would not be lit again. The halcyon days of Queen Victoria, still comfortably ensconced in the memories of Sherlock Holmes and his biographer, were gone for good. No wonder, then, that the tales explore a fateful theme: the "quarter-century of rivalry and tension" that led Great Britain and the German Empire to a ruinous trial of strength.

As the Great Detective noted, events recounted in these stories had "an unfortunate cumulative effect." Frederick III is almost a forgotten figure; yet, in 1870 he foretold the course of German history for the next seventy-five years. The *Liebestod* at Mayerling, the fate of the beautiful Sisi, are remembered as personal tragedies afflicting the stoical old emperor who presided over his decaying realm for seven decades, to the tune of a Strauss waltz. Franz Josef appears within these pages in a rather different light. Watson also reveals the true nationality of "The King of Bohemia," whose even more inept successor was overthrown by rivals who would light the "Balkan powder keg," igniting a cataclysm that would bring down Holmes and Watson's "vanished world."

Prior to taking up his pen in 1928, the Doctor had consulted contemporary sources on the origins and outbreak of the war: Allied propaganda, Emil Ludwig's biography of Kaiser Wilhelm (who wrote his own memoir), Sir Frederick Ponsonby's collection of the Empress Frederick's letters, and the opinions of revisionist historians such as

Sidney Bradshaw Fay. The present editor has augmented these accounts with recent studies. It is remarkable how frequently the words of Watson's royalty, courtiers, soldiers, and doctors are echoed in letters, diaries, and reminiscences found in the published works. For all this confirmation of his work's veracity, the Doctor's chief accomplishment is to show the "human" side of eminent figures his readers have encountered (if at all) only in the history books.

More than ever before in his stories, Watson also shows the human side of Sherlock Holmes. We are privy to his last encounter with The Woman whom (as the Doctor finally reveals to us) Holmes loved. We see Our Hero fail, far more ignominiously and tragically than in the Irene Adler case. And on this occasion, Holmes not only exhibits but admits to his emotions, explaining how he dealt with them as he pursued his work. He reproaches those of us who would define him as a "reasoning machine" incapable of feeling. "The 'great detective,' we are admonished sternly, "must not be equated with the inner man."

Readers may become annoyed by the relative inconclusiveness of the four stories. An unhappy reviewer of "A Scandal in Serbia" (which first appeared in the anthology *The MX Book of New Sherlock Holmes, Part VI*) complained that "There seemed to be no clear outcome to the adventure. . . ." Please note, therefore—as Watson does regretfully in his Introduction—that he and Holmes could not arrest the destined course of history. Despite the best efforts of Our Heroes, in the "fateful summer" of 1914 the cases' "long-delayed results combined with terrible effect." Two shots rang out at Sarajevo, the Great War began, and The Crowned Heads of Europe eventually fell victim to their folly. "Our endeavours," concluded the Doctor, "had but postponed their fall and preserved our own country from immediate destruction. Yet," as he consoled himself, "that in itself is a good deal." Whether it is enough to satisfy readers of these stories I shall leave to them.

* * *

In a way, *Crowned Heads* has been percolating since my childhood, when my mom gave me *A Treasury of Sherlock Holmes*. Although HOUN and SPEC were my favorites, I also liked the stories that dealt with espionage and military matters: NAVA, BRUC, and (of course) LAST. By the time I arrived in graduate school at the University of Tennessee and Vanderbilt, I had developed special interests in Anglo-German relations, Austria-Hungary, and Sarajevo. A student job at the Vanderbilt medical library brought to my attention Sir Morell Mackenzie's fascinating (if sad, polemical, and gruesome) account of "Frederick the Noble's" tragic end. Thus was laid the groundwork for my senescent editing of Watson's notes. I started the project soon after retiring from the Alabama state archives in 2016, having no idea that I would take so long to finish it.

Thanks are first due to several people from my distant past, some of whom, alas, are long deceased. University of Tennessee professors Galen Broeker, Paul Pinckney, and (in a back-handed fashion) Arthur Haas helped to stimulate my interest in the topics covered here, as did my doctoral committee at Vanderbilt. *Crowned Heads* might be seen as a belated sequel to my Ph.D. dissertation on late-Victorian British defense policy, although surely not the one my professors had expected. One more thank-you from those days: my fellow grad student and long-time friend John Shedd, now retired from a distinguished career in education, offered astute criticism and support throughout the project.

On the Sherlockian side, the list is even longer. Publisher Steve Emecz has been unfailingly helpful and encouraging from the time he accepted my first story seven years ago. My friend and editor, David Marcum, not only forgave me for a shockingly un-canonical beginning, but allowed me to invade his own literary universe, as cited in the bibliography. Marcia Wilson, whose striking illustrations illuminate this volume, wrote my first positive review. Her books on

Lestrade and his fellow Scotland Yarders remain a constant inspiration. It is to the most "literary" of Sherlockians (and retired English teacher), Daniel D. Victor, that *Crowned Heads'* readers owe the absence of 117 end notes that swamped the e-book edition of "The Dying Emperor." S.F. Bennett gave that work a kind review, and her depiction of the edgy relationship between the two best-known Holmes brothers has informed my own. Other Sherlockian colleagues I should thank are: Brian Belanger (who designed the book's cover), Derrick Belanger, Richard Gillman, and Chris Redmond.

Several friends and family members (Greg Parsons, Larry White, my daughter Catherine, and my son Bryan) have read and offered encouragement about these stories. So has my wife Paula, who—having gone through this before back in the 'Eighties—was incredibly patient with the hours I spent each day wandering in Sherlockian Europe. Her love sustained me, as it has for over forty years.

February 20, 2021

Introduction

By John H. Watson, M.D.

During the long and distinguished career of Mr. Sherlock Holmes, he was often called upon to serve the British government, or one of the then-reigning monarchies of Europe, in cases of exceeding delicacy. As my friend's biographer, I was required to exercise more than usual discretion when writing of such cases, or those that could be presented to the public if suitably disguised. Some of these disguises were inadequate, I fear, for readers with more than a passing knowledge of contemporary politics. No doubt they identified "Lord Bellinger" or "the Duke of Holderness" with ease, aware that no "King of Bohemia" had ruled an independent kingdom for four centuries. Nevertheless, given the gravity of the events behind them, these mythical figures had to populate my stories in order for them to be read at all.

Surely, the necessity for such feeble deceptions has now passed. Our Victorian statesmen have long since departed the political arena. The Great War has swept away the dynasties of Europe. It becomes possible, therefore, to write openly of cases Holmes could not have permitted to be published, a decade ago, even in the fictionalised manner I have hitherto employed. All but one of the royal principals are dead, and the survivor's reputation cannot be diminished further by my revelations. These four inconclusive cases—two of which date back over thirty years—may finally be recorded, although they shall not be published until well beyond my lifetime. Had the facts behind them been made public at the time, each would have resulted in a European scandal. But in every instance, Holmes's scrupulous investigation remained unresolved, my own account unwritten, and the historical facts behind the cases faded with each passing year.

Until, one fateful summer fourteen years ago, their long-delayed results combined with terrible effect, erupting in the cataclysm that brought down our vanished world.

John H. Watson, M.D.
October 12, 1928

The
Case of the
Dying Emperor

Charlottenburg, Germany

1888

CHAPTER 1

Important Visitors

With the horrors of the Great War still fresh in our memories, it seems strange to recall that Great Britain's relations with Imperial Germany were not always marked by mutual antipathy. Indeed, for much of my lifetime, our traditional European enemies were France and Russia; with the new German Empire, we shared both a common racial heritage and close dynastic ties. The events I shall narrate fatefully transformed that relationship, beginning a quarter-century of rivalry and tension that eventually would lead to war. Naturally, there were many other causes of the breach, but those I shall leave to the historians. In a symbolic sense, the change occurred with the untimely passing of one German Emperor, Frederick III, and his succession by another whose name would become anathema in our new century. This was, of course, "The Kaiser," William II, who led his empire to destruction and engulfed all Europe in its ruin.

The case was also a beginning for my friend Sherlock Holmes, initiating an anti-German espionage campaign that would occupy him, intermittently, until the very week the war began.[1] Unmasking the plot behind William's premature accession was the first of Holmes's diplomatic missions in which I was permitted to take part. For almost forty years, my notes on this case have languished in my tin despatch box. However, with Sir Frederick Ponsonby's recent publication of the Empress Frederick's letters, the time at last seems right to set down the full story, although I shall withhold it from the public for many years to come.

---

[1] An obvious reference to "His Last Bow," which took place on the night of August 2, 1914, two days before Great Britain declared war on Germany.

1

By the time this tale is published, no one will remember, as I do, the splendid impression made by Crown Prince Frederick, our late Queen's son-in-law, in the procession of thirty-two mounted princes that escorted Her Majesty to Westminster Abbey during the Golden Jubilee. One newspaper described the German Heir-Apparent as "a golden, bearded Charlemagne," uniformed in white beneath a silver breastplate, with his nation's eagle on his helm. On that June day in 1887, few of us in the admiring London throng would realise that even as he rode, the gallant horseman was already stricken with a dread disease that would kill him in a twelvemonth.

During the autumn, I followed Frederick's case with interest, for both the British and the German press continued to report it in remarkable detail. Much ink was spilt over an ongoing dispute between the Crown Prince's German doctors and the eminent British laryngologist Morell Mackenzie, called in at the supposed insistence of Frederick's wife Victoria, daughter of our Queen. In May, before the royal couple's trip to London, Dr. Mackenzie had refused to certify the Crown Prince's ailment as cancer, thereby preventing a dangerous operation that the German doctors insisted was the only cure. He later removed the laryngeal tumour orally without invasive surgery. After months of remission, a new tumour was discovered in November while Frederick was visiting the Mediterranean resort San Remo. This time, a diagnosis of laryngeal cancer was confirmed. Thus began a macabre race between Germany's ninety-year-old Emperor, William I, and his son and heir-apparent to see who would die first.

At about that stage, I ceased taking notice of the matter. My young wife Constance, whom I had met in San Francisco and married just a year before, had never thrived amid the dank and filthy fogs of London. In November and December, her health declined even more precipitously than Crown Prince Frederick's, although—like him—she had vainly sought relief at various resorts and spas. Four days after Christmas, I lost her to diphtheria.[2] Abandoning my practice, I returned to Baker Street, where Holmes and Mrs. Hudson showed every kindness and did their utmost to save me from despair. Gradually, settling back into my old routines began to mitigate my grief, especially when I rejoined my friend in our detective partnership. The Birlstone murder, which occurred just after my return, was but the first in a series of exciting cases that carried us through the early months of 1888.

On the morning of the eighth of April, I was late arising, for we had spent the previous afternoon, and most of the evening, involved in that strange affair in Norbury. I came downstairs to find Holmes lounging in his dressing gown, having finished his share of the ample repast prepared for us by Mrs. Hudson. As I approached the table, he snatched away a letter lying on its corner, but not before I saw that it was signed with the initial "M."

"Merely a note from one of the clerks in Whitehall, Watson," he assured me. "I've rung for another pot of coffee, but do hurry with your breakfast. We are expecting important visitors at half past nine."

"Rather early for important visitors," I grumbled. "Is it an important case?"

My friend was saved from replying by our landlady's arrival with the promised pot, which she delivered with a glance that mildly reproved me for my tardiness. Only when she had departed did I receive an answer to my query.

---

[2] Dr. Watson's brief, tragic marriage to Constance Adams was first recorded in W.S. Baring-Gould's biography *Sherlock Holmes of Baker Street* (Avenel, NJ: Wings Books, 1995 [1962]), pp. 67-70. Watson told the story fully in "A Ghost from Christmas Past," which appeared in *The MX Book of New Sherlock Holmes Stories, Part VII: Eliminate the Impossible*, edited by David Marcum (London: MX Publishing, 2017), pp. 130-152. An illustrated version, featuring an original painting by artist Nuné Asatryan, was published in *The Art of Sherlock Holmes: West Palm Beach Edition*, edited by Phil Growick (London: MX Publishing, 2019), pp. 196-211.

"Yes, I believe that you will find it so. We might dress with a bit more care than usual. The person whom these emissaries represent is of indisputable importance." I was intrigued that the usually cavalier consultant—who had denied his aid to Cabinet ministers and even shown the King of Serbia his back—should for once be taking special pains. By now, I knew better than to question him further, but at nine twenty-eight we were dressed to the nines and waiting in our places for Mrs. Hudson's knock.

Precisely two minutes later, that knock sounded, and the good lady announced our visitors with less than her usual aplomb. "Sir Henry Ponsonby," she quavered, "and Sir William Jenner." Holmes and I both rose. In my case, it was with astonishment, for these gentlemen were, respectively, the private secretary and physician-in-ordinary to Her Majesty the Queen.

They looked an oddly matched pair: the ex-soldier tall, bearded, and patrician; the eminent physician squat, bald, and almost toad-like. As befitted his military training, it was Ponsonby who took the lead, responding to Holmes's introduction of me by offering his hand.

"I'm told you were wounded at Maiwand, Surgeon-Major Watson," he said warmly, "fighting with the Berkshires. I regret your loss to the service, although Mr. Holmes must find such a man invaluable in his own work for the Crown."

Holmes cleared his throat meaningfully as I stammered a reply. "It is a little early to discuss that work, Sir Henry," he suggested, waving our visitors to the settee before taking the armchair across from them. I occupied the basket chair beside him, rather than my usual seat before the hearth. "Perhaps you gentleman might begin by explaining how Watson and I may be of service to the Crown today."

General Ponsonby's face showed briefly that he was unaccustomed to instruction, at least from anyone other than the Queen. However, his equanimity remained unruffled, and he nodded to my friend with no hint of condescension.

"Quite so, Mr. Holmes. I must first apprise you both that this visit is purely unofficial, as are any actions on your part that may arise from it. Naturally, Her Majesty's ministers have been informed, but government itself plays no part in the matter. We are not acting for the Queen in her capacity as *monarch*, but (if I may so express it) simply in her position as a *mother*. Of course, you will already have heard this from—"

"From the clerk in Whitehall who notified me you were coming," my friend broke in quickly. "Indeed I have, though I am sadly confused as to Her Majesty's intentions. This proceeding strikes me as irregular from a constitutional perspective."

"Perhaps, sir." This time, the Queen's private secretary regarded Holmes severely. "But it is hardly my place—and certainly not yours—to criticise Her Majesty's intentions or proceedings."

With a snort of disgust, my friend sprang from his chair and glared down from our window on the denizens of Baker Street. It was fully half a minute before he turned back to reply. "And *yet*, Sir Henry," he insisted, "once Watson and I are in Berlin, it is we who must answer to men who could misapprehend Her Majesty's intentions. You may blithely send us off as 'unofficial emissaries.' Chancellor Bismarck may regard us as no more than spies."

At this point, old Sir William Jenner, who had watched the developing acrimony through half-closed eyes, came to my relief. "For God's sake, Ponsonby," he growled. "Would one of you please explain to Dr. Watson what this is all about? The poor man's bewildered."

His intervention stilled the troubled waters. Both disputants gave a shamefaced laugh, and my friend resumed his seat. "My apologies, Doctor," said the General. "Let us start from the beginning. What do you know of Germany's new emperor?"

"From what I've read in the medical reports, his reign will be a short one," I replied. "Cancer of the larynx is a terrible disease."

"You've followed the case closely, then?" asked Jenner, now fully awake for the first time.

"Not for several months. The last thing I recall reading, other than the newspapers, was Sir Morell Mackenzie's defence of his actions in the *British Medical Journal*."

"That was in mid-December. Mackenzie was writing—damned imprudently, in my opinion—to answer the ill-informed and virulent attacks he'd been receiving in the Berlin press. As you know, he and von Bergmann, the leading German surgeon, have been at odds over Frederick's treatment from the first."

"Ah," said Sherlock Holmes. "When doctors quarrel, the outlook for the patient is indeed gloomy! Is Sir Morell Mackenzie a contentious man?"

Jenner shifted restlessly, as though reluctant to reply. "Mackenzie's eminence in *laryngology*," he emphasised, "is universally acknowledged. As a surgeon, he exhibits remarkable deftness and manipulative skill. Also—unlike too many of us—he takes a kindly interest in his patients and seems to inspire them with great trust. As a *colleague*, however. . . ." He turned to Sir Henry for support.

"There is no question," Ponsonby assured us, "of Sir Morell behaving other than honourably and straightforwardly in Germany. However, events have shown that he is perhaps a little indiscreet, a bit too oversensitive, and—yes—inclined to be polemical."

"In short," said Holmes, "you consider his judgement unequal to his skill."

"I believe that puts it fairly. He is in a difficult position for a doctor, due to his patient's extraordinary eminence and the international rivalries involved. We had no idea last May that Mackenzie's participation in the Crown Prince's treatment would set off an Anglo-German press war. Yet, his reputation was already such that Her Majesty hesitated to despatch him."

"Did the Crown Princess not insist upon it?" I enquired. "I recall the Berlin papers attributing the responsibility to her."

"No, Doctor, that is one of many calumnies heaped upon the daughter of our Queen. It is asserted that she distrusts German physicians owing to Prince William's injury at birth, which sadly resulted in a withered arm. But that charge is as baseless as the other. In fact, it was Chancellor Bismarck who ordered Frederick's doctors to find the best laryngologist available, and *they* called in Mackenzie. The Crown Princess did not write to her mother until the following day."

"But *was* Dr. Mackenzie the best choice?" asked Sherlock Holmes. "As I understand the matter, he disputed the original cancer diagnosis and opposed the operations recommended by the German doctors, both in May and in November. With the result that the Emperor is now a dying man."

Again, Sir William Jenner showed discomfort. "The course of events was not that simple, Mr. Holmes. In May, Mackenzie could find no conclusive evidence of cancer. Indeed, its presence remained unconfirmed in five tissue samples later removed from Frederick's larynx, the last as recently as January. Those microscopic evaluations were conducted by Professor Virchow, the greatest pathologist now living. Even the Germans admit that it has been a baffling case. But the operation they proposed in November—complete excision of the larynx—would have been far more likely to kill their patient than to cure him. Its survival rate is very low, and even if successful it would have left Frederick in no fit condition to rule Germany."

"The Crown Prince himself rejected that option, Mr. Holmes," put in Sir Henry Ponsonby. "He did agree to undergo a tracheotomy, in order to assist his breathing, when the cancer was sufficiently advanced. That procedure was performed in February, a month before Frederick ascended to the throne. Alas, his condition since that time has continued to deteriorate."

"Then what can be the purpose of our journey?" wondered Holmes. "It appears that His Imperial Majesty has passed beyond whatever aid we can provide."

"Regrettably, sir, that may be so," Ponsonby admitted, "but you and Dr. Watson may still be of service to your Queen."

"How?" my friend demanded, with a gesture of ill-suppressed impatience.

"Later this month, Her Majesty, who has been on holiday in Florence, proposes to visit the Emperor and Empress before returning home. Given the state of Anglo-German relations, her plans have aroused great uneasiness in both London and Berlin. Unfortunately, even the Prime Minister cannot dissuade her. We should like you gentlemen, therefore, to precede the Queen to Germany, in order to assess the situation in Charlottenburg before her arrival."

"'Unofficial emissaries,' Watson, as my Whitehall correspondent put it."

"For Surgeon-Major Watson," laughed the General, "a better analogy would be 'reconnaissance by skirmishers.'" All three men, to my dismay, gazed at me expectantly.

"I doubt, Sir Henry, that I would pass muster as a diplomatic skirmisher."

"Perhaps not," replied Sir William Jenner, "but you *are* a doctor. And at this juncture, a doctor's arrival at the palace will seem more natural than a diplomat's."

"But how can I possibly assist? The most renowned specialists from both countries are already in attendance."

"No special expertise is needed, Doctor," Jenner answered, "only your impressions as a qualified observer. Even now, for example, the Empress writes to her mother as though Frederick may recover, or at worst have months or even years before him. Is her attitude mere wishful thinking? Is Sir Morell misleading her? Or do the medical facts justify her confidence?"

8

"Will Watson and I have access to His Majesty?" Holmes queried.

"Mackenzie is in charge of the case, and usually he sees the Emperor apart from his German colleagues. He has agreed—reluctantly—to cooperate in your investigation."

"It is imperative, gentlemen," urged Sir Henry Ponsonby, "that we fully understand the Emperor's condition. The future course of Great Britain's relations with the German Empire will depend on his prognosis."

My friend groaned in response to this pronouncement. Rising from his chair, he took from the mantelpiece a box of fine Havanas he had procured for the occasion. The General and I accepted one; Jenner declined; and Holmes replaced the box after choosing a cigar himself. Once the three of us were smoking peaceably, the detective made his reply to Ponsonby.

"Does it truly matter, Sir Henry, who sits on the German throne?" He waved his cigar dismissively. "Bismarck has held the power in Berlin for a quarter of a century. He has dominated all Europe for a decade. Whether the Emperor Frederick lives or dies, are those facts likely to be altered?"

"Her Majesty believes so, Mr. Holmes. She has always regarded her son-in-law as the best hope of liberalising Germany. In the early years of his marriage, Frederick spent much time in England; he sincerely admires our institutions. Although old Emperor William never allowed him a political role, as Crown Prince he spoke publicly against the Iron Chancellor's militarism, anti-Semitism, and restrictions on freedom of the press. We understand that Frederick wrote an edict, prior to his accession, that would limit the powers of the emperor and chancellor. If effected, it would transform the empire into a constitutional monarchy on British lines."

"But this decree has not been published?"

"Not as yet. The Emperor's accession manifesto mentioned no immediate changes, and he sent a conciliatory letter inviting Bismarck to remain in office. Their relations are superficially correct, and until recently each man seemed content to bide his time."

"The question is, how much time *have* they?" rumbled Sir William Jenner. "Frederick has a mortal illness. The Chancellor is ailing and just turned seventy-three."

"A race to the grave," my friend remarked sardonically.

"A race of grave import to Europe's future, sir," snapped Ponsonby. "Behind the scenes, Bismarck has worked for months to undermine the Emperor and Empress. Last November, the doctors' private report on Frederick's illness was somehow published in the court gazette. It included the speculation that he might have syphilis! The official press depicts the Emperor as a doomed man, dominated by his English wife, whose chosen doctor thwarted the surgery that might have saved his life."

"You feel certain that Bismarck inspires these attacks?"

"Not a word is published in Berlin without the Chancellor's approval. The Prime Minister has long deplored his vast, corrupt influence on the German press."

"Unfortunately," Jenner added, "he also has a willing tool in Crown Prince William, who supports the position of the German doctors. His conduct towards his parents has been infamous! In November, when Frederick would not agree to the removal of his larynx, the young man traveled to San Remo and made quite a scene, trying to force the operation on his father. Then, with Bismarck's aid, he persuaded his grandfather to name him—instead of Frederick— regent in case of the old man's incapacitation. William's sycophants already treat him as emperor in all but name. The Chancellor has no scruples about flattering his vanity."

"Infamous, indeed," Holmes murmured. "So, whenever Frederick passes from the scene, the prospect of a liberal Germany dies with him, and the Bismarckian principles of 'Blood and Iron' will be secure. Is that the essence of Her Majesty's concern?"

"Properly speaking, that is her government's concern," General Ponsonby replied. "The Queen's personal interest is in learning how long her son-in-law is likely to survive. Yet, I cannot deny Her Majesty's hope that time remains to accomplish the reforms that Frederick and her daughter cherish."

"Which would greatly diminish Bismarck's power," my friend noted. "Obviously, it is in his interest to speed his young disciple's accession to the throne."

"Pardon me, Sir Henry," I now interposed. "Has not the contest between Emperor and Chancellor already been decided? The papers are full of Bismarck's intention to resign over the impending Sandro marriage."

"Possibly, Doctor," Ponsonby agreed, "though intentions do not always end in resignations. The marriage crisis is another reason for anxiety over the Queen's proposed visit to Berlin."

"What, pray tell, is a 'Sandro?'" wondered Holmes.

"Prince Alexander of Battenberg," I reminded him, delighted for once to have the advantage of my friend. "You remember: the former ruler of Bulgaria, who defeated our friend King Milan in the war of '85. His elder brother married Beatrice, the Queen's youngest daughter. Alexander is called 'Sandro' within the royal family."

"Thank you, Watson, I had quite forgotten him." Sherlock Holmes seemed slightly nettled. "How fortunate that your obsession with royalty is there to cover any lapses on my part. So, Sir Henry, whom does 'Sandro' intend to marry, and why do his prospects of connubial bliss arouse dismay in diplomatic circles?"

"The Prince's engagement to Frederick's second daughter, Princess Viktoria ["*another* Victoria!" lamented Holmes], is rumoured to be imminent. The Chancellor has threatened to leave office if a betrothal is announced. He interprets the marriage as a plot by the Empress and her mother to embroil Germany with Russia. As you recall, it was the Tsar who sponsored the Bulgarian coup that overthrew Prince Alexander."

11

"No doubt," my friend said blandly. "And *does* the Queen support the match?"

"Her Majesty has no objection to the Prince, but he is said to be enamoured of an actress. In any case, she has advised her daughter not to proceed without the consent of Crown Prince William, who is supporting Bismarck's opposition to his parents' wishes. Whether the Empress is set upon the marriage, and whether the Iron Chancellor would then carry out his threat of resignation, will likewise be subjects for your investigation."

"Dear me," said Holmes, "we are developing quite an agenda!"

"The crux of the matter is this," intoned Sir William Jenner. "Is Frederick's health still good enough for him to serve—at least in the foreseeable future—as a counterweight to Bismarck? If so, how long is that situation likely to continue?"

"The Chancellor, for all his faults, is a known quantity," Ponsonby concluded. "Since 1871, when Germany united, his sagacious foreign policy has kept the peace in Europe and been invaluable to British interests as a stabilising force. Crown Prince William, I regret to say, allies himself with men who would abandon Bismarck's prudence and launch preventive wars on those they deem to be the empire's enemies. For Great Britain, Mr. Holmes, the question now becomes: How soon must we contend with an erratic, untried, and possibly dangerous young ruler whose nation has grown strong enough to challenge us, and will grow stronger still? Under Frederick III, we can still regard the German Empire as a friendly Power. Under William II, will it be a friend, a rival, or an enemy?"

Holmes sighed and came slowly to his feet, dropping his cigar into the coal scuttle. "Well, gentlemen, you have given us much to ponder as we depart for Berlin. I cannot promise answers to all the questions you have posed, but Watson and I will do our best. To whom do we report?"

"Mackenzie reports by telegram to Dr. Reid, my colleague at the palace," replied Jenner. "He keeps Her Majesty apprised of the

Emperor's medical condition. However, I expect that much of the information you provide will be political in nature."

"Those reports you may address to me," said Ponsonby. "Sir Edward Malet is aware of your mission, but do not involve the embassy unless an emergency arises. It is best for this matter to remain entirely unofficial."

"Of course. How soon do we begin our journey?"

"We had hoped that you would leave tomorrow morning, allowing your arrival in Charlottenburg by Tuesday afternoon. I have your itinerary here from—"

"*Thank* you, Sir Henry," Holmes once more interrupted, taking the folded document before Ponsonby could complete his thought. He guided the Queen's emissaries to our door, ushering them onto the landing with "We shall be in touch!" as his only parting word. Not knowing then that my friend was determined to forestall any mention of his brother Mycroft (whom I had yet to meet), I could only marvel at his lack of awe in the presence of great men. Even now, I have not decided whether it is a mark of his own greatness—or rather the reverse.

CHAPTER 2

An Evening in Charlottenburg

Early on the afternoon of April tenth, Sherlock Holmes and I were comfortably ensconced inside a spacious, velvet-lined compartment, while our express rolled over what my friend unkindly called "the featureless north German plain." Having enjoyed a delicious and satisfying luncheon, and noting that we were on schedule for Berlin, I could not fail to be impressed by the luxury and efficiency of German railways. I saw, on consulting my *Baedeker*, that we were approaching Magdeburg—once a stronghold of Reformation Lutheranism, now the headquarters of an army corps. I pointed out to Holmes the great citadel built upon an island in the middle of the Elbe, with bridges extended to both banks and bastions advanced to fortify the town in all directions. The very symbol of German military might!

My companion only grunted. Although this journey was my first lengthy one with Sherlock Holmes, I was aware that he valued rail travel chiefly as an opportunity for undistracted thought. He had said little since departing Hanover, engrossed in the voluminous materials provided by his contact in Whitehall. As always, he had rebuffed my efforts to discuss our mission before he had fully mastered all the facts.

Finally, Holmes abandoned his papers with a sigh, smiling ruefully at the desiccated contents of his luncheon tray, delivered from the dining car but soon forgotten.

"What are you reading, Watson?"

I handed him my book: Melville Landon's *The Franco-Prussian War in a Nutshell*, purchased several years before in San Francisco. "I had not remembered," I remarked as he ruffled through its pages, "that Frederick, as crown prince, played so heroic a role in the Wars of German Unification. His army's arrival at Königgrätz saved the battle for the Prussians, and later he won several victories against the French."

My friend shook his head. "Alas, Watson, his wartime service may prove to be the Emperor's only lasting legacy. It seems ironic that a man of his temperament should win fame as a soldier. For all his valour, Frederick had hoped to unite Germany by peaceful means. He and his wife opposed Bismarck's policy of 'Blood and Iron.'

"He has had a long wait for the throne."

"Yes, it is sad to see the years of a man's prime wasted. Our own Albert Edward is hardly an example of patience in adversity."

I laughed, recalling Holmes's disdain for the Prince of Wales. "But Crown Prince William seems more impatient still."

"Indeed. I had an interesting conversation in Whitehall on Sunday concerning that young man—if nine-and-twenty can really be considered 'young.'"

"I wondered where you'd gone. Mrs. Hudson was not pleased that you missed luncheon, especially after you evicted our visitors before she could serve tea."

"Tea, so soon after breakfast?" My friend had little time for the travails of our good landlady. "Doctor, do you know a surgeon named John Erichsen?"

"Only by reputation, Holmes. He is past president of the Royal College of Surgeons and has an appointment to the palace. We seldom move in the same circles! An elderly man now, I believe, originally Danish. Was he the person whom you met in Whitehall?"

"No, my informant was in government. However, he showed me some notes that Erichsen had written, recording the results of a long-distance consultation last year with Prince William's surgeons. One was Professor von Bergmann, the chief opponent of Mackenzie. Erichsen's memorandum outlined possible mental effects of the chronic inner ear infections William has suffered since his youth. I have a copy of it here."

I read the document with growing horror. "Good heavens, Holmes! It says here that the Prince 'is not, and never will be, a normal man!' That 'when angry, he will be incapable of forming a reasoned or temperate judgement.' That 'some of his actions will probably be those of a man not wholly sane'! Has the German government been apprised of this report?"

"Not entirely, Watson. Erichsen felt it prudent not to communicate his concern for William's sanity, so he restricted

16

himself to a purely medical diagnosis of the case. His conclusion was that should the purulent discharge from the diseased ears ever cease, the infection could attack Prince William's brain—in which case he would be in grave peril not only of his mind but of his life. Do you think that outcome likely?"

"I would hardly set my judgement against that of an expert in the field. But if there is even a chance that Erichsen is right, then William's accession would be a danger to all Europe!"

"The Prime Minister agrees. His private secretary has instructed me to deliver this document to Bismarck when we reach Berlin. Perhaps it will convince him that the devil he knows—Frederick III, that is to say—is preferable to the one who would succeed him. I am to moot the idea of setting the Crown Prince aside and passing the succession to his brother Henry, either directly or as regent for William's little son."

"Let us hope the Chancellor sees the wisdom of that course." It was I who sat silent as we rode through Brandenburg, the ancient seat of Hohenzollern power. All too soon, I feared, that royal house and its great empire would be ruled by a potential madman.

"What a *dull*-looking town," sighed Sherlock Holmes. "What is *that* monstrosity?"

"The *Rathaus*," I replied, glancing at my guide-book. "It dates from the fourteenth century, but—as even *Baedeker* admits—was 'disfigured' by its modernisation in the eighteenth."

My friend gave one of his sardonic barks. "How much longer, Doctor, before we arrive in Berlin?"

"About an hour." Typically, Holmes had been too absorbed in his research to consult anything so mundane as a timetable.

"Time enough to tell you of my second interview on Sunday. It was with another laryngologist, Dr. Felix Semon. I was able to see him just prior to his departure for the Isle of Wight." In response to his glance of enquiry, I could only shake my head.

17

"Dr. Semon is a German Jew, who has lived in England since the middle 'Seventies. He is still a young man and was once Mackenzie's protégé, but he described his mentor's character in *most* demeaning terms. In Semon's view, Sir Morell is 'a money-grubbing charlatan'! Realising from his first examination that Frederick was doomed, he sent the dying man from Germany to Britain, then to the Alps and Riviera, merely to increase his travel fees and the scenic beauty of their periodic consultations. Mackenzie also, Semon said, colluded with Empress Victoria to hide the nature of her husband's illness until it could no longer be denied."

"Surely, all that is preposterous, Holmes!"

"Is it? Well, Watson, I should normally discount the opinion of a rival, for Semon admitted that he had hoped to treat the Emperor himself last year in London. He is also a childhood friend of Herbert Bismarck, the Chancellor's son, and regularly primes him with information to use against Mackenzie. Yet, however venomous, Dr. Semon remains a leading laryngologist; and he confirmed the German doctors on the one essential point."

"Which is?"

"That the removal of his larynx—despite its probability of killing Frederick or reducing him what Semon called 'a deplorable, even suicidal mental state'—was nonetheless the *only* possibility of saving him. Now, even with his tracheotomy, the Emperor will survive two years at best, in what Semon described as 'ever-increasing agony.' If that is the prognosis, it places the actions of Prince William in a rather different light."

"How so? He tried to force an exceedingly dangerous operation on his father, and when that failed, usurped his position as putative regent. Given what we now know of the young man's mental state, such actions to me seem quite in character."

"As for 'usurping the regency,' Watson, how could Frederick have exercised the powers of a regent from San Remo? Whatever her motives, the fact that the Crown Princess kept the heir to the throne out of Berlin for nine full months, while his aged father slid slowly towards the grave, created a political vacuum. It was not unreasonable, given the circumstances, that Bismarck proposed the old emperor's grandson as the best option to take his father's place."

"From that perspective, I suppose you have a point."

Holmes glanced fleetingly outside our window, where a tower commemorated the Brandenburgers killed in Bismarck's wars. "Remember, Doctor," he reminded me, "that we have received conflicting information from many different sources, all of whom have interests of their own. We must weigh this information *without prejudice*, and draw our own conclusions when we reach Berlin."

By this time, the environs of that great city could be seen on the horizon. We arrived at its western terminal at sunset and, after retrieving our baggage, hired a diligence for the short drive into Charlottenburg. Our route took us through the Thiergarten, Berlin's most famous public park. Had I been less weary, I might have been receptive to its beauties. As matters stood, the overhanging trees seemed ominous in twilight, and the well-wrought statues of Prussian kings and poets vaguely threatening. Holmes, to my relief, was as hungry as I was when we reached the town. A fine dinner of pork knuckles and sauerkraut, washed down with a tankard of beer, soon dispelled my gloomy thoughts. Departing the café, we traversed a gracefully arched bridge over the canal, with the lights from Schloss Charlottenburg reflected in the darkening water.

The Schloss itself was a study in Rococo elegance. Designed two centuries before, it was built of yellow stone, with two front wings in opposition to its central portion, which was crowned by a rather outsized dome. Unlike the Gothic fantasies of Bavaria's mad king, the impression Charlottenburg conveyed was of serenity and grace, qualities that seemed appropriate for the enlightened ruler we had come to meet.

Yet, all was not serene when we arrived. A crowd had gathered in the well-lit street outside the gates, where a large man in clerical garb was delivering a stentorian address. With a sharp word to the driver, Holmes halted our equipage and proposed that we proceed on foot.

"That is Adolf Stoecker, he informed me, "a right-wing politician and notorious anti-Semite. The former emperor appointed him court chaplain." He restrained me from approaching any closer. "Let us stop and hear whatever poison he is spewing."

My German was too poor to follow the harangue; but my interpreter reported that Pastor Stoecker was roundly denouncing the English, the doctors, and the Jews—who in his exposition all seemed intermixed. We heard encouraging shouts from his audience of: *"Nieder mit den Juden!"*, *"Nieder mit den Englisch!"*, and *"Nieder mit Moritz Markovicz!"* At this last bit of invective, Sherlock Holmes broke into a hearty laugh.

"It appears, Watson, that the Berlin newspapers—along with the venerable man of God before us—have just learned that the English doctor attending their emperor is actually a Jew! His real name is now asserted to be 'Moritz Markovicz.'"

"But that is nonsense, Holmes!"

"Of course it is." Momentarily distracted, he looked beyond Stoecker towards the palace gates, where the *Gardes du Corps* had remained stolidly oblivious to the uproar in the street. Now the guards were letting through a young, clean-shaven man who set out in our direction. Having his back to the crowd, he failed to attract either their attention or the orator's.

"Dr. Watson?" With a pleasant smile, this harbinger—who was obviously British—looked uncertainly between myself and my companion. I nodded in acknowledgement.

"Mark Hovell," he informed us. "I am assistant surgeon to Sir Morell Mackenzie."

"How do you do, Dr. Hovell? May I introduce Mr. Sherlock Holmes?"

"Delighted, Mr. Holmes," he said, "but I am likewise 'mister'— a humble M.R.C.S. Welcome to Charlottenburg! Sir Morell has asked me to offer his regrets. We weren't quite sure when to expect you, and he has an audience with the Emperor this evening."

"An audience, you say?" my friend enquired, "rather than a consultation?"

"In this instance, it was not a medical matter, but a private one." Our new acquaintance seemed slightly ill at ease. "Shall we go in? I presume that cab is yours."

Holmes did not reply, and I noticed that the booming voice in the background had now fallen silent. I turned to find Stoecker and his flock regarding the three of us with undisguised hostility.

"*Also*, Herr Hovell," intoned the formidable cleric in heavily accented English. "You bring *more* Englishmen into the Schloss? More Jews to assist Moritz Markovicz in murdering our Kaiser?"

Hovell remained admirably calm, despite the angry murmurs. "You know perfectly well, Parson Stoecker, that Sir *Morell Mackenzie* is not a Jew. Nor are these gentlemen. And, yes, I am bringing them into the palace."

"*Are* you?" jeered the Parson, his porcine face creased into an evil smile. "Well, now, perhaps we will not permit it. Perhaps, when Kronprinz Wilhelm comes into his own, you Englishmen and Jews will all be dealt with!"

"Perhaps so," Hovell steadily replied, "but you may rest assured that Sir Morell and I are working to postpone that day as long as possible."

"*Ja*, we know what you and Moritz Markovicz are working for!" the cleric snarled. "But tonight, *so Gott will*, we will keep you here with us!" He gestured briefly; and his followers (most of whom were burly, ill-dressed Aryans of military age) quickly dispersed to block us from the palace gates.

"I think not," said Mark Hovell. Taking from his pocket a small whistle, he blew three long blasts. Instantly, we heard orders being

21

shouted from the courtyard of Charlottenburg, and a squadron of the *Gardes du Corps* (with their eagle-crested helmets, glittering cuirasses, and drawn swords) came marching at the double-time. Opening the gates, they pushed through Stoecker's mob and cordoned off our diligence, while their officer respectfully—but firmly—kept the livid clergyman from interfering. Hovell, Holmes, and I quickly climbed into the cab; and a moment later we found ourselves before the entrance to the Emperor Frederick's palace.

Its imposing doors had been thrown open; and a balding, bearded man, of wary and distrustful mien, stood waiting in the outer hall to greet us. "Good evening, gentlemen!" he called out cordially, bowing and clicking his heels in a parody of Teutonic salutation. "I am Count Radolinski, the Kaiser's *Hof-Marschall.*

"I am also," he confided, when Holmes and I had entered the hall and introduced ourselves, "the resident spy for Chancellor Bismarck, just as you gentlemen"—with a genial nod, he included Hovell—"are the resident spies for Queen Victoria. *Jawohl*, Herr Holmes, we have heard of you in Germany! Why else would a noted detective travel to Charlottenburg, mere days before his sovereign is scheduled to arrive? My apologies for that disturbance in the street—although, I must confess, I had some part in organising it."

My friend smiled but did not bother to reply, for it was clear, as we passed through the Baroque splendour of several drawing rooms, that the Count was in full flow and did not require an answer. Holmes, I knew, was mentally recording every detail of his chatter. Only once was Radolinski distracted: when we came into a beautifully frescoed room that was filled with shelves and cabinets of blue-and-white ceramic pottery ("Ah, the Porcelain Chamber!"). Many of its finest pieces were Chinese and might, a few years hence, have aroused the acquisitive urges of our future adversary Baron Gruner. Others (Radolinski told us) were locally produced at the royal porcelain factory nearby.

Eventually, we arrived at a grand staircase, where the Count suggested to Hovell that he rejoin the Emperor and Sir Morell Mackenzie ("I believe they are expecting you") while he showed us to our rooms. The young surgeon bowed and departed, promising to see us the next morning. As we ascended, our guide resumed his monologue.

"I am sorry that the great English doctor could not welcome you, but tonight His Imperial Majesty is investing him with the Cross and Star of the Hohenzollern Order. Herr Hovell is to receive a somewhat lesser medal. It is our custom here in Germany to decorate the surgeons who have done so excellent a job of murdering our Kaiser! You, Herr Doktor Watson, may hope for a bauble in your turn.

"Later tonight," he warned us as we crossed a landing, "I suspect that you will meet the Kaiserin. She, too, gentlemen, has played her part. Having swallowed every lie the English doctor told her, for thirteen months she pretended to all that dear Fritz was only slightly ailing, that he would soon be well! All through the past autumn, she climbed in the Alps, *tête-à-tête* with her 'English Sportsman,' or toured art galleries in Venice, keeping our German surgeons always at bay. Then, when the Crown Prince's true condition became known at last, we were told that no operation would take place! Even after the tracheotomy in February, Her Highness assured me that her husband was to be *completely cured*, for Sir Morell was now *quite* certain that it was only *perichondritis*, which is not in any way malignant!"

In response to my friend's raised eyebrows, I quietly mouthed, "A severe form of inflammation, Holmes." Meanwhile, I was inwardly fuming at this blackguard's slander of the Empress, but Radolinski rattled on obliviously. When we finally turned into a long and richly panelled corridor, with great chandeliers illuminating works of heraldry upon its walls, he turned to face us with an expression of dismay.

"But *now*—having dragged her poor invalid from death's door to the throne—she will surely make an end of him over this Battenberg marriage! A week ago, after the Chancellor had finally talked the Kaiser out of it, Her Majesty intercepted the telegram telling Prince Alexander not to come. Back she stormed to her sick husband and—*in front of witnesses*—accused him of breaking his sworn promise and their poor daughter's heart! So humiliated was the Kaiser that he lost patience, banged his fists upon the table, tore the bandage from his throat and tried to speak (only the words *'Leave me alone!'* were clearly heard), and finally stamped his foot and pointed to the door. The Kaiserin, for once, was worsted; she retired white as a sheet!"

Taken aback when neither Holmes nor I responded to this lurid tale, the Count concluded rather lamely, "And here, gentlemen, are your rooms." Although less opulent than the public areas downstairs, our small chambers looked comfortable enough, and two of the palace servants were already unpacking our belongings. We bowed our thanks.

"You have been an entertaining host, Count Radolinski," my friend told him. "As you seem resolved to consider us adversaries, may I say that it will be an honour to cross swords with such a one."

"*Friendly* adveraries, I hope, Herr Holmes!" cried Radolinski. He lowered his voice as the servants made their obeisance and departed. "Do not, I beg you, be deceived into doubting that your valets understand the English language, though they may show no sign of doing so. These walls," he added conspiratorially, *have ears!"*

"Well, Holmes," I said crossly, when, after a last exaggerated heel-click, the Count had finally left us, "we know there is at least *one* scoundrel in Charlottenburg!" We were lounging in armchairs before the fireplace in my room, sipping the fine whisky my untrustworthy valet had left upon the sideboard. Assuming the decanter was not poisoned, we might almost have been at home in Baker Street.

"Did you think so?" Holmes airily replied, puffing the old brier pipe he used when travelling. "The *Hof-Marschall* impressed me as an

24

honest rogue, quite transparent in his knavery. Recall your Shakespeare, Watson! It is the villain who 'smiles and smiles' we must beware."

"Who," I wondered, "is this 'English Sportsman'? Radolinski had the impudence to hint at some impropriety between him and the Empress."

"Would that be so surprising?" As ever, my friend was willing to think poorly of the fair sex. "Her Majesty is a relatively young and handsome woman, whose husband has been too ill for months to share her bed. Count von Seckendorff—for that is the gentleman's name—is said to possess both physical attractions and seductive charm. He is from an old Franconian family, but served with our army in India and Egypt, which accounts for his *nom de guerre*. According to my Whitehall correspondent, there were indeed rumours of a liaison between them in the Italian Alps last year. One wag even called Seckendorff 'the Crown Princess's right hand—and something more besides!'"

"Holmes! You are speaking of the daughter of our Queen!"

"I would fain speak ill of neither Queen nor Empress, but have *all* the queens of history been paragons of virtue?"

"All the same—" I countered, when I was interrupted by a knock upon my door.

"Herr Holmes?"

The two of us exchanged a weary look, for it was nearly ten o'clock at the end of a long and tiring day. Then I recalled Radolinski saying that an audience with the Empress might keep us from our beds. With a sigh, I rose and admitted our unwelcome visitor.

The man who entered was strongly built and handsome, his russet beard agreeably tinged with grey. He seemed oddly familiar, and I searched my memory on the chance that we had met somewhere in India. Later, I realised that he bore a passing resemblance to John Brown, the Queen's Scots servant. His clothes and bearing, however, were undoubtedly a gentleman's.

25

"I am Count von Seckendorff," he informed us, quite unnecessarily. "Her Imperial Majesty apologises for the lateness of this summons, but she wonders if you could meet with her for a brief time before retiring." He gazed on us benignly, with no indication that he had heard himself discussed, still less of "seductive charm."

"We are always at Her Majesty's service," answered Sherlock Holmes. After taking a moment to tidy our apparel, we followed Seckendorff along the corridor, down another gilded staircase, through more splendid rooms, and up the servants' stair into a narrow hallway, which ended at a whitewashed door. When our escort opened it, we entered a small and plainly furnished ante-room, where the Empress Victoria awaited. Her chamberlain retired into a corner, where he did his best to look invisible.

The consort of Frederick III was then in her late forties. Like her mother, she was short and statuesque, with dark hair and an unlined, rounded face that allowed her to look younger than her years. Her smile was gracious yet somehow insincere, as though smiling had become a tiresome duty that no longer reflected her emotions.

"Thank you, gentlemen," she said, "for coming at so late an hour. As Sir Henry has telegraphed that you are *unofficial* visitors—his wife Mary is my *dearest* friend—I thought it best to see you when our meeting would arouse the *least* attention. I believe that you have not spoken with Sir Morell Mackenzie?"

"Not as yet, Your Majesty," Holmes admitted. "We expect to meet that gentleman tomorrow morning."

"We owe *so* much to him," the Empress sighed. "The bleeding from my husband's awful tracheotomy has been *much* better since Sir Morell changed the tube! And I am *very* thankful that Professor Virchow's reports are as good as they have been. The Emperor is anxious to be *cured* and to recover!

"Of *course*," she added, when Holmes and I remained uncomfortably silent, "you will hear that this Professor *Waldeger* has found undoubted evidence of cancer—an immense quantity of *nest-*

cells in Fritz's sputum.[3] This *quite* convinces Professor von Bergmann and the other *German* doctors. Yet, Sir Morell tells me that *Virchow* is the great pathologist, and *he* does not consider mere nest-cells as *undoubted* proof!"

"Perhaps, Your Majesty," I carefully replied, "we can clarify that difference of opinion with Sir Morell tomorrow."

"*Please* do, Dr. Watson." Her Majesty offered me a grateful look before her voice turned scornful. "Did you know that von Bergmann has told Willy that his Papa has *six months to live?*" She exchanged a glance, I saw, with Seckendorff; and Sherlock Holmes suppressed a smile.

"I confess to you, gentlemen, my *boundless* disappointment in my eldest son." The Empress began moving restlessly about the room, no longer regarding us directly. "Naturally, it has *never* been easy for me here. When I married Fritz and first came to Berlin, we hoped that dear Papa's dream of a *liberal*, united Germany could still be realised. But from the *first*, the Prussian court saw me only as 'the *English* woman'—suspected of *free-thinking* tendencies, of *cosmopolitan* and *humanitarian* sentiments—all *abominations* in the eyes of those who are all-powerful now! For all of Willy's life, Fritz and I have worked *tirelessly* to educate him in the *constitutional* tradition so dear to my own parents, so that he would one day become the liberal, enlightened ruler *they* wished for him to be."

Turning from the window, she raised her hands in a gesture of baffled resignation. "But it seems *evident*, gentlemen, that we have *failed!* The conservatives, the court, the military, the government people—in short, the *Bismarck* clique!—all have rallied now to *William!* They criticise; they slander us; they intrigue behind our backs. They treat our son as though he was *already* emperor! And all this adulation has *quite* gone to his head. Not a *word* of sympathy or

---

[3] It was actually Dr. Heinrich von Waldeyer who found cancer "nest cells" in Frederick's sputum in early March 1888. Yet, even on the 24th, Mackenzie wrote to Reid that the illness might still be perichondritis.

affection does Willy offer us, and it distresses me to see what *airs* he gives himself."

"Possibly, ma'am," my friend suggested gently, "it would have been wiser to accept that in the end, your son will become a German Emperor, not a King of England."

"*Well*, Mr. Holmes," the Empress huffily replied, "it is *easy* to be wise in hindsight. But even today, I know that the *whole nation*— the *true* people of Germany—are behind my husband in his liberal aims. I *still* believe that Fritz and I may do some good for"—here her voice faltered—"*however* long he reigns. *Oh*, if I could *only* think we had a year before us!" She looked away again, but not before I saw the glint of tears.

"But it is a *hard* thing, gentlemen, to see our *son*, the heir to a great empire, surround himself with the most *reactionary* representatives of Junkerdom! Count von Waldersee, who is soon to head the General Staff, will start a *war* unless Fritz can have him transferred to the provinces. There is also Herr Puttkamer, a politician so *corrupt* that even *Bismarck*—his own brother-in-law—cannot abide him! You have already, I am told, met that *odious* man Stoecker, whom Willy calls 'a second *Luther!*'"

"We had that pleasure earlier this evening," Holmes said drily, "but were rescued in a timely manner by the palace guard."

Her Majesty surprised us with a girlish laugh. "We *thought* you might have trouble from that quarter! The Emperor sent an order to alert the *Gardes du Corps*. We are not, you see, *altogether* without allies!"

"What of the Chancellor?" asked Sherlock Holmes. "It is no secret that he and your husband do not see eye-to-eye. Has His Majesty found Bismarck possible to manage?"

"Their relations are *better* than before Fritz ascended to the throne," the Empress conceded. "One *must* respect the man's accomplishments. But you cannot expect from *him* that which modern Germany thirsts for: *peace* among its classes, friendly relations with

28

its neighbours, *liberty* and the respect for *right* instead of force, and the protection of the *whole* against the strong. None of *those* blessings will ever come from our 'Iron Chancellor.' *Despotism* is the essence of his being!

"Take this *crisis* over poor Moretta's marriage," she went on, resuming her agitated pacing. "Prince Bismarck has orchestrated it merely to place *me* in the wrong! My own dear Mama tells me that the Tsar no longer cares a *straw* whom Sandro marries! There is no prospect *whatever* of his returning to Bulgaria, although I *had* hoped to place him there, with Moretta at his side, to give Germany and England a secure presence in the Balkans. Yet, the Chancellor casts me as an *hysterical mother*, ready to risk war with Russia merely to ensure her daughter's happiness! It is *all* a plan to ingratiate himself again with *Willy*—who hates Sandro—after the two fell out last November. Naturally, it is *Bismarck's* version that everyone believes! Even my husband complains that I 'give him no peace' about the matter."

"Yes, we heard something of the sort tonight."

Her Majesty regarded my friend with mild distaste. "No doubt from our loyal *Hof-Marschall!* As you may *not* be aware, the Chancellor seldom goes out now or mixes in the world. He is *thoroughly* dependent on the tales carried to him by his satellites, which he always *implicitly* believes. So Fritz and I are *quite* used to being spied upon!

"But when he *does* come here," she added, "Prince Bismarck treats us with cold courtesy. At least *he* is able—unlike William—not to look at Fritz as though calculating how much longer he may *live!* Civility is *easy* for him now. He knows that despite his age, he is nearly *certain* to outlast us. What worries the old man, Mr. Holmes, is what comes *after*. Because, you see, the great 'Iron Chancellor' is even more frightened of my son than *I* am!"

Wry amusement fading from her eyes, the Empress nodded graciously in parting. "Gentlemen, I have kept you *far* too long

29

tonight. Forgive my *un-imperial* outspokenness, which dear Mama would *surely* disapprove! But since Mary Ponsonby went home, there are so *few* people here to whom I can speak *openly*. I mean, you understand, people who are *English!*"

We bowed our own way out the door and to the landing, for Her Majesty had asked her chamberlain to remain behind before he took us to our rooms. Once we were alone, I could not forbear to comment on the audience.

"What a remarkable woman, Holmes! I was relieved to find her more realistic about her husband's dire prognosis than at first she seemed."

"No thanks, it appears, to Sir Morell Mackenzie!" my companion snapped. "Indeed, Doctor, the Empress seems to combine her father's intellect with her mother's strength of character. Had Frederick come to the throne a healthy man, *she* would have been the *de facto* ruler of the empire. Instead, thirty years of waiting have all come to naught. It must break her heart to know that Prince Albert's dream of a liberal Germany will not now be fulfilled. Certainly, it will never happen under William II!"

Our talk ended abruptly when Seckendorff emerged. On arriving at the bottom of the stairs, we glimpsed Count Radolinski as he slipped around a corner.

"Please excuse me, gentlemen," our guide said grimly. He was already in pursuit of his rival before adding, "I trust that you can find your own way back."

"Well, Watson," grumbled Sherlock Holmes, "we will leave Counts Rosencrantz and Guildenstern to practice their *duello*. I for one am ready for my bed."

Precisely on cue, our valets emerged from behind the servants' stairway. Bowing wordlessly, they politely gestured in the direction of our rooms. As we followed them through the darkened, empty halls of Schloss Charlottenburg, the only sound I heard was my friend's laughter.

CHAPTER 3

Frederick the Noble

Bright sunlight filtered through my window the next morning, and I awoke to find a tray of coffee, rolls, cheese, and liverwurst upon the beside table. My ubiquitous valet, it seemed, had come and gone again in silence.

Stifling a yawn (for it was half past seven), I looked down upon the palace gardens, which had not been visible the night before. They were designed to replicate an English landscape park, having been converted from the Baroque style a century before. Beyond the central fountain lay a placid lake and wooded paths along the Spree. A fine place for a ramble, I decided, sadly recalling morning walks with Constance through the gardens near Kensington Palace. Alas, those walks had ended all too soon, for my bride now rested in a churchyard by the sea in Brighton. Already our early days together seemed very long ago.

I was rescued from my reminiscences by the sight of a lone figure striding briskly towards the palace, which I first mistook for Sherlock Holmes. No, despite the Inverness cape and soft grey hat, the man was hardly tall enough to be my friend. I surmised that it must be Mackenzie, as I could not imagine any German dressed in such a way. At the same moment, there came a knock upon my door, and I opened it to find Holmes likewise wearing a checked Inverness, along with his deerstalker. I could not withhold an incredulous chuckle.

"Well, either you ran up several flights of stairs, or you have a *Doppelgänger* in the garden!" I led him to the window, but the caped walker had already disappeared.

"No, Doctor," Holmes answered with a slightly puzzled frown, "I came in from the street. I walked to town early this morning, hoping to elude the vigilance of Radolinski's spies. Someone did follow me—likely one of the military attachés—but I lost him before catching a tram into Berlin. There I visited the telegraph office and remained to see the message sent; it was a report to Ponsonby on last night's meeting with the Empress. No doubt Bismarck's agents will bribe or bully the operator into giving them a copy, but at least the report cannot be lost or altered. I see that you have been a slugabed, as usual!"

"By no means; I have consumed an excellent breakfast and half a pot of coffee! Would you like a cup?"

"No, thank you. I enjoyed *Frühstück* in a Charlottenburg café. Do finish dressing quickly, Watson. I expect another interview to occupy our morning." He left me and returned to his own room. I had finished shaving and was knotting my necktie when another knock sounded on the door.

"Dr. Watson?"

This time, it was our new friend Hovell. Having heard him, Holmes soon joined us as well. The assistant surgeon had come to take us to his chief, who, as I suspected, had just returned from an early-morning walk.

After the usual ascents, descents, and wanderings, we arrived in a part of the palace I had not visited before. Here we entered a small but exquisitely shelved and panelled library, which Mackenzie—who had been in residence, of course, for several weeks—had turned into a replica of his consulting-room. Besides his medical treatises, it was adorned with pictures of his family, which vied for space on the handsome desk with a plethora of case notes. Holmes and I sank into a pair of plush armchairs to await the great man's pleasure. He did not keep us waiting long.

Sir Morell Mackenzie was at that time aged fifty. He was spare of face and figure, a bright-eyed, dapper man with thinning hair and the side-whiskers typical of our profession. Although of cheerful countenance, he looked tired and overworked, and I thought that I detected signs of the asthmatic. Hovell told me later that Mackenzie seldom got a full night's rest. I noted with amusement that he appeared to be wearing the order the Emperor had presented him the night before.

"Ah, gentlemen," he greeted us. "I regret that I was not on hand to welcome you last night, but quite unexpectedly I was afforded an audience with His Imperial Majesty. He has—as you see here—honoured me with the Hohenzollern cross and star, which will now accompany my knighthood from the Queen."

After Holmes and I had dutifully expressed our congratulations, Sir Morell politely dismissed his subordinate to attend upon the Emperor. "As you know, Mr. Hovell, he should be dressed by now and will no doubt wish to go down to the Orangery. These gentlemen and I shall join you there presently." He settled himself comfortably behind his desk, regarding us as though we were prospective patients, or perhaps applicants for a position on his staff.

"I understand, Mr. Holmes," Mackenzie said to my companion (who had watched his pontifications with a sardonic eye) that upon arriving last evening you were subjected to an unfortunate reception by a rabble in the street! Was it, as I was told, an anti-Semitic demonstration?"

"It was," the detective replied gravely, "although we ourselves were not initially its targets. I regret, Sir Morell," he added with an impishness only I discerned, "that several crude placards carried by the mob referred to *you* as 'Moritz Markovicz.'"

"That is ridiculous, of course!" the doctor snorted. "Dr. Krause—my one remaining German colleague—is in fact a member of that remarkable race, but my own ancestry is Highland Scots. Nevertheless, gentlemen, I for months have been a victim of the same hostility that you encountered. At the time of the Emperor's accession, there were actual threats upon my life! The *Kölnische Zeitung* has claimed I am afraid to venture from the palace, because the German people would either tear me to pieces or stone me to death! Well, Mr. Holmes, I *did* accompany the Emperor when he visited his capital at the end of March. Naturally, he was greeted with *tremendous* enthusiasm, and I myself was met by the populace with both kindness and respect. Men took off their hats to me, and ladies bowed in the most *friendly* way. We really should not pay too much attention to these ravings of the reptile press!"

Having delivered himself upon that subject, Sir Morell suggested that we proceed to the business of our meeting. "While I am

34

delighted to see you in Charlottenburg, I must confess to having no idea of the *purpose* of your visit."

"Her Majesty's ministers," said Holmes, "have asked us to investigate one or two diplomatic matters that have recently arisen in Berlin, due to their possible impact upon the Queen's intended visit, which will occur later in the month."

"Yes," Mackenzie mused, "there *has* been a good deal of public excitement over Princess Viktoria's proposed marriage. But if your concerns are purely political," he added, "what is another doctor doing here?" His smile of polite enquiry held a touch of frost. Before I could answer, my companion smoothly intervened.

"Dr. Watson's presence provides a 'cloak of plausibility' for our political investigation. He is here, Sir Morell, merely to observe, not to consult with you professionally or to participate directly in the Emperor's treatment."

"I assumed that was the case. Otherwise, London might have been expected to send someone more qualified." For the first time, Mackenzie spoke to me directly. "Forgive me, sir, but I understand that you are simply a retired army surgeon."

Sir Morell probably intended no offense, so I decided to show none. "Your understanding is correct, sir. I served in the late Afghan war. Until recently, I also maintained a private practice."

"Have you any knowledge of, or experience in laryngology?"

"I once examined a suspected case of laryngeal cancer."

"Indeed? How did you undertake to treat the patient?"

"Not feeling myself sufficiently versed in the disease, I sent him to a specialist."

"Very wise of you. And did the gentleman survive?"

"I believe he died, Sir Morell, a short time after I referred him to you."

"To *me?* What was the gentleman's name?"

I told him. "Strictly speaking, he was not a gentleman, but a factory worker. As such, I was told he found himself unable to afford your fee."

"How unfortunate!" To my surprise, Mackenzie seemed genuinely pained. "I make a point of reducing my fees for patients from the lower classes. Surely there was some misunderstanding!

"Well, gentlemen," he concluded in a rather shaken voice, "at least we shall not encounter *that* difficulty in the present case. No doubt you will wish to hear my latest news about the Emperor."

"To be sure," said Sherlock Holmes. "The Queen's physicians have instructed us to request from you a definitive statement of her son-in-law's prognosis, assuming that such a thing is possible."

"So your visit's purpose is medical as well! In this case, sir, a 'definitive statement' is hazardous indeed!" Obviously flustered, Sir Morell turned to me as a potential ally. "As *you* may know, Dr. Watson, the slow progress of laryngeal cancer is widely recognised. The organ's hard, encasing cartilage resists the growth of the disease. *On average*, the duration of life is two years after onset, but there are well-documented instances of untreated patients living three years or even four."

"You are convinced, then," I guardedly enquired, "that the disease *is* cancer, and not perichondritis? I ask only because others with whom we have spoken seem unsure upon that point." (*"Excellent, Watson!"* I heard my friend mutter.)

"I never said it was *not* cancer," cried Mackenzie, "not from my first examination of the patient! I only said that cancer was not *proven*. And lacking proof, I refused to sanction surgical procedures which—as even you, Doctor, must surely be aware—are *always* dangerous to life; nearly always destructive to the voice; and which, even when technically 'successful,' often leave the patient in a condition worse than death! Should I have inflicted *that* fate upon the Emperor?"

36

"Why not," demanded Sherlock Holmes, "if it was the only chance of saving him?"

"Saving him for *what*, Holmes," I retorted, "a life of abject misery? Remember that Sir William Jenner and even Dr. Semon shared Sir Morell's view of the effects of laryngectomy!" I turned back to Mackenzie, who was regarding me with some surprise.

"I fully understand your reservations, Sir Morell, about the surgery. Had I been in Frederick's position in November, I would have refused the knife as well. Yet, surely it is time to be definitive about the diagnosis! Dr. Waldeyer's discovery of cancer cells in the Emperor's sputum demonstrates that more than perichondritis is involved."

"It *was* stronger evidence than any I had hitherto received," the specialist admitted. "Nevertheless, perichondritis is certainly present. This sloughing of cartilage from the trachea and larynx is more characteristic of that disease than cancer. His Majesty coughed up two large pieces yesterday. Cancer may be there as well—although," he doggedly insisted, "the first pathologist of the world found nothing of the kind!"

"Dr. Semon," Holmes interjected, "was convinced that it was cancer from the first."

"I *trained* Felix Semon, sir, and *his* opinion"—Mackenzie returned my friend's derisive smile—"is one I should undoubtedly respect. Need I remind you, however, that *he has never seen the patient?*"

"Well, well," sighed Sherlock Holmes, "we have wandered rather far afield. I apologise *most* humbly, Sir Morell, if our questions have offended you. Let us return to our original query. If—as Dr. Watson has reminded us—the *preponderance* of evidence suggests that His Imperial Majesty is suffering from cancer, how much longer do you expect him to survive? I might add (without any intention of offending further) that Professor von Bergmann has given him six months."

"I am aware of that prediction, Mr. Holmes. As usual, my renowned colleague was unduly pessimistic when he spoke to Crown Prince William. I myself told the young man in November that *if* his father's tumour was malignant, he might reasonably hope to live for eighteen months. Sadly, a great deal has happened since that time."

Mackenzie shook his head indignantly. "You must understand, gentlemen, that the case has been deplorably mismanaged by the German doctors. When the tracheotomy was performed in February, Dr. Bramann insisted upon using a canula that was much too large. It damaged the trachea and led to chronic coughing, bleeding, and infection. In the weeks before I was permitted to replace it, that canula caused as much destruction as the disease itself would have done in as many months. If not for Bramann's error, and the patient's resulting loss of strength, the operation recommended by von Bergmann might have been attempted when the disease's nature was confirmed by Dr. Waldeyer."

"An operation you had *consistently opposed*," sneered Holmes. "So, you do *now* admit that the diagnosis of cancer is confirmed?"

The eminent laryngologist stared at his tormenter like a beaten man. "I can no longer find sufficient reason to deny it," he said finally.

"Then possibly you should convey that fact to the Empress! And Frederick's life expectancy? Your *best guess* will naturally suffice."

Sir Morell waved a weary hand, his exhaustion all at once apparent. "He has recovered a good deal in recent days. Barring any further setbacks, he could well last another year."

"And for the duration of his life, the Emperor will remain capable of ruling?"

"Mentally capable, you mean? Laryngeal cancer, Mr. Holmes, kills the body, not the mind. At present, His Majesty is suffering no pain, and there will be none of any consequence before the end. For as long as his physical strength endures, Frederick III should remain in full possession of his faculties and able to fulfill his role as sovereign."

"For, you say, another year. Still long enough, in theory, to implement the political reforms that he and the Empress have envisioned."

"Well, sir," laughed Mackenzie, having at last recovered his composure, "you take me from my province there. I can offer little aid to you in predicting the political future of the German Empire! I speak as His Majesty's physician. Have you or Dr. Watson any other questions for me?"

"No, sir," said Sherlock Holmes. I mutely shook my head, appalled at this merciless interrogation and feeling nothing but sorrow for its victim.

"Then, gentlemen, I suggest we pay a visit to the Emperor. No doubt it will enable you to draw your own conclusions, rather than humouring the fantasies of us poor fools who have attended him these past eleven months." Sir Morell rose and quit the room, not waiting for us to follow him.

As we left the library, I noticed a youngish, military-looking fellow who stood just across the hallway, admiring one of Boucher's voluptuous renderings of unclad female flesh. Although I had never met the man, I learned afterwards that it was Major Lyncker, one of the two attachés.

"Good day to you, sir," called Sherlock Holmes. I trust you enjoyed our morning stroll into Charlottenburg? On your next visit, do try Appelmeyer's. The *Brötchen* there are quite delicious!"

The attaché bowed and silently departed. We did not pursue him, for Mackenzie was fast disappearing in the opposite direction.

The Great Orangery of Charlottenburg was in a side wing of the palace, a handsome edifice built of the same yellow stone. Save for its entrance, it was all upon one level, with large, arched windows that gave it a relatively light and airy look. We overtook Sir Morell just before he entered. He immediately turned to challenge Holmes.

"I wonder, Mr. Holmes, if you are truly aware of the lamentable state of a patient who survives a laryngectomy. The conditions of existence are so utterly miserable, with food having to be taken in so distressing a way, that suffocation is constantly imminent, and death from starvation not infrequently occurs. Only last week, a Socialist deputy of the Reichstag died in Breslau, *one week* after extirpation of the larynx. Very few 'survivors' live more than a few months. Several I know of have committed suicide!

"I would also have you know," he continued, raising a hand to forestall my friend's response, "that last November it was Professor von Schrötter, from Vienna, who communicated to Crown Prince Frederick the situation facing him, with all of his physicians present. For reasons you may understand, I declined to take *that* responsibility upon myself. After hearing the surgical alternatives, and consulting briefly with his wife, the Crown Prince declined extirpation but agreed to tracheotomy. It was not *I*, sir, who urged upon him that decision!"

Holmes took a breath before replying. "Dr. Mackenzie, I am neither a physician nor a surgeon, although I *have* spent time in Barts to gain a knowledge of anatomy. Possibly, it was presumptuous of me to question your professional conduct or advice. The fact that Dr. Watson supports your view carries far more weight with me than the opinions of your German colleagues. My quarrel with you, sir, is that you have not been forthright with the Empress about her husband's prospects of survival. I have not yet met the Emperor and can form no judgement there. But you have allowed Her Majesty to hold onto hopes which the facts—as you yourself explain them—can no longer justify."

Sir Morell looked deeply troubled. "That may be true, sir. Over the past year, I have spent much time with the Imperial couple, and I have come—perhaps unwisely—to think of them as friends as well as

40

patients. I know of their enlightened and far-reaching plans for the internal development of Germany. Having met their son, I also know that all those hopes and plans now hang upon a very slender thread. It is possible that my respect for them, and my sorrow for the end that almost certainly awaits His Majesty, have at times clouded my professional judgement."

"As has, perhaps, the responsibility of a mistaken diagnosis?"

Mackenzie gave my friend a bitter smile. "You are a hard man, Mr. Holmes. But, yes, there may be that as well."

"Then I propose that we begin again." Sherlock Holmes held out his hand, which, after a slight hesitation, Sir Morell accepted.

"Shall we go in, gentlemen?" he asked.

The interior of the Orangery, which preserved the imperial fruit collection over the winter months, belied its promising façade. The old, thick-stemmed orange trees had not yet been moved outdoors for spring. Their leaves covered most of the windows, blocking the sunlight and giving the long corridor a dark, depressing air. The place, Mackenzie grumbled, had been "better than nothing" for the Emperor to walk in during the snowy weather of mid-March; but it was hardly equal to the sunshine of San Remo.

"But there is no one here!" he noticed suddenly.

The remark was not entirely accurate, for an unknown apparition was now lurching towards us through the gloom. Upon arrival, it bowed with studied insolence and handed a note to Sir Morrell. Then, to my surprise, the man gave me what appeared to be a letter. Having received a warning look from Holmes, I put it unopened in my pocket.

"That was Beerbaum," Mackenzie confided when Beerbaum had disappeared. "He is, at best, an adequate nurse to wait upon our patient; but his more important role is as von Bergmann's spy. Ah," he continued upon examining the note, "Mr. Hovell writes that he has taken His Majesty to the palace mausoleum. So, gentlemen, we have another walk in store."

He led us from the Orangery and down a cobbled avenue lined with lofty pines. Visible at this alley's end was a stone mausoleum, built in the Doric style. Originally, Sir Morell informed us, it had housed only the tombs of Frederick's grandparents; but in March the late emperor's bier had been placed there as well.

"His Majesty had hoped to arrive from San Remo before his father's death, and I had quite a struggle to dissuade him from marching in the funeral procession. Unhappily, the weather last month was far too inclement. He has visited the mausoleum twice since then, both times with an unfavourable effect upon his health. As you know, Dr. Watson, melancholia can be a deadly foe in cases of this kind."

Indeed, on entering the mausoleum we beheld a distant figure, bowed in grief before a coffin crowned with laurel wreaths. In a fresco just above the altar, the long-dead king and queen knelt in adoration of their Saviour. Light from two elaborately carved candelabra cast its glow upon the marble walls. It was an affecting scene; and Mr. Hovell, who stood respectfully aside, put a finger to his lips to silence us. For the moment, I gave my attention to the tomb of Queen Louise, who had implored the first Napoleon in vain to spare Prussia from dismemberment. The lady was as beautiful in effigy as she had been in life; and I fancied that I saw something of my own, dead Constance in her face. A cough from Holmes recalled me from this idle vision. The imperial mourner had finally turned to greet us, and we bowed in unison to Emperor Frederick III.

His Majesty was much changed from the commanding horseman I had admired, ten months before, in the Jubilee procession. He wore civilian dress, his hair and beard were greying, and he had lost at least two stone in weight. His eyes had now a haunted look, and the noise of his breathing through the canula was audible from where we stood. Yet, on that morning few would have taken the Emperor for a dying man. He held himself erect, regarded us with interest, and smiled with genuine warmth as we approached. When we reached him, he playfully tapped the order on Sir Morell's lapel, as

42

though gently chiding him for wearing it. After Holmes and I had been presented, Frederick took a pad and pencil from the pocket of his coat, scribbled for a moment, and handed the note to Mr. Hovell.

"His Imperial Majesty apologises for receiving you in such a solemn setting," the young surgeon self-consciously recited. He writes: 'At times of late, I feel more at home among the dead than with the living.'" The Emperor waved a hand to deprecate the force of this remark, but I saw the remnants of tears upon his cheeks. He resumed writing and soon handed a second note to Sherlock Holmes, who had been introduced to him as an emissary from the Queen.

"'Please assure my august mother-in-law,'" my friend declaimed, "'of the love and reverence I feel for her, and of my sincere and earnest wish for a *close* and *lasting* friendship between our two nations.' The words 'close' and 'lasting' have been underscored. I shall, indeed, Your Majesty," he added, with an inclination that approached a bow.

The third and longest note went to Mackenzie, who read it aloud with signs of discomfiture. "'I shall look forward to seeing *Dr. Watson*'"—Sir Morell paused to glance at me uncertainly—"'along with you and Mr. Hovell, at our evening consultation.' In *fact*, Your Majesty. . . ." Frederick, after an enquiring look, gestured for him to continue. Instead, the specialist abandoned whatever he had been about to say and went on reading. "'And now, gentlemen, let us return to the palace. I wish to take an early luncheon, for I have much work to do this afternoon.' Very well, sir . . . as you command, of course."

On our walk back up the cobbled pathway, His Majesty set a steady pace, and it was obvious to all of us that he enjoyed being out-of-doors. Before re-entering the Schloss, he took us on a tour of its gardens, pointing out a belvedere across the pond and various shrubs and statues for Hovell or Mackenzie to describe. Sherlock Holmes said very little; but he intimated by several covert glances that Frederick, in this initial meeting, had both surprised and impressed him. From a medical perspective, the Emperor seemed stronger

43

physically than I had expected, and more than capable of exercising his imperial prerogatives. I saw no reason, on that sunny April morning, why he should not remain a wise and benevolent ruler to his people for many days to come.

CHAPTER 4

An Unexpected Invitation

After leaving the Emperor Frederick with his doctors, Holmes and I returned to our rooms to read the letter in my pocket. It came as no surprise that the message delivered by von Bergmann's spy had been written by von Bergmann. His missive was quite short and ran as follows:

> *Honoured Colleague!*
>
> *By now, you have met His Majesty and consulted with the omnipotent Mackenzie. Would it interest you to hear a German perspective on the case? If so, please join me for luncheon, this afternoon at two o'clock, at the Hôtel S_____ L_____ , Zimmer-Str. 20, on the corner of the Friedrich-Str. I look forward with pleasure to our meeting.*
>
> *Ernst von Bergmann*

My friend had subjected this letter and its envelope to his usual meticulous scrutiny. Now he returned it to me with a smile.

"What do you make of it, Watson?"

"Quite surprising, Holmes. I had hardly expected to consult the leading German surgeon in the case, or to be addressed by him as 'honoured colleague.'"

"Yes, such condescension seems unnatural for a surgeon of von Bergmann's stature. But the note itself? What deductions do you draw from it?"

"Short and to the point. As you say, excessively polite to me while derisive of Mackenzie, which I suppose we must expect."

"Nothing else?" he cried with disappointment. "Surely you can begin to apply my methods by this time!"

"Well. . ." I said doubtfully, knowing that an effort was required, "the paper is of indifferent quality, and the writing far from neat. His pen either spluttered or ran dry three times while composing this brief note."

"Better. What may we infer from that?"

I thought a short while before the obvious conclusion dawned. "It seems unlikely, Holmes, that he wrote from his consulting room. I would refill my ink bottle and find a reliable pen before sending a professional communication."

"Excellent, Doctor! It is probable, in fact, that von Bergmann wrote from the hotel where he has invited you to lunch. Not one of the first or second class, judging from its stationery. What does *Baedeker* say of it?"

I retrieved my guide-book and turned to its description of Berlin hotels. "Very little, it appears. Merely the name and address, with the word 'unpretending.'"

"Ha!" barked Sherlock Holmes. "So, Watson, our renowned surgeon has evidently spent the night, or at least consumed a very early breakfast, for his letter to have reached you when it did, in an establishment that leads *Baedeker* to be discreet. What does that fact suggest about von Bergmann's invitation?"

After puzzling a moment, I could only shake my head. "I fear I have exhausted my deductive powers for one morning."

"Then allow me to refresh them. It *suggests* (for our logical deductions do not amount to proof) either that this invitation was a sudden inspiration, on which von Bergmann decided he must act at once, or that *someone else* at the hotel—who may have observed his late-night revels—induced him in some way to write the note."

"My dear Holmes," I remonstrated, "you have ridden a long way on a wobbly cycle! Is there really enough here to accuse an eminent surgeon of succumbing to debauchery and blackmail?"

46

"Well," he laughed, "*possibly* not." It said much for our relations since my return to Baker Street that my protest amused rather than affronted him. "Nevertheless, there is a reek of beer about this envelope, just as the capital letters in von Bergmann's message reek of self-esteem. What do the medical journals say of him? Beyond the fact that he was born a Balt and taught at Dorpat before coming to Berlin, I have little information."

"He is a strong proponent of anti-septic measures," I remembered, "and insists upon boiling instruments and dressings before use. His practice of clothing himself and his surgical assistants in white coats is more controversial, but I can see the idea's merit. Undoubtedly, he is among the foremost surgeons at the Charité."

"I shall be eager to hear your impressions of him, Watson. It will be an interesting encounter, given the tone he has taken in this note."

"You do not wish to accompany me?"

"No, I have an appointment at the Chancellery this afternoon. I saw Radolinski this morning after my return from town. He agreed to send a message to Bismarck requesting an audience on my behalf. Thus, Doctor, we shall divide our forces and attack upon two fronts: you the medical, and I the political. Let us rendezvous to compare notes before your examination of the Emperor this evening."

I wondered whether this divided strategy would have earned General Ponsonby's approval, deep as we were behind enemy lines. Even so, it was heartening to be entrusted with my own command. At half past twelve, I left the palace, walked to Charlottenburg, and took a cab into Berlin. After traversing the Thiergarten, it passed beneath the Chariot of Victory crowning the Brandenburg Gate and emerged onto the broad avenue of Unter den Linden, the very heart of the German Empire. The ancient lime trees were by now sadly decrepit; but the Baroque palaces, spacious hotels, and vast commercial arcades preserved an atmosphere of splendour. Turning south onto the

47

Friedrich-Strasse, I came to my destination just prior to the appointed hour.

The hotel's restaurant, despite its proximity to Berlin's centre, looked less than prepossessing when I entered it. While no doubt well-managed and (like everything in Germany) scrupulously clean, it had nonetheless an air of raffishness that I remembered from my army days. Its clientèle seemed largely composed of businessmen and soldiers, and the laughter from the American-style bar was too loud for strict propriety. Some of the young women lunching with much older gentlemen would not have been admitted to the Kaiserhof or Hôtel Continental.

In the middle of the room, a well-dressed, portly figure had risen from his table and raised a hand to welcome me. Having seen photographs of all the German doctors, I recognised von Bergmann. He smiled behind his beard as I approached, greeting me with a loud *"Guten Tag!"* before continuing, to my relief, in English. The first half-hour of our luncheon passed quite pleasantly. Obviously, the great surgeon was well-known at this hotel, for we were served with a degree of ceremony. As course succeeded course, my host ate heartily and drank freely of the wines provided, although he showed no ill effects. We found a good deal in common to discuss. Like myself, von Bergmann had been a military surgeon, most recently with the Russian army in the Balkans. He listened to my Afghan tales with interest and asked several questions about King Milan of Serbia. I mentioned that ruler, a former client,[4] only after learning that von Bergmann was fully aware that I had been accompanied to Germany by Sherlock Holmes. It seemed clear that despite his temporary absence from the palace, he was communicating regularly with Radolinski and the "Bismarck clique" of Frederick's court.

---

[4] As will be revealed later in this volume, Irene Adler's so-called "King of Bohemia" was actually King Milan Obrenović, who ruled the small Balkan state of Serbia from 1868 until 1889.

In this atmosphere of seeming frankness, our talk turned finally to the Emperor. *"Also,* Herr Doktor, *"* my host rumbled, "what is your opinion of our illustrious patient? Several days have passed since I have seen him. Does his progress continue to fulfill Mackenzie's sanguine expectations?"

Not liking the tenor of this query, I cast my reply in neutral terms. "I have not yet been able to examine His Majesty myself. However, today at our first meeting he looked both healthier and stronger than I had anticipated. My impression was that he may live for quite some time. Sir Morell thinks perhaps another year."

"Ach! Wenn das nur möglich wäre! If only it were possible! He can never recover and will soon rapidly get worse. Two months ago I told the Kaiserin, but *natürlich* she did not believe.

"Do not mistake me, colleague," he went on before I could reply. "In politics I am a liberal. For many years, as our first Kaiser lived on and on into his dotage, I awaited the accession of my good friend *'unser Fritz.'* He is a noble fellow, but—alas!—he is now doomed. There can be no help for it, and we must accustom ourselves to a new order. For His Imperial Majesty, the kindest outcome would be an affection of the lung, leading to a quick and painless death. From what my nurse in the Schloss reports to me, I suspect that such an affection already may be taking place."

"Do your own observations indicate pneumonia?"

"Nein, nein, not as yet," von Bergmann answered, "but it is coming, all the same. On Sunday, when last I examined the Kaiser, cancer cells had begun to accrue around the tracheotomy. I showed them to Mackenzie, but he babbled about 'granulation tissue' and refused to see. The *Dummkopf* blames perichondritis for the breakdown of the trachea. Bah! The larynx is disintegrating. Morbid cells have descended to the trachea and will soon afflict the lungs."

I felt an obligation to defend my British colleague. "In fact, Professor," I cautiously began, "Sir Morell attributes the initial damage to the patient's trachea to the large canula employed by Dr.

49

Bramann. As he explained the matter, it caused chronic bleeding and a serious infection, which the Emperor was lucky to survive."

"I see that our magician 'Moritz Markovicz' has cast a spell on you as well! Do you truly believe, Herr Doktor, that an experienced German surgeon cannot properly utilise a canula? I was not present for the Kaiser's tracheotomy, but my assistant Bramann has performed that procedure in my presence many times. *Nein, nein,* the gangrenous process in the larynx is at the root of all the evil. *Bitte, mein Freund,* do not allow yourself to be deceived."

Despite his declaration of friendship, Professor von Bergmann now seemed ready to bring our luncheon to a close. When I enquired (perhaps imprudently) what he thought of Dr. Erichsen's report on Prince William's ear infections, he affected not to understand. Mumbling that he was due at the Charité for surgery, my host summoned our waiter, settled the bill, bowed, and departed—all within a minute and a half. I was left to find my own way to the street.

In the hotel's foyer, I was briefly accosted by a "fallen flower" of the sort I had once treated in a San Francisco clinic. My experience there, however, had left me proof against her charms; and I caught the tram for Charlottenburg without further incident. Suspecting that Holmes was still at the Chancellery, I decided to stop and tour the Thiergarten before returning to the Schloss. It was a far more beautiful and restful haven than it had seemed the night of our arrival. The zoological garden was the largest and finest I had ever seen, though it reminded me poignantly of the afternoon I had proposed to Constance. After wandering past the various enclosures, enjoying the animals and the music of a military band, I walked back to Charlottenburg. There I stopped to drink a stein of beer before arriving at the palace, shortly after half past five.

It was another hour before Sherlock Holmes rejoined me. Without deigning to knock, he swept through the door into my chamber, threw himself into an armchair, and took out his cherrywood—the one I called his "disputatious" pipe.

"Watson," he cried, "you are looking at the greatest fool in Europe!"

"You exaggerate, Holmes."

He acknowledged my quip with a gruff chuckle, puffing fretfully until his pipe began to draw.

"I arrived at the Chancellery for my three o'clock appointment, then waited for *two hours* in an ante-room without a word. When a smirking aide at last appeared, he told me that Prince Bismarck was still at Friedrichsruh—*his estate in Schleswig-Holstein!*—and was not expected back before tomorrow night. In the vernacular of the criminal classes, Doctor, I have been *had!*"

"Well! So much for Radolinski's reputation as 'an honest rogue.'"

"Pray do remind me of a gross misjudgement. It is evident he will do everything in his power to delay or thwart us. And behind him lies the infinitely greater power of the chancellor he serves."

"What are we to do, then, Holmes?"

"We can do nothing tonight on the political side. How was your luncheon?"

I provided a recapitulation of the meeting, but admitted having no idea of why von Bergmann had desired to see me. "He could not have found enlightenment in *my* opinion of the case, and his spy keeps him informed of all that happens in the palace."

"His claim to be a liberal in politics is interesting. It must have saddened him to urge an almost surely fatal operation when his liberal emperor's era was about to dawn. Yet now, you say, von Bergmann obtains information on us from the Bismarck party and consigns poor Frederick to 'a quick and painless death.' Hardly a consistent character! He and Mackenzie are as jealous as a pair of professional beauties."

"Like Gregson and Lestrade. It's a common fault in our profession, but unfortunately the stakes are higher here."

51

"Indeed. Not only one man's life, but the future of a nation. Good-night, Watson. You have done well today. It is time for me to lock myself in my own room, replace this pipe with my old brier, and reconsider the case from its beginning. I wish you an informative discussion with the *English* surgeons."

Moments after Holmes's departure, Hovell came to fetch me for the consultation. Its results, alas, were not encouraging. On examining the Emperor, I realised that the energy he had shown during our morning walk had but disguised his true condition. In the sickroom, dressed in a simple nightshirt that accentuated how wan and gaunt he had become, our patient looked and acted very much the invalid. His throat, with the canula removed, was a depressing sight. Around the wound, I could see the rough, discoloured patches that von Bergmann had called "cancer" and Mackenzie insisted were only "granulations." Whatever their real nature, the tracheotomy site emitted a faint but unmistakable odour of decay. I could now well understand the German surgeon's pessimism.

His Majesty had greeted me with cordiality before submitting to our ministrations. Mackenzie, however, could not altogether mask his resentment of my presence. Even so, he made a conscientious attempt to treat me as a colleague, explaining the non-invasive, "endolaryn-geal" method he had used to extract Frederick's original tumour by instruments passed into the larynx through the mouth. To my surprise, he even offered me a turn with his laryngoscope, a remarkable instrument for viewing the organ indirectly with the aid of mirrors and an external source of light. Unfortunately, though I was able to introduce the mirror into the Emperor's throat, I had great difficulty in focusing the lamp. Its luminous disk seemed to bob about everywhere save on the laryngeal mirror. Not wishing for my clumsy efforts to cause our patient pain, I soon abandoned them. Sir Morell received my apologies with smiling condescension.

"Be of good cheer, Dr. Watson. You were no less successful as a laryngologist than my colleagues Drs. Bramann and Kussmaul, both

52

of whom are surgeons of considerable experience. It is a difficult instrument for a novice to master."

Despite his condolences, I could not but feel that the experiment had been intended to put me in my place. From a personal if not professional standpoint, therefore, I was not sorry to see the consultation end.

On my way back to my room, I heard quick steps approaching, and a voice called out "I say—Watson!"

I turned to find Hovell trotting after me. "A word with you, Doctor, if I may."

"Of course."

"I wanted to say," he gasped, having apparently run all the way from His Majesty's bedchamber, "that you really must not mind Sir Morell. I have never known a better doctor or a kinder man, but he is always mistrustful of what he calls 'outside interference.' Although I believe he likes you personally, you are not under his *control;* and therefore your presence makes him nervous, especially in a consultation with the Emperor."

"I understand completely, Hovell. It did not help matters, I am sure, that Holmes gave him quite a drubbing in our interview this morning. As for my poor self, Mackenzie can hardly be expected to regard me as a colleague. Considering my qualifications, from a medical perspective I should not be here at all. My only defence is that our mission to Charlottenburg is not entirely medical in nature."

"I suspected that Mr. Sherlock Holmes's true interest might lie elsewhere. In fact, Watson, there is a subject in the political line that I should like to discuss with both of you as soon as possible."

"Come with me now, then. I'm sure that Holmes would welcome a distraction. He has just returned from a rather trying visit to the Chancellery."

"No, it cannot be tonight. He did not like to say so in front of you, but Sir Morell is not happy with the Emperor's breathing. I don't

53

know whether you noticed, but there was a distinct rasping sound coming through the canula."

"I did notice, Hovell, but it hardly seemed my place to comment."

"We fear that the wall of the trachea is collapsing and pressing on the canula's rear opening. Its front portion seems to be extruding from the wound. If His Majesty has trouble breathing in the night, I must try to adjust it."

"Ah, night duty! The bane of the *locum tenens,* as I discovered in my early days. Hard luck, old man."

"As the junior, it's often my sad lot. Oddly, both Their Majesties seem to find my presence comforting. Perhaps it's because I *don't* remind them of their eldest son!"

With a laugh, we said good-bye and went our separate ways, having little inkling that disaster would befall us on the morrow.

CHAPTER 5

A Fatal Day

Soon after I awakened the next morning, Hovell sent a note advising me that the Emperor's breathing had worsened in the night. His adjustments of the canula had not prevailed; and Sir Morell, now deeply concerned, was consulting his remaining German colleagues. Sherlock Holmes did not answer to my knock, so I assumed that he was either out upon some mission or still enshrouded in tobacco smoke, oblivious to my presence and all other non-essential factors as he ruminated on the case. After I had dressed and eaten, I retraced my steps to Frederick's suite and, receiving a nod from Mackenzie, joined in the consultation.

"Good day, Dr. Watson," the specialist said cordially, with no trace of the reserve he had exhibited the night before. "I believe that you have not met Dr. Krause, my fellow laryngologist, or His Majesty's personal physician, Dr. Wegner." I nodded to these gentlemen and greeted Hovell, who looked tired and worried.

"We tried the effect of a shorter canula," he told me, "but it seemed to do no lasting good. Sir Morell is about to go into Berlin to retrieve several new ones he had ordered. He thinks their design will better suit the fragile condition of the Emperor's trachea."

"His Majesty is perfectly well for the present," Mackenzie assured us, his confident words belied by the anxiety in his demeanour. "Please look in upon him, Dr. Watson, if you wish. I shall be gone no more than an hour." His departure was regarded with misgivings by Drs. Krause and Wegner. They exchanged some words in German, bowed to us, and re-entered the Emperor's bedchamber.

"Do you want to go in, Watson?" Hovell asked. His tone revealed that my presence would be merely a distraction.

"No, I should probably report to Holmes. Is there indeed no danger?"

"I think not, although old Wegner says that Frederick has complained of pressure in his chest. His breathing is still noisy, but freer than it was earlier this morning. That rascal Beerbaum has absconded, by the way. You and Mr. Holmes are welcome to attend at any time. I'll send you word when Sir Morell returns."

Feeling rather like the fifth wheel on the coach, I walked back to my own part of the Schloss, where I found Holmes pacing up and down the hall outside our rooms.

"Where were you, Watson?" he greeted me impatiently. "I looked for you before I went into Berlin. This time, I made my way to the telegraph office without being followed. Ponsonby will be glad to have Mackenzie's prognosis that His Majesty is likely to survive another year."

"Let us hope that prognosis has not changed." I quickly apprised him of the crisis. Holmes seemed less disturbed by the Emperor's condition than by Beerbaum's disappearance. "It was he, you say, who reported Frederick's worsened breathing?"

"So Hovell told me in his message. It seems His Majesty had a sudden coughing fit just after midnight, when Hovell left the room and Beerbaum was on duty."

"Indeed? That is suggestive, though hardly conclusive. And then von Bergmann's agent fled his post—off, no doubt, to take the tidings to his master."

It was now past noon, and I had received no word from Hovell. Being somewhat at loose ends, Holmes and I occupied an hour by walking in the palace gardens. I had no expectation, naturally, that we would discuss the case. Instead, I was treated to a disquisition on the waterfowl inhabiting the Spree. My friend's vast store of arcane knowledge was often used to foil my curiosity about more relevant concerns.

On emerging from our ramble, we found a messenger waiting with a note informing us that Mackenzie had at last returned. We departed at once for the Emperor's chambers, Holmes accompanying me as a matter of course. Sir Morell, who stood talking with Hovell in an ante-room, looked displeased to see my friend. However, he voiced no objection, directing his remarks to me.

"There you are, Dr. Watson. As I was telling Mr. Hovell, the canulae I ordered in Berlin were not yet ready. I have instructed the instrument-maker to make a temporary one of lead, so that it can be re-shaped quickly if the need arises. It will be delivered by mid-afternoon. Meanwhile, I have written to invite Professor von Bergmann to attend the new tube's fitting. It will be a different model than any we have used before."

"Is his presence essential?" I involuntarily blurted, appalled at my own temerity. Before Mackenzie could respond, my friend said quietly, "I should advise against that invitation, Sir Morell."

"It is required by professional courtesy," the laryngologist insisted. "An elementary rule of civilised medical practice, Mr. Holmes, is that all those associated in a case be acquainted with any new treatment that is carried out. May I remind you, sir," he added, "that you claim to be here as a political observer. It is not your place to intervene in the discussions of His Majesty's physicians on an issue of medical procedure."

The detective bowed. "On your own head be it," he said coldly before stalking to the window. Hovell and I exchanged unhappy glances, but Sir Morell seemed unperturbed as he turned back to me.

"If you wish to be useful, Dr. Watson, you may take this message and ask Count Radolinski to provide a mounted courier. He should ride *ventre à terre*[5] to reach von Bergmann's house as soon as possible.

"Now, Mr. Hovell," he concluded, after handing me the note, "I think it is time that you and I returned to our patient. Good afternoon, gentlemen."

With a nod in our direction, Mackenzie marched to the Emperor's bedroom, trailed by his mortified assistant. Sherlock Holmes and I were left standing like a pair of schoolboys dismissed by the headmaster.

"Well, Watson," my friend sighed glumly, "we have made a pretty mess of things. In our defence, I doubt the British medical profession could produce a greater ass. Surely *he* is more than capable of killing Frederick without his rival's aid!"

"Why," I asked, as we made our way down now-familiar corridors, "were you so opposed to calling in von Bergmann?"

"Why were *you?*" retorted Holmes. "It was an instinct, Doctor, and one you would do well to cultivate. The Professor's conduct is the one inconsistent factor in this case, and that inconsistency makes him suspect in my eyes. A surgeon who insists upon the safety of an operation which three experts assure us means almost certain death? A liberal who consults with minions of the Iron Chancellor? A friend of the still-reigning emperor who speaks of 'accustoming ourselves to a new order?' And his henchman in the palace was alone with Frederick when he took his sudden turn."

"Well, you have convinced *me*, Holmes. Perhaps I should tear up this note."

"No, Doctor, we had best play the cards we have been dealt. That stubborn fool would only send another, and we should be excluded henceforth from his councils. If, indeed, we are not already banished!"

---

[5] According to Merriam-Webster, "belly to the ground," "full speed," or "flat out" (https://www.merriam-webster. com/dictionary/ventre%20%C3%A0%20terre).

We found the *Hof-Marschall* at his post and made Mackenzie's wishes known. Holmes—still smarting from his wasted visit to the Chancellery—treated the Count with some asperity, but Radolinski remained as glibly courteous as ever. To my surprise, he seemed genuinely distressed about the Emperor; hence (my friend remarked) we could be reasonably certain the message would be delivered to von Bergmann's home and not to Paris or East Prussia. A rider was immediately summoned and took off at a gallop. When an hour passed and neither he nor the German surgeon had appeared, Holmes's patience (never bottomless) had nearly reached its limit. At that moment, happily, the instrument-maker arrived from Berlin with the new canula; so we took the opportunity to escort him to the doctors. It was I, in fact, who took the last few steps, for Holmes prudently remained outside the door.

I was greeted by the anxious Hovell, while Sir Morell, without acknowledging me, began to inspect the leaden canula. "No word?" I asked.

"None." The young surgeon shook his head in exasperation. "I telephoned the house. The royal messenger had been there, but the Professor's servants were unsure of his whereabouts. I left a message urging him to make all haste." He lowered his voice, although Mackenzie and the workman were deep in conversation. "Frankly, Watson, I am seriously worried. His Majesty's breathing is no better, and to my mind he shows signs of oxygen depletion. Sir Morell is still convinced there is no danger. Do you think we could persuade him to proceed without von Bergmann?"

"I have another idea that might be more successful. I met von Bergmann yesterday at a hotel where he apparently spends quite a bit of time. Suppose that Holmes and I look for him there? If we don't find him and he still has not arrived, I'll do whatever I can to help you with Mackenzie."

It was so agreed, and I slipped from the room without further notice. Holmes likewise acceded to my plan, and we hired a diligence outside the palace gates. Though I had proposed that borrowing horses would be faster, my friend (who considered the creatures "dangerous at both ends and crafty in the middle") demurred. He urged our driver not to spare his own, however, and we came to the Hôtel S_____ L_____ shortly before three o'clock.

With his habitual caution, Holmes dismissed our cab well down the street, and we approached the place on foot. As we turned onto the Zimmer-Strasse, he seized my arm to halt my progress.

"Do you see those two men, Doctor?"

An unlikely pair were emerging from the hotel lobby. The first—short, stout, and mustachioed—wore the uniform of the Imperial General Staff. The other was a dour civilian: stooped, grey-bearded, and cadaverously thin, like a malign incarnation of the Emperor. They were deep in conversation and too far away to notice us.

"The general," my friend muttered, "is Count von Waldersee, deputy chief to old von Moltke. The evil-looking fellow is Herr Puttkamer, Minister of the Interior. Both—as you recall Her Majesty informing us—are members of Crown Prince William's faction. What do you suppose *they* were doing at our missing surgeon's hideaway?"

"Taking a late luncheon, Holmes?"

He shot me a disgusted look. "This is not the time for pawky humour, Watson. A change of tactics is in order. *You* will see von Bergmann and—if necessary—drag him to the palace. I shall follow those two gentlemen to learn whither they are bound."

Without further parley, we undertook our missions. I entered the hotel and enquired of the idle desk clerk whether "Herr Professor Doktor von Bergmann" might be on the premises. His answer (which my knowledge of German sufficed to comprehend) was that the Professor had reserved a room. After my request for its number yielded but a smirk and shrug, the transfer of a golden mark secured the information. I trotted up the stairway (the old-fashioned S_____

60

L_____ did not boast a lift) and soon was pounding on von Bergmann's door.

Inside, there was a muffled curse, followed by the protest *"Nicht noch einmal!"* Next came a squeak of bedsprings, and heavy steps advanced. A slurred voice queried, *"Wer ist da?"*

"It is John Watson, Professor," I called loudly. "His Majesty's breathing is obstructed, and Sir Morell would like your help in fitting a new canula. He asks for you to come at once!"

I heard a noise between a grunt and groan. After a pause, von Bergmann opened the door just wide enough to answer me, hulking to block my view into the room. Red-faced and disheveled, he wore no coat or waistcoat, only a wrinkled shirt half-fastened over his considerable paunch.

"Ja ja, Watson," he muttered, breathing brandy fumes into my face. "I know of this already. I shall be going soon."

"You received Mackenzie's message?" I exclaimed. "Why in Heaven's name did you not leave at once?"

"I am in the middle of a consultation," answered the Professor, before his pretence of dignity was shattered by a giggle from inside the room. For an awful moment, we stood staring at each other. Then the renowned surgeon gathered himself and told me quietly: "Tell Mackenzie I shall collect my colleague Bramann and arrive within the hour. *Natürlich,* Herr Doktor, I shall value your discretion in this matter."

Too astonished by such dereliction to reply, I turned blindly for the stairway. As I descended, I passed the royal courier, who saluted as he hastened towards von Bergmann's room.

Contrary to his promise, von Bergmann had not come to Charlottenburg an hour later. Nor, to my dismay, had Sherlock Holmes. Upon my own arrival, our friend Hovell had quietly re-admitted me to the Emperor's suite, while Mackenzie and his instrument-maker, Herr Windler, were busy completing the new

61

canula. The specialist was less than welcoming initially, but both men heard my circumspect account of the condition of their German colleague with horrified concern.

"Drunk, you say?" cried Hovell. "My God, Sir Morell, we cannot allow him access to His Majesty!"

"I may not have the power to prevent it," Mackenzie countered. "The Emperor, on his accession, appointed von Bergmann one of his medical attendants, in part to calm the ravings of the reptile press against myself. Count Radolinski has repeatedly urged me to work harmoniously with the Professor, whom, he says, is greatly trusted by the official classes. There must be no ground for complaint against me, Hovell, for any violation of the decencies of professional intercourse.

"Besides," he added doubtfully, "I cannot imagine that *any* physician would attend upon a patient while the worse for drink. If Professor von Bergmann still feels himself intoxicated, he will surely place the consultation in the hands of his assistant Bramann."

It was five o'clock before the missing surgeon joined us, appearing without Dr. Bramann or any explanation for his absence. The Professor was immaculately dressed and seemed in full possession of his faculties, if perhaps a little flurried. His British rival had begun to welcome him when Sherlock Holmes burst in upon us.

"Sir Morell," my friend announced dramatically, "this man *must not* be admitted to your consultation! I have every reason to believe that he intends to harm the Emperor."

Von Bergmann blanched, then reddened, turning a furious gaze upon the interloper. *"Wer ist dieser Mann?"*

"You know my identity quite well," said Holmes, "having learned it from Prince Bismarck's minions. Unless, of course, you are too inebriated to remember! Tell me, why was your assistant left sitting in your carriage?"

Recovering his English, the offended Teuton appealed to his professional colleague. "Mackenzie, it is an outrage! Throw this

Schweinhund out, or I shall have him arrested. I am a privy councillor!"

Sir Morell seemed hardly less irate. "Mr. Holmes," he snapped, "I have suffered all the interference from you that I intend to tolerate! Professor von Bergmann is here under His Imperial Majesty's authority. This is a *medical consultation*, sir, in which you have no standing. Leave us at once, or I shall summon the *Gardes du Corps* and have you forcibly removed!"

To my surprise, my friend accepted his dismissal with a growl of weary resignation. While Mackenzie tried to soothe his angry colleague, Holmes took me aside and told me grimly: "Well, Watson, I expected nothing else. You must be my eyes and ears inside the sickroom. I doubt that you can stop that blind fool's folly; but watch von Bergmann's every move, and—as Haydn's noble anthem puts it—*'erhalte den Kaiser!'* I shall be in the hallway, within ear-shot, when the crisis comes."

I nodded and turned back to the doctors, who were gathering up assorted canulae prior to entering the Emperor's room. It was with trepidation that I followed; but Sir Morell seemed not to notice, and the German surgeon remained silent after one quick, anxious glance. As we went through the door, he seemed to stagger slightly.

Inside, we found His Majesty (who had insisted on arising in the afternoon) seated at his desk, quietly engaged in correspondence. Although he showed no obvious distress, I noted cyanosis in the cheeks and lips, and his open coat revealed the muscles of the neck involved in respiration. His breathing was far harsher and more audible than it had been the night before.

"Mein Gott!" von Bergmann cried, "the man is suffocating!" Rushing forward, he urged the startled sovereign to stand, moved his chair beneath the window, and directed Frederick to resume his seat. Snatching a canula from Mackenzie's hands, the surgeon gestured for his rival to stand behind His Majesty and support his head. The canula he had chosen was not, I saw, equipped with a protective pilot,

63

leaving its knifelike metal edge unguarded. Quickly, von Bergmann undid the bandage holding the existing tube in place, removed the latter, and stood swaying for a moment. Then, with far more force than needed, he plunged the canula he held into the Emperor's throat.

Our patient gasped in pain and half-rose in his chair, but no air came through the tube. When it was withdrawn, he began coughing furiously as a thick stream of blood gushed from the wound. Undeterred, the German surgeon picked up a second canula, cut off its covering sponge, and attempted to insert it. Again no air came through, and again the Emperor coughed and copiously bled after von Bergmann had given up the task. At that point, Sir Morell could restrain himself no longer.

"For Heaven's sake, Professor, you are making a false passage! You have missed the windpipe and are ploughing through soft tissues of the throat!"

"*Unsinn,*" growled von Bergmann mulishly. "The cancerous granulations inside the opening are blocking entry to the trachea. I must try to remove them." Whereupon—to our consternation—he *thrust his unwashed finger* deep into the wound, and on removing it failed for a third time to insert the canula. It was Frederick III who finally ended his own torment.

"*Nicht mehr,*" he wheezed, using a blood-soaked hand to cover the tracheotomy and sound what little of his voice remained to him. Even as he was overcome by another fit of coughing, the Emperor pushed his privy councillor aside. Von Bergmann collapsed onto the floor and lay there, groaning, until Hovell and I lifted him into a chair. "Bramann," the drunken surgeon moaned, "bring Dr. Bramann."

"I shall summon him at once," said Sherlock Holmes. He stood in the doorway, regarding the gory scene before him with horror and disgust. "My God, Watson," he bitterly exclaimed, "could not the three of you together thwart this butchery?" I flushed with shame, for I had failed His Majesty, and—far worse than that—had failed my friend.

Hours later, the four of us sat despondently in Sir Morell's consulting-room, holding what might easily have been a literal post-mortem. Holmes had quickly returned with Dr. Bramann. Although shocked by the condition of his patient, the junior German surgeon had readily inserted a new canula and restored the Emperor's breathing. With a brusque word of apology, he took the stupefied von Bergmann and departed. His Majesty continued to cough and bleed for two hours afterwards, but he had largely recovered by the time that he retired to bed.

Now, as we shared a restorative decanter, which all of us quite badly needed, the laryngologist addressed my friend remorsefully.

"Mr. Holmes, I owe you a profound *mea culpa*. I would never have dreamed that any surgeon could so unconscionably violate his Hippocratic Oath. Indeed, I still cannot believe the Professor's harmful actions were intentional. His random stabbing must have resulted from a loss of dexterity brought on by his inebriation."

"What amazes *me*," Hovell interjected, "is that von Bergmann—who, as we know, is Europe's foremost proponent of anti-septic surgery—should have neglected to wash his hands, at least, before introducing his finger into the tracheal wound. Such forgetfulness is surely evidence of the disorder of his wits."

Sherlock Holmes smiled sceptically at the doctors' efforts to redeem their colleague. "Alas, gentlemen, however disordered the Professor's wits, I do not accept that simple drunkenness explains his conduct. I am sure it was indeed intentional, although inebriation—no doubt the product of a guilty conscience—lessened its effects. In that, if in nothing else, His Majesty was fortunate."

"But what could have possessed von Bergmann to do so mad a thing?" mused Hovell. "I had always understood him to be a friend and supporter of the Emperor."

"Who knows?" In keeping with his Vernet ancestry, my friend essayed a shrug. "Perhaps blackmail, to which a man of the Professor's habits must always be exposed. In any case, his motives are irrelevant. What matters is that His Majesty must be protected from any further danger from the man."

"Of that there is no question, Mr. Holmes," Mackenzie answered stoutly. "His Majesty has expressly informed me that he wishes to endure no further consultations with his privy councillor. And I have respectfully assured him that I can no longer accept the honour of attending him if that gentleman is ever permitted to touch his throat again."

Afterwards, when the two of us discussed the day's events before retiring, I asked how Holmes had been so sure that von Bergmann planned to harm his royal master. The detective sighed ruefully as he extinguished his cigar.

"Well, Watson, I had hoped to tell this story to Mackenzie when it might have done some good. By now, any account of my sad blundering is no more than a cautionary tale for my biographer."

"Whatever do you mean?"

"Simply that you overestimate my powers, Doctor, a fact seldom more evident than it was today. I made an elementary error that might have cost His Majesty his life.

"To my surprise," he recounted (ignoring my look of disbelief), "Waldersee and Puttkamer continued strolling up the Friedrich-Strasse when I followed them from the hotel. They stopped at a tobacco shop, so it was nearly half an hour before they regressed to Unter den Linden. There they parted company. The old man hailed a cab travelling in the direction of the Wilhelm-Strasse; I therefore surmised that he was reporting to the Chancellery. General von Waldersee remained afoot. He turned right, towards Crown Prince William's palace, which is exactly where I expected him to go. Yet, *I shadowed him*, Watson, wasting another quarter-hour in the process. Only when he entered the building did I take my own cab to the Chancellery, contrive a pretext for my visit, and confirm that Herr Puttkamer had signed the log of visitors. I was further delayed when my cab departing from the city broke a wheel. Hence—as you witnessed—I arrived at Charlottenburg too late to forestall von Bergmann, or to explain myself to those who might have prevented his attack upon the Emperor."

"I fail to see what else you could have done. You could not follow both of them."

"No, but Waldersee is known to be William's military advisor and confidant. If *he* was suborning Frederick's surgeon, it could only be at the behest of the Crown Prince. Puttkamer was the variable factor. Given his poor relationship with Bismarck, I could not be sure that he was acting on the Chancellor's behalf. It was he, if anyone, I should have followed. Yet, it was a pointless exercise to follow them at all! Were I indeed the ideal reasoner whom you depict, their very presence at the Hôtel S_____ L_____ should have led me to the obvious conclusion."

There was no consoling the detective when he fell short of his own standards of deduction. I could but rail against the murderous plot we had uncovered against a noble monarch, whose chief minister and heir ought to have been the strongest bulwarks of his throne. My complaints, however futile, assisted in my friend's recovery by awakening his cynical amusement. Sherlock Holmes fully agreed with Lord Acton's dictum concerning the corrupting tendencies of power.

Later, as I lay still wakeful in my bed, I recalled our conversation with the Empress Victoria, whom Holmes and I had met in a corridor while making our way to the *post-mortem* with Mackenzie. The lady had greeted us with a radiant smile.

"Gentlemen, I have just come from His Majesty's apartments. He is *ever* so much better, thanks to Sir Morell, *despite* von Bergmann's bungling. And he had such *splendid* news! Prince *Bismarck*, at last, has settled *nine million marks* upon my daughters and myself, as our share of the *late* Emperor's estate. Now *all of us* will be financially secure *throughout* my widowhood, *whatever* my son may wish to do in future!"

Her Majesty nodded graciously and proceeded down the hallway, leaving the two of us without a word to say. However, one who overheard her aria of thanks did not neglect (as was his wont) to comment. Emerging from his hiding-place behind the staircase, the *Hof-Marschall* said sadly:

"Herr Holmes, whatever you may think of me, I do feel sorry for that woman. But she should not *smile* so much in public. It does her harm, for one cannot help thinking that she does not *feel*. That is not true, even though it often seems so. Only when she is alone does she give way to grief."

We bowed to Count Radolinski and continued to the meeting. Of all our strange encounters on that fatal day, these last two were perhaps the most incongruous.

CHAPTER 6

The Founding of the German Empire

In contrast to the previous morning, Friday, the thirteenth of April, began with a knock upon my door by Sherlock Holmes. It was hard to imagine the new day, for all its evil reputation, being any more ill-omened than its predecessor. My friend, however, seemed to have put the disasters of the twelfth behind him, and even to have reached an accommodation with our adversaries.

"Good morrow, friend Watson," he hailed me cheerfully. "I have just returned from an amiable stroll into the capital with Major Lyncker. After I despatched my telegram to London, he treated me to *Frühstück* in our favourite café. There he regaled me with the morning papers. It looks as though the Bismarck clique has wasted no time in reinterpreting yesterday's events to their own satisfaction."

He deposited a pile of well-thumbed newsprint beside my breakfast tray. "As you know quite well," I grumbled, "my German is hardly up to making sense of these."

"My apologies, Doctor," murmured Holmes. "Let me translate for you a few of the relevant paragraphs quoted by the military attaché. He seemed to take a great delight in them, although I fear that our medical cohorts will be less pleased.

"Here is the latest from the *Kölnische Zeitung*, one of the Chancellor's most reliable supporters. It accuses our friend Hovell of injuring the Emperor's trachea on the night of the eleventh, while trying to adjust the canula. 'Diseased matter was forced into the patient's lungs, leaving him at the point of suffocation for the next *fifteen hours.*'"

"Impossible—" I began, but my friend raised a hand to halt the interruption.

"'*Fortunately*,' the article continues, 'Professor von Bergmann arrived in time to snatch His Imperial Majesty from the jaws of death, rectifying the criminal ineptitude—or worse—shown by the English doctors.'"

"But that is monstrous, Holmes!"

"Is it? Then let us try *The Times*. Ah, that distinguished journal's Berlin correspondent has simply reprinted an item from the *Cologne Gazette*. 'It was resolved,' the British public are informed, 'to insert a new and larger cannula, and this was deftly done'—*deftly*, mind you, Watson—'by Professor von Bergmann himself.'"

"'*Deftly*'?" I cried in outrage.

"Indeed. Now for the *Kreuz-Zeitung*, the organ of the Prussian court. It accuses Sir Morell of being utterly *rathlos* (or, loosely translated, 'at his wit's end') when confronted by the Emperor's alarming state. 'Care has now been taken,' we are told, 'to have either Professor von Bergmann or Dr. Bramann always at hand in future, so as to obviate such accidents.'"

Imagining how the laryngologist would react to this report, I could only join Holmes in helpless laughter. "What barefaced effrontery! How can any reputable newspaper print such lies? It's downright libellous!"

"No, Doctor, it is merely the manipulation of compliant editors by politicians highly skilled in controlling information. Remember, Ponsonby warned us of Bismarck's 'vast, corrupt influence on the German press.' I have no doubt that von Bergmann—or, more likely, Bramann—quickly reported yesterday's fiasco to Count Radolinski, and that clever fellow set the wheels in motion to transfer the blame. Poor Hovell was the obvious scapegoat: His Majesty's only attendant on the night of the eleventh, save for von Bergmann's spy."

We decided to visit Hovell and Mackenzie and offer our condolences. However, on arriving at the Emperor's quarters, we encountered neither the English doctors nor the Emperor himself, only Drs. Wegner and Bramann. Those gentlemen simply stared at us disdainfully, turning their backs when we enquired as to their colleagues' whereabouts. More auspiciously, the pretty maid who followed us into the corridor informed my friend that *"der junge Engländer"* was walking in the palace gardens. We found Mark Hovell slumped upon a bench beside the central fountain, staring at the pond as though contemplating his immediate immersion. Nevertheless, he accepted our words of commiseration with a rueful smile.

"If you think *I* am angry, gentlemen, you should talk with Sir Morell. He would happily consign every reporter on the planet to the fires of Hell, starting with the *Times'* correspondent, Mr. Lowe. 'This, too, shall pass,' no doubt, but my chief is determined to write *The Times* a letter of rebuttal."

"Speaking of Mackenzie," queried Holmes, "what has become of the laryngologist and his imperial patient?"

A mien of care returned to the young surgeon's face. "They have taken a drive into Berlin," he said reluctantly. "His Majesty felt well when he awoke this morning, but he was running a slight fever. Even von Bergmann advised against the trip—"

"Von Bergmann?" I nearly shouted. *"He* had the nerve to show his face?"

"Oh, yes, although the Emperor refused to see him. Naturally, he arrived before we had seen the morning papers! He wanted Sir Morell to issue a bulletin announcing the successful changing of the canula. Sir Morell thought it better to quiet public anxiety by having His Majesty make an appearance in the capital. Tomorrow," he added bitterly, "they are visiting the Thiergarten!"

"Once again," snarled Sherlock Holmes, "the patient's welfare is imperilled merely to preserve the reputations of his two physicians! In this matter, Mr. Hovell, your chief has no less to answer for than does his German rival."

Hovell nodded unhappily but made no reply, and we sat for a long while in silence.

"But what does it all *mean?*" the detective finally blurted. "The Emperor Frederick is doomed. Even if he lives another year—even if he implements the liberal reforms that he envisions, those reforms can easily be undone by his successor. Why attack him *now*, merely to shorten a life that cannot last much longer? And why, Mark Hovell, make *you* the scapegoat of this needless plot?"

The junior surgeon smiled and rose, his equanimity restored. "I believe I can answer at least your second question, Mr. Holmes. Walk with me, gentlemen, and I will tell you a story.

"As late as last December," Hovell recounted as we strolled beside the Spree, "there was still reason to hope that Crown Prince Frederick would recover. Despite the cancer diagnosis in November, his symptoms largely abated over the next month. The recently discovered tumour nearly disappeared; the congestion and swelling in adjacent tissues were substantially reduced. Sir Morell, who returned to San Remo after several weeks in London, decided once again that his patient might not have cancer after all. Indeed, it did not seem so. The Crown Prince was in fine spirits and looked very fit; he out-walked us all in the hills above the Riviera. Our main problem was to keep His Highness from using his voice too frequently at dinner! He would rail against the Berlin press for reporting he was sicker than he really was."

The surgeon sighed a little wistfully. "It was a happy time, gentlemen—perhaps the last happy time the poor man knew. Lady Ponsonby arrived to visit the Crown Princess; Her Highness seemed more relaxed and cheerful than she had been for many months. The couple was even looking forward to their children visiting for Christmas.

"*Well*, Mr. Holmes," he broke off, noting my friend's impatient frown, "I shall spare you any more nostalgia. There was just one cloud on our horizon: the safety of the Crown Prince's war diaries. During the Jubilee, he had deposited part of his archives in Windsor Castle, but the diaries had been left behind. With Frederick's health uncertain, and surrounded by Chancellor Bismarck's spies, Their Highnesses sought to move all their private papers to safekeeping against the eventual accession of their son. It was decided that the diaries must be smuggled from the Villa Zirio, and I was selected to undertake the task."

Sherlock Holmes gave a cry of surprise, startling a small flock of ducks that flew off quacking in alarm. "You impress me, Mr. Hovell! I had not counted espionage among your many talents."

"Believe me, sir, I was an utter novice in the field. Yet, in the end it was a fairly simple matter to arrange. My father had been ill— still is, unfortunately—and late one night I received an urgent call to return forthwith to England. The diaries had been left open in plain view upon a table in the drawing room, so I quickly slipped the three small volumes into my coat as I walked by. Their absence was not noted until the following morning. Naturally, Count Radolinski responded with his usual efficiency, telegraphing every agent in the German Empire to watch all routes to England and extract the diaries from my luggage. But it was all to no avail."

"Fascinating!" enthused Holmes. "However did you manage to elude their snares?"

"Quite simply, Mr. Holmes: I never left for England. The call from London was a ruse. Instead, I took a fast train to Berlin, went directly to the embassy, and awoke Sir Edward Malet in the early hours of the morning. It was at that point that I came closest to arrest, but after considerable wrangling I persuaded him to take the diaries. By now, they are certainly safe somewhere within the British Isles."

Both Holmes and I burst into admiring laughter. "But surely, Hovell," I exclaimed, "you must have been suspected?"

"Oh, undoubtedly. I received some dark looks from the attachés when I returned to the Villa Zirio. My room had been ransacked with deliberate clumsiness, reminding me that my hosts were not quite the fools that they appeared. Still, I was never interrogated, although the

73

Hof-Marschall was most solicitous in enquiring after the health of my poor father. Otherwise, there were no further repercussions—until today, that is."

"A remarkable story," my friend marvelled, "and one that reflects great credit upon your courage and inventiveness. My congratulations, Hovell." Flushing slightly, the young surgeon accepted a well-earned handshake from us both.

"But what," I mused aloud, "was in the diaries that made Bismarck so determined to retrieve them? Surely, Frederick's part in the Wars of Unification is already quite well known."

"I cannot tell you, Watson," Hovell answered. "I was chosen for the mission due to my utter ignorance of German. I have no idea whatever of the diaries' contents."

"I know one man who does," said Sherlock Holmes.

The *Hof-Marschall* received us in a small but elegant salon, where he had ordered an afternoon tea served in the English fashion. As we sipped Darjeeling from exquisite Chinese porcelain, our host cheerfully acknowledged Hovell's exploit.

"*Jawohl*, gentlemen, it is quite true. The young rascal got the better of us that time. Who would have thought an English sawbones could outwit the Chancellor's best spies? *Also*, you can be sure, we were not sorry to do *him* an ill turn when the opportunity arose. Do have another scone, Herr Doktor. Her Majesty is quite fond of them, so we try to keep her happy in that way, if not in others."

In reply to Holmes's inquiry regarding the war diaries' significance, Radolinski hesitated only briefly. "Perhaps I owe you both a little of the truth. Do you wish to hear how our great German Empire was proclaimed? Then have another cup of tea, and I will tell you." Having poured, he settled back a moment to collect his thoughts.

"You must understand that as the year 1871 began, Crown Prince Friedrich's fame was at its zenith. His army was before the

74

gates of Paris, having won two early victories and played a crucial part in the decisive Battle of Sedan. The Crown Prince was beloved by his troops, admired even by his French opponents, and—at the time—the apple of his father's eye. And it was he, not Bismarck, who persuaded King Wilhelm to don the imperial crown." From the corner of my eye, I saw my friend suppress a whistle.

"The King's outlook, you see, was purely Prussian. Already in his seventies, he had ruled the realm for many years. Incredible as it seems to us today, as a boy he had seen his parents humiliated by the *first* Napoleon and his beautiful young mother driven to an early grave. The old man hated France with all his being, but once her humiliation was achieved, he was content. That is Indian chutney, Herr Holmes, if you are not partial to anchovy paste." Holmes opted instead for the smoked salmon.

"Even after Napoleon III's defeat," the Count continued, "Paris would not fall. New French armies, formed by the recently proclaimed republic, had risen to come to the capital's relief. By mid-winter, our German armies were exhausted and faced an entire nation armed against them. Everyone—myself included—wanted to go home. While the Chancellor was painfully negotiating to bring Bavaria and Württemberg into the Confederation, thus uniting all the German states, the King of Prussia still stubbornly opposed the imperial idea. He cared nothing for an emperor's crown; he likened it to 'a brevet rank as a lieutenant-colonel' conferred upon a major!'"

Recalling my own ambition for higher military rank, I could not withhold a rueful chuckle. It failed to distract our storyteller from his course.

"On the day before the empire was to be proclaimed in Versailles' Hall of Mirrors, King Wilhelm threw a tantrum and would have nothing more to do with the event. Count Bismarck, too, was in hysterics. By that time, he had already quarrelled with von Moltke and the generals, with half the German princes, and now even with the King himself. His whole, carefully prepared edifice threatened to come crashing down! The Crown Prince knew well what Bismarck was; he had freely expressed that knowledge in his diaries. *He* looked forward to a very different sort of German Empire, one in which a man such as the Iron Chancellor would have no place. *Natürlich*, the fearsome Otto knew the Heir-Apparent's feelings very well. At this juncture, gentlemen, his political future was not bright!"

The *Hof-Marschall* paused to sip Darjeeling, knowing that he held us rapt. Quite unexpectedly, the keeper of Chancellor Bismarck's secrets had revealed an episode in German history few foreigners were privileged to be told.

"In the end, it was *'unser Fritz'* who persuaded the old King to seize his destiny. He spoke to his father patiently and kindly, as one would to a child, reminding him that the House of Hohenzollern had risen from the dignity of Burggraf to Elector and then to the Crown, each step taken without prejudicing the family or the country. Now one last step was needed to restore the old German Empire of a thousand years ago, in a far truer sense than ever had the 'Holy Roman Empire' of the Habsburgs. This final step the entire world was waiting for His Majesty to take.

"But at this"—Radolinski raised a hand dramatically, enjoying his own performance—"the King sprang up in a fury, ordered us all from the room, and declared *he would not hear another word* of the ceremony appointed for tomorrow! We left his quarters in despair. The Chancellor was ashen-faced at the ruin of his magnificent ambitions. . . . Do you object to Viennese strudel as our third course, gentlemen? I am afraid Battenberg cake has quite gone out of style."

Once the strudel was distributed, the Count resumed his tale. "The next morning, there came news of another victory that prevented the relief of Paris. The Crown Prince called for a Guard of Honour to parade beneath his father's window. Old King Wilhelm emerged smiling broadly, and it was evident that he had reconsidered the wise words of his heir. *Also*, the imperial ceremony that afternoon went off without a hitch! The Heir-Apparent knelt to kiss his father's hand; the newly proclaimed Kaiser raised his son up and embraced him—all this while the man who regarded *himself* as Germany's creator stood and glowered in the throng below.

"Thus, in a very real sense, gentlemen," concluded Radolinski, "it was the Crown Prince of Prussia—not Otto von Bismarck—who finally brought the German Empire to fruition. And the Chancellor will do whatever he must do to guard his legacy and keep that fact from being widely known."

"It seems he has already done so," remarked Sherlock Holmes. "Yet, *your* loyalty, Count Radolinski, remains with the Iron Chancellor, not with the Emperor whom you have sworn to serve."

"Alas, Herr Holmes, some of us find ourselves on the wrong side of history. But it is still the *winning* side. We accept our place; we even try to profit from it. Nonetheless, I would ask you to believe that in our hearts, we wish the outcome had been different."

The *Hof-Marschall* rose, offering us a melancholy smile. "And now, my dear opponents, I must ask you to excuse me. Prince Bismarck will be awaiting my report."

Shortly after ten o'clock that evening, I consulted briefly with the English doctors. Sir Morell, having returned from a late dinner, had just looked in upon the Emperor. He found His Majesty still feverish and breathing rather rapidly.

"There is no hindrance to air passing through the canula, however," the specialist assured me. "Such quickened respiration no doubt results from shock, which is to be expected after yesterday's ordeal. Mr. Hovell," he added, smiling at his junior colleague, "has advised cancelling our visit to the Thiergarten tomorrow. There, I must be guided by the wishes of my august patient! If he is no worse in the morning, there should be no harm."

With that, Mackenzie left us to report to the Empress on her husband's condition. Hovell and I exchanged despairing looks.

"Watson, I cannot fathom Sir Morell's complacency! He told me earlier that he feared an infection, or even pneumonia, would develop from von Bergmann's mutilation of the Emperor's throat. Yet, he permits His Majesty to continue his usual routine, even though he has complained of chills as well as fever."

At that point, we were accosted by the spectral Beerbaum, whom Mackenzie (to my surprise) had allowed to resume his duties as orderly. I declined to join Hovell in a new examination of the Emperor, deciding instead to retire early for a good night's rest.

As I left the imperial apartments, I saw the stout, bearded figure of none other than von Bergmann in the hallway. With him was a young man of middle height, deceptively mild of countenance and less fiercely mustached than he would be in later years. His left arm, I noticed, was slightly shorter than his right. Even without that disfigurement, his ostentatious uniform—worn at this late hour in his family's rooms—would have told me that I had encountered Crown Prince William, heir-apparent to his father's throne.

His Highness evidently knew my identity as well. After whispering a word to his companion, he approached me with a smirk of patent insincerity.

"*Guten Abend*, Herr Doktor Watson! How fares my noble Papa?"

"Not well, Your Imperial Highness. I expect that he would welcome a visit from his son and heir."

"No doubt he would; but not just now, I think. My friend von Bergmann is no longer admitted to the imperial presence—thanks to you!"

I half-bowed to the Professor, who returned a scowl. "Regrettably, I cannot take full credit for that accomplishment, Your Highness."

"Certainly not! There is also Mr. Sherlock Holmes. Rest assured, I shall remember you two gentlemen when I come into my throne. Perhaps I shall send you both a minor decoration, as my father is so fond of giving to his doctors."

"I thank Your Imperial Highness. Holmes and I will likewise remember our visit to Charlottenburg. Even now, his reports provide enlightening reading for the gentlemen in Whitehall."

The bland young face suffused with anger, although the voice remained quite calm. "*Sehr gut!* When you return to London—and you shall, quite soon—pray give my greetings to dear Grandmamma. Tell her I look forward to welcoming her into my realm as Kaiser! Remind her of the photograph I sent her several years ago. The one that says: *'I bide my time!'* I am nine-and-twenty, Herr Doktor, and my memory is long."

He nodded curtly and, ignoring my bow, rejoined the Professor. The two of them stalked silently away, in the opposite direction from the Emperor's suite. I returned to my own room in the palace, but I cannot say that I slept well that night.

CHAPTER 7

Dénouement

Frederick III awoke on Saturday morning even more unwell than he had been the night before. To the relief of his physicians, he agreed to postpone his visit to the Thiergarten and remained indoors, dealing with state papers. Sherlock Holmes and I, meanwhile, had troubles of our own. Just after ten o'clock, we received a courteous note from Radolinski, which apprised us that in late evening we would occupy a first-class compartment in the last west-bound train to leave Berlin. The Crown Prince, it seemed, had made good upon his promise.

Naturally, my friend was furious. We departed for the capital immediately to post a telegram to London, reporting our impending deportation and requesting permission to dispute it until the uncertain status of the Emperor's health had been resolved. Although I had suggested calling at the embassy, Holmes demurred, citing Ponsonby's instructions. We did stop at the Chancellery, but were not surprised to hear that the Chancellor himself was unavailable.

Our return to Charlottenburg, early in the afternoon, was equally frustrating. A note from Hovell left in our quarters informed us that His Majesty, upon finishing his work, had gone to the Thiergarten after all with the Empress and Mackenzie. Neither the junior surgeon nor the German doctors were in evidence. The *Hof-Marschall* was also absent, and even our own valets had disappeared. It was as though Holmes and I had already been banished from the empire.

The detective was as restless as a caged tiger under these conditions. After fretting for an hour, he decided to go to the Thiergarten and appeal to the Emperor directly. Upon arriving there, however, we learned that the imperial party had just left—only moments before, apparently, for we had not met them on the road.

Holmes snarled his displeasure; yet, he insisted on detouring to the telegraph office before following Their Majesties. There, he left instructions for any telegram to him to be instantly delivered to the palace. With some difficulty, I persuaded him to stop at a Charlottenburg café, as we had eaten nothing of any consequence since breakfast.

It had been, my friend bitterly remarked, an altogether wasted day. Church bells in the village had tolled seven long before we passed the palace gates; our home-bound train was to depart the station at nine-thirty. Once indoors, we went directly to the Emperor's suite, only to find Major Lyncker on guard at the entrance. Apologetically but firmly, the attaché told Holmes that we were not to be admitted. He did agree, albeit reluctantly, to inform the English doctors that we desired to see them. To our surprise, the doctor who emerged was not Hovell but Mackenzie.

Sir Morell looked tired and drawn, as though he had aged a decade overnight. "Good evening, gentlemen," he sighed. "I am told you must return to London."

"Indeed," replied Holmes grimly, "We leave tonight, barring any new instructions, which I am still in hope of receiving from Whitehall. As you can understand, the government will wish to know the Emperor's condition."

"I'm afraid it is extremely serious. His Majesty returned from the Thiergarten this evening with chills and a temperature of 103 degrees F. He appears to have developed bronchitis and has begun to expectorate a malodorous pus through his canula. It is the sign of a virulent infection, undoubtedly originating in the 'false passage' inflicted by von Bergmann. I have expected such a complication since that gentleman put his finger into the Emperor's throat."

"And yet," I found myself observing, "today you allowed His Majesty to make an excursion to the park."

The laryngologist's glare of indignation subsided into guilt. "His Majesty was most insistent, Doctor. His congestion, chills, and sudden rise in fever did not begin until after his return."

"Once more, Sir Morell," said Sherlock Holmes, "I must ask you for a definitive statement of the Emperor's prognosis."

"Most unfavourable, Mr. Holmes. The wound to His Majesty's throat has mortified into an abscess. Even if it bursts and he survives the immediate crisis, the injury itself is permanent, and his current symptoms are unlikely to abate. Gentlemen, I fear it is a fatal complication that will almost certainly lead to chronic infection and further gangrenous destruction of the trachea. There is no doubt whatever that von Bergmann's attack upon the Emperor has, at the very least, shortened His Majesty's life. It is no longer a question of years or months, but of weeks—perhaps only days."

"*Thank* you, Sir Morell," cried Holmes with scarcely veiled irony, "for so *unequivocal* a statement. And now, Watson and I must say farewell. Please extend our good wishes to His Majesty, and our warm regards to your invaluable assistant, Mr. Hovell."

"He will be sorry to have missed you," Mackenzie answered coolly. "Not liking to leave my patient in a crisis, I sent Hovell to the capital an hour ago to report to Dr. Reid. I wish you both a safe journey back to London."

He did not offer his hand; nor did Holmes and I extend our own. With a civil nod, Sir Morell Mackenzie turned away and reentered the Emperor's bedchamber. It was our last meeting with that eminent physician.

After departing the imperial quarters, Sherlock Holmes and I returned to our rooms to pack up our belongings. We were assisted in the endeavour by our valets, who miraculously had reappeared, silent and obsequious as ever. It was past eight o'clock by the time we made our way into the palace's imposing entrance hall, where, four nights before, we had been so flamboyantly welcomed by Count Radolinski.

Of him there was no sign. Instead, we were met by Major Kessel, the senior military attaché, who—after favouring us with a formal bow and heel-click—handed Sherlock Holmes a telegram. It was the reply from London. Having inspected the envelope, Holmes gave the German officer a steely glare.

"This has been opened, Major."

"Not by *my* hand, sir!" The attaché drew himself up as though preparing to issue or repel a challenge.

"Oh, I have no doubt of *that*," my friend replied. "May I crave your indulgence to read the thing myself in private?"

"*Natürlich*, Herr Holmes. But please be swift. When you have finished, I am to escort you and the Herr Doktor to His Highness Prince Bismarck. He is awaiting you in the drawing room behind that door."

"Is he, *indeed?*" marvelled the detective. "Well, *Gott sei Dank!* At long last, Herr Doktor, we have been granted audience!"

After Kessel had withdrawn discreetly to a corner, Holmes read through the *communiqué*, his face darkening in proportion to his progress. Finally, with a snort of absolute disgust, he crumpled the thing into a ball and tossed it to me.

"Put *that* in your notebook, Watson, as our mission's official seal of failure! Myc—that is, my *correspondent* in Whitehall—writes that the government has instructed us not to oppose our ignominious eviction. We are to tuck our tails between our legs and meekly flee to London!"

"But why?" Taking Holmes's arm, I propelled him through the palace doors into the courtyard, where we could confer beyond the Major's hearing.

"Oh, no doubt it all makes perfect sense to the official mind! The Prime Minister has decided that the true nature of von Bergmann's attack upon the Emperor is not to be disclosed. He was advised that with Frederick's death inevitable, and perhaps imminent (Hovell, you remember, telegraphed as much to Reid), revealing the truth would embitter Anglo-German relations to no purpose, complicating the Queen's visit to Charlottenburg and possibly endangering the Empress after the accession of her son. Therefore, the heir and Chancellor's attempt at murder will be swept beneath the carpet, and Her Britannic Majesty's son-in-law dies unavenged!"

Having vented his spleen, my friend assented to reentering the Schloss, where we were at once confronted by the anxious Major Kessel. He led us, without further ado, into the presence of Germany's Iron Chancellor.

I had, of course, seen many photographs of Otto von Bismarck, most often scowling ferociously under a spiked helmet. The scowl and heavy mustache were still evident; but without his helmet, and in a rumpled uniform, the aging chancellor was revealed as a fat and bald old man, leaning heavily upon his cane and looking every one of his seventy-three years. When we entered, he was admiring a painting of the lovely Queen Louise, who appeared to be offering her beauty to Napoleon I. I found it an odd subject for her grandson's drawing room.

Then Prince Bismarck turned to greet us, and the signs of his physical decay became irrelevant. Above their pouches, the deeply-set brown eyes were still as hard as agates, bespeaking the survival of both remarkable intelligence and inflexible, unbroken will. It was obvious to both of us that inwardly, at least, Bismarck had lost very little to the years.

He offered what might have been intended as a genial smile. "*Guten Abend, meine Herren!* Tonight I deputise for Crown Prince Wilhelm. He had hoped to meet the well-known Sherlock Holmes before the two of you left Germany, having already made the acquaintance of Herr Doktor Watson." After an amused glance in my direction, the Chancellor directed his remarks to Holmes.

"Unfortunately, it seems a more important matter has detained him. It may be just as well, Herr Holmes. The young prince is an inveterate talker, and I should not like for you two gentlemen to miss your train."

My friend returned Bismarck's ironic chuckle. "There would be little point, in any case, in our remaining longer. The goals of our mission have been substantially fulfilled, in spite of your best efforts to impede them."

"Pray do not be impertinent, Herr Holmes," the Chancellor growled, "for it does not become you. You likewise are a young man still, and therefore you have much to learn. *Jawohl*, you have done well in your mission to Charlottenburg! You have drawn the right conclusions and identified the true men, the scoundrels, and the fools. But I am too old a fox to be caught by a young hound, for all his eagerness! It has not been difficult to stay a trick or two ahead of you. Even so, I have been impressed by the accuracy and thoroughness of your reports to Whitehall, which *Grandmamma* will surely find as entertaining as I did before she visits here. If I may so observe, sir, your talents are wasted on those 'petty puzzles of the police-court,' as I believe they have been called."

I saw Holmes blanch at this remark, although at the time I had no understanding why.[6] Although obviously shaken, he complimented Prince Bismarck in turn upon the deviousness and dedication of his minions. "They serve Your Highness with a skill and loyalty that would be more honourably reserved for their Emperor, whose reign you have now brought prematurely to a close."

The Iron Chancellor's weathered face assumed a look of sorrow. "Indeed, Herr Holmes, I fear our noble Kaiser Friedrich must soon lay down his heavy burden. It is a tragedy, for had he only married wisely

---

[6] The cause of Holmes's discomfort was that this gibe originated with his brother Mycroft, showing that the Germans were aware of the reclusive analyst who would soon become, at times, "the British government." Although Watson recorded Mycroft's banter in "The Bruce-Partington Plans" (1895), the senior Holmes may well have employed it from the time his younger brother took up detective work.

85

he would have been in all respects a worthy man. Regrettably, his wife—whose will, alas, is so much stronger than his own—has never accepted that Germany is not England, and will never be. Neither she nor her husband understood that only blood and iron could build the German Empire! Such was the verdict of 1848. History, *meine Herren*, is written by the victors, but not necessarily by them *all*. In our case, history will record that Otto von Bismarck was the founder of the German Empire. 'Fritz and Vicky' will quite soon be forgotten. As I have said, it is no doubt a pity. Yet, a man who could not rule his wife—or even speak!—was hardly fit to rule an empire."

"What of a man who may go mad at any moment?" my friend responded sharply. He took from his coat pocket Erichsen's report on the lurking danger of insanity behind Crown Prince William's ear infections. The Chancellor accepted and began to read the document, albeit with the demeanour of a man humouring a fool.

"*Ja, ja,*" he grumbled, "we knew of this already. Herbert provided such a report last December. This evil malady—should it occur—will be dealt with at the necessary time, as were all the other misfortunes that have plagued the Crown Prince since his birth. If there should be a fatal outcome, then Prince Heinrich will make an admirable regent for his little nephew. A whole, man, at least, and less erratic than his elder brother. I was saddened when the other two boys died so young. One thing that must be said for your queen's daughter: she made a fine brood mare!"

At that point, I could tolerate this ogre's callousness no longer. "You go too far, sir! As you have admitted, you are speaking of the daughter of my Queen!" Bismarck gave me a mocking smile before turning back to my companion, who placed a reassuring hand upon my arm.

"Herr Holmes," sighed the Iron Chancellor, "I know full well that Crown Prince Wilhelm's accession poses risks. While no longer a boy, he retains all the impetuosity of youth. He cannot hold his tongue, and he allows himself to be swayed by flatterers. More dangerously still, the young lord wants a war with Russia! He would draw his sword tomorrow if he could. Unless Wilhelm can learn self-control, as Kaiser he could lead the Reich into a general European war—without even realising or wanting it. Assuredly, he will require much direction, but I am long accustomed to providing it. Under my tutelage, there will be no liberal experiments in the reign of Wilhelm II, just as there were none in the reign of Wilhelm I. Instead, the German Empire will continue to be governed under my policy of 'Blood and Iron!'"

"And what will be the empire's fate, Your Highness," Holmes enquired softly, "if its new ruler should disdain your tutelage, or fail to mature sufficiently before your time as chancellor is done?"

The cynical smile faded from the old man's lips, and he regarded my friend with a look of deep foreboding. "If that contingency occurs, Herr Holmes, then woe to my poor grandchildren! If that contingency occurs, Kaiser Wilhelm II will become the nemesis of history!"

We left the Schloss to find the street outside it filled with ordinary Germans. All had traveled there, by carriage, tram, or foot, to keep a solemn vigil for their stricken Kaiser Friedrich. Meanwhile, in a secluded corner of the courtyard, the Heir-Apparent was talking urgently with the commander of his father's guard. Keeping to the shadows beneath the palace wall, Holmes and I stealthily approached and hid ourselves behind a stand of shrubbery.

"The moment you hear of the Kaiser's death," the Crown Prince was saying, "occupy the Schloss and let no one in or out, without exception. Search every room until you find my parents' private papers. I want them seized before my mother can arrange to have them sent to England."

Clicking his heels, the commandant saluted. As William went on to issue further orders, the crowd beyond the palisade began to stir. I heard glad cries of *"Unser Fritz!"* followed by a curse from the

Crown Prince. Turning, we saw Frederick III standing in the half-lit window of his bedroom, the smaller figure of his wife beside him. Dressed in a beautiful white uniform, erect and dignified as always, the dying emperor raised a hand to his people in benediction and farewell.

"Come, Watson," muttered Sherlock Holmes. Stepping from our hiding place, we bowed to the venerable couple in the window; then Holmes shot a brief, contemptuous glance at the man who would succeed his father all too soon. We passed the palace gates, saluted by the *Gardes du Corps*, and made our way unnoticed through several hundred anxious Germans. As we crossed the cobblestones and turned our backs upon Charlottenburg, I heard the crowd begin to cheer.

EPILOGUE

Inquest on a Murdered Monarch

Although the weeks that followed our return to London were extremely busy, we continued to monitor events in Germany as reported in the British press. Against all expectations, Frederick III survived his latest crisis, and the Queen's visit to Charlottenburg took place as planned near the end of April. Her Majesty accepted a bouquet of forget-me-nots from her son-in-law; delivered sound, if unwelcome, advice to her daughter; reviewed the imperial guard with her grandson William; and, just prior to her departure, held a private interview with the Iron Chancellor. It was agreed between them that Princess Viktoria would *not* marry the former ruler of Bulgaria.

The Emperor's reprieve was brief. On the first of June, when Frederick left Schloss Charlottenburg by yacht for his palace in Berlin, thousands of his subjects lined the banks of the Spree to honour him. Five days later, his doctors published a bulletin stating that His Majesty's health was so satisfactory that further reports would be issued only if there was a need. On June fifteenth, the Emperor died. "Delusional to the end!" was my friend's comment, referring to Mackenzie. He was no less disgruntled, over the next few days, by William II's accession proclamation (which contained no mention of his father); by the Dowager Empress's quick exile from Berlin; and by the German doctors' highly polemical account of Frederick's illness, published in July.

Afterwards, events upon the Continent receded in our minds. During the month of August, Sherlock Holmes was much distracted by the gruesome murders in Whitechapel, as I was by the sudden death of my brother Henry, which required an unexpected voyage to America. When I returned to Baker Street in mid-September, Holmes and I were soon involved in new investigations, among them the case of the Greek interpreter. It was then that I met my friend's elder brother. Although I privately deduced that Mycroft (the mysterious "M") was the detective's contact in Whitehall, my friend continued to withhold the true nature of his sibling's service to the British government.

On the following Sunday, a rare day of drizzle in an otherwise fine month, we were enjoying an afternoon of leisure. Holmes, who had been growing restless since his recent consultation with the French detective Villard, was engaged in researching his voluminous, if ill-ordered, archives. I was immersed in the latest of Clark Russell's sea-stories. It was with some asperity, therefore, that Mrs. Hudson's more irritable lodger responded to her knock.

"I'm sorry to disturb you, Mr. Holmes, I'm sure," that much-tried lady snapped, "but you have a visitor. A nice young man, by all appearances; his name is Mr. Hovell. He says you will remember him from Germany."

Needless to say, if the interruption was unwelcome, our visitor was not. Holmes and I hailed the young surgeon with enthusiasm. When he was provided with a whisky and a comfortable seat before the fire, we extended our condolences on the recent death of Hovell's father. My friend then demanded an account of his adventures since our last encounter.

"Well, Mr. Holmes, I'm sure that you and Dr. Watson followed the sad progress of Emperor Frederick's demise. The cancerous growth eventually breached his oesophagus, so we were forced to feed him through a tube. Fortunately, pneumonia intervened, and the poor man endured but a few days of suffering. The end was quite serene. Certain events after His Majesty's death, however, caused something of a scandal."

"Yes, the newspapers made those facts quite clear," my friend acknowledged. "You needn't rehearse the sorry tale."

"There was one incident a few weeks ago that should amuse you," Hovell said more cheerfully. "It was a bit of retribution that

90

vindicated Sir Morell. I wasn't there myself; I had the story from a German surgeon, Dr. Carl Schleich. You know of him, Watson. He is a pioneer in local anesthesia."

I nodded silently, for Holmes looked impatient for our friend to continue.

"In mid-July, it seems—only a month after the Emperor's death—Professor von Bergmann announced with great pomp and circumstance that his students at the Charité were to witness the surgery that would have saved their Kaiser. He had located a patient (some luckless aristocrat) who had—according to von Bergmann—the same type of laryngeal cancer that had afflicted Frederick. So, before a vast, appreciative audience, he and his assistants began the laryngectomy. After an hour or so, there were mutterings of dismay among the surgeons. Suddenly, the Professor removed his mask and angrily announced: 'Gentlemen, we have been misled! This is not carcinoma after all; it is tuberculosis of the larynx. I am discontinuing the operation!' As you might well imagine, the poor patient died, two hours after he left the operating table."

Quite inappropriately, considering the outcome of this tale, all three of us burst into a roar of laughter. We were interrupted at this stage by our landlady. Having failed to serve tea for an earlier visit by more exalted guests, Mrs. Hudson was not to be denied on this occasion. Ignoring Holmes's protests, she performed the rite with grace and triumphantly departed, leaving one of us annoyed and all of us refreshed.

Following the interlude, Hovell resumed his recollections in a more serious vein. "Gentlemen, I fear that my story's epilogue is less amusing. Just after this public display of gross incompetence, Kaiser Wilhelm II invested Professor von Bergmann with the Hohenzollern Cross and Star, the same award—for butchering his father—that Frederick III had given to the man who tried to save him!"

My friend sighed almost sympathetically. "How *is* Sir Morell Mackenzie? For all his love of baubles, I did admire the man's devotion to his patient. The German doctors were exceedingly severe with him in their reports. Has he managed to bear their attacks with equanimity, or will he make an effort to retaliate?"

Holmes's question was highly disingenuous, for he had already informed me that the laryngologist was writing his own book. Hovell looked at him askance before replying.

"Mr. Holmes, he is as angry as a man whose honour is impugned should be! Most of the German doctors' claims are utterly without foundation. Professor Gerhardt, the throat specialist who had treated Frederick before we were called in, accused Sir Morell of removing *healthy* tissue from the patient's larynx so *it* would be sent to Professor Virchow for analysis. This from a man whose idea of treatment is burning the throat with a hot wire! In *his* report, von Bergmann asserted that splitting the Crown Prince's larynx (the procedure he first proposed in 1887) is no more dangerous than routine tracheotomy. He cited seven of his successful cures, without revealing that none of them had cancer! As for his account of his butchery in April, it is no more than a pack of lies!"

"His conduct has been despicable," remarked Sherlock Holmes, "but hardly more so than I expected after four days in Charlottenburg. Were I permitted to advise Mackenzie, I should urge him to exercise restraint. There are powerful interests, both here and in Berlin, who seem quite determined that the truth shall not come out."

"My chief has been made aware of that, " said Hovell drily. "Some days ago, Sir Morell received a visit from a gentleman in Whitehall, who stated in the most *emphatic* terms that he was not to accuse von Bergmann of intentionally injuring the Emperor."

"Indeed?" The detective paused, no doubt trying to decide whether Mycroft had summoned the energy to go himself or delegated the task to a subordinate.

"So, Hovell," he eventually continued, "I trust that Mackenzie will be wise enough to heed this warning, and restrict any self-defence that he may make to the medical issues disputed in the case?"

"I hope so, sir, but he chafes a good deal under those restrictions. Even on the terms you mention, the draft I have read is injudicious. Sir Morell has indulged in petty personal attacks and side-issues, as well as counter-charges against his German colleagues that he cannot prove. Dr. Donelan and I have tried to discourage him from publishing the book at all. We shall urge him, at the very least, to cut large portions of it."

"Surely," I suggested, "it would be better for Mackenzie to write a sober article for the *British Medical Journal* or *The Lancet*—or, if he must reply in kind to personal attacks, the newspapers. He has often made use of them before! The sort of book you say he's writing will only destroy a distinguished and honourable career."

"You're quite right, Watson," Hovell sighed. "Donelan and I have made that argument repeatedly, but I doubt that Sir Morell will ever listen. If nothing else, he wants his book to pay a tribute to the Emperor—whom he mourns, I believe, as much from guilt as grief. His journal entries concerning His Late Majesty are quite moving."

My friend's derisive grunt was our last comment on Mackenzie. Afterwards, we sat pondering in silence for so long that I rose and lit the lamps, for those outside our windows had been burning for an hour. Mark Hovell seemed the most thoughtful of us all. At last, he asked Holmes quietly:

"Would you tell me something, Mr. Holmes?"

"If I can," replied the detective, but I could see that his antennae were fully on alert.

"In your last report from Charlottenburg to Whitehall, what were your conclusions? What did you tell those gentlemen regarding the attack upon the Emperor?"

"I can answer that quite simply, Mr. Hovell." With a slightly absent smile, Holmes took up his cherry-wood pipe and occupied himself in lighting it. "I told my contacts in Whitehall that the Emperor Frederick had been murdered."

"Murdered, Mr. Holmes?" cried Hovell. "I can accept your calling von Bergmann's 'random stabbing' an *attempt* at murder, for I must reluctantly agree that his actions were deliberate. Even so, His Majesty survived that attack, and in any case he was a doomed man from the start."

"Does *that* matter?" queried Sherlock Holmes. "Cannot a dying man be murdered? If actions were deliberately undertaken that curtailed the Emperor's life, then do not those actions—however delayed their effect—qualify as murder?"

"I have often wondered." I put in, "whether, upon the evidence, the Professor would have been convicted by a British jury."

"At the time, Doctor," my friend chuckled, "I suspect *His Majesty's* evidence would have been decisive! However, gentlemen, the focus of your investigation is too narrow. The villainous von Bergmann—while admittedly the perpetrator of the act itself—was by no means the only one responsible for Frederick's death."

"Indeed not, Holmes! We successfully unmasked both Crown Prince William and the Chancellor for their roles in the conspiracy."

"Still too narrow, Watson," answered Holmes, frowning as he placed a warning finger to his lips. "Has it not occurred to you that almost *everyone* in his immediate circle conspired in some way to kill the Emperor? From the beginning, the self-serving rivalry between the English and the German doctors (from which I exempt *you*, Mr. Hovell) was of the worst possible service to their patient. Regardless of who was right or wrong concerning Frederick's treatment or his chances of survival, both sides placed their own egos and ambitions above their fealty to the Hippocratic Oath.

"Worse still for His Majesty, he became a pawn in a one-sided chess match between his own wife and the Iron Chancellor. I have concluded that the Empress most valued her husband as the embodiment of her parents' political ideals, a part that *she* could never play in Germany. If so, her tactics were deplorable. Motivated by her overly protective love, she kept Frederick off the board so long that politically he had become a nullity by the time he ascended to the throne. The wily Bismarck, left unchallenged in Berlin, had nine full months to subvert the couple's impatient and unloving son, ensuring that the liberal dreams they both had cherished would never be fulfilled.

"Thus, it was the errors of his friends, as well as the malice of his foes, that cut short the Emperor's life. Frederick's enemies also

95

succeeded in diminishing his legacy, which ought to have ensured the gallant, visionary, but ill-fated monarch a lasting place in European history."

Sherlock Homes subsided and re-lit his pipe, favouring the two of us with a world-weary smile. "Well now, gentlemen! If you do not concur that all of *that* amounts to murder, perhaps we had better redefine the word!"

The Adventure of the Inconvenient Heir-Apparent

Geneva, Switzerland
1898

CHAPTER 1

A Summons to Geneva

In November 1913, Great Britain was honoured by a visit from the heir-apparent to the Habsburg throne. Archduke Franz Ferdinand, accompanied by his morganatic wife, stayed several days with Their Majesties at Windsor, then departed for a shooting party to be held at Welbeck Abbey, the home of his friends the Duke and Duchess of Portland. Through the intervention of a certain gentleman in Whitehall, Mr. Sherlock Holmes and I were invited to attend that shoot, despite our humble status in such exalted company.

That, however, is not the tale that I shall tell today. For the Heir-Apparent's advent recalled to us a journey which had occurred years earlier, but which presaged a tragedy of momentous import to Europe and the world. Because of the shame it caused him, this is the most daunting to record of all the cases undertaken by my friend. Nevertheless, the sad events at Mayerling, and in Geneva, provide a necessary prelude to the Archduke's visit. On the day Franz Ferdinand arrived in London, he was still seven months removed from Sarajevo. Yet, according to the great detective, his fate had long since been foretold.

The late summer of 1898 brought days of unusually hot, dry weather to the British Isles. Though it was not yet noon on Friday, the second of September, the thermometer was rising steadily towards eighty. Holmes and I, thoroughly enervated, lounged in our oppressive sitting-room, the side panels of its bow window open to catch the slightest stir of breeze.

Still jaded from my breakfast, I leafed lethargically through the London dailies. The Sirdar's army was advancing rapidly on Omdurman, soon to avenge the long-abandoned general whose

97

portrait hung above my writing-desk. At Fashoda, farther south, a small but gallant band of Frenchman awaited Kitchener's arrival, portending a crisis that could well set off a European war. Meanwhile, a noted British physicist had perished, with three of his children, in an Alpine mountaineering accident; and a new American breakfast cereal ("Corn Flakes") was threatening to infiltrate British markets. None of these events, I knew, was likely to engage my friend. The crumpled pile of newsprint beside his own armchair showed that the latest criminal tidings had likewise failed to interest him. Instead, the detective, who was presently without a case, was postponing his inevitable return to boredom by a listless investigation of the morning's mail.

A cream-coloured envelope, marked with a foreign stamp, caught Holmes's eye. I watched as he eagerly tore into it, and a low whistle escaped him when he read the note.

"Well, Doctor," my friend murmured, "it seems I have surpassed myself." With a transparent air of carelessness, he tossed the epistle more or less in my direction. I rose, containing my annoyance, and retrieved it from the floor. "The author of this letter," Holmes went on behind me, "exceeds even our old client 'The King of Bohemia' as the highest-ranking potentate who has solicited my services."

Resuming my seat with a non-committal grunt, I scanned the letter. Dated two days earlier, it had been written on stationery from the Grand Hôtel de Caux, near Montreux, Switzerland:

Herr Sherlock Holmes!

I need your help to rectify a grave injustice to the memory of one whom I held dear. Please arrange to meet with me, at the Hôtel Beau Rivage on Lake Geneva, one week from the day you will receive this letter—that is to say, at nine o'clock on the morning of Saturday, September 10th.

Having received assurances of your integrity, and knowing that a degree of curiosity must attend your career as a detective, I feel confident that you will not only honour this request, but will take every precaution to maintain my anonymity and privacy. It goes without saying that you are to come alone.

Elisabeth
Countess von Hohenembs

I regarded the recipient of this appeal with some perplexity. "See here, Holmes," I reminded him, "this appears to have come from a mere countess. Surely her station falls far below a king's—even the king of a minor Balkan nation."

"Ah, Watson, I notice you have used the word 'appears.'" Taking his brier pipe from a coat pocket, my friend reached to retrieve the Persian slipper from the hearth. "Are you aware that the 'Countess von Hohenembs' also bears a more exalted title?"

"Do I *seem* aware of it?" I replied gruffly. "Who is the lady, then?"

"Why, none other than the Empress Elisabeth of Austria!" With a smile of satisfaction, he began packing the pipe with his accustomed shag.

"The beauteous Sisi!" I chortled, fully mollified as I returned the letter. "Without a doubt, the loveliest queen in Europe when you and I were young. Her portrait by Winterhalter held pride of place in our officers' mess while I was with the Fusiliers. There was no one to touch her as an equestrienne, not even our friend Skittles."[7]

"That is indeed the lady," the detective said. "Evidently," he added, with a glance at the recovered missive, "Her Majesty

---

[7] For Holmes and Watson's encounter with the famous Victorian courtesan Catherine "Skittles" Walters, see "A Game of Skittles" in *The MX Book of New Sherlock Holmes Stories, Part XIX: 2020 Annual (1882-1890)* (London: MX Publishing, 2020), pp. 221-246.

overestimated the time it would take her appeal to reach us from Montreux."

"You will accept the commission, I presume?"

"Of course, likewise presuming I am allowed to go. Brother Mycroft will have to be consulted."

"Would his involvement not violate the Empress's conditions?" I protested. "She asked specifically that you protect her 'anonymity and privacy.'"

"Oh, no, Doctor," Holmes replied as he puffed serenely on his brier. "Her Majesty is aware of the political necessities in a country such as ours. She would expect for government to be informed. It is the vulgar gaze of the public or—God help us!—the newspapers that she wishes to avoid. That is why she always travels incognito."

"But whose memory does Her Majesty believe to have suffered 'grave injustice'? She refers only to a person whom she once 'held dear.'"

"It cannot be anyone except her son, the late Crown Prince. Surely, Watson, you recall the sad incident at Mayerling, where Rudolf died with his young mistress. It was generally accepted that he had first shot her and then himself. For a Catholic royal house, there could hardly be a more ignoble scandal. It shook the Austro-Hungarian monarchy to its very core!"

"And yet," I pondered, "the Empress rejects that verdict as unjust. If Rudolf was innocent, it would mean they *both* were murdered. What new evidence could Elisabeth possess? It's been nine years since Mayerling."

The detective essayed a Gallic shrug. "We shall obviously have to wait and see. You know my dislike of attempting to theorise without data. However, even at the time, the official version of the tragedy seemed at variance with several details reported by the foreign press—for whatever *that* is worth. I telegraphed offering my services to Vienna's police when they started their investigation. I was rebuffed in no uncertain terms."

"Really? I don't recall your making such an offer."

"You and Miss Morstan were out of London at the time, spending a few days of your engagement with Mrs. Cecil Forrester." My friend smiled sadly at the mention of my dear, departed wife.

"Of course! It was at the end of January, 1889. I remember how shocked Mary was to read of the Crown Prince's death. It was an appalling crime!"

"Indeed." Having apparently come to a decision, Holmes strode to his writing-desk. He scribbled hastily, then pulled the bell. The latest incarnation of our "boy in buttons" dutifully appeared and was directed to take the note to Mr. Mycroft Holmes. Disdaining my proposal of an early luncheon, the detective announced that he would nap for an hour before meeting with his brother. I contented myself, on the advice of Mrs. Hudson, with the remnants of last night's steak-and-kidney pie. Upon arising, Holmes laughed incredulously at the message Billy had delivered.

"So," I ventured, "we are bound for the Diogenes Club."

"Oh, no, my dear fellow," replied the younger brother. "For once, the Mountain is coming to Muhammad. Mycroft says that he will see us here!"

CHAPTER 2

The Mountain Comes to Baker Street

"You're joking!"

When I first met Mycroft Holmes, he had just turned forty and was no more than moderately corpulent. Over the past decade, he had grown increasingly obese, and correspondingly less willing to engage in any sort of physical activity. Beyond short daily jaunts between his Whitehall office and the Diogenes Club, it was unknown for him to travel. That he should walk from Pall Mall to Baker Street, on such an afternoon as this, aroused my professional dismay. What had possessed his brother, I enquired of Sherlock Holmes, to alter his lethargic habits in so dangerous a way?

"I fear that Mycroft has fallen victim to his own success," sighed Holmes. "Having finally reached the apex of that strange cabal in which he labours for the Queen, he was recently called for the first time into the royal presence. Her Majesty (who, I am told, has become rather caustic in old age) remarked to her new informant that he was even fatter than her eldest son. She proposed that he take exercise, and—given Mycroft's veneration for the lady—he took her suggestion as a royal command. Hence, I surmise, his journey here today."

As though our talk had summoned him, we heard the senior Holmes's arrival in the hall below. There came a deep but incoherent grumble (presumably his greeting to the landlady), then a painfully slow ascension of the stairs. A far lighter step made quicker progress, and the door burst open to reveal young Billy, looking terrified.

"Get ready, sir, he's almost here—and, Doctor, you'd better get your bag!" He turned and fled, and we could hear him urging Mycroft towards the summit. The last step was at length surmounted; the heavy tread and ragged breath grew nigh. Our page re-entered to announce, with creditable aplomb: "Gentlemen, Mr. Mycroft Holmes."

102

A huge, scarlet-visaged apparition lurched into our sitting-room and staggered to the settee. There it collapsed like a downed elephant, nearly shattering the frame. Sherlock Holmes rushed to loosen Mycroft's collar and wipe his brow, while I poured out a glass of water and warned him not to gulp it. After a dose of smelling salts and perhaps five minutes' rest, our visitor's breathing slowed, and his face regained an almost normal hue. Mycroft hoisted himself upright and lay back against the cushions, regarding his sibling with a look of baffled indignation.

"Never again, Sherlock," he gasped hoarsely, "not even if Her Majesty demotes me to the consulate in East Timor!" Another moment, and he handed me the empty tumbler. "Fill that with whisky, Doctor, if you please." Glancing about himself vaguely, as though searching for someone, the Queen's advisor queried: "Who *was* that boy?"

I explained that a succession of "Billys" had filled the post of Mrs. Hudson's page. Although most had come from the ranks of her family or acquaintances, the present incumbent had been a promising Irregular, as Holmes cheerfully confirmed. "I should not have made it here alive without his aid," acknowledged Mycroft. "That boy will go far. In future, however, I shall not attempt to follow him!"

Once fortified by the tray of sandwiches our good landlady prepared, Holmes's brother heard his account of Elisabeth's commission. Mycroft grunted sceptically, however, at the implication of new evidence concerning Rudolf's death.

"I have no idea what evidence the Empress might conceive she has uncovered, but the tragedy was investigated thoroughly at the time. Would Franz Josef have allowed his only son to be dishonoured as a murderer and suicide had there been another explanation of the matter?"

"But other theories *were* put forth," insisted Holmes. "The newspapers were full of rumours in the early days of February."

103

"Oh, yes, the sort of romantic foolishness that usually accompanies such cases. The Crown Prince was murdered by a disgruntled gamekeeper, whose wife he had seduced. Or he was shot by the uncles of his seventeen-year-old paramour—who, in the course of avenging the girl's honour, managed to shoot her as well. *Or*, there was a wild, immoral party in the hunting lodge at Mayerling, during which a drunken crony smashed a bottle of Champagne on Rudolf's head. A German pamphlet to that effect appeared last year. I didn't read its explanation of how his mistress—whose name I have forgotten—"

"Mary Vetsera," I supplied, recalling my own Mary's sympathy for the poor girl.

"—Mary Vetsera died," the senior Holmes finished, acknowledging my contribution with a nod. "Talking of the Germans, both the French and the American papers concocted sinister tales of German hunting parties roving the Vienna Woods near Mayerling before the tragedy."

"Now *that*," opined the detective, "sounds rather more intriguing."

"Piffle, Sherlock!" Mycroft snorted. "One expects such nonsense from the French, but you and the *New York Times* should know better. As it happened, we had spies among the crowd outside the lodge by eleven in the morning. Mayerling is not an isolated place; but no one with whom our agents spoke had seen anyone other than servants, gamekeepers, and Rudolf's usual companions in the hunt. That is not to say conclusively that no one else was there—the Crown Prince, after all, had sneaked in the Vetsera girl—but another hunting party in the region would not have passed unnoticed."

"Tell us what else your department knows about the matter," Holmes requested, "or as much of it as you are able to reveal. As you recall, Mycroft, I had hoped to investigate the deaths at Mayerling myself, but the Austrian police would have no part of me."

"Well, brother-mine," the Mountain rumbled, "for once I can be reasonably forthcoming. A glance at my department's archives confirmed that we know remarkably little, beyond what was reported in the press or acquired through the usual diplomatic channels." Having secured the last sandwich, Mycroft settled himself more comfortably and removed a slender file of papers from his coat's voluminous depths.

"If I may simply read that," my friend observed, "it will save considerable time."

"Certainly not! I shall summarise the facts, and you gentlemen may draw your own conclusions." Leafing through his documents, Mycroft sipped the tea with which Mrs. Hudson had replaced his tumbler of whisky. Holmes and I regarded him attentively, my friend taking the opportunity to re-light his brier.

"Rudolf and Baroness Vetsera," the senior Holmes began, "arrived at Mayerling in late afternoon on the twenty-eighth of January. *Her* presence, however, was unknown to anyone except the Crown Prince's coachman, Bratfisch, and his valet, Loschek. Rudolf, it appears, had not intended to start his hunting-trip so soon. Unfortunately, he had recently been observed in an altercation with his father at the opera, and the previous night his mistress had rudely snubbed Crown Princess Stéphanie at a ball in the German Embassy. There were also rumours linking the Heir-Apparent to the uproar in Budapest over a bill that required Hungarian reserve officers to learn the German language. It seemed a most convenient moment, therefore, for the prince and his young concubine to disappear from the capital for a few days."

I began to raise a point about the army bill, but my friend lifted a restraining hand. Mycroft, undeterred, continued.

"The remaining members of the hunting party, Prince Philipp of Coburg and Count Josef Hoyos, came to the lodge as scheduled on the morning of the twenty-ninth. They did not see Mary Vetsera or even realise she was there. However, Crown Prince Rudolf excused himself from the day's hunt, claiming a mild illness. That afternoon, he also telegraphed his wife, declining to attend his sister's engagement dinner at the Hofburg. It was then that the imperial family grew concerned. Meanwhile, Baroness *Helene* Vetsera, alarmed at her daughter's disappearance, was urging the authorities to undertake a search. I regret to say that owing to the reputation of both ladies, she received no satisfaction until it became evident that Rudolf had decided to isolate himself at Mayerling.

"The last person to see the Crown Prince alive, other than his mistress and his valet, was Count Hoyos. The two of them had dinner while the young baroness remained in hiding. Rudolf seemed to his friend in excellent spirits; he ate and drank copiously, even remarking on the beauty of the Vienna Woods in snow and moonlight. He retired at nine o'clock, after ordering his coachman to return Mary Vetsera to Vienna in the morning, and his valet to 'Let no one in, not even if it is the Emperor.'"

"Were those the Heir-Apparent's final words?" I wondered.

"By no means, Doctor, for Rudolf emerged just after six o'clock on the morning of the thirtieth. He instructed Loschek to call for him at seven-thirty and went off whistling a tune. *That* was the last time the Crown Prince was seen alive."

"You say that snow covered the estate," Holmes noted. "Did your men examine the grounds for signs of an intrusion?"

"They made an inefficient search," admitted Mycroft, "not being trained observers of your calibre. Along with servants and gamekeepers, Austrian police were on the scene by the time our men arrived. A crowd of lookers-on soon gathered. My agents could not search assiduously without arousing suspicion and revealing their identity. It appeared, however, that there had been no attempt to infiltrate the grounds or break into the lodge where Rudolf and his mistress were residing."

"'*Appeared*'!" snorted the detective. "If only *I* had been there!"

"Shall I continue," his elder brother queried, "or do you prefer to rant?"

"Proceed."

Henceforth, Mycroft acknowledged, his account was based in part upon conjecture. British spies had remained at Mayerling throughout that afternoon and on into the night. While never able to enter the sequestered lodge, they had talked cautiously to members of the Heir-Apparent's retinue and witnessed those who came and went. Thanks to their observations, and to intelligence passed on by diplomatic contacts, an outline of the subsequent events was known.

Before the appointed time to call his master, Loschek had heard two shots fired in Rudolf's room. His frantic knocking went unanswered, and he was unable to open the locked door. After some delay, the valet summoned Hoyos, who was observed crossing the courtyard at eight o'clock. "The remarkable thing," mused our informant, "is that an hour earlier, Rudolf's driver Bratfisch had advised the chief huntsman to cancel the day's shoot. 'The Crown Prince,' he declared, 'is dead.'"

"Did no one question the man upon that point?" fumed Holmes.

"As I have told you," Mycroft snapped, "our spies were incognito. Nor had they any standing to interrogate members of the imperial household. Worst of all, dear brother, Bratfisch had departed before they came upon the scene!"

"Were they able to discover anything at all?" my friend enquired sarcastically.

The answer to his gibe was largely in the negative. Nothing more had been visible to those outside until Prince Philipp of Coburg arrived at half past eight. Soon afterwards, Count Hoyos—who appeared extremely agitated—emerged from the lodge and was driven by Bratfisch to the station in Baden. There he commandeered a train coming from Trieste, having blurted to the stationmaster, "The Crown Prince has shot himself!"

"*Well*," Mycroft chuckled grimly, "the stationmaster immediately notified the owner of the train, who happened to be Baron Nathaniel Rothschild. *He* telegraphed his brother Albert, who promptly informed the British and the German embassies. Thereby, gentlemen, I daresay *we* learned of Crown Prince Rudolf's death before his parents did!"

The detective was unimpressed by this digression. "So Coburg and Hoyos were the first to find the bodies," he impatiently remarked.

"It was Loschek who first looked through the bedroom door, which the three men had broken into with an axe. He assured the courtiers before they entered that both occupants were dead. Prince Philipp wrote to the Queen later that the pistol shot left Rudolf's head 'terribly disfigured.' Mary Vetsera was also killed by a single bullet to the brain."

"Was that the entirety of the medical report?" I questioned doubtfully, receiving an approving nod from Holmes. "Surely, someone at Mayerling summoned a doctor!"

"The physician from the Hofburg arrived shortly after noon. Obviously, none of our agents witnessed his examination, but he was heard to say upon departing that Mary Vetsera died at least six hours before the Heir-Apparent."

"Demonstrating," I asserted, "that he first shot her and then himself."

"Not necessarily, Watson," Holmes objected. "So long a delay might also suggest that the unfortunate girl took her own life, and that on discovering her body, the Crown Prince shot himself out of remorse."

"You are *both* forgetting," interjected Mycroft, "that the valet Loschek heard two concurrent shots, indicating that the deaths were almost simultaneous."

"But that contradicts the doctor's evidence!" I cried out in bewilderment, accompanied by a merry laugh from Holmes.

"Well, brother, you have sadly demolished our *ex post facto* efforts at deduction! I suppose none of your agents saw Baroness Vetsera's body, and might allow us to resolve her time of death?"

Mycroft shook his massive head. "Neither body was visible to our men at any time. Just before dark, a squad of police evicted all observers and surrounded Mayerling. Our men remained on watch outside the grounds. About an hour later, a horse-drawn hearse emerged from the forest and disappeared through the lodge gate. It reappeared soon after midnight and drove away in the direction of Vienna. Only one corpse could have been inside, and that undoubtedly was Rudolf's. We later learned that the Vetsera girl's family were permitted to remove her body on the following night. It was taken to Heiligenkreuz Abbey and buried in an unmarked grave."

"Soon after," recalled Sherlock Holmes, "the initial press reports that Crown Prince Rudolf died of heart failure, or in a hunting accident, or from poison administered by his rejected mistress, were all disavowed. Within a week, the imperial court admitted that the Heir-Apparent had taken his own life while mentally deranged."

His elder brother nodded. "Derangement was required to ensure a suicide a Catholic funeral. It may have been quite true, of course. Our informants reported that the Crown Prince's behaviour grew increasingly erratic during his last weeks."

"And yet," I reminded them, "his mother denies all charges of suicide and murder."

"What mother would not?" Mycroft grumbled. "Even so, the Doctor has recalled us to the point at hand." Not without difficulty, the Queen's advisor rose and poured himself another glass of whisky. Holmes and I accepted one as well. "How do we—or, more precisely—how do *you*, Sherlock, intend to respond to the Empress's commission?"

"Why, brother-mine, that is why we called *you* here," my friend responded blandly. "What are Her Majesty's ministers likely to say about the matter?"

The senior Holmes resumed his seat with an ironic grunt. "They are likely to say a great deal, but nothing of any use in crafting policy. As for reaching a decision. . . ." Leaving this remark unfinished, he sat pondering a moment, while my friend and I waited in respectful silence. Suddenly, Mycroft's countenance altered and he gave a guilty start, drawing his watch from his expansive waistcoat's pocket.

"Great heavens, gentlemen, is that the time? I am expected to meet with the Prime Minister in twenty minutes. I must leave at once!"

"But you *will* return for dinner," Holmes entreated, "so that we may conclude our discussion? I am sure I can prevail on Mrs. Hudson to whip something up."

"No, no, Sherlock," cried the elder brother, rising almost quickly to his feet. "I have no wish to impose upon your landlady. Besides, my schedule has been disrupted as it is. After disgracing myself before Lord Salisbury, I shall return to the Diogenes Club and restore my appearance to a more gentlemanly state. You and Dr. Watson are welcome to join me for dinner in the Stranger's Room at eight o'clock."

"Very well, Mycroft," my friend responded meekly. "Is there anything Watson and I can do for you before you leave?"

Looking nearly as flurried and disheveled as he had on his arrival, Her Majesty's corpulent advisor paused within the open door. "Yes, my dear brother, there *is* one thing you can do for me. Have that excellent young page of yours summon a cab!"

CHAPTER 3

Dinner in the Stranger's Room

That evening, having made our way to the Diogenes Club and partaken of a joint of beef that rivalled Simpsons', Holmes and I sat sipping port across from Brother Mycroft. That gentleman, his toilet and attire once more immaculate, was likewise restored to his usual complacency. He sat nursing his own glass while eying the last surviving pudding. Though it was well past nine o'clock, no more had been said of the letter from Montreux or the deaths at Mayerling. The senior Holmes, having elected to forgo a last foray on the platter, was now prepared to correct that omission.

"The Empress Elisabeth," he announced without preamble, "is no longer a political factor in Franz Josef's empire. For a time, she wielded considerable influence; indeed, the *Ausgleich* with Hungary in '67 would not have been achieved without her aid. Since her son's demise, however, Her Imperial and Royal Majesty has indulged herself in aimless wanderings across the Continent, alone save for a small retinue of trusted servants. She spends almost no time in Vienna and sees her husband only once or twice each year. In essence, therefore, she has become a private person."

The detective was fully alert to this narrative's significance. "If I take your meaning, Mycroft," he replied, "you imply that Her *Britannic* Majesty's government would take no official interest in my investigation."

"Not quite, Sherlock. I am advising that you may approach the Empress on the same basis as any other, ah, client. Nearly ten years have elapsed since Rudolf died; Austria-Hungary has a new heir to the throne. As a practical matter, it makes little difference to Great Britain whether the late Crown Prince was truly guilty of suicide and murder. Even if he himself was murdered, that fact is of no importance to us, *so long as his murder was a private crime!* Conversely, should Elisabeth possess reliable evidence documenting the involvement of any other European power—or of dissident or traitorous elements within Austria-Hungary itself—either contingency would interest Her Majesty's government very much indeed!"

"So, in the end," my friend chuckled, "we come back to German hunting parties prowling the Vienna Woods." I could not help joining his laughter, but Mycroft did not share in our amusement.

"That idea, Sherlock, was ridiculous; but Germany may still have been aware if not involved. We noticed at the time that its ambassador to Vienna seemed surprisingly well-informed about events at Mayerling. Quite early on, he telegraphed the Wilhelmstrasse a detailed account. The Dowager Empress apprised Her Majesty that the 'Iron Chancellor' by no means regretted Crown Prince Rudolf's death."

"Was not Rudolf known to hold liberal opinions?" I remembered. "From what we saw in Charlottenburg of Bismarck's attitude towards his own liberal emperor, the accession of an allied ruler with similar ideals would have been anathema."

"Quite so, Doctor," the elder Holmes agreed. "Moreover, it was widely believed that on coming to the throne, Rudolf would cast Germany aside and pursue an Anglo-French alliance. The Chancellor despised and feared him, and those sentiments were passed on to the new Kaiser. William II and Rudolf were much of an age, but they found little else in common. One of our most reliable contacts in Vienna—Frau Wolf, the proprietor of a multinational, highly exclusive house of pleasure—relayed an intriguing account of William's indiscreet admissions to an Austrian *demoiselle* early in 1887."

"Some of your department's contacts, Mycroft," his younger brother noted primly, "are as disgusting as they are reliable. Is information gathered from such sources really worth the price?"

"Oh, yes, Sherlock," the head of British intelligence imperturbably replied. "It does no good to be squeamish where information is concerned. In the event," he continued, returning to his file, "while in his cups, Prince William spoke candidly of his belief that the Habsburg monarchy was very near to dissolution. Its German-speaking regions, he forecast, 'would soon drop like ripe fruit' into the Hohenzollerns' lap. As for the empire's Heir-Apparent, Prince William placed Rudolf in the same category as his own father . . . 'a Judaized, vain, arty, popularity-seeker without ability or character,' as it says here."

"Good heavens!" I laughed, "I trust you forwarded those slanderous remarks to the Austrian Crown Prince?"

"There was no need, Doctor," Mycroft smiled, "for Frau Wolf had already done so. Though I must admit," he added, "that we did not take the drunken tirade seriously. At the time, two lives still stood between Prince William and the German throne, and we had no inkling then that Crown Prince Frederick was destined for an early grave."

"A more relevant question," opined Sherlock Holmes, "is whether, two years later, the new Kaiser knew of or assisted in the murder of his ally's heir."

"We have no evidence for that hypothesis," his elder brother answered. "However, assuming that Rudolf's death *was* murder, German involvement cannot be discounted as a possibility. It will be interesting to learn whether Empress Elisabeth has any thoughts about the matter. If she believes her son to be a victim of the crime at Mayerling, rather than its perpetrator, she presumably has some idea of who was actually responsible."

By this stage in the evening, port and our large dinner had combined to make me rather sleepy. "So, gentlemen," I wondered, stifling a yawn, "how do you propose that we begin this new investigation?" I rose to stand before the fire and lit up a cigar, which I have often found a useful aid to thought and to digestion.

113

The brothers Holmes exchanged a wary glance. "As you must recall, Watson," my friend began with an embarrassed air, "Elisabeth's instructions were quite explicit that I was to meet with her alone."

"Oh . . . yes, indeed," I haltingly replied, quite flummoxed. It had not occurred to me that I would have no part in what promised to be a memorable case. "Very well, then. How do the two of you propose that *Holmes* should start?"

To my relief, my two companions laughed uproariously. "Surely, old friend," cried Sherlock Holmes, "you did not think you would be left behind? Why, I should be lost without my Boswell! It may be necessary to keep you outside Her Majesty's purview, but you will definitely have a role to play."

"Doctor," Mycroft rumbled, taking cigars from a pocket for his brother and himself, "a decade may have passed, but I have not forgotten your invaluable service during the mission to Charlottenburg. Though you were not aware of *me* in those days, I was already quite aware of *you!* I have given the matter much thought since our meeting earlier today, and on this occasion I should like to entrust you with an assignment of your own."

"You have evolved a plan of campaign, then, brother?" Holmes eagerly enquired. I returned to the table as the Queen's adviser poured us all one final round of port. Well content to have our full attention, Mycroft sat back comfortably and began to expound.

"The key to this matter is that we have a week in hand before your meeting with the Empress. Such a delay allows time for consultation with others involved in the events at Mayerling. Obtaining various perspectives should be useful in evaluating the veracity of Elisabeth's presumed new evidence."

"Surely," I remonstrated, "the word of an empress may be trusted!" From the corner of my eye, I saw Holmes sneer at this latest example of what he frequently derided as my "fascination with The Great."

"I do not question *Her Majesty's* veracity," Mycroft patiently explained, "or, rather, her willingness to impart the truth as she perceives it. Unfortunately, in her latter years the Austrian empress has grown increasingly . . . eccentric. She exercises obsessively and undertakes starvation diets. On a visit to Egypt, she spent eight hours each day walking in the desert sun; yet, she is equally fond of taking long sea voyages in the dead of winter. She has developed the habit of dropping in on fellow monarchs, or even total strangers, unannounced; the Dowager Empress Victoria's household guard once mistakenly imprisoned her. Even Empress Carlotta of Mexico— herself no model of stability—noted that Elisabeth's spirit 'seems to dwell within another world.' Rumours abound in the Continental press that the poor woman is no longer sane."

"It is remarkable," Sherlock Holmes indeed remarked, "how many empresses still clutter the European landscape with the twentieth century about to dawn. May we *please* move on, elder brother, to the plan you have in mind for our investigation?"

"Of course, *younger* brother," Mycroft snarled, "after I have finished the point I was about to make. My point being that while the Empress is not now taken seriously by the espionage services of Europe, that fact could change quickly if she begins raking through the coals of Mayerling. Assuming that her son *was* innocent, and his assassins discover her efforts to reveal the truth, your mission will become exceedingly dangerous, not only to Elisabeth, but to you and Dr. Watson."

"I am sure I speak for Watson," Holmes announced—without, I was proud to see, a glance in my direction—"in stating that we are both prepared to take that risk."

"I expected nothing less," the Queen's advisor answered. "Let us consider, then, gentlemen, who else might provide us with useful information."

"Prince Philipp of Coburg," my friend put forth, "was among those present on the scene at Mayerling."

115

"Prince Philipp of *Saxe*-Coburg *and Gotha*," Mycroft corrected him, "is too closely connected to the Royal Family to be approached. I shall say nothing to the Queen, still less to the Cabinet, until we know a good deal more of this affair."

"What about Crown Princess Stéphanie?" I offered. "Apart from the matter of her husband's infidelity, she may know more of what was in his mind than anyone."

"Excellent, Doctor! My brother informs me that 'the fair sex' is *your* department, and she is the lady I intended to assign to you. Stéphanie presently resides with her young daughter at Miramar Castle in Trieste. By train, it is an overnight journey from Geneva, so you will easily have time to rejoin Sherlock there before the tenth day of September."

"What am *I* doing in the meantime?" Holmes demanded.

"Well, brother-mine, there is another participant in the Mayerling tragedy whom I should like for you to interview: Count Josef Hoyos. The problem is that we are uncertain where he now resides. Presumably, it is somewhere in Vienna."

"I *do* have some experience, Mycroft, in tracing a subject's whereabouts."

"I know it, Sherlock. But remember that in Austria-Hungary you will be perpetually surrounded by police spies. Your usual methods of enquiry would be indiscreet and time-consuming. Fortunately, there is an old friend of yours currently visiting Vienna. He was once an intimate of the Crown Prince and his inner circle. I expect the gentleman can still direct you to Count Hoyos."

"And who, brother, might this gentleman be?"

"Why, 'The King of Bohemia,' of course!"

116

CHAPTER 4

An Interview with an Ignoble King

It is on occasions such as this that I realise how unjustly I have denigrated my friend Watson's literary efforts. When, after nearly thirty years, he asked me to write an account of my work upon this case (which I acknowledge as my most grievous failure), I became aware of how little of that work derived from my own unique talents of observation and deduction, and how much of it required no more than simple "leg-work" of the sort that Gregson, Lestrade, or even Athelney Jones might have performed as well as I.

Thus, there will be little scope within these pages to explicate the principles of "The Science of Deduction," as Watson pithily christened the body of knowledge on which my reputation has been built. For it must be admitted, I suppose, that the chief interest of *this* case lay in its "romantic" aspects—ultimately, it was merely a tale of murdered princes and mad queens—i.e., in the very features of the Doctor's writing that I most deplored. Moreover, I admit that my old friend's literary talents are better-suited to recounting such a tale than are my own.

Watson's unfortunate self-deprecation in his narratives has masked the fact that his contribution to my cases frequently went well beyond the role of chronicler. Although, despite forty years of tutelage, he absorbed amazingly little of The Science of Deduction, and even now remains blind as a beetle in the observation of physical details, as an observer of the human race the Doctor's perspicacity is actually superior to mine. Perhaps his greater reliance on the unpredictable factor of emotion, rather than the dictates of pure reason, accounts for the difference and serves him surprisingly well in this regard. Few other humans, after all, are as resistant to the impact of emotion as am I.

Be that as it may—and to begin the story I was asked to write—on that particular morning in Vienna I needed no help from my friend to analyse the character of the man I was to meet. Eleven years had passed since our only previous encounter; but I remembered Milan Obrenović, now ex-king of Serbia, all too well.

The Doctor and I had departed London on Sunday, the fourth of September, arriving at Vienna's *West-Bahnhof* the following evening. On Tuesday the sixth, having enjoyed an excellent breakfast of coffee and strudel, Watson hailed a cab for the city's southern terminal, where he would catch a Semmering Line train bound for Trieste. I, meanwhile, made my way to the address where Mycroft had indicated I would find the former king. Because my name, though not my face, was known to the Austrian police, I had adopted the persona of my eldest brother, posing as "Sir Robert Sherrinford, Bart.," a simple country squire. Disguising my appearance was unnecessary, but merely for amusement I applied a touch of talcum powder to my temples and pasted on a grey mustache.

My cab dropped me in an older section of Vienna's central district, near a large complex of buildings left from the conversion of a Baroque palace. One of them was now the Hôtel Klomser, later to gain notoriety as the site of Colonel Redl's suicide.[8] It was not, I saw immediately, a hotel of the first class. It appeared that Milan, after giving up his crown, had been placed upon short rations by his Austrian protectors. In happier days he would have been welcome at the Hofburg. Entering the run-down lobby, I approached the desk, wrote a note on the reverse side of Sir Robert's card, and asked to have the card delivered to King Milan's rooms. A bribe for the clerk, and a tip for the bell-boy, were required to secure the transaction; but within five minutes a swarthy Balkan page arrived to conduct me to

---

[8] Colonel Alfred Redl (1864-1913) was an intelligence officer on the Austro-Hungarian General Staff. His homosexuality left him vulnerable to blackmail. When it was discovered that Redl had sold his army's war plans to the Russians, he was allowed to shoot himself rather than face a public trial.

the royal presence. As we headed for the lift, I noticed the retired hussar who had been eyeing me across the lobby scribble on his cuff. It was thereby proven that the Serbian ex-monarch's contacts were still of interest to Franz Josef's spies.

I found Milan lounging in a splendid suite that in no way reflected his diminished status. It had obviously been furnished with possessions of his own, including a magnificent Turkish carpet and three superb Impressionist paintings by an artist I did not then recognise. (In later years, I identified them as Cézannes.) A young woman, whose blonde attractions were more suited to the hotel in which she found herself, rose from the divan where sat the King and exited, though not without a meaning glance in my direction. As for Serbia's erstwhile ruler, he also stood and offered me an ironic grin of welcome.

"Ah, Mr. Sherlock Holmes—unless you prefer to continue as 'Sir Robert' or 'SH'? Does 'Miss Adler' truly 'send me her regards'? Somehow, I tend to doubt it. That mustache, sir, does not become you."

The years since our last meeting had not dealt kindly with my host. Following his sudden abdication—which occurred within weeks of Crown Prince Rudolf's death—he had enjoyed the life of a sybarite in Paris. In 1897, his son and successor had recalled him to Belgrade. There (my brother had informed me) Milan was doing the best work of his life, rebuilding the Serbian army he had once led to disaster in his Bulgarian war. Yet, the legacy of the King's unruly reign, and his ineradicable Habsburg sympathies, left him unredeemed in the eyes of the Slav populace. It was also evident that years of dissipation had undermined the ex-king's health. The handsome uniform he wore could not disguise a paunch. His cat-like eyes were pouched and rheumy. His once thick hair had thinned and grizzled; only the heavy mustache retained its virility. Milan's visage bore an air of disillusionment, as though the melancholy that had always underlain his braggadocio had now come to the fore. Although King Milan

Obrenović was eight months younger than myself, I felt sure that Watson would have marked him for an early death. In fact, on that morning he had slightly more than two years left to live.

Thus, the real "King of Bohemia" was an even more ignoble figure than the alter ego who appeared in Watson's fable. Nevertheless, the man seemed gratified to see me, and as I had need of his assistance I decided to be cordial.

"I must admit, Your Majesty," I replied to his enquiry, "that Miss Adler's greetings were an invention of my own. It may interest you to know, however, that she was well when I last had word of her."

"Which, I believe, was earlier this year, when you visited her home in Montenegro," the King said smoothly. "Oh, take no offense, my friend! It is only prudent for a man in my position to monitor the meetings of a former adversary. Most happily for all of us, Dr. Watson's depiction of your service to me was admirably discreet. I was amused to find myself portrayed as a Bohemian, having led so bohemian a life. As for the divine Irene, now that the Queen and I ostensibly have reconciled, you are welcome, Mr. Holmes, to *any* of my cast-off mistresses!"

Before I could answer this contemptible remark as it deserved, Milan abruptly asked how he might be of use to me—"for long have I desired to compensate you for your most invaluable aid, although even then I realised that you do not think well of me. Pray, sir, allow me to discharge my debt, so that henceforth we may go our separate ways."

"I wish to locate another of your former friends," I told him coldly. "An Austrian nobleman named Count Josef Hoyos."

"Hoyos!" His Majesty's sallow countenance blanched further. He turned uneasily away, crossing the room to a sideboard and pouring himself a glass of cognac, which he quickly drank. "Mr. Holmes," he sighed, "you take me back to a most unlucky era in my life!" Pouring again from the decanter, Milan lifted a second glass invitingly. When I declined (for it was not yet eleven in the morning), he shrugged and returned to the divan, motioning me to take a chair across from him. "May I ask," he queried, "what—or rather *who*—has prompted this enquiry?"

I was aware that anything I told my host would be repeated to the Hofburg. "Your Majesty will understand that *all* my clients must receive the same discretion that I once afforded in your case."

"Oh, indeed, sir!" Milan sniggered irritably. "Well, if you are looking into Rudolf's death—for *that* is the only reason Hoyos could be of any interest to you—it is not hard to guess who is behind it. Not his *father*, certainly. But have no fear; my lips are sealed!"

The nod I gave him combined my admiration for the King's intelligence with a degree of doubt. Having reached an impasse, we sat in glum silence for an interval while His Majesty sipped cognac. I longed for my cherry-wood pipe but had no desire to smoke it in the royal apartments. At last, Milan raised his eyes and asked me slyly:

"Have you never wondered, Mr. Holmes, *why* it was the Crown Prince died? Could it really have been for love of a young baroness? Not *Mary Vetsera*, I assure you! That pretty child was a mere whore, as had been her mother. Why, the Emperor himself, for all his sterling reputation, could verify the latter fact! We have these women— aristocratic whores, I mean—in Serbia as well. My fool of a son intends to marry one of them!"

Having drunk himself into an evil humour, King Milan retreated to the sideboard to stoke his ire. This time, in order to keep his reminiscences flowing, I agreed to join him.

"Can Your Majesty be sure of Rudolf's feelings?" I enquired sceptically as I took my glass. As expected, his cognac was first-rate. "I was unaware that your relationship with the Crown Prince was sufficiently close to permit such confidences."

"Why, sir," cried the King indignantly, "I went hunting with him only a day or two before he died! Myself, Rudolf, and his cousin Archduke Otto—*Otto*, Mr. Holmes, the wildest fellow of the three! Rudolf spoke to us quite freely of his latest mistress. 'I've known many far more beautiful,' he said, 'though never one more faithful. But now the little minx has turned into a perfect devil! She threatens

122

to immerse me in a scandal—which would not matter much if it did not clash with more important things.'"

"What do you suppose he meant?" I asked, my tone implying that the matter was of no importance.

"Oh, there was some affair in Hungary that worried him. Of that he did not speak. My point, Mr. Holmes, is that while he was indeed quite fond of her, the Crown Prince was eager to be rid of the Vetsera girl. She had become more trouble than her love was worth. It is often so with these young girls, who have little to offer but their bodies."

Disgusted by such callousness, I decided to attack the problem from another angle. "Your Majesty's abdication, I recall, followed closely upon the deaths at Mayerling. But I was told that you had granted Serbia a liberal new constitution; the kingdom was at peace after many years of strife. Why choose such a time to go? Was it merely a coincidence, or was your departure related to the demise of the Crown Prince?"

To have asked these questions of a sober king would have been impossible. But I was aided by the fact that Milan, long before noon, was near to drunkenness. Clearly, our discussion had awoken painful memories, and it was my duty to learn what I might.

"Your *client* has heard this tale already," the King responded thickly. Yet, when he spoke again, it was with unexpected dignity and eloquence. "Mr. Holmes, when I visited Franz Josef and Elisabeth to express my grief at their son's death, I had seen a man I very much admired not only *die*, but die condemned as a murderer and suicide. Perhaps my friend was neither, perhaps both; I do not know. But I *do* know, sir, that Rudolf would have been a very different ruler than his hidebound father. I had great faith that one day he would *unite* the Southern Slavs under the Habsburg banner. He would have been a *liberal* monarch, as had been—so briefly—the German Emperor Frederick, and as even *I*—so futilely—had once aspired to be. Oh, yes, the fate of my two predecessors shocked and saddened me. But more than that, it *frightened* me, coward that I am. You dare to ask me, sir, how I could renounce my throne, placing my poor country in the hands of a twelve-year-old boy? Because, Mr. Holmes, *I did not wish to be the next to die!"* Venting a Slavic oath with which I was unfamiliar, Milan Obrenović leapt to his feet and smashed his empty glass upon the hearth.

Needless to say, it was not long afterwards that I took my leave. After apologising for his "unseemly loss of equanimity," the King provided me with Count Josef Hoyos's address, as well as a letter of introduction sealed with his own ring. It was only when we were at the door that he asked of me one favour in return.

"When next you see her, Mr. Holmes—as I am sure you will—pray give Miss Adler my respectful greetings. What a queen she would have made! But, you see, she would not understand that much to my misfortune, I already possessed one." With a rueful smile, His Majesty concluded: "Of all the many women in my miserable life, that fair young songbird was one of very few whom I came close to loving."

"The King of Bohemia" offered his hand, just as he had done eleven years before. This time, rather to my own surprise, I shook it.

CHAPTER 5

A Meeting with a Banished Princess

It was with a touch of pride that I bade farewell to Sherlock Holmes, leaving Vienna on the assignment I was to carry out alone. True, that assignment was merely to conduct an interview, but the interview's subject was a member of "The Great." I found it satisfying that my long-ago efforts at Charlottenburg, and in the Baskerville case a few months later, had convinced Her Majesty's advisor to entrust me with an independent role.

The trip itself was most enjoyable. My first-class compartment, as luxurious as the German one ten years before, was likewise comfortable and airy. The food in the dining car was excellent. Approaching Graz, our route bridged the river Mürz and passed several picturesque ruined castles, then rose to an eminence with a fine view of the Styrian Alps. In mid-afternoon, we entered Carniola, which my *Baedeker* identified as Austria's chief mining district. Night fell long before we reached Trieste, the empire's largest seaport. It was also, since her husband's death, the residence of Dowager Crown Princess Stéphanie, the lady I had come to meet.

My day ended with a late arrival at the Hôtel de la Ville, whose manager fortunately spoke English. The next morning, I telephoned the British consul, Mr. Harry Churchill. As it happened, Churchill and I had once been school-fellows at Wellington. Mycroft had already instructed him by cable to assist me, and he had arranged an audience with Her Imperial and Royal Highness for four o'clock that afternoon. After we spent a pleasant day touring the city, I boarded a steamboat that would take me to Schloss Miramar.

The castle was quite different from the vast *Schlösser* of Berlin. Small and elegant, it was designed to suit its seaside setting, as well as the whims of its creator. For Miramar had been intended for Archduke

Ferdinand Maximilian, Franz Josef's younger brother, who lived there briefly with his Belgian wife Carlotta (aunt of the Crown Princess) before voyaging to his untimely end as Emperor of Mexico. It was an idiosyncratic place but very beautiful, built at the end of a rocky peninsula that overlooked the harbour and was surrounded by a wooded park. As our boat approached the headland, the towering white walls of Miramar glowed radiantly in the waning sunlight, with the Adriatic's deep-blue water shimmering below. I could not withhold a gasp of admiration.

We tied up at the quay beside the castle. Looking towards the small, hedged garden visible from my vantage point, I was surprised to see two figures strolling there. One was easily recognisable as Stéphanie, the other a dark-suited gentleman of comparable age. As I walked down the causeway that led into the garden, I realised, to my embarrassment, that I had arrived before my time. A servant who stood guard at the entrance intercepted me, challenging my intrusion with words I failed to comprehend. Providentially, as I attempted to explain myself, the Crown Princess came to my relief.

"*U redu je, Aleksandar!*" she called gaily, adding, for my benefit, in English: "Our visitor is a little early, but he *is* expected." With a sullen nod, Cerberus stepped aside and motioned me to proceed in the direction of his mistress.

"How do you do, Dr. Watson?" Her Highness unexpectedly offered me her hand before she turned to her companion. "Here is another of my guests: Count Lónyay. Dr. Watson, Elemér, is the author of the famous tales of Sherlock Holmes."

"Alas, sir, to my regret I have not read them," the handsome count replied serenely. Despite a strong Hungarian accent, his English was impeccable. "For it seems to me that in our unhappy world, there are crimes enough without resort to *fictional* detectives."

I nodded politely, although the Crown Princess seemed nonplussed. Considering the confidential nature of my mission, so much the better if this unknown aristocrat believed my friend to be a *"fictional* detective."

"Well, I shall leave you now, Stéphanie. I am pleased to have met you, Dr. Wilson." Obviously able to subdue his pleasure, the Hungarian magnate bowed and turned away to mount a staircase leading to the ground level of the castle and its outbuildings beyond.

"Count Lónyay is staying in the Castelletto," the Crown Princess informed me, no doubt for propriety's sake. "If you will follow me, Doctor, I thought we might have our tea in the Emperor Maximilian's study, a room I am sure will be of interest to you."

It was indeed a fascinating room, built to replicate the captain's cabin of an old-time frigate. Her ill-fated uncle, Stéphanie explained, had once commanded SMS *Novara* on a voyage round the world. Like many of the halls of Miramar, the study's upper walls and draperies were deep red. Rich wooden panelling and bookshelves opposed a long, curved gallery of windows like those on a ship's stern. The Crown Princess seated herself at a small table near Maximilian's desk, motioning me to take the chair adjacent to her. A tea service, its pot steaming, stood awaiting us. Rather to my disappointment, the tea was Chinese instead of Indian; but it was accompanied by the usual, delicious Viennese confections and—of all things—Belgian chocolate. Not until we had begun to sip our second cup did my hostess raise the subject of our meeting.

"Now, Dr. Watson, please tell me how I may assist you."

After due consideration of the matter, I had decided to be forthright. "The Empress," I carefully began, "has recently commissioned my friend's services. Although she has not directly said so, we believe her interest may concern the tragedy at Mayerling."

Stéphanie's deep flush almost matched her draperies. "Well, Doctor," she snapped angrily, "I can save you and Mr. Holmes a good deal of work in your investigation. If you wish to know whom that bitter old woman blames for her son's death, you need look no farther than myself! She told me so quite plainly at the time."

127

Unsure how to respond, I endeavoured to look sympathetic and encouraging. The Crown Princess, as I had expected, continued on her own.

"From the moment she met me, Dr. Watson, it seemed that my mother-in-law's only concern was to ensure that my marriage would be no happier than hers. 'The mighty bumpkin,' she would call me, or 'the Belgian cow.' Oh, I know I am not beautiful." (Alas, this was an accurate assessment; while she had retained a youthful prettiness into her thirties, Stéphanie's snub nose, full cheeks, and narrow eyes fell well short of beauty.) "But, after all," she cried, "it was not as if I had married an *Adonis!*" Remembering the sad-eyed, balding prince in Rudolf's photographs, I could not repress a smile.

"When Rudolf died, the Empress said to me: 'You hated your father, you did not love your husband, and you do not love your daughter!' The first item in her wicked list was true; the rest were lies. My father, Doctor—as the world is beginning to discover—is a cruel, vindictive man. He has despised my sister and me ever since our brother died, so he forced us both to marry in our teens.[9] Louise's marriage, to the Prince of Coburg, has been even worse than mine.

"Yet, at first," insisted Stéphanie, "the Crown Prince and I were happy. We lived in Prague then, on our own, while he was with the army. Our daughter was born there, and Rudolf *adored* little Erzsi. It was only after we returned to Vienna that it all went wrong."

After his recall to the capital, the Crown Prince and his new family were virtually imprisoned in an apartment in the Hofburg. They were under constant scrutiny, stifled by the rigid Spanish etiquette of Franz Josef's court. For the same reason, Rudolf's once-beloved mother was seldom at his side. The Heir-Apparent's perceptive memoranda on political reform were ignored by the Emperor. In General Staff meetings presided over by his father's

---

[9] Stéphanie's father was Belgium's King Leopold II, whose only son had died of pneumonia at the age of nine. The King was soon to become infamous for the atrocities in the Belgian Congo, his personal domain.

uncle, Archduke Albrecht, his suggestions about military matters were treated with contempt. Under these circumstances, her husband began (as Stéphanie expressed it) to "lose his moral balance." Rudolf soon abandoned his young wife and daughter for "an unceasing round of pleasure." He drank, took drugs, and womanised voraciously, the last with the assistance of the notorious Frau Wolf.

By the late 'Eighties, their marriage had broken irretrievably. "You see," sighed the Crown Princess, "my husband had given me a venereal disease. No, not *that* one, thank God, but it prevented me from bearing him a son. Afterwards, I could not fail to notice an alarming change in Rudolf. It was not only that he became more restless and distraught; he was now prone to outbursts of fierce anger, even over trifles. Often, he was unrecognizable as the man I had once loved." Again she sighed; again I was unable to conceive a suitable reply.

"It was not *all* bad, Doctor," Stéphanie laughed softly, noticing what was no doubt a look of distress upon my face. "My no-longer-loving husband may have been unfaithful to me, but at least my reprieve from child-bearing allowed me to have an adventure of my own. I took a lover. It was *not* Count Lónyay!" she added impishly.

Appalled, I sought to dam this flow of reminiscences. Even more disturbing than the tale itself was the fact that the Crown Princess had revealed to a stranger such intimate details. "If we may, Your Highness," I said uneasily, "I would like to move on to the days immediately before your husband's death. I am aware, of course, of his relationship with Baroness Vetsera. Other than that episode, what can you tell me of his state of mind?"

My hostess sat silent and thoughtful for perhaps a minute, gazing out the study's windows at her formal garden. Unlike Charlottenburg's, it had retained a Baroque design. When Stéphanie spoke again, any tone of levity had left her voice. It was as though she was reliving the last awful days before the deaths at Mayerling, the end not only of her marriage, but of the reign she would have had as empress.

"Rudolf was rarely sober then. He would speak of horrible things, sometimes toying cruelly with a revolver he carried about. In so despicable a state, I would not permit him to see little Erzsi. He would have terrified her! I myself had become afraid to be alone with him."

"Did you have any inkling then, Your Highness, that he would take his life?"

"No, for at times Rudolf would be quite exalted. He would speak of 'secret plans,' of being 'predestined to inaugurate a marvellous new era' in the empire's history. Once—not long before the end—he shouted wildly that he was 'prepared to hazard every-thing on a single throw of the dice!'"

"What could he have meant?" I asked. In fact, I believed I knew! It was exciting to envision reporting my suspicions—if correct—to Holmes as the key to the investigation.

The Crown Princess had evidently thought the matter through and reached the same conclusion. "I suppose that there was some conspiracy," she answered. "A plot, in which the Heir-Apparent was involved, to act against the Emperor."

"But you had no idea, Your Highness, of the details of this plot?"

"Of course not, Dr. Watson!" cried Stéphanie indignantly. "Do you think I would have abetted my husband in an act of treason?"

"By no means!" I hastily assured her. "I am only trying, Your Highness, to establish a plausible motive for your husband's death, other than the facts already known to us."

"You mean the facts regarding the Vetsera girl," sniffed the Crown Princess. Her exasperation faded as an idea occurred to her. "Doctor, there is one fact of which we have not spoken. It might seem to concern that little harlot, but I have since decided that such was not the case. Before his death, my husband was seeking to annul our marriage."

"Surely not to marry Baroness Vetsera!"

"Undoubtedly not. I knew the Crown Prince's mind quite well by then. Oh, yes, he would use that silly child for his own purposes, and to humiliate his wife, but he would *not* have married her. His father would never have permitted such a marriage, and the last thing Rudolf wanted was to endanger his succession to the throne. No, Dr. Watson, I suspect that his desire for an annulment was connected to the greater matter."

"You mean the conspiracy against the Emperor." As Holmes would have remarked, my talent for the obvious had seldom been in better form. "Then why do you believe the Heir-Apparent died?"

Just at that moment, the door from the library flew open, and a striking adolescent swept into the room. No more than fifteen, she was even blonder than her mother, and the promise of beauty once denied to Stéphanie was now redeemed in her.

"*Maman,* where is Elemér? He promised to teach me backgammon this afternoon."

"*Count Lónyay,*" the Crown Princess answered sternly, "is resting in his room. He will join us for dinner." Seeming rather disconcerted, my hostess turned to me. "Doctor, this is my daughter: Archduchess Elisabeth Marie. Erzsi, this is Dr. John H. Watson, who writes those wonderful Sherlock Holmes adventures you admire so much."

I bowed. So this was Rudolf's daughter!

The young archduchess merely nodded to me, obviously unimpressed. "But where is Mr. Sherlock Holmes?" she asked accusingly.

"I fear, Your Highness, that he did not accompany me today."

"Oh! How disappointing." Without another word, Erzsi turned back into the library, leaving her mother and me to contemplate our private discomfitures. After an awkward silence, Stéphanie laughed resignedly.

"You see, Doctor, what I must contend with? But it will not last forever! I have been writing my memoirs of late, and before many years have passed the world will know the truth. Moreover, when Erzsi comes of age I shall remarry. The court in Vienna will force me to renounce my titles, but of what use are they now? Once *that* is done, Rudolf's parents can do no further harm to me. I know too much not to be allowed my freedom—unless they wish to murder me as well! Surely, after all these years alone, even I deserve a *little* happiness."

Before I left, we watched the sunset from a balustrade that overlooked the Adriatic. I congratulated the Dowager Crown Princess on the beauty of her home.

"Indeed," she smiled ruefully, "it makes a pleasant exile for a woman who might have been an empress but is now not welcome at the court. Will you not stay for dinner, Dr. Watson, or even for the night? The Castelletto where Count Lónyay sleeps has more than one spare bedroom."

"I thank Your Highness, but I have already accepted an invitation from my friend, the British consul." Churchill had expressed a wish to introduce me to his family.

"Very well," Stéphanie graciously replied, again extending me her hand. "I shall not ask you to remember me to Empress Elisabeth, but I hope the result of your investigation can bring that unhappy woman peace. And—if it is not *too* painful for you, Dr. Watson— please give my daughter's greetings to Mr. Sherlock Holmes!"

Thus ended my much-anticipated, independent mission to Trieste. Although I rather regretted losing an opportunity to spend a night at Miramar, it was no doubt just as well. I was willing enough to risk another snub from the Hungarian, but the prospect of facing Archduchess Elisabeth Marie across the dinner table was a daunting one!

CHAPTER 6

The Emperor's Good Servant

King Milan had apprised me that Count Hoyos was a patient at Löw Sanatorium. Located on the Mariannengasse in Vienna's Ninth District, it had become the city's most exclusive private hospital, a place where prominent Austro-Hungarians often went to die. (Gustav Mahler, later my disgruntled client, also spent his last days at Löw.[10]) The Count, regrettably, was ill with cancer and would survive our interview by only a few months. With a callousness that typified the man, Serbia's ex-monarch had predicted that Hoyos would speak freely to me, "for he now has little left to lose."

Arriving at the hospital in mid-afternoon, I followed the same procedure as I had that morning: another note upon another of Sir Robert's cards; another minion to deliver it, along with His Majesty's sealed letter, to the appropriate room. The attendant returned within ten minutes, bearing a reply from Hoyos's physician. His patient was indisposed, while undergoing treatment, but had agreed to meet with me on the following day. Would nine o'clock in the morning be convenient? In fact, the delay was highly *inconvenient*, as I had intended to leave for Geneva before the day was out. Obviously, nothing could be done to hasten matters, so I acquiesced with an appearance of good grace.

The next morning, Count Hoyos awaited me in the sanatorium's tree-shaded garden, looking fairly well. The site of our interview was a considerable relief, as there are few things I detest more than a sick-

---

[10] Holmes met Gustav Mahler on the 1902 visit to Vienna discussed later in this story. For the composer's case, see "The Solitary Violinist," found in *The MX Book of New Sherlock Holmes Stories, Part XVIII: "Whatever Remains . . . Must Be the Truth (1899-1925)*, (London: MX Publishing, 2019) pp. 212-242.

room. He was a grey-bearded gentleman approaching sixty, unduly gaunt and pale, but retaining the distinguished countenance of his Iberian progenitors. (The House of Hoyos, Mycroft's notes informed me, had followed Emperor Ferdinand I from Spain to Austria in 1525.) Despite his illness, Hoyos had dressed formally for our encounter. Had Watson been writing this account, I am sure he would have mentioned the Count's "deep-set, haunted eyes."

"Good morning, Your Illustrious Highness," I greeted him.

My host blinked agreeably in surprise. "*Sehr gut*, Herr Holmes! Few Englishmen can properly address a Count of the Holy Roman Empire. Most often, I am required to tolerate 'Your Excellency.'" With a courtly gesture, he invited me to join him on a bench beneath a maple tree.

"Not that it much matters," Hoyos sighed. "Soon my line will be no less extinct than the empire that conferred my title." I recalled that he had neither wife nor progeny. "You wish, I understand, to speak to me of Mayerling?"

I began to explain Elisabeth's commission, but the Count lifted a restraining hand. "The former King of Serbia has told me. *Also*, I must choose between breaking the oath I swore to Emperor Franz Josef or refusing the commission of his wife! Herr Holmes, you place this old courtier in an impossible position."

I feared that our interview was over, but Count Hoyos met my dismay with an ironic smile. "I have written," he informed me, "a full, if circumspect, account that will provide posterity with a palatable version of the Crown Prince's end. It was locked away inside the Hofburg long ago. For all my life, Herr Holmes, I have been the Emperor's good servant, and as such I am content to die. Yet, I shall renounce my oath today by speaking with you. Why, you may ask? Because poor Rudolf was my friend, and his father has suppressed the inconvenient facts of his demise. Before my own time comes, I should like one man, at least, to hear the entire story."

Inevitably, "the entire story" began with an account of facts irrelevant to my investigation. As a boy, Rudolf had been rescued from a brutal military tutor by his mother, who saw to it that henceforth he received a liberal education. Count Hoyos had accompanied the Crown Prince on a hunting trip to Egypt in 1881, where he was impressed by the young man's intelligence and thirst for knowledge. The Heir-Apparent's book about their journey reflected his scientific interests; moreover, he had subsequently commissioned an encyclopaedia, *The Austro-Hungarian Monarchy in Word and Picture*. "Rudolf," recalled Hoyos, "wrote part of the first volume himself. When his research was completed, the Crown Prince knew more about his father's realm than Franz Josef had learned in forty years as emperor. His Majesty, *natürlich*, was completely unimpressed! Rudolf should have been a scholar, not a prince."

I attempted to recall His Illustrious Highness to the case at hand, reminding him that the Empress's interest lay in Mayerling. To my disappointment, the aspect of that subject that occurred to him was the Vetsera girl. Hoyos deplored the ruin of his friend's "once noble mind and character," which were gradually eroded by his dissolution.

"Rudolf had indulged himself in love affairs for years," the Count admitted sadly, "but Mary Vetsera seemed to cast a spell on him. I recognised it at a party at the German embassy, only days before they died. It was not that the girl was particularly beautiful, for she was small and dark; yet, her eyes sparkled with alluring mystery. That night, when she had insulted Stéphanie and knew that every eye within the room was fixed upon her, her whole personality seemed to blaze. Poor Rudolf was even more humiliated than his wife. 'Oh, if someone would only deliver me from her!' he cried."

"If we may abandon melodrama," I proposed, "I would like to move on to the Heir-Apparent's death. You arrived at Mayerling, I understand, the day before the tragedy?"

"That is correct. Prince Philipp and I were to join the Crown Prince for a hunt."

135

"But he elected to take no part in it."

"*Ja*. Rudolf claimed to have a cold, but I suspected he had planned an assignation. One of his former mistresses—an actress married to the nobleman who had sold him the estate—still lived nearby. I did not see the young baroness at any time; indeed, I had no idea that she was on the premises."

Clear and concise! If one kept him to the subject, Count Hoyos made an excellent witness. "Did anything unusual," I asked him, "occur during the hunt? For example, did you see any sign of strangers, such as other hunting parties, in the area?"

"Certainly not. Mayerling was then imperial property and closely guarded. The hunt itself," he shrugged, "was disappointing. I had only one shot all day and failed to kill my stag. The keepers chased the poor creature for half the afternoon to finish it. By then, Prince Philipp had departed for Vienna. He and Rudolf were to attend Archduchess Marie Valerie's engagement party in the evening."

"Which the Heir-Apparent did not, in fact, attend."

Hoyos shook his head. "When I returned to the lodge, I was astonished to find a note from him inviting me to dinner. His refusal to appear at the Hofburg would have been regarded by his parents and his sister as a grave affront."

"Very well, Your Illustrious Highness. If we may, let us discuss your dinner with the Heir-Apparent: the last time anyone—other than his servants and, of course, Baroness Vetsera—saw him alive." I searched my host's face for signs of reluctance or weariness, but he regarded me impassively. After taking a moment to collect his thoughts, the Count recited quietly:

"We dined at seven in the billiard room, as Rudolf often did at Mayerling. His valet, Loschek, served us; he was the only other person whom I saw. The meal, as I recall, was excellent: soup, goose liver pâté, roast beef, and venison. The Crown Prince ate heartily and drank much wine, but no more than usual. Afterwards, we sat and talked. My friend seemed in good spirits—until he took from his

136

pocket and read three telegrams that had arrived that afternoon. His face paled then, and I heard him mutter, with a curse: 'Disastrous! Károly has left me in the lurch. I have signed my own death warrant!'"

"Did you read the telegrams?" I asked, controlling my excitement.

"I did not, for Rudolf quickly threw them in the fire and changed the subject. But his buoyant mood had vanished, and I could see he wished me gone. I left soon afterwards—at nine o'clock, it was— when the Crown Prince said he was retiring for the night."

I elected to move cautiously. "These telegrams . . . could they have concerned the disturbances in Budapest—resulting, I was told, from a new bill to impose the German language upon reserve officers in Hungary?"

The Count's bushy eyebrows lifted. "You are well-informed, Herr Holmes! *Jawohl*, Prime Minister Tisza had introduced such a bill the week before. Naturally, it aroused great opposition in the Diet, and there were riots in the streets. Count Károly, the leader of the nationalists, made a fiery speech that all but called for Hungary to declare her independence. He implied that 'a very trustworthy source' in Vienna fully supported the Magyar cause."

"Meaning, I assume, the Heir-Apparent." I gave Rudolf's old courtier a direct look. *"Would* he have supported the dissolution of his father's empire?"

"It would not necessarily have come to that," Hoyos replied imperturbably. "Under the *Ausgleich*, Hungary was in theory free to choose her king. Years earlier, Tisza himself had proposed that Rudolf might replace Franz Josef and rule in Budapest without dismembering the empire. The Crown Prince rejected the idea—in part because their conversation had been reported to old Archduke Albrecht. But as time went on and his frustration grew, my friend began to regret his decision. You may be sure that the Magyar nobles worked steadily upon him. Finally, during a shooting party in Transylvania a few

137

months before he died, Rudolf signed a document pledging to support a revolution that would give him the Hungarian crown. He was, of course, quite inebriated at the time."

"He *admitted* this to you, Count Hoyos?" I queried in amazement.

"Not explicitly, but there were sometimes slips, as during our last dinner. Since that dinner, Herr Holmes, I have spoken with several other gentlemen who signed the document. The Diet's rejection of the army bill was to be the catalyst: Tisza's government would fall, and the Crown Prince would be called to Budapest as king. But on the day the historic moment came—with Rudolf awaiting the result at Mayerling—too many traitors lost their nerve. Vienna's bill was approved by a slim majority; Tisza did not fall; and the Hungarian revolution was over before it began."

"Would not the Heir-Apparent," I suggested, "have regarded such an outcome as a fortunate escape?"

"He might have," Hoyos replied grimly, "had not he signed the damning document. Any one of the Hungarian magnates implicated would have betrayed the Crown Prince to save his own neck from the gallows. Moreover, I believe that by that time, the Emperor knew of his involvement. On the eve of Károly's speech in Budapest, Franz Josef and his heir were seen having an intense—if whispered— argument in Vienna's opera house. Rudolf admitted at our dinner that the telegrams had left him 'compromised.'"

"Was this the reason, Illustrious Highness, that the Crown Prince killed himself?"

"It could not have been the only reason, or Mary Vetsera need not have died. Rudolf left a note for one of the Hungarians, stating that death was now 'the only way to leave this world like a gentleman.' It is obvious," Hoyos sighed, "that my friend was no longer thinking clearly. The Emperor would not have publicly acknowledged his son's treason; that family prefers to hush up all its scandals. Yet, I am sure the Heir-Apparent realised that henceforth his freedom would be even more restricted, his credibility as a future emperor destroyed for anyone who knew. In that sense, Rudolf's life was over before he ever put a pistol to his head."

As eager as I was to hear more revelations, it was apparent that Count Hoyos was now extremely tired. When he asked for an adjournment until after luncheon, I complied, reluctantly discarding my plan to leave Vienna by mid-afternoon. I enquired whether our next interview might not be held more comfortably indoors, but the Count preferred to return to an alfresco setting. "Herr Holmes, it is a fine September, and I shall not live to see another. I also fear," he added quietly, "that our privacy inside the sanatorium would not be assured."

Hoyos's fears proved justified. As I walked along the Mariannengasse to look for a café, I was inexpertly shadowed by another of Franz Josef's spies. This one—a former postal clerk—sat down at a table almost adjacent to my own. He began scribbling notes, glancing at me surreptitiously from the corner of his eye. I considered inviting the poor man to share a glass of wine, but decided that it might embarrass him. Nevertheless, his amusing company, coupled with a filling plate of *Tafelspitz*, offered a welcome respite as I pondered what might comprise the last installment of the tragic story that awaited me.

"My room, Herr Holmes," Count Hoyos responded to my question, "was in the old gamekeeper's cottage. It was perhaps five hundred meters from the Crown Prince's quarters, so I heard nothing of what happened in the lodge that night."

The Count's first inkling that something was amiss occurred early the next morning. Shortly before eight o'clock, Rudolf's valet sent a message urgently requesting his assistance. Despite repeated knocking, he had been unable to rouse his master at the appointed time. "I assured Loschek," Hoyos remembered, "that the Crown Prince was only tired. Recalling my friend's mood when I had left

him, I believed that he had taken morphine to help him sleep."
Eventually, however, the Count proposed breaking down the door.
"Poor Loschek was curiously reluctant; at last, he confessed to me that
Baroness Vetsera was also in the room." Under the circumstances, the
two agreed to wait for Prince Philipp of Coburg, Rudolf's brother-in-
law, to take responsibility when he arrived at half-past eight. "Our
nicety seems foolish to me now," sighed Hoyos, "but on that morning
it seemed inconceivable that the Heir-Apparent could be dead."

"Please describe what you found when the door was finally
opened," I requested, "and be *precise* as to details."

"I assure you, Herr Holmes, that the scene is graven on my
memory." Hoyos took a deep breath before continuing. "After we had
taken an axe to Rudolf's bedroom door, it was Loscheck who first
peered through the opening. He announced to us at once that both the
Crown Prince and his paramour were dead."

"One moment. At this time, how much light was in the room?"

"Very little. The curtains were drawn and the windows
shuttered. We later saw a candle on a night table beside the bed, but it
had been extinguished."

"Yet, the valet reported *immediately*—without even entering the
room—that both its occupants were dead. Did he seem surprised?
Shaken? Horrified?"

"Horrified, of course, as well as shaken. But not, I think,
surprised." My host, I saw, was eying me with interest, as if
anticipating the deduction I was about to make. Quickly, I inwardly
reviewed the details Mycroft had given us in his account of
Mayerling.

"It was approximately eight-thirty in the morning, Count Hoyos,
when the three of you broke into the Heir-Apparent's bedroom?"

"That is correct," Hoyos acknowledged.

"Yet, I have been informed that Rudolf's coachman, one
Bratfisch, told the imperial gamekeeper *an hour and a half before that*

time that there would be no hunt that day—because (he said) 'the Crown Prince is dead.'"

This time, the Count only nodded, again awaiting my conclusion. It was so obvious that I saw no need to keep him waiting long.

"Then it is undeniable, Your Illustrious Highness, that Rudolf's servants knew—not merely suspected, but *knew*—he was dead long before they requested your assistance. Do you believe they were complicit in his murder?"

"I do not, Herr Holmes. I believe the delay arose not from guilt, but from a desire—misguided though it was—to protect their master's reputation. Remember," he reminded me, "that they alone, aside from Rudolf, knew that Mary Vetsera was at Mayerling."

Again, I sat and pondered, cursing myself for having left my pipe in my hotel room. Blue skies and sun-dappled woods—while delightful to the eye—I find less conducive to deduction than the "poisonous atmosphere" my friend the Doctor so persistently derides. On this occasion, the absence of my tobacco-infused haze must have been unusually inhibiting, for I found myself unable to penetrate the mystery hovering before me in clear air. I decided to rehearse the facts, as they were known, aloud.

"The valet, Loschek, heard two shots fired in the bedroom well before he was to awaken the Crown Prince," I expounded. "Undoubtedly, he would have been alarmed—all the more so when his master failed to answer his entreaties—but how could he have known for a *certainty* that Rudolf was dead? He evidently said so to Bratfisch, who (I am told) was waiting in his coach to return Baroness Vetsera to Vienna. Bratfisch passed on the news to the head gamekeeper as a *fait accompli*. Yet, Rudolf might easily have been alive—perhaps only wounded—and the girl his assailant. Why, in so dire a situation, be reluctant to reveal *her* presence? Surely, the fact that the Crown Prince was sleeping with his mistress was the least of anyone's concerns!"

141

So long as I did not look at my companion, I could almost persuade myself that it was Watson acting as my sounding board. When I did turn to the Count, he was regarding me with a grave smile. "Mary Vetsera," he said softly.

Then I remembered the contradiction that had so flummoxed the good Doctor. "The fatal shots, Count Hoyos," I responded, "were supposedly fired almost simultaneously. Yet, the court physician who examined the girl's body was overheard to say that she had died *six hours* before her body was discovered. Assuming that the man was not a gross incompetent, which seems unlikely, then Loschek either lied or left out crucial evidence. Evidence proving beyond doubt that the Crown Prince was a murderer!"

"Bravo, Herr Holmes! You have reasoned as I did—long after the fact, of course. In later years, I confronted Johann Loschek, who was by then enjoying his full pension and a medal from the Emperor. We met in secret, and I paid him well. To me, he told a different story than he had told the newspapers. In fact, *one* shot was fired at Mayerling that morning. The first shot had come the night before."

After the Crown Prince had retired to join his mistress, Loschek heard sounds of a serious quarrel behind the bedroom door. Exactly what was said he did not reveal, even to Count Hoyos. But about midnight, having gone to bed in the adjacent room, he heard a pistol fire not twenty feet away from him. When Loschek knocked on Rudolf's door, his master opened it just wide enough to answer him, said that the shot had been an accident, and ordered the valet back to bed. The Crown Prince's face was ashen, but Loschek had been reassured by his cheerful demeanour the next morning. The second shot, fired soon after Rudolf had last spoken to him, had come as a complete surprise.

Although it appeared that the essentials of the case were solved, I asked the Count to describe the scene that he and his companions had encountered on entering the bedroom. Not surprisingly, it was the dead girl's body the three men noticed first.

"The press accounts," grumbled Hoyos, "gushed of young Baroness Vetsera clothed in faerie raiment, lying peacefully with a white rose clasped unto her breast. In fact, the girl was naked, although for decency's sake I dressed her when writing my memorandum to the Emperor. She sat upon the right side of the bed, slumped back against the headboard. Her hair was loose, her eyes wide open. She still held in her hand a handkerchief, and blood had pooled about her waist. It had flowed from a bullet hole in her left temple. Somehow, it appeared to me the shot had come as a surprise."

"And the Crown Prince?" While obviously deeply moved, the Count was bearing up remarkably. Even so, he could not repress a shudder when talking of his friend.

"The top of Rudolf's skull was blown away. He had sat upon the left side of the bed to shoot himself. His body had slumped forward. He was dressed in the same hunting clothes he had worn at dinner. The revolver lay beneath him on the floor."

"You were satisfied that the wound was self-inflicted?"

"I was. You see, there was a hand mirror lying on the bed. My thought was that the Heir-Apparent must have used it to improve his aim."

"Indeed. One last query, sir: The windows, you are sure, were all firmly shuttered, the door locked. So the shot, or shots, could not have originated from outside the room?"

"I do not see how that would be possible."

"*Thank* you, Count Hoyos." My host looked thoroughly exhausted, so I suggested that we return to the sanatorium. To my surprise, he declined the invitation.

"There was one more occurrence, Herr Holmes, of which I wish to speak. It may have no significance, but at the time it puzzled me."

"Please proceed."

"You may know that it was I who took the news of Mayerling to Rudolf's parents. Prince Philipp was prostrated by grief, so Bratfisch drove me to the rail station in Baden. When we left the lodge that morning, the roads were still muddy from the recent snow. At first, I saw only the tracks of Coburg's carriage. Farther on, as we approached a road that led directly to Vienna, I noticed that the sodden ground was much disturbed."

"Indeed?" Had my assumption that the case was solved been premature?

"I stopped the carriage to investigate. It appeared that a small party of horsemen had ridden within two kilometers of Mayerling, only to turn round and return the way they came. Their tracks ran in both directions. When we arrived at the fork, I told Bratfisch to follow the Vienna road for a short distance, confirming that the riders had come and gone along its way. Unhappily, my mission was too urgent to pursue them far. We turned back to the station, where I caught a train and reported to the Hofburg."

"Can you be certain that these unknown horsemen did not go to Mayerling?"

"By no means. There are many side roads through the Vienna Woods, even trails that riders might traverse in single file. I could only be certain that they had not gone to Mayerling by the main road."

"You saw no signs of their presence at the lodge?"

"Not in the courtyard, Herr Holmes, but I had not looked elsewhere. My mind was upon other matters at the time."

"Of course. Again, my thanks, Your Illustrious Highness. This occurrence may or may not be significant, but I am glad to be informed of it. Allow me to congratulate you on your powers of observation at what was surely a most stressful time."

We walked back together to the hospital, silent in the late-afternoon sunlight that filtered through the trees. Though I am seldom attuned to the emotions of casual acquaintances, I divined that Count Hoyos was sad and thoughtful. Not until we reached the sanatorium's entrance did he turn and speak to me.

"I shall not implore you, Herr Holmes, to give Her Majesty my greetings. It was to Elisabeth, you see, that I gave the news of

Rudolf's death—for only someone of *her* rank could impart such tidings to the Emperor. I have never seen a woman bear her grief with greater courage, but afterwards it was for the Empress as though I did not exist.

"The next day, I saw Franz Josef. To him I offered to accept the blame for Rudolf's death, for reasons I now fail to comprehend. I would say that I had shot the Crown Prince in a hunting accident. (The death of Baroness Vetsera, you may be sure, was a minor inconvenience, one of which the court took no official notice.) His Imperial and Royal Majesty graciously declined my offer. Instead, he commanded me to write a full account of his son's death, and to swear an oath never to reveal the facts I knew. That oath, Herr Holmes, I have kept faithfully—until today. Strangely, for a man who has thus forfeited his honour, I feel much the better for it."

He held out his hand to me, and *his* hand I accepted without hesitation. Indeed, even now I regard "the Emperor's good servant" as the sole redeeming feature of the case. In his own mind, perhaps, Count Josef Hoyos had forfeited his honour. Speaking for myself, I consider it an honour to have known him.

CHAPTER 7

Rendezvous at the Beau-Rivage

Although I had departed from Trieste as early as possible on Thursday, my arrival in Geneva was delayed. Our express had been detained in Venice, and again in Milan, by Italian police in search of anarchists. King Umberto, it appeared, had become their target after his brutal suppression of labour riots in the spring. The officers seemed sure that any train from Austria, Italy's purely nominal ally, was bound to be teeming with bloodthirsty assassins.[11] Fortunately, my British passport secured me from suspicion, but it could not retrieve the hours lost.

It was nine o'clock on Friday morning before we reached the station in Geneva, and half an hour longer before I came to my hotel. Appropriately for an empress's refuge, the Beau-Rivage was an elegant establishment of the first class. I crossed its lofty atrium and approached the desk, where I learned that Holmes and I had been assigned to rooms on the third floor. A curt note from that gentleman awaited me:

> *My dear Watson,*
>   *Whenever you at last appear, meet me at the Cathédrale Saint-Pierre. It should easily be visible, across the lake, from your room's balcony. If you have not yet*

---

[11] Their concern was not unfounded. In 1900, Umberto I fell victim to an anarchist avenging the hundreds of workers killed or wounded in Milan. Most unwisely, the king had presented a medal to the general who fired upon the crowd (http://www.unofficialroyalty.com/king-umberto-i-of-italy/).

eaten, I shall make an effort to accommodate you, despite
your having missed the excellent English breakfast I had
ordered for us at eight o'clock this morning.
Your sincere, if impatient, friend,
Sherlock Holmes

Despite my friend's impatience, it was such a pleasant morning, although overcast, that I decided to walk to the cathedral. I set off down the Quai du Mont-Blanc, which ran in front of the hotel. Disappointingly, clouds blocked my view of the great mountain, the highest in the Alps. But the lake itself, and the sights of the Old Town along its opposite bank, offered ample compensation. Crossing the broad Pont du Mont-Blanc that bridged the Rhône, I glanced down upon the Île Rousseau: once a stronghold of Geneva, now a public park honouring that mischievous philosopher. On attaining the river's left bank, I turned past the English Garden and, after a short climb, came to my destination a quarter-hour after leaving the hotel.

Begun in the twelfth century, the Cathédrale Saint-Pierre had since evolved into a massive hotchpotch. It combined two Romanesque towers with a Gothic spire and—most unsuitably—a Corinthian portico tacked on in Georgian times. The interior (I would soon discover), lost much of its Catholic splendour to the Reformation, for the church had been the headquarters of Jean Calvin's stern regime. Finding the door of the portico bolted, I made my way along the Rue Farel to the rear of the great edifice. There, my guide-book had informed me, lived the verger.

This ancient fellow had evidently been expecting me. "*M. le révérend Bosquevalle,*" he confided, awaited me in the Chapelle des Macchabées. He pointed to another Gothic accretion that stood close beside us, while I considered the garbled surname and decided that it must be "Baskerville." I followed him expecting to meet Sherlock Holmes.

148

Perhaps a dozen worshippers occupied the chapel; its vaulted, stained-glass windows glowed serenely in the gauzy light. Obviously, this magnificent structure had been exempted from Calvinist austerity. A few elderly couples huddled in the pews, while a tall, white-haired gentleman wearing clerical garb stood examining the pulpit. It was he, of course, who turned to us.

"Ah, Dr. *Wilson!*" Reverend Baskerville cried gleefully, nodding his thanks to the departing verger. "So happy you could finally join me!" He pumped my hand enthusiastically, beaming behind his spectacles, then murmured, "This way, Doctor, if you please."

I followed Holmes out a side entrance and through an unlocked door that led to the cathedral. There we began to climb a long, spiral staircase in the southernmost of the two towers. I was winded before we reached the top, but the view when we emerged onto the balcony was worth the effort. The entire city lay beneath us in panoramic glory, with the blue of Lake Geneva fading into the horizon. I looked to see the famous *Jet d'Eau*, before remembering that it was out of season. My friend—not normally a devotee of scenery—seemed satisfied with the effect produced.

"Impressive, is it not? And quite private, which is what I wanted."

"Would it not be equally private *inside* the tower? This wind is rather piercing."

"Oh, very well, Watson." As we retreated from the elements, the detective removed from his coat and handed me an unidentifiable lump wrapped in wax paper.

"What's this?"

"*Rösti*, I am told. It's supposed to be a national dish. I bought it from a street vendor on my way to the cathedral. Of course," he added anxiously, as I peered into the greasy paper, "that was now some time ago. How is it?"

I had taken a dubious bite of what proved to be shredded, fried potato, topped with bacon, egg, and cheese. "Quite cold, unfortunately, but I do appreciate the thought. What are we *doing* here, Holmes?"

"It was essential that we not discuss the case in the hotel. The 'Countess von Hohenembs' has not arrived, but there are one or two characters lurking who must not be privy to our counsels. Do you remember the name 'Adolf Meyer,' Doctor?"

"Vaguely, but I cannot place him."

"He was on Mycroft's list of suspects in the theft of the Bruce-Partington plans. Oberstein, you recall, turned out to be the culprit."

"Is Meyer, then, another German spy?"

"No, someone far more dangerous: an Austrian of Pan-German sympathies and, thus, no admirer of Franz Josef. We have crossed swords once or twice before. I saw him at the Beau-Rivage last night, and I fear he may have recognised 'Sir Robert Sherrinford.' Hence my disguise today."

"Do you consider him a danger to Elisabeth?"

"Assuredly, if he is aware of the 'Countess's' true identify. Moreover, I witnessed him in conversation with a man of the *foulest* antecedents: Baron Adelbert Gruner. He is another Austrian, and undoubtedly a murderer. I am certain that he killed his wife last year in an 'accident' in the Splugen Pass, although he was acquitted at his trial in Prague. So far as I am aware, Gruner is not involved in espionage, but he would be a willing tool of Adolf Meyer if well paid."

"What do you intend for us to do?"

"We can do very little before the Empress arrives. It may be, of course, that Meyer intends Her Majesty no harm; but remember Mycroft's warning that her interest in Mayerling could be dangerous. For the present, Watson, let us compare notes. What did you learn from Crown Princess Stéphanie?"

150

Eagerly, I began to recount Rudolf's involvement in the Hungarian conspiracy, only to be apprised that my friend already knew of the affair. Mastering my disappointment, I listened to his own account, which culminated in Count Hoyos's fortuitous discovery that mysterious riders had approached Mayerling on the night before the tragedy. In answer to my query, Holmes stated his belief that the balance of evidence still pointed to the Heir-Apparent as the author of the deaths. "However, that is merely a provisional conclusion, Doctor, until I have heard what Elisabeth may have to say."

By this time, we had left the tower of Cathédrale Saint-Pierre and were walking in the English Garden, for an Alpine chill had come into the air. Although the detective cast a wary eye upon the park's few other occupants, our privacy was undisturbed. I began to consider the misfortune of Crown Prince Rudolf's life, imparting some of the details I had acquired from Stéphanie. It was tragic, I reflected, that this intelligent and ambitious heir—so full of new ideas and zeal—had not been spared to lead his father's antiquated realm into the modern world. Holmes wearily dismissed my sentiments.

"No, old friend, Rudolf's fall was utterly predictable. Such has been the destiny of innumerable crown princes throughout history. Your ambitious heir is neither trusted nor appreciated by the reigning monarch and an obeisant retinue of courtiers, ministers, and generals—all irredeemably committed to the stultifying *status quo*. He is given nothing to do, no outlet for his energies. And so he waits . . . and waits . . . and waits . . . until, little by little, his energy begins to flag, his zeal to wane. He begins to doubt his own ideals, and his frustration—with no end to his predicament in sight—turns inward on himself."

"That is precisely what I'm saying, Holmes!"

"*And yet*, Doctor, in the same years that Rudolf suffered, Crown Prince Frederick of Germany, and even our own Prince of Wales, would have recognised his plight. Indeed, they had carried their own crosses far longer than did he, and to their cost. Unhappily, as every

151

account that we have heard of him makes clear, Austria-Hungary's heir-apparent lacked their degree of stamina. Before he reached the age of *thirty*, Rudolf's intellectual machinery had torn itself apart."

My friend's verdicts, though seldom merciful, were always just. It was a sad epitaph for a man who might have saved an empire.

The Empress appeared at half-past three that afternoon. Holmes and I, ensconced in the lobby of the Beau-Rivage, witnessed a sudden flurry among the hotel staff. We heard repeated exclamations of *"die Gräfin!"* as clerks and porters hurried to and fro, creating more uproar than any countess could possibly have caused. Eventually, two ladies, both elegantly if severely dressed, were escorted into the atrium by the fawning manager, as their belongings disappeared behind them in the direction of the lift.

It would be my closest approach to the legendary Sisi. She had not on this occasion worn a veil, her habitual defence against the public gaze. I made an effort not to stare, but Holmes seemed utterly oblivious, scarcely raising his eyes from his newspaper. Ungallant as it is to say so, I admit to being disillusioned. In 1898, Elisabeth was sixty. Though she remained a handsome woman for her age, ten years of grief and wandering had wrinkled her once flawless face, and she was gaunt to the point of emaciation. Her manner to the hotel staff was gracious but reserved, before she retired to her suite within moments of arriving. Only as they departed did I notice the younger, mildly pretty woman who accompanied the Empress. Mycroft's notes identified her as Countess Irma Sztáray, Her Majesty's Hungarian lady-in-waiting.

The thoughts of Sherlock Holmes did not concern Elisabeth's appearance. Having heard her inform the staff (in perfect French) that she intended to go shopping, he decided immediately to shadow her. When I offered to accompany him, my friend's gentle laugh was sufficient to dissuade me.

"My dear fellow, you have *many* invaluable qualities, but I regret to say that stealth is not among them. He stalks best, in any case, who stalks alone. Why not take a well-earned rest? A late night lies ahead of us; and I shall undoubtedly have need of you."

I could hardly argue, although I had been proud of my stalking prowess in Afghanistan. In fact, I *was* quite weary, having slept little on my interrupted journey from Trieste. I therefore bade farewell to the detective, while he (still disguised as Reverend Baskerville) remained in the lobby to await the Empress's return.

A belated luncheon delivered to my room enabled me to sleep until the evening. It was well after seven when I was awakened by a knock upon my door. Holmes, formally attired and fully restored to his usual appearance, met my enquiry concerning the success of his expedition with a rueful smile.

"I quickly discovered, Doctor, that the Empress is remarkably observant, extremely averse to being followed, and incredibly fleet of foot for a woman of her years. She also knows the streets of Geneva much better than do I. Not to put too fine a point on it, I lost her! It was the most deplorable lapse of its kind since I failed to perceive 'The Woman' stalking me in '87. Even now, it appears, the shadow of the 'King of Bohemia' looms above this case.

"For the present, Watson," he concluded more prosaically, "I must ask that you join me in donning evening dress. We have a soirée to attend."

"For the 'Countess von Hohenembs,' I presume?"

"Ostensibly, though her presence here will not be acknowledged and she will not, in any case, attend. After Her Majesty eluded me, I repaired to the hotel lobby to wait for her return. Elisabeth and her attendant lady came in bearing a collection of toys, which I can only surmise must be intended for her grandchildren. I was rather touched—until she gave poor 'Reverend Baskerville' a look that would have frozen Hell itself! Loudly, for my benefit, the Empress remarked to Countess Sztáray that she was retiring for the night.

Therefore, Doctor, as neither of my disguises is of any further use, I have no choice but to attend tonight's event as a very chastened Mr. Sherlock Holmes!"

The soirée took place in a small, ornate salon adjacent to the hotel's atrium. To my friend's relief, it was merely a reception. There was not room enough to dance, although a string quartet (playing the inevitable Strauss waltzes) occupied a corner. I was pleased to see that food and drink were amply supplied. Some thirty people clustered in the room, comprising the élite of the Hôtel Beau Rivage's clientèle. The men wore either uniform or formal dress; the ladies' finery looked worthy of the Hofburg. While several of these ladies were quite lovely, the only one I recognised was Countess Sztáray. She was talking to an immoderately handsome gentleman who leaned too close for strict propriety. From his place beside me, Sherlock Holmes grunted with disgust. "*That,*" he sneered quietly, "is Baron Gruner."

When the Austrian at last bowed and departed, we approached Countess Sztáray to introduce ourselves. Elisabeth's lady-in-waiting greeted us politely, but she repeated her mistress's instruction that Holmes was to meet Her Imperial and Royal Majesty alone. My friend, on this occasion, was at his most urbane.

"Dr. Watson," he assured the Countess (rather to my irritation), "stands in much the same position to myself as you do to the Empress. His function is primarily to assist me, and he will be nowhere in evidence when I have the honour to attend upon Her Majesty tomorrow morning."

"You remind me, Herr Holmes," replied our new acquaintance, "that Her Majesty required me to inform you that she wishes to postpone the interview until a later hour. Would twelve noon be acceptable? Our steamer to Montreux does not leave until early in the afternoon, so you will still have ample time to talk."

"Of course. I trust Her Majesty is not indisposed?"

"Oh, no, but she was very tired tonight. You see, we were pursued this afternoon by a mad old clergyman who followed us from the hotel. It took some time to shake him off, so that we could get on with our shopping." Countess Sztáray's blue eyes gazed into the detective's grey ones without a hint of guile, as I struggled to turn my snort of laughter into a choking cough. Holmes covered his discomfiture by summoning a steward to bring us glasses of Champagne.

"The man with whom you were speaking earlier," he guardedly enquired, "Did you know him, Countess?"

"No, we met tonight." Was it my imagination, or were the lady-in-waiting's open features enlivened by a blush? "His name is Baron Gruner—Baron *Adelbert* Gruner, I believe. One would not think so to look at him, but he collects rare china. He wished to enquire about purchasing certain pieces from the imperial collection. Naturally, I had to tell the Baron that it was quite impossible to approach Her Majesty on such a matter. It is a pity, really. . . . He had such magnetic eyes!"

My friend's eyes gave the Countess's a very direct look. "If I may presume upon our short acquaintance to advise you, madam," he said earnestly, "I would urge *for your own safety*, as well as for Her Majesty's, that you keep clear of Baron Gruner. I am reliably informed that he has acquired an exceedingly dangerous and dishonourable reputation, particularly where women are concerned."

As Countess Sztáray regarded him with mild astonishment, Sherlock Holmes was suddenly distracted. I saw him eyeing a strongly built man in evening dress who had just entered the soirée. He had close-cut, ginger hair atop a brutish countenance, smirking disagreeably underneath his "Kaiser Wilhelm" mustache. When the newcomer noticed the detective, his smirk widened, and with a mocking bow he turned and left the room.

"You must excuse me, Countess," muttered Holmes. "Watson, please join me in my room at ten o'clock. We have a great deal to discuss." He left us with no further explanation, exiting through the door from which his enemy had come.

The lady's look of astonishment now turned on me. "My goodness, Herr Doktor! Is Herr Holmes always so abrupt? If so, he must be a difficult employer."

While I am not unduly egotistical, I did not let the imputation pass. "Herr Holmes can put things badly. I am his friend and colleague, not his employé. No doubt," I could not forbear adding, "he would rightly claim to be 'the brains' behind our partnership."

Countess Sztáray apologised at perhaps unnecessary length. "I have more empathy for your role than you imagine," she concluded. "Her Majesty likewise can be difficult. I *hope* that she considers me a friend, but it is impossible to base real friendship on terms of inequality."

The lady's frankness encouraged me to ask a question that had never been resolved. "Holmes and I," I cautiously began, "have operated on the assumption that the Empress desires him to investigate the deaths at Mayerling. Is that in fact the case? Our work so far has focused on learning all we can regarding the late Heir-Apparent."

Once more, I had embarrassed my companion. "Her Majesty has not confided to me her wishes in the matter," she admitted, "and my service to her began only after the death of the Crown Prince. She does not often speak of him, at least to me, and *never* of the sad events at Mayerling."

"But surely," I insisted, "she must have her own ideas about the matter. From all we have discovered, Rudolf was in torment for weeks before his death. I cannot imagine that a woman of the Empress's sensitivity could remain entirely ignorant of the misfortunes afflicting her own son!"

Countess Sztáray responded with a look informing me that I had gone too far. "You must not forget, Herr Doktor, that persons of the highest rank live quite differently than you and I. They find out less, and in that way they are most unhappy, because the truth only rarely reaches them, and even then never completely. I do believe (for what little *my* belief is worth) that Her Imperial and Royal Majesty once loved Crown Prince Rudolf very deeply, far more than she ever loved her husband. But all that is behind her now. She longs only for death, and I cannot help but feel that death will not be long in finding her. We may feel pity for the Empress, but we must not presume to judge her."

I could but bow and extend my own apology. Elisabeth's lady-in-waiting departed the soirée, after apprising me that her mistress had ordered luncheon for herself and the detective in a private dining room. As much as I might once have yearned to meet the Empress Sisi, I did not altogether envy Sherlock Holmes.

Long after ten o'clock, my friend and I sat discussing preparations for the morning. The fire in the hearth had died to embers. Holmes had left the draperies to his balcony undrawn, so I watched the lights of Old Town shining on the lake below. Having shared a bottle of Bordeaux from the hotel's excellent cellar, I lit a cigar while the detective took out his favourite brier, bent on creating the 'poisonous atmosphere' he found well-nigh indispensable to concentration.

Holmes began by reporting his confrontation with Herr Adolf Meyer. "I confess myself baffled, Doctor, as to the man's intentions. He did not, so far as I could tell, shadow Elisabeth on her shopping expedition—although my own efforts there were so inept I can be sure of nothing! Tonight, when I caught up with Meyer after he looked into the soirée, I found him disturbingly amiable. He professed to be spending a few days in Geneva following a mountaineering holiday, having had no idea (he claimed!) that Her Majesty was even in the region."

"Do you believe him?"

"Certainly not, but it seems unlikely that Meyer would show himself so openly if he was plotting to do our client harm. When I challenged him regarding his relationship with Baron Gruner, he told me that the fellow had approached him—as he approached Countess Sztáray—about a piece of pottery. He had an answer to everything, you see! Yet, all my instincts warn me that Adolf Meyer intends some deviltry tomorrow. His presence at the Beau-Rivage cannot be coincidence."

"What will you do, Holmes?"

"What will *we* do, Watson? For while I am lunching with Elisabeth, the burden of guarding her from an avowed and dangerous enemy must be left with you."

"But the Empress will not tolerate my presence. Besides, stealth—as you so kindly informed me—is not among my 'invaluable qualities.'"

"It will not be needed in this instance. Early in the morning, I shall make a thorough reconnaissance of the hotel and its surroundings, especially regarding access to the room in which Her Majesty and I shall meet. Your task will to shadow Meyer's every move. Whether or not he sees you doesn't matter; in fact, I should prefer him to know that we are keeping him in view. Here is the number of his room, which is on the floor below us. I want you outside watching it no later than six o'clock a.m."

"So I'm to spend six hours lurking in the hallway? Suppose Meyer escapes from his balcony in the middle of the night? Must I disguise myself as a chambermaid to ascertain his presence in the room? Your plan is hardly foolproof, Holmes!"

With a curse, the detective sprang from his chair and threw open the windows onto his own balcony. He stalked outside and stood glaring down on Lake Geneva. I allowed him a moment to compose himself before I followed.

Holmes met me with a bitter smile. "You're right, of course, old friend. My plan is rubbish! It takes no account of Baron Gruner, who may be far less negligible in this affair than I suppose. But there are only two of us; the hotel detective is useless in dealing with an empress and a spy. The maddening thing, Watson, is that my precautions—inadequate as they are—may be entirely needless. Leaving aside my brother's warning, and Meyer's known Pan-German sympathies, we have no evidence that Her Majesty is in any danger. Yet, those two factors alone do not permit me to put my mind at rest."

"Another factor in the case remains uncertain," I reminded Holmes as we relapsed into our seats before the fire. "Countess Sztáray could not confirm our supposition that her mistress wishes you to reexamine Mayerling. Suppose that all she really wants is your opinion of her skills as an equestrienne, compared to those of Skittles?"

"In *that* event, Doctor," my friend facetiously replied, "henceforth, whenever you feel that I have grown too confident of my own powers, pray whisper 'Geneva' in my ear instead of 'Norbury.'"

Sherlock Holmes laughed heartily, but those words still haunt him after thirty years.

CHAPTER 8

September 10, 1898

My "Boswell" Watson, in his chronicles of my career, too often depicted me as an emotionless reasoning machine. No doubt he sought in his protagonist a contrast to the frequently romantic—indeed, occasionally lurid—content of his stories. It is true that I regarded my personal feelings as a distraction to my work, and I tried to minimise their impact upon The Science of Deduction. Inevitably, this habitual suppression of emotion carried over to my private life, a part of life already limited for a man as immersed in his vocation as was I. Readers of the Doctor's tales should not conclude, however, that I am, or ever was, *incapable* of feeling. Sherlock Holmes is no automaton; the "great detective" must not be equated with the inner man.

Surely, our half-century of friendship—for Watson is the truest friend a man could have—provides evidence of human feeling. My relations with Mycroft exhibit our competitiveness and mutual exasperation, but there is also a degree of brotherly affection. Contrary to the fictional disclaimer attributed to me by my biographer, I have indeed experienced romantic love. Readers who recall the hatred I once felt for Moriarty (who corrupted his own brilliant mind long before I slew his body), the contempt with which I dismissed young James Ryder, or the horror that nearly overcame me under the malign influence of the Devil's Foot, will understand that the darkest of emotions have come to me as well. However, in the case involving Empress Elisabeth, I was subjected to an emotion I have seldom felt before or since, and that was shame.

It was not the first occasion on which I lost, or nearly lost, a client. John Openshaw died because I misread the imminence of the danger facing him. I solved the cipher of the dancing men too late for

Hilton Cubitt. Sir Henry Baskerville could easily have ended as the final victim of the Hound. My defeats, when they have come, have been attributable to circumstances I did not foresee or errors in the execution of my plans. On two occasions only was I out-thought and out-maneuvered by a superior opponent. The first of these was Irene Adler. Whatever self-respect I lost to her was later compensated by a thousandfold. The second foe who bested me was Adolf Meyer. Neither I nor my client recovered what we lost to him on that September afternoon.

My morning reconnaissance of the hotel and grounds proved eminently satisfactory. As I had now resumed my own persona, the concierge agreed to show me the private dining room chosen for my meeting with the Empress. It had but a single window, and by moving our table slightly I was able to ensure that it did not fall within that window's line of sight. I questioned the hotel manager closely, ascertaining that all staff who would wait upon Her Majesty had been long in his service and were beyond reproach. With Watson unavailable, I asked the hotel detective to forestall guests or strangers from entering the room. Beyond the walls and grounds, the adjacent, tree-lined park (site of the Brunswick Monument) initially caused me some anxiety. However, it was likely to be busy on a Saturday and faced a different side of the hotel. All things considered, I was reasonably certain I had done everything required to ensure the safety of our meeting. And my confidence, in this regard, was not misplaced.

As we had agreed, I met Watson in the hotel lobby an hour before luncheon. The Doctor—despite his scepticism of my plan—had posted himself faithfully in the hall outside Meyer's room at six a.m. Forgoing the masquerade he had ironically proposed, he inveigled from the presiding chambermaid (who happened to be pretty) the intelligence that our adversary had remained inside. At eight o'clock, Watson was startled when the door he was observing opened suddenly, and the Austrian appeared before he was able to slip around a corner. To my proxy's surprise and probable relief, Herr Meyer was quite friendly. In fact, they had breakfasted together.

"Well, Doctor," I remarked, "you are surely taking literally my injunction to watch Meyer's every move. What on Earth did you discuss?"

"Mountaineering, primarily. Having learned that I spent time in northern India, he wanted to hear my impression of the Himalaya. Meyer actually proposed that we meet him in Zermatt next spring! I was able to beg off by pleading my bad leg. He asked me to say that the invitation is still open as it applies to you."

"No, thank you; I have no desire to end my days in a crevasse. The nerve of the villain! I almost find myself admiring him. What did you do next?"

"Meyer next invited me to join him in sailing on the lake. I declined, of course, for reasons similar to yours. However, I accompanied him to the landing to assure myself that *he* had gone aboard a boat. To judge by what he paid the boatman, he ought to return to the hotel before much longer."

"*If* the hotel is his destination. Was there anything in Meyer's conduct that struck you as unusual?" This enquiry I made without much hope, but for once my unobservant friend surprised me.

"No . . . *Yes*, there was, by Godfrey! although it may mean nothing. As we crossed the street in front of the hotel, Meyer nodded briefly to someone on the opposite side. I followed his glance, and I saw a young man watching him intently."

"Indeed? Describe this young man."

"Well, he was a common sort of person, Holmes. In his twenties, I would guess . . . short of stature . . . close-cropped hair, and a mustache. He had an ugly countenance."

"How was he dressed?"

"A striped smock beneath a workman's suit of clothes . . . and a soft hat. Definitely of the labouring classes. I thought he might have been a beggar to whom Meyer had previously given money."

"But this beggar, or workman, did not approach Herr Meyer?"

"No, when Meyer ignored him, beyond nodding, he turned away into the crowd of passers-by."

"Excellent, Watson! We shall make a detective of you yet! Happily," I added, after consulting the lobby clock, "I have just time enough to look around a bit outside and see if I can spot the fellow. You stay here and continue to dog our adversary's footsteps, if and when he should return. Let us meet again at two o'clock. By that time, Her Majesty will have departed and I should have a better idea of how we shall proceed in future."

My search for a man matching the description the Doctor had provided was without result. I therefore regressed to the private dining room, arriving shortly before twelve o'clock. My client, attended by Countess Sztáray, did not appear until twenty minutes later. The Countess sat down at a table beyond hearing distance and ignored my presence. The Empress, whom I saw had worn a veil, nodded silently as I helped her to her chair. Receiving her permissive gesture, I bowed and sat as well.

Elisabeth seemed ill at ease, and several moments passed before she brought herself to speak. "My thanks, Herr Holmes," she began formally, "for acceding to my wishes in this matter. I realise that I have put you to considerable inconvenience, and I am prepared to compensate you fully for your time and trouble."

It seemed best to play the courtier card until I got my bearings. "I am honoured," I assured my client, "to be of service to Your Majesty. It is also a pleasure to return to this beautiful city. Geneva is among my favourite destinations on the Continent."

"It is my favourite place to stay as well," the Empress acknowledged. "The lake is altogether the colour of the ocean, and I can become quite lost among the cosmopolites. Geneva confers— however briefly—an illusion of the true human condition."

In this vein, I had the inspiration to dare greatly. "Might I request that Your Majesty remove your veil? It makes natural

164

conversation difficult, and as it happens I was in the hotel lobby when you and Countess Sztáray arrived."

Even without seeing her face, Elisabeth's start of annoyance informed me that I had displeased her. "*Also*, it was *you*, Herr Holmes—in that absurd disguise—who pursued us through the city yesterday! I suspected as much but did not like to think it."

"I intended to provide Your Majesty protection. Although," I ruefully admitted, "I quickly found myself providing that protection from afar."

An ironic chuckle issued from the veil. "My husband's police, Herr Holmes, have 'protected' me for many years. I have become quite adept at eluding them. I hope your other skills as a detective," she added tartly, "are somewhat more impressive!"

It was perhaps fortunate that at this stage we were interrupted by the *maître d'hôtel*, the head *sommelier*, and a swarm of subsidiary waiters. Less to their surprise than I might have expected, Her Majesty ordered a large glass of milk and a dish of scrambled eggs. My request for a cup of Turkish coffee evoked more consternation, but I had no energy to spare for digestion at that moment. When our meagre fare arrived, it was accompanied by a plate of violet macaroons, a speciality of the hotel and (as I learned later) a favourite of the Empress.

Meanwhile, Elisabeth—perhaps impressed by my culinary self-restraint—relented upon her refusal to converse face-to-face. "If you truly desire to behold the Gorgon for a second time, Herr Holmes," she offered coyly, "I shall not deny you." And the veil arose.

"I behold no Medusa, Majesty," I assured her vanity, "only a beautiful 'lady whom time hath surprised.'" Watson at his finest could not have bettered *that*, and to my satisfaction my client responded with a girlish laugh.

"The Dowager Empress Victoria did not describe you as a gallant, Herr Sherlock Holmes! *Jawohl*, it was she who suggested I consult you—after her guards had let me out of prison. Now, I believe, it is time for me to speak of your commission, for the Countess and I must board the lake steamer to Montreux within the hour."

"I am all attention, ma'am."

"I desire you, sir, to avenge the murder of my son."

"Indeed!" My sigh was pure relief that a week-long investigation was not wasted.

"You do not seem surprised."

"It was the likeliest explanation, given the reference in Your Majesty's letter to 'one whom I held dear.' I must point out that nine years have elapsed since Mayerling. What has led you to suspect, after such an interval, that the late Crown Prince was murdered?"

"It is not a mere suspicion, sir! Rudolf himself informed me of the fact."

As the Doctor might write, *my heart sank within me,* for it was now apparent that I was dealing with a madwoman. For the moment, I would humour her.

"When did His Imperial and Royal Highness impart this information?"

"He warned me during our last Christmas together, only weeks before he died. My poor boy"—Elisabeth's voice quavered momentarily with what I assumed to be maternal grief—"had given me a book of Heine autographs. When he embraced me, Rudolf began to sob and whispered softly, 'Mother, I know that soon I shall be killed.'"

"He did not explain?"

"Before the entire family? How could he?"

"A premonition and a warning, ma'am, do not amount to fact."

The Empress ignored my remark. "After Mayerling, I went by night into the crypt where Rudolf's body was entombed. I felt sure my son would send some message to me, some explanation as to *why* he died. I sent away the friar, and I waited for an hour in the torchlight by the coffin. But no message came."

166

"Your Majesty astounds me."

"The spirits can only materialise when permitted by the great Jehovah," snapped Elisabeth, "and *His* destructive power you would do well not to mock! I no longer believe according to the Church, for to do so would require accepting that my son is damned. I was in despair, Herr Holmes, for I came to realise that our pleas are powerless against the divine Jehovah's inscrutable will. For *nine years*, He has condemned me to wander in the wilderness, in search of His enlightenment. Yet, when enlightenment came to me at last, it was from the most unlikely source imaginable—my husband!"

It seemed that, after all, there might be method in the lady's madness. Before I could press her for details, a waiter (this time only one) intruded to enquire into our satisfaction. After repulsing him, Her Majesty returned to the subject of her own accord.

"The Emperor and I met earlier this summer at Bad Ischl, where we endured two weeks together. There he spoke to me more openly of our son's death than at any time since it occurred. I have no idea what possessed Franz Josef; it has been many years since we confided in each other. Even so, our memories of Rudolf still unite us, and perhaps my husband felt he owed me all the truth at last." Here my client's courage must have faltered, for she picked fitfully at her untasted plate of eggs.

"Once more, I am all attention, Majesty."

"I was already aware, Herr Holmes, that shortly before Rudolf died, the Emperor had refused to annul his marriage and made him promise to give up the Vetsera girl. His Majesty's command was for the best, although I must excuse my son for looking elsewhere to ease the emptiness of his own home. Things would have been different had the Crown Prince possessed a wife who understood him!"

"But the Emperor's commandments were not new to you," I prompted her.

"*Nein.* My husband's revelation was that eighteen years before the deaths at Mayerling, he had conducted an affair with Baroness

Helene Vetsera. In other words, he may have been the father of his own son's paramour. You understand what this would mean?"

"All too well, Your Majesty," I answered grimly.

"I assure you, Herr Holmes, that the disgust I see reflected in your face would also have afflicted the Crown Prince. It was not that he and his mistress could not marry; *that* would never have occurred. But the awe in which our son held His Apostolic Majesty—a pillar of rectitude whom he could only hope to emulate—was damaged irreversibly. What a blow to Rudolf's self-esteem! In a sense, he had been cuckolded by his own father!"

With an appeasing gesture, I sought to escape this mire of melodrama. "I recognise, Your Majesty," I told my client, "that the Heir-Apparent would have been distressed by such distasteful news. But what has this to do with murder? If anything, it would merely predispose your son to suicide—which was, as I recall, the verdict on his death."

Elisabeth gave me a contemptuous look. "I shall come to that, Herr Holmes. When the Emperor met Rudolf in a private audience before he left for Mayerling, the possibility of a half-sister was but part of the 'distasteful news.' His Majesty also ordered the Crown Prince to explain his connexion to disturbances in Hungary—disturbances that demanded Rudolf's replacement of his father as that country's king. My husband, quite naturally, was furious. 'You are no longer worthy to be my successor!' he rebuked our son."

"I have already heard something of this matter," I wearily replied. "It provides, in my view, no direct evidence to support Your Majesty's contention that the late Crown Prince was murdered."

"Then assuredly you have not heard all! Nor *could* you have, Herr Holmes, for I did not learn the whole truth myself until this summer at Bad Ischl. Now, will you *please* be silent and let me finish my account?"

I bowed to the extent possible while remaining in my chair. The Empress took a moment to recover her composure, seizing a violet macaroon and munching it—the first bite she had eaten since the meal began. At last, she regarded me with a pitying smile.

"You have never married, I believe, Herr Holmes?"

"Indeed," I admitted, "that privilege has so far been denied me."

"I advise you not to change your happy state. Marriage is a nonsensical institution. One is sold as a child of fifteen and takes an oath one does not understand but can never undo. Do you wish to know when my marriage to the Emperor ended—or ended, at least, in my own eyes?"

"If Your Majesty wishes to enlighten me."

"It was in 1859, after my husband went to war in Italy. He brought home to me not victory but a venereal disease. Afterwards, our relations ended for some years—until I agreed to bear him one more child (alas, another daughter!) following his next defeat. My price was equality for my beloved Hungary. After Königgrätz, I took my son and went to Budapest—like Maria Theresia—to rally support for the imperilled Habsburg Crown. But I fell in love with that wild country, and with Count Andrássy!

"So you see," she went on when I did not respond, "Rudolf's treasonous adventure was to some degree my fault. Those months in Hungary were the only time the two of us were truly close, and my boy never lost his childhood fascination with the place. Had I been there for him to confide in, I could have stopped him before matters went too far."

Elisabeth's eyes had filled with tears, but I could offer her no consolation. Instead, I enquired: "What was 'the whole truth' His Majesty told you at Bad Ischl?"

After sighing deeply, my client resumed a neutral tone. "As you may not know, at the time of Rudolf's death our army was commanded by the Archduke Albrecht. He was my husband's uncle— and the victor of Custozza in 1866!—but still Inspector General although past seventy. Needless to say, Albrecht opposed all ideas of reform and held the forward-thinking Heir-Apparent in contempt.

Unfortunately, the Emperor notified him of Rudolf's Hungarian activities, and he was closely monitoring events in Budapest. When my son failed to attend Marie Valerie's engagement dinner, the old archduke concluded that he was preparing to depart for Hungary to launch the coup d'état. On his own authority, he sent ten Roll Commandoes—they are an élite regiment of sharpshooters—to arrest the Crown Prince at Mayerling. Only after they had left did he inform my husband."

So these were Count Hoyos's mysterious horsemen! Suppressing my excitement, I managed to ask without undue urgency: "And what was the Emperor's response?"

"Why, he put a stop to it, Herr Holmes! At once, His Majesty despatched his aide-de-camp by train to Baden to intercept the riders. The aide-de-camp overtook them before they reached the lodge at Mayerling, and all of them returned to Vienna. Or such was the tale reported to the Emperor."

By this time, I could anticipate Elisabeth's account. "But this report was not entirely accurate, as Your Majesty discovered at Bad Ischl."

Once again the Empress sighed. "It was on the old man's deathbed, six years later, that my husband finally heard the truth. Only *eight* Roll Commandoes had returned from Mayerling; the other two had disappeared. The Archduke had been furious, of course. He cashiered the traitors in absentia, yet made no attempt to find them. You see, if they *had* been responsible for the Crown Prince's murder, to him it was not altogether a bad thing. Albrecht confessed his treason to the Emperor with almost his dying breath, and naturally he was forgiven. Indeed, it was a surprise to me that he did not receive a medal—as did Bratfisch, Loschek, and all the other fools who failed my son at Mayerling!"

Elisabeth was trembling with anger, and it was I who sat back with a sigh. "*Well*, Your Majesty, that is truly a remarkable story. While there are several objections to this theory of the Heir-

Apparent's death, it is sufficiently plausible to merit an investigation. *Proving* it may be another matter. For the present, how does Your Majesty intend for me to treat this information?"

"To make it public, sir!" The Empress nodded to Countess Sztáray, who brought her a small journal bound in leather. "This book contains the evidence I have collected in the years since Mayerling. All the facts we have discussed today are documented there. Take this record back to England, find the proofs you need, and see that they are published. It is impossible to have such things done in Austria, or even in Geneva; my husband's spies are everywhere. The Empress Victoria informed me of your political connexions. If proof of Rudolf's murder is published in the *Times*, and endorsed by the British government, it *must* be taken seriously!"

Elisabeth passed me the journal, which I placed carefully inside my jacket's inner pocket. Coming from a woman I had dismissed as mad, my client's plan seemed sound—even though I shuddered to anticipate how Mycroft would receive it. Unfortunately, one obvious objection to her hypothesis would be difficult to circumvent.

"There is one point to which I must regretfully direct Your Majesty's attention. The medical report at Mayerling stated conclusively that the death of 'the Vetsera girl' (whom everyone appears to have forgotten in this business) occurred at least six hours before that of the Crown Prince. To me it seems inescapable, therefore, that *her* murder could not have been committed by these renegade Commandoes, but rather by . . . someone already on the scene."

My client's face turned ashen, and for a long moment she did not reply. When at last she raised her eyes to mine, it was with a bitter but courageous smile.

"That fact, sir, I have known for many years—indeed, from the very day that Rudolf died. He left a note for me, you see. It read only: 'Mother, I no longer have a right to live, for I have killed.' I tell myself, of course, that the foolish girl ended her own life, and my

171

poor son merely felt responsible. In *that* were true, I could still have faith that one day the great Jehovah would forgive him."

The bereaved mother rose. "Come, Irma," she said softly, and it was the Empress of Austria who turned back to me. "I see no need for us to meet again, Herr Holmes. Please write to me after you return to London and read the evidence I have entrusted to you. A note sent to the Grand Hôtel de Caux will find me."

"Where is Your Majesty bound next?" I enquired.

"Who knows?" she laughed. "I am free and my 'seagull flight' has begun! I want to cross the seven seas, like a female 'Flying Dutchman,' until I drown and am forgotten. Goodbye, Herr Holmes. Pray do not follow me—this time."

I bowed as Elisabeth swept from the room, followed (after a furious glance in my direction) by Countess Sztáray. It was, to my surprise, now thirty-five minutes after one o'clock. Suddenly hungry, I pocketed the remaining macaroons before the hotel staff arrived to clear the table. As Watson not due for half an hour, I walked into the lobby to await him and examine the journal Elisabeth had penned.

Readers of the Doctor's stories will attest that I am not normally a fanciful man. Yet, the instant I had installed myself upon a sofa, I was overcome by a premonition of disaster so powerful that it seemed have come directly from 'the great Jehovah.' Without any clear intention, I rushed outside onto the Quai du Mont-Blanc. There, at a distance, I beheld the Empress and her lady, en route to the boat landing to board their steamer for Montreux. They had just passed the Brunswick Monument, apparently unrecognised by the few passers-by. While I watched, a man—matching exactly the description Watson had provided—leapt from the adjacent trees and collided roughly with Elisabeth. Simultaneously, a sharp blow to the head struck me from behind. As my knees collapsed, a hand stole into the inner pocket of my jacket. Lying half-stunned beneath the sunlight's glare, I saw a vague figure looming over me. A voice I failed to

172

recognise sneered mockingly, "*Vielen Dank*, Herr Sherlock Holmes!" Then the sunlight faded, and I knew no more.

After Holmes left me for his meeting with the Empress, I remained inside the lobby, strategically placed to detect Adolf Meyer whenever he appeared. The spy did not return until nearly half past twelve. When I caught his eye, he nodded brusquely, all pretence of friendliness quite gone. I followed Herr Meyer into the hotel café, where we ate a quick, uneasy luncheon, seated separately but occasionally staring daggers at each other from across the room. By the time the meal was over, the clock had sounded one.

The Austrian marched directly past my table, his only greeting a sarcastic smile. I waited thirty seconds before leaving but was still in time to see him exiting the lobby for the street. Because the crowds along the Quai du Mont-Blanc had diminished since our earlier excursion, I kept a good fifty yards behind my quarry. Herr Meyer seemed entirely unaware of being shadowed. He crossed the great bridge over the Rhône and entered Old Town, strolling as casually as any tourist on a holiday. Gradually, it dawned upon me that I was heading once again to the Cathédrale Saint-Pierre.

The ancient church was busier than it had been the day before, but still by no means crowded. Meyer made his way swiftly through the nave and (as I somehow had expected) turned into an alcove that led to the south tower. I gave him two minutes' start before I, too, began to climb. Although the lower sections of the spiral stairway were composed of stone, near the top my ascent was interrupted by a wooden floor, which I had to cross before reaching the next set of stairs. On this, of course, my footsteps echoed hollowly. Having lost the advantage of surprise, I climbed into the tower's topmost room knowing that my adversary would be well prepared for me.

It was immediately proven that I had walked into a trap. Herr Meyer sat lounging on a windowsill that overlooked the balcony, the barrel of his new Rast & Gasser pistol pointed at my chest. When he noticed that my faithful Adams covered him as well, the Austrian chuckled in appreciation.

"*Sehr gut*, Herr Doktor! Careless of me to forget that I was dealing with a fellow soldier! Shall we put away our pistols and discuss this matter amicably?" He slipped his revolver back into the pocket of his coat; I, after a brief hesitation, did the same. Again as genial as ever, the spy waved me to another windowsill across the room. It was in following his gesture that I saw the sniper's rifle, equipped with both a forked rest and a telescopic sight, aimed directly at the row of grand hotels across the lake. Herr Meyer met my look of consternation with a smile.

"A beautiful weapon, your old English Whitworth, is it not? And far more accurate at such a range than the new German Mausers. Were I to allow you to peer through the rifle's sight, you would see the corner window of the Empress's suite. My instructions were to despatch both Her Majesty and Herr Sherlock Holmes today. Alas! the idea of entertaining a detective in her rooms was too bohemian even for Elisabeth!"

"So, Herr Meyer, you are now a soldier making war on women. How heroic!"

My opponent did not disagree. "Sadly *un*heroic, it is true," he sighed, "but the once-beautiful Sisi has become an inconvenience to my colleagues in Berlin. Even now, I fear, she is telling Herr Holmes an unfortunate story. A tale of traitorous sharpshooters who, deserting their commander, returned to Mayerling to assassinate her son."

"And is that story true?"

"*Nein*, for who can know whether the two sharpshooters succeeded? But they were *never* traitors! They served the *true* German Kaiser, not the sad old fool who misrules his mongrel empire from the Hofburg."

"Has the true German Kaiser also ordered the assassination of Elisabeth?"

"Wilhelm?" scoffed Herr Meyer. "In his youth, Wilhelm was quite smitten by Franz Josef's wife! The Kaiser knows not his own mind from one day to the next. But there are those of us who *do*, both in Berlin and in Vienna. Prince Bismarck was the best of us,[12] but there are many others. We work for the creation of a greater German Reich—one in which neither Habsburg nor Hohenzollern will ultimately have a place."

"I am not sorry," I responded, "that your work to build the Reich will not succeed today. By this time, Elisabeth will have told my friend her story. Soon, she will come walking down the promenade to board her steamer for Montreux. And if you believe that I am going to let you fire that rifle at her"—here I once more drew my revolver—"then you have misjudged your man."

I moved quickly to the side of the tower facing the hotels, intending to tip Meyer's deadly Whitworth over the sill. To my chagrin, the villain merely laughed at me, not even bothering to rise.

"Herr Doktor, *please* do not damage my fine rifle! It will only fall onto the balcony, and I have no wish for either of us to be shot. Besides," he added as I fumed, "I assure you the Whitworth is not even loaded. You see, I have made alternative arrangements; all of this is but a blind."

"A *blind!*"

"*Natürlich!* It was necessary to draw you away from Herr Holmes and the Empress, and I have found allies to carry out my work. One is an unsavoury rascal whom I bought with a Chinese vase from Charlottenburg's Porcelain Chamber. For the main task, there are always anarchists lurking in Geneva. It was only required to put one on the scent. Events will take their course, but the outcome is unlikely to be traced to me."

---

[12] Prince Otto von Bismarck, Germany's "Iron Chancellor," had died at 84 on July 30.

I suddenly remembered the disreputable-looking labourer Meyer had nodded to that morning. If he was an assassin, poised to strike somewhere along the Quai du Mont-Blanc, I had no time to lose. Elisabeth's lake steamer for Montreux departed in less than fifteen minutes. Without another word, I threw myself back down the spiral stairway, pursued by the spy's scornful laughter: *"Too late, Herr Doktor Watson! You and the great detective Sherlock Holmes will be too late!"*

Pushing past a dozen startled visitors inside the cathedral, I made my way out into the street. Although the distance to the Hôtel Beau Rivage was little more than half an English mile, I was a middle-aged man with a game leg and sadly out of training. Yet, I ran that afternoon as I had never run before, not even on the night I had outpaced my friend Lestrade when we raced to save Sir Henry Baskerville. At every step, I expected to feel my head explode from the impact of a bullet from Adolf Meyer's Whitworth. No bullet came, but a gendarme shouted at me angrily as I dodged through the pedestrians upon the bridge across the Rhône.

Then, as I descended from the Pont du Mont-Blanc and turned the corner, my mind was set at rest. Some distance ahead, the Empress Elisabeth and Countess Sztáray came walking rapidly along the promenade, approaching the quay where their boat waited. Her Majesty appeared somewhat flustered; the Countess brushed anxiously at her mistress's sleeve. But they were both, thank God, alive and well, and not too late for their departure. To my relief, they swept up the ramp and boarded safely. The steamer's whistle sounded, and she began to move away.

There was no sign of Sherlock Holmes, so he had not—as I would have expected—accompanied our client to the quay. I wondered how their interview had gone, and where the case might take us next. Having caught my breath, I quickened my pace, realising that I needed to report promptly on Meyer's failed attempt at murder. The opportunity to do so came sooner than I thought. Beyond the intersection with the Rue des Alpes, I saw a man I recognised propped up against a tree, attended by a gendarme and an elderly fellow who appeared to be a doctor. The man beneath the tree was Holmes.

"Hallo, Watson," he hailed me groggily. "Where have you dropped from?" With a bandaged head, bleary eyes, and rumpled clothing, my friend looked quite forlorn.

"Never mind that for the present," I responded, dropping to my knees beside him. "Tell me what has happened, Holmes, to leave you in this state."

"It is over, Doctor," he replied despondently. "I have made a complete hash of this business, and the case is lost." Lying down upon the ground, Holmes threw an arm across his brow, offering no further explanation. In my confusion, I turned to the gendarme.

"*Monsieur* was injured," the policeman told me in a kind of English, "at the same time the lady was attacked."

"Lady? What lady?"

"*The Empress*, you dullard!" Holmes cried furiously, half rising on an elbow. "What other lady would be worth attacking in this godforsaken place?" He grabbed his head and fell back groaning, as the doctor clucked reproachfully.

"The Empress is perfectly well, Holmes," I assured him evenly. Given my friend's condition, I would forgive the insult, although it cut me to the quick. "I saw Her Majesty and Countess Sztáray approaching when I passed the docks. They boarded their steamer without incident, and are now bound for Montreux."

"That is irrelevant. They got what they came for," he added vaguely. "The journal is gone, and Elisabeth's charge cannot be proven. How can I face her after this? My most prestigious client, and I failed her utterly. *Fool* that I was to underestimate that scoundrel Gruner!" Again the old physician chided him, and he said no more.

Between the gendarme and the doctor, I eventually received a partial explanation. An unknown lady (for my informants had still not taken in the Empress's identity) had been knocked down in the street

177

by a young thief. Other gendarmerie were already in pursuit of him. Happily, the lady was only slightly shaken. She had risen immediately, and she and her companion had proceeded to the docks. The attack upon the gentleman was even more deplorable, but not necessarily related to the first event. Such regrettable incidents (the gendarme shrugged) occurred even in Geneva. According to the doctor, the gentleman would certainly recover; it was a minor concussion, nothing more.

There was a rustling in the grass behind us, and I turned to see two more splendidly uniformed gendarmes approaching with the "thief" in custody. He was undoubtedly the tool of Adolf Meyer I had seen that morning; a face like his was unmistakable. When I rose to confront the failed assassin,[13] he grinned insolently in recognition.

"Well, sir," I informed him, "your dastardly attempt did not succeed. Instead of winning infamy as the assassin of an empress, you can anticipate a lengthy prison term."

Whether the villain understood me was uncertain, for he was gazing intently across my shoulder at the lake beyond. *"Guarda!"* he commanded, and there was an unpleasant note of triumph in his voice. Reluctantly obeying, we turned to Lake Geneva, where the recently departed steamboat was returning to the quay.

The Empress of Austria was dead. Her heart had been pierced by a blade so thin that blood seeped slowly into the pericardium, so that the organ ceased only gradually to beat. Not until Elisabeth fainted upon boarding the steamer did Countess Sztáray realise that her mistress had been wounded. Her Majesty, who sank almost at once into unconsciousness, never realised it at all. The fabled Sisi was

---

[13] For more information on Elisabeth's attacker, the anarchist Luigi Lucheni, consult the webpage: http://www.unofficialroyalty.com/assassination-of-empress-elisabeth-of-austria-1898. Until Watson's account revealed Adolf Meyer's role, it was uncertain how Lucheni had learned of the Empress's one-night stay at the Hôtel Beau Rivage.

taken on a stretcher to the Hôtel Beau Rivage, where the death she had so longed for was pronounced.

I had an account of Elisabeth's post-mortem from the hotel physician, who, having examined the dead empress, collaborated with me in treating Sherlock Holmes. To my dismay, the detective awoke with a fever on Sunday, the eleventh of September, and was bedridden for the next three days. Had we been in Baker Street, he would never have tolerated so long a spell of forced inaction, but it was evident that my friend's emotional as well as physical well-being had suffered a traumatic blow. He seemed almost relieved when informed of the Empress's assassination, perhaps because it allowed him to consign the case—and his own failure—to the past. Having recovered his wits and heard my story, Holmes apologised for his bitter words to me following the journal's theft.

"It was unforgivable, Watson, but I hope you will forgive me, nonetheless. While I was ensuring that my client's final moments would be filled with grief, you were risking your life to forestall a crime that I could not prevent. Had my efforts in this case matched yours, old friend, Her Majesty would be alive today."

Although I hardly merited such praise from Caesar, I saw Holmes's contrition as a hopeful sign for his recovery. Unfortunately, reestablishing his equilibrium was not to be an easy task. On the morning that we left Geneva, our train shared a platform with the imperial funeral express, onto which Elisabeth's elaborate, three-tiered coffin was being loaded just as we arrived. My friend was mostly silent for the duration of our journey.

I did not accompany Holmes when he went to Whitehall to report to Mycroft, but it must have been for the two brothers an excruciating interview. Upon returning, my friend informed me that he wished never to speak again of our visit to Geneva. He seldom mentioned those events in later years and always refused to discuss them in detail. There were certain outcomes in which I was involved, one the case I have chronicled as "The Adventure of the Illustrious

Client." There the detective, assisted by "a woman scorned," exacted a terrible revenge on Baron Gruner, although nearly at the cost of his own life. When I wrote up the story, I was forbidden any reference to Holmes's earlier encounter with the Baron. Nor did we find Empress Elisabeth's lost journal among that reprobate's disgusting files. No doubt it was passed successfully to Adolf Meyer and destroyed.

It was not until 1911 that Holmes told me of his visit to Vienna, nine years earlier, to inform the Emperor Franz Josef of our ill-fated mission for his wife. On the night that I first learned of it, the detective was departing the next day for the United States, in order to begin a far more significant assignment.[14] It was two years later on the train to Welbeck Abbey, as we travelled to the shooting party where we would meet the latest Habsburg heir, that I finally heard my friend's epilogue to the Geneva story.

---

[14] See "The Solitary Violinist," as cited in note 5. The "far more significant assignment" was, of course, Holmes's "Altamont" mission against Germany prior to World War I, as described in "His Last Bow."

The Inconvenient Heir-Apparents

"I shall spare you most of my morning at the Foreign Ministry, Watson. From the moment I entered the Austro-Hungarian Empire, I was shadowed by Franz Josef's police, and with rather more efficiency than in 1898. On arriving at the ministry, I was informed by Count Goluchowski that the imperial delegation had desired to question me concerning Her Majesty's death when they came to Geneva to retrieve her body. Naturally, the Swiss authorities had refused permission, and in any case I was in no condition to receive them. At one stage in the morning's proceedings, I was compelled to remind my hosts that I was visiting Vienna at the invitation of their emperor, and that Her Britannic Majesty's government would look most unfavourably upon any effort to detain me. The tone of the interview changed markedly thereafter, although my interlocutors declined to accept the theory of the Mayerling and Geneva crimes I offered them. Nevertheless, I was permitted to keep my appointment with His Imperial and Royal Majesty, whom I saw at Schönbrunn Palace.

"I did not greatly relish, Doctor, my meeting with this emperor. He was a monarch whose reign, in a span of over fifty years, had witnessed an unprecedented series of disasters. Early on, Franz Josef's realm had suffered revolution and two ruinous wars. It was thereby evicted from a dominant position in both Germany and Italy as those countries unified. In consequence, His Majesty had been forced to grant equality to once-rebellious Hungary, while many of his Slav and German subjects seethed to break away. Through it all, the Emperor's stubborn resistance to all change, coupled with a rigid outlook typified by his mediaeval protocol, had made an exile of his wife, driven one heir-apparent to despair, and forced the second into a morganatic marriage. Verily, Franz Josef's was a record of futility that made Milan of Serbia seem a veritable Sun King! Yet, thanks to his impenetrable dignity, and his iron devotion to his duty as he saw it, the Austro-Hungarian Emperor remained the most respected ruler in all Europe, even as his ramshackle empire threatened to disintegrate around him.

"His Majesty received me in his study, a modest room chiefly notable for its many images of the lost Sisi. At seventy-one, Franz Josef was still erect and handsome (if now completely bald), wearing an immaculate, white uniform matched by equally white side-whiskers. He began the interview by questioning me about my meeting with Elisabeth. Surprisingly, the imperial widower unbent sufficiently to mourn: 'No one will ever know how much we loved each other!' As head of state, however, he was no more willing than his foreign minister to consider the possibility that elements in Berlin had connived in the murders of his wife and son. Having listened to me patiently, the Emperor made what I imagine he conceived to be a shrewd remark.

"'I had hoped, Herr Holmes,' he noted, 'that your country's negotiations with my German ally in these past years would result in Great Britain joining the Triple Alliance. Now that your King Edward has turned instead to France, it is no doubt the policy of his government to sow discord between Kaiser Wilhelm and myself.'

"'I assure Your Majesty that neither I nor my government has any such intention. If my evidence has not convinced you, sire,' I challenged him, 'may I ask how *you* believe the Crown Prince died?'

"'God's ways are inscrutable,' the Emperor mused. 'Perhaps he sends these trials to spare me yet a harder one.' Noting my impatient look, Franz Josef sighed. 'My poor son, Herr Holmes,' he said eventually, 'had never truly vexed me until the day he died. Yet, as my heir-apparent, he had become . . . something of an inconvenience. It was difficult for me—both as Rudolf's father and as the guardian of

182

our dynastic legacy—to contemplate placing the future of my empire in my son's unsteady hands.'

"'Then how do you believe he died?' I quietly insisted.

"'*By his own hand*, sir, as the world has known since 1889!' At last, the impervious façade had cracked. 'Any other verdict, at this late date, would be unthinkable! . . . And if not,' the Emperor added after a long pause, 'surely it is best for everyone that the truth of Mayerling died with my beloved wife.'

"No doubt my contempt for the man was evident upon my face. 'Unfortunately,' I sneered at him, 'Your Majesty is now saddled with *another* inconvenient heir-apparent.' I was thinking, Doctor, of the remark you had passed on from Stéphanie: 'Poor Franzi will be the next to go. He has had the temerity to fall in love with a lady-in-waiting!'

"By now, Emperor Franz Josef had regained his composure. He scowled at me with an Olympian disdain. 'You refer to my nephew's impious marriage. The Almighty, Herr Holmes, does not allow Himself to be challenged with impunity. One day, a higher power will restore the order that I, regrettably, was unable to maintain.'

"'And where, Your Majesty,' I wondered, 'does that higher power reside? With the Almighty in the heavens, or with the Kaiser in Berlin?'

"Needless to say, my imperial audience abruptly ended. I was dismissed with frosty courtesy and left Schönbrunn Palace. Nor does it surprise me, Watson, that I have never been invited to return."

And so, dear Readers, it was with a feeling of foreboding that I arrived at Welbeck Abbey to join the Duke of Portland's shooting party. But that, I fear, must be a story for another day.

A Scandal in Serbia

Belgrade, Serbia
1903

CHAPTER 1

An Appeal from Belgrade

In October, 1902, as he has written elsewhere, I "deserted" Sherlock Holmes for a new wife. What he charitably called my "only selfish action" by no means ended our long friendship, but it did ensure that for several months I was unable to visit my old domicile. My bride, a recent widow, brought with her two young children to disrupt (delightfully) the settled order of my middle-aged existence. Reestablishing my long-neglected medical practice also occupied a considerable portion of my time. Only in the spring of 1903 did I find myself again in Baker Street, where I reunited with my friend to solve two cases that appear in Sir Arthur's latest compilation of my annals. The second of these took place near the end of May.

I had no more than arrived back in Queen Anne Street when I received a note from Holmes, summoning me to return to him immediately. My wife was understandably annoyed, and I considered an outright refusal before replying that I would call at our old quarters the next morning. It was in no very pleasant humour that I climbed the seventeen steps to that well-remembered sitting room. Fortunately, Holmes was at his most urbane and took pains to be conciliatory, but I could sense an underlying tension beneath his calm veneer.

"My dear Watson, I owe you a thousand apologies! I had no idea, when you left yesterday, that there would be any necessity for you to return to Baker Street so soon."

"You should direct your apologies to my wife and stepson," I answered gruffly. "I had promised Peter to take him to the zoo this afternoon."

"Bring him along next time!" cried Holmes, waving me to my usual chair beside the hearth. "It's no distance at all to Regent's Park. The three of us could go together." Noting my sceptical demeanour, he barked briefly in amusement. "Quite so, Doctor. Not for me to play the doting uncle. But I *am* glad, my dear fellow," he went on more kindly, "that you have a son at last." We exchanged pained smiles at a bitter memory[15]; then my friend turned brisk again.

"As to why I requested your return, I have received a letter from 'The Woman.'"

My readers will know that there was but one woman to whom Sherlock Holmes applied that honorific title. I must admit to being less than honest in the past about his true relationship with Irene Adler, the lady whose memory I libelled in "A Scandal in Bohemia" by describing it as "dubious and questionable." On the contrary, given an experience of women that spans three continents and half a century, I have known none who possessed a higher or more honourable character. That was one of many fictions in the story, required for reasons I shall now reveal.

Shortly after his presumed death in 1891, Holmes had attended a performance by Miss Adler at an opera house in Montenegro, for she had resumed her career after the untimely death of her husband, Godfrey Norton. What followed, simply put, was the only romantic attachment I have known my friend to form in all the years of our acquaintance. Surely it is no wonder that two people who had shared so strong an intellectual attraction should fall in love under the charged circumstances that attended their reunion. Fleeing the horror at the Reichenbach Falls, pursued by the most formidable of Moriarty's minions, robbed of his very identity while disguised as

---

[15] For Watson's "bitter memory," see "Sherlock Holmes and the Adventure of the Tainted Canister," an e-book or audio book from MX Publishing (https://www.amazon.com/Sherlock-Holmes-Adventure-Tainted-Canister-ebook/dp/B00J3QS5CW). It also appeared *The Art of Sherlock Holmes: USA Edition 1*, edited by Phil Growick (London, MX Publishing, 2019), pp. 94-108, paired with a painting by artist Angela Fegan.

Sigerson, my friend was in as vulnerable a state as any man who affects to disdain all emotion can be. In Irene Adler, he discovered—besides a companion of surpassing beauty, charm, and sympathy—a mind that matched his own as well. It was truly a mating of equals; and though it did not lead to marriage, the result of their union did credit to them both.[16]

"Miss Adler!" I responded, for both of us still referred to her as such, despite her recent remarriage. Her latest husband was a Montenegrin nobleman, an older gentleman named Vukčić.[17] "And how are things in Montenegro?"

"Better than they are in Serbia," Holmes muttered grimly. Rising from his armchair, he removed the jackknife that transfixed unanswered correspondence to the mantelpiece and retrieved the topmost letter, leafing through it as he strode fretfully about the room. "Tell me what you know, Doctor, of the current situation there."

"Very little, I'm afraid. I did read, some months ago, that our old friend the 'King of Bohemia' had died. In Vienna, wasn't it?"

"His spiritual home, Watson! It appears that his son and successor is still trying to live down that legacy—and not succeeding, from what Miss Adler tells me."

---

[16] Irene Adler's 1891 affair with Holmes was revealed in William S. Baring-Gould's *Sherlock Holmes of Baker Street* (Avenel, NJ: Wings Books, 1995 [1962]), pp. 207-212. David Marcum also mentioned it in "The Adventure of the Other Brother" from *The Papers of Sherlock Holmes: Volume One & Volume Two* (London: MX Publishing, 2014), p. 290. Near the end of the present story, and in the one that follows, Dr. Watson appears to confirm Baring-Gould's conclusion that "the result of their union" (Scott Adler Holmes) became Rex Stout's almost equally famous detective, Nero Wolfe.

[17] I am indebted to David Marcum for allowing me to borrow his account of Irene Adler's remarriage from "The Adventure of the Other Brother." Vukčić translates in Serbo-Croatian as "coming from a wolf," another link between Sherlock Holmes and Nero Wolfe.

Here I must once more interrupt the narrative to confess to a deception in my early works. As I have admitted elsewhere, Irene Adler's "King of Bohemia" was not, in fact, Bohemian, the crown of Bohemia having passed to the House of Habsburg centuries before. Rather, he was King Milan Obrenović of Serbia (1854-1901), father to young King Alexander, the troubled monarch Holmes and I were currently discussing. Milan's disastrous reign had been marked by discord and rebellion, a lost war against Bulgaria, and (though it was not then widely known) a private convention that reduced his small country to an Austrian dependency. His home life was equally chaotic, for his marriage had been unhappy from the start. As a result, the King spent much of his time away from Serbia, running up enormous debts and using his personal attractions to woo other ladies—titled or otherwise—in England and across the Continent. One had been the young American contralto Irene Adler, whom Milan courted in the mid-'Eighties while negotiating to divorce Queen Natalie. ("There was some talk of marriage," he admitted to us later.) Failing to set the Queen aside, he deserted Miss Adler and returned to Serbia, but not without attempting to recover a photograph imprudently left in her possession. The stage of those efforts involving Sherlock Holmes I chronicled as "A Scandal in Bohemia." Although Milan abdicated in 1889, two years before my story was published in the *Strand*, he remained a power and still employed many agents in his interests. I felt it advisable, therefore, to alter the details and disguise the identities of both the King and the wronged lady whom I called—and shall still call—"Irene Adler."

"It seems strange," I remarked as Holmes relapsed into his armchair, "that Miss Adler should greatly care what happens to King Milan's son. Surely she feels no residual loyalty to her betrayer, and she has never met King Alexander."

"Ah, Watson, how can we poor fools of men be sure what motivates a woman? Why has she remained in Montenegro all these years, so near to Serbia? You will note that she did not marry Vukčić until word had reached her of her former lover's death. However, according to this letter, Miss Adler's concern is less for the young king than for his consort. It is Queen Draga who has appealed for her assistance."

"Draga? How does she know the Queen?"

"It appears that they met in Belgrade years ago, at an opera Queen Natalie commissioned. Draga was a mere lady-in-waiting at the time. She was quite a common person, Watson: the pretty widow of a drunken engineer who left her penniless. Her reputation was not, alas, altogether without blemish; but Miss Adler thinks it unlikely that Milan's queen—whose personal morals are the antithesis of her late husband's—would have tolerated any looseness in her court. So all might have been well for Draga had not the young king fallen violently in love with her."

"Indeed?" I chortled. "And how did that occur?"

"Legend has it that she saved the boy from drowning. Alexander was only twelve when his father abdicated. Even today, at twenty-six, he is not a prepossessing man. Where did I—?" Here Holmes leapt from his chair and rummaged wildly through untidy shelves of reference books, pulling down the one he sought with a yelp of triumph. "Page one-forty-three, Doctor."

He dropped the heavy volume in my lap. Its right-hand page exhibited a photograph of a uniformed, bemedaled youth, whose aggressively bristling mustache was belied by spectacles, an exceedingly bad haircut, and epaulettes that seemed too large for his thick torso. He stood protectively beside a somewhat older lady seated stiffly in a chair. While Queen Draga was impressively attired and retained much of her dark beauty, she held the King's hand lifelessly, staring before her with the glazed, helpless eyes of a cow awaiting slaughter.

"Is it my imagination, Holmes, or is that woman frightened?"

"If so, one can hardly blame her, for in Serbia she is universally despised. Even before the royal marriage, her age, low birth, and reputation had condemned her in the people's eyes. Miss Adler writes that Draga and the King have acted most unwisely. He revoked the liberal constitution promulgated by his father, then quarrelled with the pro-Russian party Draga and his mother had urged him to support. With the *Skupština*—that is to say, the parliament—suspended, Alexander's only loyal general now rules the country by decree. Meanwhile, the Queen's family followed her into the palace. Her two loutish brothers have infuriated many of their fellow officers, who were already ill-disposed against the dynasty."

"That sounds ominous," I interjected. For although nothing can shake the British Army's loyalty to King and Country, I know from my Afghan experience how quickly one bad apple in a regimental mess can sour the whole barrel.

"But it is not the worst," Holmes went on gravely. "The Queen is barren, Doctor, which equates to mortal sin in a superstitious Balkan culture. Draga admits to Miss Adler that she compounded the problem by claiming she was pregnant and failing to produce an heir. Rumours have spread that she is pressuring the King to name her brother as successor. In April, riots against the Obrenovićs broke out in the streets of Belgrade. A poisoner was caught inside the palace kitchen by the royal cook. Each day, the Queen awakens not knowing whether, before nightfall, she and the King will be overthrown and murdered. He—with more courage then good sense—refuses to take the danger seriously. Draga is not merely frightened, Watson; she is terrified."

"What help does she expect from Irene Adler? And why has Miss Adler written to you?"

"She has told the Queen a little—*only* a little—of our friendship and my contacts in the British government. Her husband Vukčić, who has sources of his own in Serbia, has acquired a secret list of officers who are conspiring to overthrow the dynasty. Miss Adler implores me, on behalf of Draga, to go to Belgrade and lay this evidence before King Alexander. A warning delivered under British auspices, even unofficially, may compel him to see reason. Naturally, I must obtain the government's permission first."

"It would appear, then, that our next step is to visit Brother Mycroft."

"Bravo, Watson! As always, the obvious course appears with blinding clarity before you. Mycroft is expecting us in Whitehall at half-past two. Perhaps a bite at Simpson's first would not be unwelcome."

By 1903, I had been long aware that Holmes's elder brother often *was* the British government. Officially no more than a senior clerk, Mycroft had become indispensable to ministers for his uncanny ability to absorb, classify, and disseminate intelligence acquired from many sources. His conclusions often decided policy on questions of international importance. That afternoon, he sat behind a desk piled high with documents, a bit greyer and stouter than when I had last seen him, reading through the letter his brother had just summarized at length.

"I must admit, Sherlock, that Madame Vukčić's intelligence— confirmed, she says, by her husband's contacts in Serbia—agrees in every particular with the reports my own informants have provided. The conspiracy to overthrow Alexander Obrenović is common gossip in the coffee-houses of Belgrade. There is no doubt that the King and Queen are in considerable danger."

"You agree then, brother, that a warning would be efficacious?"

"Possibly," ruminated Mycroft, "quite possibly. We can only do so unofficially, of course. The question, Sherlock, is whether such an act is really in our interest."

"Surely," I expostulated, "His Majesty's government cannot sit idly by and allow the royal couple to be murdered!"

"The King's abdication most likely would preserve them. I admire your indignation, Doctor, but inaction may truly be the wiser course. These Obrenovićs have never been very satisfactory, but

Alexander seems bent on following a suicidal course. His incessant wrangling with Pašić's pro-Russian party, and more than that his unwise marriage, have destabilized not only Serbia but the entire Balkan Peninsula. No doubt the conspirators will bring in Peter Karadjordjević, the descendant of 'Black George' who won Serbia its freedom from the Turks. He is known to be an altogether sounder man."

"Come now, Mycroft," scoffed Sherlock Holmes. "That seems a bit cold-blooded, even for my taste. Now, what do you intend to do?"

"Well," his elder brother grumbled, "I can hardly send a gunboat down the Danube to protect the palace. At least allowing you to deliver Vukčić's message would give His Majesty fair warning. The Serbs seem bound to have a bloodbath either way."

"Should we not urge the King to abdicate," I suggested, "as his father did? Or to banish Queen Draga, who is evidently the cause of all the trouble?"

"That would be a poor return for her appeal, Watson," my friend grumbled, "as well as Irene Adler's."

"Even so," I insisted, pointing to the map behind us, "Austria-Hungary is just across the river from Belgrade. The Queen could be safely over the frontier within an hour."

"An excellent point, Doctor," conceded Mycroft, "geographically speaking. Draga Mašin may be less reluctant to depart than we suppose. In 1900, Alexander's ministers had persuaded her to flee across the Danube before His Majesty could marry her, but he intervened before she could depart. However foolhardy he may be, Alexander is made of stronger mettle than King Milan. He may fight to save his queen and throne, if we arm him with a list of traitors."

"Miss Adler's husband can assist us there," Holmes put in impatiently. "How long will you require to complete your arrangements?"

"These things take time, Sherlock! The Cabinet must be consulted. A week, at best, assuming the Prime Minister proves himself as mad as I. Belgrade is quite accessible by rail, but you will need to stop in Montenegro on the way. That is no easy journey."

Until Mycroft spoke, I had not realised that soon I would be travelling to Serbia. It was a shock to discover that the idea held no appeal for me at all. To leave my new family and go traipsing off with Holmes into the wildest corner in all Europe, on a secret diplomatic mission that could last for weeks and prove dangerous as well as difficult: it was the last thing I wanted at that moment in my life. Having never experienced such a reaction during my earlier marriages, I was at a loss to understand my own emotions. Had I grown so old that the prospect of adventure daunted me? Whatever my responsibility to my wife and stepchildren, had I not also a responsibility to Sherlock Holmes? Was I simply to wish my old friend well and lay aside our years of partnership?

In the end, of course, I went with Holmes to Belgrade. Withdrawing at that stage would have meant deserting not only him but Irene Adler, Mycroft and the Cabinet, and Their Majesties of Serbia. Nevertheless, before leaving I made a promise to myself—and confirmed it to my tearful, angry wife—that this would be the last extended journey I would make with Sherlock Holmes. I did not agree to give up either him or our detective work entirely, for both were still important in my life. Henceforth, however, I resolved that my family would come first. Little did I know, when we departed England, how easy it would ultimately be to keep that promise.

CHAPTER 2

The Land of the Black Mountain

Inevitably, we were delayed in leaving London. The Cabinet, divided by a tariff policy dispute, proved hard to assemble, and harder to convince that the affairs of a small Balkan kingdom were worthy of their time. While I passed uneasy days in Queen Anne Street, Holmes met again with Mycroft to receive the Prime Minister's instructions. As my friend remarked, they seemed designed less to ensure our success than to shield Mr. Balfour's government from blame for failure.

"Upon arriving in Cetinje," Mycroft had informed his brother, "you are to negotiate only with Count Vukčić, avoiding all communication with Prince Nicholas and the Montenegrin court. I shall leave it to you and Vukčić to decide how best to approach King Alexander. It would be far, far better, Sherlock, for Queen Draga to leave Serbia. Her departure might in itself restore stability, but the King is unlikely to agree. Remember that at no time are you to involve the British ministers in Cetinje and Belgrade. I shall keep both men informed, of course, but we cannot be seen as having any part whatever in this venture. Indeed, the longer I consider, the less I believe that we have anything to gain, aside from the obvious humanitarian objective."

Undeterred by this vote of meagre confidence, Holmes and I left London on the second day of June. We crossed the Channel to Calais and caught the fabled "Orient Express," steaming across northern France in the small hours of the night. The next day offered splendid vistas of the Bavarian Alps, recalling our ill-fated Reichenbach journey of twelve years before. Holmes, as ever, was indifferent to scenery, chafing at the rate of progress as our locomotive laboured up the mountain slopes. After a night in Vienna, we headed south towards the Illyrian coast, as I had done five years before. Unfortunately, a landslip in the Carniolan mining district halted our express and forced us to spend the night in Laibach. Our departure from Fiume, near the head of the Adriatic, was postponed until the fifth.

"It is infamous, Watson!" cried Sherlock Holmes. He had just been told that our Lloyd's steamship would not reach Cattaro (its nearest approach to the Montenegrin capital) until the following evening, further delaying our arrival at Count Vukčić's villa. "Nine days gone since I received Irene Adler's letter, and we are still not even to Cetinje, much less Belgrade!"

"Cheer up, old man," I consoled him, brandishing my *Baedeker*. "It says here that Montenegro and Serbia still use the Julian calendar. On arriving, we gain thirteen days!"

"Fie, Doctor!" snorted Holmes. "Must I always be subjected to your pawky sallies?" Nonetheless, he smiled. We lounged on deck throughout the afternoon, while our captain navigated skilfully among the reefs and islands strewn along that rocky coast. The sun blazed down upon our vessel from a cloudless sky; the Adriatic's waters roiled beneath the whitewashed walls of cities that "from time immemorial" (as my guide-book put it) had been way stations along "the highway of traffic between East and West." For all the grief and horror that were soon to come, I recall that afternoon on the *Pannonia* as one of the most peaceful times I ever spent with Sherlock Holmes.

The next day, my friend remained inside our cabin, researching the voluminous notes that Mycroft had provided him on Serbia and Montenegro. We entered the Bay of Cattaro just at sunset, the rugged crags of "The Black Mountain" looming high above its broad expanse. Taking a room in the town's least objectionable hotel, we found ourselves sharing it with three swarthy Montenegrins. They looked remarkably like brigands, but our innkeeper had assured us that all visitors to Cattaro's fair were obliged to leave their weapons at the border. In the event, our fellow lodgers behaved with more

194

decorum—save for snoring—than might have been encountered at an English country fair. We awoke to find they had departed well before us.

To my relief, Holmes was able to hire an open, three-horse carriage, saving us a day-long walk. As we left Dalmatia, each turning of our steep ascent afforded a more splendid view of the *Bocche di Cattaro*, its waters shadowed by the mountains from the rising sun. I remarked to my companion that we had seen nothing so beautiful since the Reichenbach Falls.

"Let us hope," he snapped curtly, "that our present journey has a happier end."

Thus rebuked, I abandoned my attempts at conversation, and we rode in silence for some miles. After a halt at the border-post to reclaim our driver's pistol, our path climbed steadily from pine-scented forest into barren hills. Soon we overtook parties of returning fair-goers. On each occasion, they would politely step aside—even to the brink of a precipice—in order to let our carriage pass. The Montenegrin men were uniformly tall and rawboned, their white, full-skirted coats festooned with weapons. The young women looked quite lovely in close-fitting black boleros and white robes, prompting Holmes to offer me a quizzical (or perhaps apologetic) smile.

In mid-afternoon, we reached a high pass in the mountains, followed by a long and serpentine descent, until the red-roofed houses of Cetinje appeared below us in a cultivated valley. We arrived at dusk, five days and nine hours after leaving London.

Count Vukčić's estate lay just outside the capital, on an open rise of land reclaimed from the pine forest. Despite its medieval origin, the house was a plain-fronted, unassuming dwelling of one storey,[18] surrounded by a low stone wall. Such lack of ostentation was evidently typical in Montenegro. Even Prince Nicholas's residence, which we had passed while driving through Cetinje, had the austerity of a hospital or orphanage, rather than a royal palace.

After a dinner of stewed lamb, smoked fish, and other delicacies, Holmes and I had fully recovered from the rigours of the day. We relaxed in the small but elegant dining room, partaking of a dry red wine, called *Vranac*, and a creamy cheese that was too salty for my taste. Earlier, we had met the two young people currently in residence: Marko, the Count's son by an earlier marriage[19]; and Miss Adler's daughter by Godfrey Norton, who at the age of twelve already showed signs of inheriting her mother's beauty.

With his large frame and iron-grey hair and mustache, Count Vukčić could have passed for a less fleshy brother of Prince Nicholas. However, he possessed an air of real nobility, unlike the sly demeanour apparent in that monarch's portraits. Although long aware of his wife's past relationship with Sherlock Holmes, the Count had welcomed us without constraint, showing the unstinting hospitality for which his country is renowned. After dinner, as we sipped our wine and lit up fine cigars, he seemed inclined to lecture. Miss Adler, who had not withdrawn, smiled indulgently as though used to hearing him.

"When Kosovo[20] was lost," intoned our host, "the Serbian warriors who took refuge in these mountains split into tribes—each

---

[18] Dr. Watson employs the British definition of "one storey," meaning a "first floor" above ground level. An American writer would consider the Vukčić residence a two-storey house.

[19] Marko Vukčić maintained a lifelong association with the future Nero Wolfe. He appears in several of Rex Stout's novels as the proprietor of Rusterman's Restaurant in Manhattan. In *The Black Mountain*, Wolfe returns to Montenegro to avenge Marko's murder.

[20] Tsar Lazar's defeat and death at the Battle of Kosovo (June 28, 1389) destroyed the medieval Serbian Empire and consigned its people to 500 years

with its own chief, like your country's Scottish clans—and carried on their fight against the Turks. They paid the price of blood to keep their freedom! We Montenegrins had been free for centuries when 'Black George' of Serbia was still a bandit, and Miloš Obrenović paid tribute to the Porte. In the battles of my prime, our own Prince Nicholas drove the Sultan's armies from our coast, while that puppy Milan Obrenović cowered in his war-camp with the gypsy girls. Then, after our Russian brothers had come to Serbia's defence, Milan sold his country to the Emperor of Austria—who stole Bosnia and Herzegovina from us—and crowned himself a king!"

"Indeed," sighed Irene Adler, "Milan was a man of many faults. But *a few* virtues."

If her husband noticed this gentle interruption, it barely broke his stride. "As for this Peter Karadjordjević, who skulks in Switzerland, has he even breathed his homeland's air since boyhood? No!" Count Vukčić cast his eyes around the table as though demanding that we share his indignation. "Who are the Karadjordjevićs and Obrenovićs to think that *they* should rule the Serbs?"

Sherlock Holmes had endured this discourse with more patience than was usually his wont. "But is it not true, Your Excellency," he queried, "that your master married his daughter to Peter Karadjordjević?" My friend had not neglected Mycroft's notes. "That was a princely gift to a man he now considers unworthy of a throne. What changed his mind about his son-in-law?"

"Alas, Mr. Holmes," replied Vukčić, "they fell out over money." He had the grace to look a little crestfallen. "If our prince has one besetting sin, it is his greed. He would steal milk from a baby at its mother's breast. But we forgive him this iniquity, for in his day he

---

of foreign rule. Over the centuries, the "Field of Blackbirds" attained great symbolic significance and became a rallying cry for the cause of Serbian independence and reunification. Archduke Franz Ferdinand was unwise to visit Sarajevo on Kosovo's anniversary in 1914.

was a mighty warrior. I have also heard it said," the Count mused absently, "that Peter Karadjordjević beat Nicholas too often at the chessboard."

"Surely, *that* is unforgivable," sneered the detective. "Now, let us discuss this list of Serbian officers supposedly implicated in the plot to murder Alexander." He waved the document our host had handed him before the meal. "I expect they are all Karadjordjević supporters?"

"Such is the information we received," Count Vukčić answered coolly, "although I object to your use of the word 'supposedly.'" The room's atmosphere had darkened, and Miss Adler and I exchanged a nervous glance. "More than a hundred officers have been identified, including a member of the General Staff. Please explain to me what you infer by your enquiry."

Holmes showed no inclination to modify his tone. "My point is this: Whatever the outcome of this so-called conspiracy, one of the rival houses to the House of Petrović-Njegoš—that is, your master's house—will be either discredited or eliminated altogether. Prince Nicholas's claim to the throne of Serbia, should he wish to press it, will thus be immeasurably strengthened. Does that hypothesis misstate the facts in any way?"

"Let us say," growled Vukčić, "that it states them in the most provocative manner possible." Our host rose from his chair and glared sternly at my friend. "Mr. Holmes, I do not relish having my motives, and those of my prince, impugned at my own table by the agent of a foreign government—even one who has come to Montenegro at the invitation of my wife!"

His wife and I looked on in consternation, for more stood between the two men now than the mere throne of Serbia. The *Serdar* held his adversary's gaze without relenting, and finally it was Holmes who dropped his eyes.

"I apologize, Count Vukčić," he said reluctantly. "I intended no affront to you, or to your master. As you have said, I am here to represent the interests of my government, so I must endeavour to obtain the clearest understanding possible of the situation that exists."

"Then allow me to explain it to you as clearly as I can." The Count was not entirely mollified, but he resumed his seat. "To an extent, Mr. Holmes," he sighed, "I admit you are correct. My prince indeed covets the Serbian throne, but the circumstances are not quite what you imagine."

"Please enlighten me."

"In 1896, after the boy-king Alexander had dismissed his regents, Prince Nicholas paid a visit to Belgrade. They agreed that if the King (who is the last of his line) did not produce an heir, the Serbian crown would pass to the House of Petrović-Njegoš. At the time, such an outcome seemed unlikely; but Nicholas wisely chose a lady from a minor Obrenović line to wed his second son, Prince Mirko. Then, to the world's amazement, Alexander married Draga Mašin. Since her plan to place her sister's baby in the royal cradle failed, all Serbia knows they will be childless. Prince Nicholas will hold the last Obrenović to his promise. If the list of traitors we provide enables him to foil this foul intrigue, the King must proclaim Prince Mirko as his heir.

"So you see, Mr. Holmes," Count Vukčić added firmly, "It would profit my prince little to invent false plots against the King of Serbia. You have my word of honour that 'this so-called conspiracy' to murder him exists."

My friend seemed less reassured than flummoxed by this resolution of his doubts. Before he could reply to Vukčić, I took the opportunity to create a diversion.

"Pardon me, Your Excellency, but I believe there is an important question still to be discussed. How are Holmes and I to obtain an audience with King Alexander?"

"Why, Doctor, that is all arranged," cried Irene Adler merrily, "and we have you to thank for it! Queen Draga," she went on, "has informed me that His Majesty is a great admirer of your works. She

199

purchased *The Hound of the Baskervilles* for Alexander the moment it was published, and it has become his favourite book! The King has invited you both to the Konak (for that is what they call the palace) to autograph his copy personally. Your audience will be on Thursday at eleven."

There was a pause, as Miss Adler smiled at me with gratitude and Count Vukčić gazed benignly on his wife. In some confusion, I turned to Sherlock Holmes. He met my eyes, the tension broke, and we all four burst into a roar of laughter.

The morning fog outside my window half-convinced me I was back in London. Warm Adriatic breezes, combined with the cool mountain air, had veiled the valley in a shroud of mist. I dressed hurriedly and packed up my belongings, for Sherlock Holmes and I were returning to Cattaro. Because our outward journey had taken a day longer than expected, the exigencies of our itinerary left no time for delay. Much to Holmes's annoyance, no rail line ran from Montenegro into Serbia, requiring us to steam back up the Adriatic and entrain for Belgrade from Fiume. We would arrive no sooner than the night before our royal audience.

The dining room was deserted when I came downstairs, so I ate a quick breakfast from the sideboard and walked out onto the lawn. Three ghostly figures loomed beneath the pine trees near the garden wall. The nearest detached itself, leaving the others deep in conversation, and glided towards me through the fog. It was our hostess, her ivory peignoir all but hidden by the woollen cloak she wore against the morning's chill.

"Good day, Dr. Watson! I must thank you for your well-timed intervention in last night's debate. It saved what could have become a very ugly scene. Jealousy is the last emotion I would have expected from Mr. Sherlock Holmes."

"I was surprised as well, Countess."

She waved aside the honorific. "I am still not used to being the wife of a *Serdar*," she laughed. "When I first came to the Balkans, I aimed much higher, as you know. Obviously, my career as an 'adventuress' has been less successful than Queen Draga's."

I bowed my head in shame. "I hope you can forgive me for that title, ma'am. At the time, it seemed a choice between sacrificing your reputation and endangering your life."

Miss Adler patted my arm reassuringly. "I understand perfectly, Doctor, so pray do not apologize. It has all come out well in the end. My husband is a worthy man, and my life has been far happier than the poor 'King of Bohemia's.'"

She glanced across the lawn, where two men could now be seen emerging from the pines, their discussion apparently concluded. "Quickly, please, before they come, I must ask a favour of you. You and Mr. Holmes will return here after your visit to Belgrade; is that not so?"

"It is indeed," I answered, barely able to suppress a groan. Reporting on our mission to the Count would further postpone our return to London, and I greatly missed my wife and stepchildren. "How may I be of service to you?"

"I should like for you to give me a medical examination. If possible, I wish neither my husband nor Mr. Holmes to know anything about it."

"What symptoms have you noticed?" I had not seen Irene Adler, who was then in her mid-forties, since the century had turned. My impression upon arriving was that she seemed unchanged. Now I saw dark circles underneath her eyes, and lines of strain that were not there at our last meeting. In the morning mist, her complexion was quite pale, with a slight bluish cast about her lips.

"Oh, nothing of real consequence. Some breathlessness upon exertion, increasing slowly for the past few years. It was the main reason I gave up my warbling—aside from the fact that the *Serdar* dislikes his wife appearing on the stage! I seem to tire more easily in general than I used to."

All this was most disquieting, and my own heart sank for her. But her soft "Hush!" silenced the response I might have made, as we were forestalled by the simultaneous arrival of Sherlock Holmes,

Count Vukčić, and Count Vukčić's carriage. While the servants brought our luggage, we quickly exchanged words of parting with our hosts. I realised, as our carriage drove away, that though Holmes had decorously embraced Miss Adler, he had merely nodded to her husband, not offering his hand. The ill will between them evidently remained unresolved.

CHAPTER 3

A Night of Horror

I shall not weary my readers with the details of our journey to Belgrade. The beauties of the Adriatic, so enchanting to us days before, began to pall upon a second viewing. After days of constant travel, Holmes and I were both exhausted. We spent most of the cruise sleeping in our cabin or, in his case, reviewing Mycroft's notes. When we passed the town of Spalato, I did emerge to see the walls of Diocletian's palace, my last venture at sight-seeing along that historic shore.

Our train from Fiume on Tuesday evening rolled through Agram in Croatia, then followed the Save River towards the Serbian frontier. Only by the next afternoon was my friend willing to confer about the object of our mission. When he began rehearsing what Vukčić had told him of the conditions in Belgrade, I interrupted with a question I was determined to pursue.

"Why on Earth," I asked him, "were you so hostile to Count Vukčić?"

"How was I 'hostile,' Watson? It has been apparent from the first that Vukčić and Prince Nicholas are using this crisis in Belgrade to advance Montenegro's designs upon the throne of Serbia. I was merely seeking to obtain complete, unbiased information."

"No, I will not accept that explanation, Holmes, at least not entirely. Your manner to the Count was needlessly offensive. I was amazed we were not ordered from the house!"

Instead of replying, Sherlock Holmes withdrew into one of his long silences. He stared out our compartment's window into the blackness of the night, appearing to ignore my question altogether. After perhaps three minutes, he enquired, "What did you think of 'The Woman?'"

"Miss Adler? What has she to do with this?"

"A great deal, Doctor, as you are aware. Do not be ingenuous."

"Well," I temporised, "I was delighted to see her again, naturally. She is certainly still as charming as I had remembered."

"You did not think she looked ill?"

"Ill? Well, no, not exactly. A little tired, perhaps." I was uncomfortably caught between our friendship and professional discretion. "Given the circumstances, Holmes, it was probably a strain for her to have us there. Your conduct after dinner," I added tartly, "must have added to that strain immensely!"

"You are as poor a dissembler as ever!" snarled Sherlock Holmes. He lapsed into another moody silence, then cried out angrily:

"Do you not think it a great shame, Watson, for a woman of Irene Adler's talent, brains, and beauty to be stuck away in a backwater like Montenegro, married to a man old enough to be her father?"

"Hardly that, I think. He is no more than sixty."

"That is *not* my point, as you well know. What can they possibly have in common? What real contact has she with the wider world? It seems no more than a sad exile from all that she once knew, and such a *waste!*"

"But that was her decision, Holmes," I answered quietly, "one that she made long ago." Despite his true concern, it was evident that 'The Woman's' diagnosis had been accurate, and that jealousy also lay behind this outburst. The same realisation must have struck my friend as well, for he subsided. We said no more of the Vukčićs for the duration of our journey. Yet, I knew that in the sense he spoke, it was not only Irene Adler's wasted life Holmes was bemoaning.

Just after half past ten on Wednesday night, our train steamed over the great bridge across the Save and into the terminal in Belgrade. It was the tenth of June at home in England, but in Serbia still the twenty-eighth of May. Our royal audience would begin within the next twelve hours, and I looked forward to some badly needed rest.

The Serbian police, on learning we had come from Montenegro, questioned us at length about our visit's purpose. Holmes could truthfully deny any official connexion to the British government, but he neglected to disclose our appointment with the King. While dubious of my friend's assurance that we hoped only "to enjoy the beauties of Belgrade," the inspectors eventually returned our passports and allowed us to depart.

Few cabs still served the station at that hour, and to my disgust we were required to pay a double fare. Our destination was the Hôtel de Paris, which Count Vukčić had recommended for its convenience to the palace. Just as we set out, a shout halted our vehicle. A young officer, wearing the dark blue uniform of Serbian infantry, scrambled onto the seat beside me. Without a glance at us, he gave an address to the driver, who promptly turned north, away from the hotel. Holmes held up a hand when I started to protest. We clattered through the almost empty streets, soon drawing up before a coffee-house that faced the old fortress and the Kalemegdan Park.

It was the liveliest scene we had encountered in Belgrade. On a long verandah, open to the flower gardens in the summer night, a crowd of officers and other patrons sat around small tables, imbibing wine or plum brandy and listening to a gypsy band. Several officers, obviously the worse for drink, had linked arms and circled clumsily in an oddly syncopated dance. It ended almost at the moment we arrived; but the soldiers—despite protests from other members of the audience—called for a repeat performance and began the dance anew. Their buffoonery seemed to amuse our uninvited fellow passenger, who laughed heartily as he descended, turning back to us with a ferocious grin.

"Queen Draga's Kolo!" he chortled before joining his comrades, who welcomed him uproariously. The kolo, I recalled, was a Serbian folk dance, and thus a bit plebian for a queen.

"Could Her Majesty be more popular with the army than we thought?" I wondered as we drove away. "Her kolo seemed quite the rage among those soldiers."

"To me, Watson, their carouse appeared to mock her." Holmes shook his head as though perplexed. "A better question might be why the officer who forced himself upon us happened to speak English."

We arrived at our hotel without further incident, but it was past midnight before I was ready to retire. As I lay abed, still wakeful, I heard the sound of singing from the street below. My window overlooked King Milan Street, and there I saw a number of officers from the revel at the coffee-house. They staggered down the cobblestones in the direction of the Konak, still pausing to dance *Queen Draga's Kolo* as they tra-la-la-ed its banal tune. Other soldiers, I now noticed, were likewise congregating in the streets. One officer, at the head of a small company, approached the group of drunkards and saluted their apparent leader. This was a young bull of a soldier who towered a full head above his fellows, the effect of his elegant mustache lessened by his balding pate and current air of dishevelment. However, he now buttoned his tunic, retrieved his hat from the gutter, and issued a brief order. The new officer swung his company in line behind the revellers, and they proceeded with more purpose towards the palace.

I thought of rousing Holmes to pass on my observations, but the lateness of the hour and our mutual weariness dissuaded me. It seemed I had slept only a few minutes when I was awakened by the roar of an explosion. This time, when I peered outside my window, the streets were full of troops hastening in all directions. Even before I could throw on my dressing gown, Sherlock Holmes was pounding on my door.

"Come, Watson! That blast came from the Konak, unless my ears deceive me. Clearly, there is some deviltry at work. I begin to doubt Their Majesties will be in a fit condition to receive us when we call tomorrow."

"There were soldiers in the street an hour ago," I told him, "heading for the palace. I saw many more when I looked out just now."

When we arrived downstairs, a crowd of disconcerted hotel guests had gathered in the lobby. The manager, a Frenchman who spoke fluent English and Serbo-Croatian, was talking with the commander of a guard of police outside the door. Even before the officer had finished his instructions, the Serbian members of our congregation began cheering wildly. It took some time for the manager to quiet his guests enough to speak. After he had addressed them in their native language (interrupted by more cheers), he walked over to the bar to offer Holmes and me a brief translation.

"I am informed that His Majesty has just agreed to the expulsion of Queen Draga and her family from the realm. He has placed Belgrade under martial law until they are safely out of the city and across the border. In the meantime, no one is to leave the hotel. These orders will remain in effect at least until the morning."

It was difficult to say who appeared more disbelieving of this news: the manager or Sherlock Holmes. "Do you accept this explanation of events?" my friend asked bluntly. "It does not account for that loud explosion from the palace, nor for the gunshots we have heard since then." Indeed, there had subsequently been fusillades of rifle fire from farther down King Milan Street.

"What you or I accept makes little difference, M. Holmes." The Frenchman literally threw up his hands in resignation. "Everything will become clearer in the morning, I feel sure. Meanwhile, I intend to go to bed. I suggest that you and Dr. Watson do the same."

Needless to say, neither Holmes nor I complied with this suggestion. We returned to our rooms long enough to dress, then reunited in the lobby. At about four o'clock, a light rain set in, and just before dawn the police departed. We stepped into the empty street and began the half-mile walk that would take us to the palace.

It promised to be a dismal outing. In deference to the diplomatic nature of our mission, Holmes and I had put on morning dress. Despite our umbrellas, our clothing was soon damp and soiled. My friend had not brought Vukčić's list, waiting for the situation to be clarified. The Konak, when it appeared upon our left, proved to be an ornate, one-storey structure built of yellow stone. Only a fence of iron railings separated its narrow garden from King Milan Street. To our surprise, the gate stood open and unguarded.

Nevertheless, there were many soldiers in the garden. Most clustered near the left-hand corner of the palace, below a balcony outside the royal apartments. Beside Serbia's defenders, in a muddy flower-bed, lay the mutilated bodies of the King and Queen, clad only in their bloody nightclothes. Even from the street, I could tell the royal couple had been butchered savagely, shot or stabbed long after the infliction of any injuries necessary to ensure their deaths. I have seen the remains of men tortured in Afghanistan, and thousands of corpses on the field of Maiwand, but neither there nor in all my years of practice did I ever witness a more brutal slaughter.

As we stepped into the courtyard, a young officer approached to block our way. He appeared to have been waiting for us, so I was not surprised to recognise our cab-mate of the night before.

"Ah, Mr. Sherlock Holmes, we meet again." His English, although accented, was excellent. "What is it you want here? There are no mysteries for you to solve in Serbia."

"You know me, then." My friend was tight-lipped, his face white with anger.

"Of course," the soldier sneered. "The great English detective and"—he spared a glance at me—"the one who writes his books. We were told that you would come to Belgrade, but you have no business at the Konak. There will be no royal audience today."

"We are serving as unofficial representatives of the British government," Holmes informed him coldly. "We wish to know what happened here."

"It is as you see. The King and Queen are dead."

"Indeed they are. Who is responsible?"

"*They* are responsible. They brought their deaths upon themselves."

"Not *by* themselves, it seems," said Holmes, "judging from this charnel house."

"Perhaps. But what is that to you, or to the British government?"

It was evident we would get nowhere with this insolent young puppy. "We grow weary of this conversation, sir," I intervened. "Let us speak with someone in authority."

"Authority? *Authority*, you say?" The officer laughed, as though marvelling at the novelty of the idea. "Wait here," he told us curtly. He strode across the garden, where a coterie of officers had gathered underneath the palace balcony, smoking, conversing, and pointedly ignoring the sodden corpses of their former rulers. After our interrogator had conferred with them, one walked towards us through the misting rain.

This man was short and heavily built, appearing to be close to our own age. His open greatcoat did not entirely hide the bloodstains on his lieutenant-colonel's uniform. Upon his collar lay the insignia of the Serbian General Staff. The face above the collar was a strong but weathered one, its deep-set eyes reflecting horror, guilt, and absolute exhaustion. He nodded brusquely, but neither introduced himself nor offered us his hand. The latter omission was a relief to both of us.

"Mr. Holmes?" With a soldier's instinct, he addressed himself to my companion.

"I am. And you are Colonel—?"

"No names!" snapped the young officer, having followed in his leader's wake.

210

"Leave us, Lieutenant," growled the Colonel. He smiled sadly as he turned back to us. "He is right, of course, although my name will soon be infamous in any case.[21]

"You, sir," he added, speaking to me. "I understand you are a doctor?"

"John Watson," I answered automatically, "retired regimental surgeon." Inwardly, I regretted my soldierly forthrightness to this man. He gave me a sympathetic nod, seeming to recognise my mixed emotions.

"Follow me, please, gentlemen." He led us towards the palace in a way calculated to avoid both the royal bodies and his fellow officers. At the head of the wide stair serving as an entrance, there stood a huge black bear. Our guide noted absently that someone had shot it during the Bulgarian war. Inside, the Konak was a scene of desolation. Its doors had been dynamited open, and a body lay amid the rubble on the floor. The Colonel stolidly ignored it.

"One of our officers," he informed us, "was severely wounded in the fighting with the palace guard. He took three bullets to the chest, and our surgeon is uncertain whether they may safely be removed. We would value the opinion of an English doctor."

"Surely," I conjectured, "such injuries must inevitably prove fatal."

"For most, perhaps. This officer is not a common man."

As we descended to the basement, I noted gouts of blood and spent shell casings littering the stairs. Upon a settee in the lower hallway lay the mustachioed giant who had drunkenly danced *Queen*

---

[21] Lieutenant-Colonel Živojin Mišić, a veteran of the wars with Turkey and Bulgaria, was the first to shoot King Alexander when he refused to abdicate. He later served heroically in the Balkan Wars and World War I and was promoted to Field Marshal after repelling an Austrian invasion. Although Rebecca West speaks highly of him in *Black Lamb and Grey Falcon*, she tactfully omits his name. See also the article in the Military Wiki at: https://military.wikia.org/wiki/%C5%BDivojin_Mi%C5%A1i%C4%87.

Draga's Kolo on his way to kill that hapless lady. He was propped against a pile of cushions, breathing harshly but still conscious, his empty pistol on the floor.

"So, Apis," the Colonel greeted him phlegmatically, "you still refuse to leave this world?"

"I know too well what awaits me in the next one!" The wounded bull (for "Apis," I remembered, was an Egyptian bull-god) produced an evil grin for his commander. That officer chuckled appreciatively but glanced at the Serbian surgeon, who could only shrug.

"Well, my friend," the Colonel sighed, "you will have much company there."

"Ah, yes," gasped Apis, "all the Obrenovićs will be there. Not only Alexander and his barren whore, but the worthless Milan . . . and Miloš, the murderer of Kara-George." His voice grew weaker as he rambled on, sagging back against the cushions.

"The Emperor of Austria," whispered Apis, ". . . old Nicholas of Montenegro . . . all those who stand against the destiny of Greater Serbia . . . all of them must die."

The executioner sank into a stupor, and it appeared he might precede his enemies as we stood watch. I held a hurried consultation with my colleague, the Colonel serving as interpreter. We concurred that if the bullets had touched any vital part, Apis would have died already. Whether he survived the shock and blood loss would depend entirely on his constitution, but an operation might prove fatal. In later years, I learned that I had almost operated on a man who did as much as anyone to bring on the Great War. I have often wondered what our world would be like in this new century had Captain Dragutin Dimitrijević died under my knife that morning in Belgrade.

This time, when we left the Konak, the Colonel took us past the murdered king and queen. My only recollection of them is that poor Draga wore one yellow stocking. Sherlock Holmes, however, was not content to let the outrage pass.

"Why have you allowed those bodies to be treated in so barbarous a manner?"

For the first time, the Colonel looked shamefaced. "We thought it prudent for them to be visible when dawn broke," he explained, "so that anyone loyal to the Obrenovićs would see there is nothing left to fight for. The dynasty is finished."

Holmes grunted noncommittally. "What do the regicides intend to happen now?"

"The provisional government will reconvene the *Skupština*, which will invite Prince Peter Karadjordjević to return to Serbia as king. We are confident that he will accept the offer."

"How confident?" enquired my friend, with a very searching look. The Colonel met his gaze with equanimity.

"Mr. Holmes," he answered quietly, "I do not expect you or your government to understand or to condone what happened here last night. I myself will make no effort to explain it, except to say that my comrades and I believe that we acted in the interests of our country. Whether our high motives can excuse so terrible a crime must be for history to judge."

"Then let us trust that history will judge you justly, Colonel," replied Sherlock Holmes. "Unhappily for Serbia, the nations of the world will not delay so long in passing judgement."

As if to prove his point, we met a fussy little gentleman at the palace gate. I learned afterward that this was M. Charikof, the Russian minister, who had watched the night's events unfold from his legation's windows. Now, he stood ready to berate the assassins beneath a huge umbrella, bravely admonishing the Colonel that his gruesome exhibition of the royal bodies was "really quite uncivilized."

"Please, sir," quavered the Tsar's representative, "take Their Majesties inside the palace now. You must clean up this mess!"

"That, Your Excellency," replied the Colonel wearily, "is what we have been trying to accomplish."

CHAPTER 4

"Good-night, Mr. Sherlock Holmes."

After Holmes telegraphed his report to London, Mycroft's return cable instructed us not to convey it to the embassy, for the Cabinet had decided to break off relations with the new regime. With no official function and the purpose of our journey gone, we took a train from Belgrade on the evening of the twelfth of June. Three days later, we were back in Montenegro. I, for one, was heartily glad to be forever quit of Serbia.

"Our mission was little more than a fool's errand, Watson," my friend had grumbled as we rolled across the plain of Hungary. "This conspiracy was far more extensive and advanced than Count Vukčić's sources had divined. With treason inside the Konak as well as out of it, the King and Queen could never have survived for long, even had they received our warning."

"Yet, the names on Vukčić's list were accurate." I nodded towards the stack of newspapers that Holmes and I had just perused. Most featured interviews of the regicides by members of the foreign press. Incredibly, these officers had described their crimes in bloodcurdling detail, unconcerned with either infamy or punishment. All were identified within the document we had been unable to deliver.

"Yes," sighed Holmes, "I have to acknowledge that I misjudged the man. Whatever the ambitions of his royal master, the plot was real enough, God knows. We must credit the Montenegrins with at least trying to avert it. What a cesspool of perdition Belgrade is! I shall apologize to Vukčić the moment we arrive."

It was now Tuesday, June sixteenth, and we were scheduled to depart for London the next day. Whether Sherlock Holmes had yet made his apology I had no idea. He and the Count had been summoned to the royal palace in Cetinje at nine o'clock that morning, in order to explain the murders in Belgrade to Prince Nicholas. It was not an interview I envied either of them.

I, meanwhile, waited in Irene Adler's boudoir to fulfill a promise. As I stood idly beside her writing desk, my eye fell on the photograph of a boy I had not seen before. Although no more than ten or eleven, he was tall for his age and already inclining to his uncle's stoutness. The lineaments of the Holmes family were unmistakable.

"That is my son Scott, Dr. Watson," said a voice behind me. "He is away at school."

I turned to see my patient in the doorway. With her stood the maid who had greeted us sixteen years before, when Sherlock Holmes, the King of Serbia, and I had called to remove an incriminating photograph from Miss Adler's London home. Now, after her mistress suggested that she tidy the adjacent bedroom, the old woman glided by me with the same sardonic smile.

"A handsome lad," I noted as I replaced the photograph.

"Very like his father, would you not agree? I fear he may grow fat at Harrow, unless his masters treat him strictly. Here in Montenegro, he has fewer opportunities to indulge his love of fine cuisine. Not that he's likely to encounter any at an English public school," she laughed, "but there *are* restaurants in London, I am told."

I decided to reciprocate her frankness. "Does Holmes know he is Scott's father?"

"Could he see him and not know? They have met three times since Scott was born. Naturally, I have not formally apprised my son, although by now he must have guessed. Sherlock—I may call him 'Sherlock,' Doctor, mayn't I? It seems ridiculous to call him 'Mr. Holmes,' given the subject of our conversation. *Sherlock*, then, has insisted upon financing Scott's education."

"He would see that as no less than his duty, ma'am."

I cursed myself for what must have seemed a cold response. Miss Adler tactfully covered my embarrassment by proposing that we proceed with her examination. Alas, it was over all too soon, and the resulting diagnosis confirmed my worst fears.

"Well, Doctor," my patient enquired whimsically, after she returned from dressing in her bedroom, "what is to be my fate?"

"Unfortunately, it is as I anticipated, Countess. You have a weakness of the heart, not too far advanced, but likely to become more serious as you grow older."

"Ah. I am not surprised to hear it. The heart has always been my weakness, after all. How long may I expect to live?" she added brightly.

"Why, for many years!" I assured her, with perhaps more feeling than with perfect truth. "You will need to take things easily, of course. It was wise to give up so stressful a career as opera singing. Moderate exercise, such as walking in the hills, is fine; but avoid prolonged or steep ascents. I regret that bearing more children would not be advisable."

"That is flattering at my age, Doctor, but it is not an issue in my present marriage."

"Very well. Obviously," I went on, "there are specialists better qualified to advise you than I am. The nearest is in Budapest. The best is in Vienna."

"Both places are eventually accessible from here, as you have seen." Irene Adler, who had been seated at her writing desk, now rose and took my hands in hers. "Thank you, Dr. Watson, for speaking to me honestly. Thank you for being as good a friend to me today as you have always been to Sherlock."

"Of course, Miss Ad—that is, Countess Vukčić."

"Oh, *Irene*, for Heaven's sake!" she cried. "You *Englishmen!* In America, where I was born, people acquainted for as long as we would be insulted at being denied their Christian name. Now, may I ask two more favours of you, *John?* Only two, I promise."

"Of course, Irene."

"See? You *can* do it! First, will you promise me to keep an eye on Scott in London? I know you have your own family to look after now, but—to the extent you are able? Sherlock will no doubt take an interest, too, in his haphazard way, but he has not your quality of *steadiness*."

"I shall be honoured. And the second favour?"

"You must not tell Sherlock about *this*." She placed a hand upon her breast. "About my condition, and"—she looked at me quite calmly—"its likely outcome."

"He already suspects, I fear."

"Oh, I daresay he does. I have never been able to hide anything from him for long. Still—unless he asks—say nothing, at least until you have returned to London. It would spoil our time together, for you know he hates a scene as much as I do."

"Very well, Irene. I promise."

"Thank you, John." She leaned across and gently brushed my cheek, a kiss that I have treasured all my life.

After breakfast the next morning, while Count Vukčić and I played a game of billiards, Sherlock Holmes and Irene Adler walked for half an hour in her garden. He has never confided to me what was said, or left unsaid, between them. I only know that when we drove away, bound for Cattaro, there were tears in my friend's eyes. It was the first time I had ever witnessed Holmes succumb to grief, and I have not seen the like again in all the years thereafter.

We arrived at Victoria Station on the twenty-first of June. For me, it was a joyful sight to see Priscilla waving from the platform, and my stepchildren positively jumping up and down with glee. However, our happy reunion was maddeningly short-lived, for Mycroft's henchmen were waiting to whisk Holmes and me away to Whitehall. There we briefed his disgruntled elder brother, whose doubts about our mission had been amply fulfilled. As he often did, the King's advisor showed remarkable prescience in predicting what would follow.

"Will a strong Serbia," he wondered, "be more likely—or less?—to promote peace and order in the Balkans? Pan-Slavic sentiment now pervades the country. Even if King Peter repudiates the regicides, he must strive to redeem his fellow Serbs in Bosnia and Herzegovina, or risk the fate of Alexander Obrenović. Should Austria-Hungary respond by annexing those two provinces—which now she merely occupies—she will certainly arouse Russia's ire. This revolution in Belgrade has made the Balkan powder-keg more volatile than ever. Far, far better, gentlemen, had we never shown our hand to the Serbian conspirators in such a hopeless cause. Wasn't it your old friend Bismarck who warned that 'some damned foolish thing in the Balkans' would set off the next war?"

During the following months, I concentrated on my family and my practice, only infrequently visiting Sherlock Holmes to assist in several cases. My friend had grown melancholy since our return from Montenegro, and I noticed that his deductive powers seemed less sharp than usual. To my amazement, Holmes even remarked that London had begun to weary him, even though he had often quoted Johnson's dictum that "a man who is tired of London is tired of life."

It was early in October that I received a note requiring me to come to Baker Street. As always, no matter how peremptory the summons, I complied. The moment I reentered our old quarters, Holmes abruptly announced his decision to retire. He then handed me a telegram from Vukčić, which informed us of Irene Adler's death. She had perished, along with many others, in a train derailment near Vienna, while on her way to consult the heart specialist I had recommended. My friend and I spent the afternoon together reminiscing. We agreed it was a kinder fate for Irene's courage, grace, and beauty to be cut down in their full flower, rather than to linger and diminish in an illness that could only end in death. At last, when Holmes haltingly began to tell me of their son, I was able to spare him the pain of that confession by admitting what I knew.

In later years, Scott Adler Holmes would become a source of pride and comfort to his father. His adventures to the present time must be a tale for someone else to tell. My purpose here is simply to abjure my long denial that Sherlock Holmes "felt any emotion akin to love for Irene Adler," and to restore the reputation of a brave and noble lady who honoured me by naming me her friend. Even at so late a date, it is a relief to set down the true story, which can now replace my early fable called "A Scandal in Bohemia."

The Welbeck Abbey Shooting Party

Nottinghamshire
United Kingdom
1913

CHAPTER 1

A Conference with the Elder Brother

On a mild but windy morning in November, eight months before the outbreak of the Great War, I found myself in Whitehall answering a summons to meet with Mycroft Holmes. It had been several months since I last encountered that remarkable civil servant; nor had I seen his brother, my friend Sherlock Holmes, since early in the spring. In those days (as I have written elsewhere), the detective was often absent in the United States, posing as an Irish-American agent known as "Altamont." The momentous results of his mission would be revealed in the case Sir Arthur has entitled "His Last Bow"—although it proved, of course, to be nothing of the kind.

I was relieved that our interview would take place in Mycroft's office, rather than inside the strange confines of the Diogenes Club. It was not often that I met alone with His Majesty's advisor, whom I found slightly intimidating even in his brother's presence. Fortunately, whatever nervousness I felt was groundless. The senior Holmes greeted me with his old-fashioned courtesy, removing a pile of documents from the chair before his desk and enquiring whether I preferred tea or sherry. Much like his brother, however, he evinced a degree of satisfaction when I declined both.

"Then let us proceed to business, Doctor, if you please." With a heavy sigh, Mycroft relapsed into his voluminous desk chair. I could not but notice that he looked older than when I visited him last. The iron-grey hair above his lofty brow was sparse; his Victorian side-whiskers had fallen victim to the modern age. While hardly slim, he was at least three stone lighter than when he served the Queen. Yet, that in itself was no bad thing. Mycroft's colour was still excellent; his lethargy seemed no more pronounced than formerly. It occurred to me that Holmes's elder brother was five years older than myself, and my

222

own countenance in the morning mirror was no longer an inspiring sight.

"In forty minutes, I must report to the Prime Minister on the Irish transport workers' strike," he grumbled, "so we are forced to make our plans in haste. I have an assignment for you and Sherlock, Dr. Watson: one that will bring you once more into the presence of European royalty."

"Holmes is back in England?" I had had no word from him to that effect.

"He docked last night in Liverpool and is on his way to London. I have arranged a room for him in the Diogenes Club. He will join you on Friday for the trip to Worksop, then return to Chicago when your mission is completed."

"Worksop?" I tried to recall the place and failed. It sounded less than euphonious as a destination for European royalty.

"In Nottinghamshire, Doctor!" Mycroft had no more patience than his cadet with slower-moving intellects. "It is the nearest town to Welbeck Abbey, the country house of the Duke of Portland, whom Franz Ferdinand intends to visit."

I knew Portland, at least by reputation. As a very young man, he had served in the élite Coldstream Guards, but a promising army career was cut short by his early succession to the dukedom. Since then, he had held several court positions, including Master of the Horse for both of Britain's recently departed Majesties. I remembered his leading Queen Victoria's Golden Jubilee Procession when I was married to poor Constance, in what seemed of late to be another lifetime.

"Is the Archduke acquainted with Portland?" The Austro-Hungarian heir-apparent and his morganatic wife were presently at Windsor, the guests of King George and Queen Mary. My own wife was following their visit with great interest.

"Yes, they met in Vienna years ago. The Portlands spend much time in Austria and have many friends there. The late Empress

223

Elisabeth even sent the Duke a number of her Lipizzaner horses, in exchange for four of his Jersey cows. As you perhaps have heard, Franz Ferdinand is an obsessive hunter, and Welbeck Abbey is renowned for its shooting parties. You, along with my brother and the Archduke, will attend one there next week."

"But why?" Had I been summoned merely to fulfill a social obligation?

"Because I've no one else to send! Ireland, Doctor, is on the verge of civil war. My best men are in Dublin or Belfast; the others are shadowing those wretched Pankhursts, lest another suffragette do worse than throw herself under the King's horse. This country has gone to the Devil since that damnable Parliament Act two years ago![22] The Austrian heir-apparent and his wife are safe enough at Windsor, but my agents—if I had any!— cannot operate effectively on a private estate like Welbeck Abbey. No, it must be you and Sherlock. As guardians of a foreign potentate, you're all I've got."

"Is Franz Ferdinand in danger?"

"'The Great,' as I believe you habitually refer to them, are perpetually in danger. No doubt your experience of Herr Anton Meyer has convinced you of the Pan-Germans' lack of reverence for the House of Habsburg. The Archduke himself is widely hated, both within and without the borders of his realm. It is rumoured that on his accession, he will revise the *Ausgleich* with Hungary to improve the fortunes of the empire's Slavs. Besides antagonising the great Magyar nobles, that course quashes the ambitions of the Pan-Serb dynasty that has ruled in Belgrade since you and Sherlock failed to save King Alexander. [Here I shifted restlessly in protest.] Fortunately, Franz

---

[22] The constitutional crisis of the Parliament Act, the imminence of civil war in Ireland, the suffragette movement, and other domestic crises facing Britain on the eve of World War I are treated in George Dangerfield's classic *The Strange Death of Liberal England, 1910-1914* (New York: Capricorn Books, 1961 [1935]) Dangerfield stresses the helplessness of Prime Minister Asquith's traditional Liberal methodology to solve them.

Ferdinand was able to restrain the Austrian military leaders who sought a reckoning with Serbia in the recent Balkan Wars."

"That surprises me. The newspapers often depicted him as a leading warmonger."

"Doctor, I have no time to correct the manifold imbecilities of the British press. Suffice it to say that the Heir-Apparent has a host of enemies. His marriage alone left him *persona non grata* with the Emperor. His wife was a lady-in-waiting, although of ancient lineage. The Duchess of Hohenberg, as she is now entitled, endures constant petty snubs at court, which naturally exacerbates Franz Ferdinand's ferocious temper. The Duchess has been treated far more respectfully at Windsor this past week than ever in Vienna."

Having been apprised of the lady's troubles by my fascinated, if sympathetic, wife, I only shook my head regretfully. "So if I understand you properly," I cautiously began, "Holmes and I—mere commoners—are to act as secret bodyguards for the heir-apparent to a European throne, attempting to look inconspicuous on a ducal estate teeming with aristocrats, all armed to the teeth with hunting weapons. How are we go about it? Do we join someone's retinue, or try to socialise on equal terms?"

Mycroft smiled with more compassion than I had expected. "I shall leave that to you and Sherlock. But guests invited to the shooting party—although admittedly august—are not exclusively nobility. Several Conservative ex-ministers from the House of Commons will attend, including Mr. Balfour. [I all but rolled my eyes; an ex-Premier, the nephew of a marquess, would bring down the tone of the occasion!] There are likewise a good many soldiers, with whom you, as a veteran of Maiwand, ought to fit in well. If possible, I shall provide a guest list before your departure. Have you any other questions, Doctor?"

I had several, but I decided to pose the one Priscilla would have asked. "Does the invitation to Welbeck Abbey—which I presume you have secured—include my wife?"

"I fear not. To avoid any questions of precedence, ladies are excluded from the party unless they are related to the Duke or are already acquainted with the imperial couple. For the same reason, His Majesty did not invite the royal princesses to attend at Windsor. Moreover, the presence of your wife would be a needless complication, given the nature of your mission."

I looked forward to offering Priscilla *that* excuse! Nevertheless, my country called. It would be exciting, even at so late a date, to share another adventure with Mr. Sherlock Holmes. As ever, I acquiesced in what was asked of me, and Mycroft quickly outlined the logistics. Then I returned to Queen Anne Street to placate my wife.

"But I don't understand why *I* can't go," Priscilla wailed, "if other wives are invited to the shooting party. It's not as though *I* take precedence over the poor Duchess! It really is too bad of Mr. Holmes, John."

We were preparing for an evening out, so I was reluctantly donning evening dress, thankful again that a retired army surgeon was not required to keep a valet.

"My dear, it was not Mr. Holmes's decision." Suppressing a sigh and retrieving a dropped stud, I repeated Mycroft's explanation, which sounded unconvincing even to my ears. The simple truth was that Priscilla would be in the way, but I could hardly tell her so. I had not been permitted to reveal the nature of our mission.

"Well, I certainly hope this will be the last time," she said sulkily, passing me my cufflinks. "You promised before Belgrade there would be no more 'royal adventures.'"

"I promised there would be no more *European journeys*," I corrected her. "Welbeck Abbey is in Nottinghamshire, three hours north of London. I'll be back within a week."

"I know that, John," my wife conceded. "It's just that I'd got used to your being at home with Emily and me since Mr. *Sherlock* Holmes left for America. And he always takes you into danger!

226

Should you—should *either* of you, for that matter—still be having these adventures at your time of life?"

"We're not *quite* at death's door, you know," I muttered, fastening my collar. In truth, I had felt that fearful portal looming nearer since turning sixty-one. Like any aging man possessed of a still young and lovely wife, I saw the contrast between us more poignantly each time we passed a mirror. My expanding girth, grey hair, and tendency to gout—two of those attributes visible at this very moment—reminded me that the man I had been once I was no longer.

Part of my wife's resentfulness, I realised, stemmed from her bitter argument with Peter during his recent leave from Eton. Now a sixth-former, my stepson was resolved to join the army, mostly as a tribute to his father but in part, I thought, to me. He had written to his paternal grandparents (the Prescotts were an old military family), who had agreed to assist in putting him through Sandhurst when he finished university. Peter's mother was dead-set against the prospect. The circumstances of her first husband's death (which had been the occasion of our meeting[23]) left Priscilla with an abiding distrust and hatred of the institution Captain Prescott and I both revered. Before our marriage, she had urged that I do everything within my power to discourage Peter from following the example of his father. I had not agreed to go so far, but I did promise not to encourage a course that I would otherwise have favoured. There the matter stood for eleven years, until Peter had stubbornly defended his decision earlier that month.

"She's very beautiful, I hear," a voice behind me murmured.

"Who's beautiful, Priscilla?"

"The Duchess. Of Portland, I mean, not the Archduke's wife. Sargent's painted her, as has Lázló."

---

[23] Dr. Watson told the story of meeting Priscilla Prescott in "The Adventure of the Disgraced Captain," to be published in May 2021 in *The MX Book of New Sherlock Holmes Stories, Part XXVII*.

"Quite so, my dear," I acknowledged, turning back to Priscilla with a manufactured smile. "The Duchess of Portland was undoubtedly the most beautiful woman I saw at the Devonshire House Ball. In 1897! She is at least a decade older than you are, and—I can honestly assure you—not half so beautiful even at the time."

My third wife *was* sufficiently beautiful that my exaggerated compliment was not an empty one. The high-waisted, flowing gown she wore matched her green eyes and suited her trim figure; her chestnut hair (confined for the evening by a feathered headdress) was a glory when released. Priscilla dimpled sweetly as she reached over to adjust my tie, and the smile I gave her this time was sincere.

"We'll say no more about the trip to Welbeck," she decided, "but you must tell me all about it—the people, I mean, not the shooting—when you and Mr. Holmes return. And tonight, John: It's only a one-act play, so, please, no longing glances towards the lobby after fifteen minutes. You know how much I enjoy Mr. Shaw."

I did, but I also knew how much *I* enjoyed Mr. Shaw. Nevertheless, I managed to maintain an amiable demeanour for the remainder of the evening, consoling myself with the thought that—come Friday—the game would be afoot!

CHAPTER 2

From London to Worksop

I arrived at King's Cross promptly on Friday afternoon, well ahead of the scheduled time of our departure. Stepping outside the first-class compartment Mycroft had reserved for us, I scanned the platform in search of Sherlock Holmes. It was eighteen minutes past three—with a mere seven minutes' grace remaining—when he at last appeared, moving through the milling crowd with the purposeful stride I well remembered. I noted that he was wearing a most atypical tweed cap, matched by a suit that looked as though it had done service in the 'Nineties. Holmes had brought with him a surprisingly small amount of luggage, and when he turned to instruct the porter I re-entered the train and took my seat, not wishing to appear unduly anxious.

"Well, Holmes," I greeted my old companion as he joined me, "That's certainly not one of your more elaborate disguises. No Italian clerics or consumptive seamen in your repertoire today?"

"As it happens," he replied with veiled amusement. "I removed my original disguise before leaving for the station. I did not wish to place *too* great a strain upon your powers of observation." We exchanged a laugh, and Holmes tapped my knee with his brier pipe, a puckish gesture prompted by the lapse of time since our last meeting. "How are you, Watson?" he enquired, pulling out a bag of shag tobacco. "Eating too well of late, I see."

"Indeed," I ruefully admitted. "I only wish that I could say the same of you." The detective was as gaunt as he had been in Baker Street when using himself up too freely. "You look tired. Was it the sea voyage? I recall from our last 'royal adventure' that you don't do well on ships."

229

"In part, I suppose," Holmes sighed. "I came over on *Olympic*— in the veritable lap of luxury—but it reminded me how close I was to embarking on *Titanic* last year for her maiden voyage. If not for a last-moment change of plans, I might be sitting on an iceberg instead of talking with you now."

"Indeed," I parrotted once more. My friend's jocularity, I knew, masked his deep emotion at that awful tragedy. Several acquaintances had gone down on the ill-fated liner, among them Senator Gibson and his second wife, our former clients. After thirty years, however, it was evident to me that something more was wrong with Holmes. A sudden jolt, as our train began to leave the station, forestalled my enquiry.

"Sometimes, Doctor," he remarked quietly, "I find myself doubting that the British Empire will survive the present century."

"Good heavens, old man!" I replied, quite shocked. "What on Earth has happened to leave you in any doubt of *that?*"

"Nothing I can coherently explain to you, or even to myself. Yet, my latest mission has convinced me that Britain lies in greater danger now than at any time since Napoleon I ruled Europe. Another emperor (you have met the one I mean) now seeks the same hegemony. Before many years have passed, his country will be far better able to displace us than ever was 'The Little Corsican's.'"

"This mission, Holmes," I prodded him, for he had previously said very little of his quest. "Of what does it consist? Why does it require these frequent journeys to America? What results have you accomplished during all these months?"

My friend stared out our compartment's window, where the environs of London had given way to countryside. It was a long while before he answered. Even then, his gaze remained fixed at first upon the passing scenery.

"It involves misleading our most likely enemy regarding our defensive capabilities. I cannot say more, old friend, even to you. However," he went on more brightly, "it has gone well of late. I have disarranged a number of my adversary's plans, and thus far he has not questioned the slightly flawed intelligence 'Altamont' has sold him. However, the crux of the affair cannot occur for quite some time. Until then, I can take no risks that would expose me prematurely or upset the scheme I have in place. For that reason, Watson"—here he turned back to me, and I could foretell the rest with dawning horror— "I cannot accompany you to Welbeck Abbey."

"What?" I nearly shouted. "You're leaving me alone?"

"I must! This morning, Altamont met in secret with the German spy to whom he has been feeding information. There I learned my 'pigeon' has been invited to the Duke of Portland's shooting party. I have not altered Altamont's appearance from my own, save for adopting American attire and a hideous goatee. How can I take the risk of being recognised? Why, I might forget myself and lapse into a Yankee twang."

"Good heavens, Holmes! Your spy may have travelled with us on this train." Rather foolishly, I glanced out our compartment's doorway in alarm.

"No, no," my friend assured me. "Herr von Bork will accompany the rest of the German contingent tomorrow, the same day the Archduke is arriving."

"Von Bork?" I queried. "Who *is* the scoundrel?"

"Hardly a scoundrel, Watson; merely a faithful—if not always scrupulous—servant of his sovereign, much like you or I. Von Bork is an amiable *bon vivant* who fills some minor position at the embassy. Since arriving here three years ago, he and his wife have become great favourites in society. *However*, beneath his charming surface, this young man has succeeded our late friends Oberstein and Meyer as the most dangerous of the Kaiser's agents. Should I be recognised at Welbeck Abbey, not only our two lives, but the safety of the British Empire would be forfeit."

"So I'm on my own to protect the 'widely hated' Heir-Apparent from your spy and every other assassin who attends the shoot. A fine plan you and Mycroft have conceived! What are *you* doing in the meantime, having tea? Why are you even on this train?"

"Don't blame Mycroft, my dear fellow; he had no inkling of my meeting with von Bork at the time he spoke to you. And it isn't quite as bad as that. I'll be within call, four miles away in Worksop. I can come to your aid if absolutely needed."

"Four miles? Why, thank—"

"And you *will* have other allies. Portland has been informed of your true function, and there are trustworthy people on the Heir-Apparent's staff. One soldier, in particular, you should get on with—a Colonel Brosch von Aarenau. He headed Franz Ferdinand's *Militärkanzlerei*—a kind of shadow chancellery in the Belvedere Palace—for five years before leaving to command a regiment of *Jägers*. His successor, young Count von Straten Ponthoz, is an unknown quantity. Finally, there is Baron von Rumerkirch, the Archduke's chamberlain, who has served him long and faithfully."

"Anyone else?" Despite myself, the prospect of another independent mission was beginning to appeal to me.

Holmes smiled, taking from his jacket a thick portfolio. "As usual, Mycroft has prepared extensive notes on everyone whom you will meet. Study them carefully, Doctor. Fortunately, neither the Austrians nor the Germans will arrive before tomorrow evening, which should give you ample time to speak privately with Portland. Ask him to find a reliable local lad to act as a messenger between us; you remember my procedure in the Dartmoor case so long ago. Make any other preparations the two of you deem fit. But *do not* say anything to Portland to give away von Bork."

"But why? Why not arrest the fellow and be done with it?"

"It would never do, Watson. In the first place, he has done nothing—nothing we can yet reveal, at least—to justify arrest. Although his presence at the shooting party makes me uncomfortable, we are in much the same position as we were with Adolf Meyer in Geneva, back in '98."

232

"Well, you know how *that* turned out!" I put in caustically.

"Of course I do, but here the stakes are even higher. In the last analysis, the life of Franz Ferdinand is secondary to my greater mission. Habsburg heir-apparents—as we have seen—can always be replaced. Whatever may happen to the Archduke, it cannot be allowed to compromise the delicate plans I have arranged. It is in Sussex, not at Welbeck Abbey, that I must entrap von Bork."

I could only accept this decision. It was then that my friend told me of his audience, eleven years earlier, with the Emperor Franz Josef, an event I have recounted elsewhere. To judge by that chilling conversation, the Heir-Apparent faced more dangers in Vienna than beyond the borders of his realm. Next, Holmes described the rest of the German contingent that would attend the shoot.

"Von Bork's 'handler'—to employ one of Mycroft's terms—is the embassy's chief secretary, Baron von Herling. A huge man, slow of speech but my no means slow of wit. Watch him closely, for he is known to be disloyal to the ambassador, Prince Lichnowsky, who has done his utmost to ease tensions between London and Berlin. Whether the Baron's ultimate allegiance is to his Kaiser or the Pan-Germanists remains uncertain."

"Are they not one and the same?" I suggested. "Your brother apprised us long ago of William's boast that he would seize the Habsburgs' German-speaking provinces."

"Ah, but that was before the present system of alliances came fully into force. Now Germany finds herself caught between France—her bitter enemy—and the Russian bear. Given Italy's unreliability, Austria-Hungary is the Kaiser's only trustworthy ally. He has therefore taken pains to cultivate her heir-apparent. Four years ago, William invited the Archduke and his consort to Berlin. There he made quite a show of treating Duchess Sophie with full royal honours, and the two men have become fast friends. Recently, the Kaiser even visited Franz Ferdinand at Konopischt to view his rose gardens."

233

"The Archduke grows roses?" I asked incredulously. "That belies almost everything I've heard about his personality!"

"Do not rely, Doctor, solely on court gossip from Vienna. Mycroft informs me that Franz Ferdinand, despite his reputation for ferocity, is a man of considerable intelligence. Nor is his wife the ambitious climber her enemies portray. They both made an excellent impression upon the King and Queen at Windsor. As I have often told you, we must not cloud our observations with pre-judgements."

"Quite so, Holmes." I meekly admitted.

"There is one other person of whom you need to be aware," my friend concluded, "and that is Prince von Fürstenberg. Frankly, I don't know what to make of him. He is extremely wealthy, with vast estates in both Germany and Austria, and serves as a trusted messenger between Vienna and Berlin. Yet, he appears to be a foolish, foppish fellow in himself. More oddly still, his friendship with the Kaiser is reputed to be of such a nature that the Kaiserin objects to it."

"Surely not!" For all my dislike of our old enemy, I was astonished to hear such an imputation made against the man.

"So I have been told. Mycroft—who, as you know, has an eye at every European keyhole—reports that William's previous 'best friend,' Prince Eulenburg, was disgraced some years ago in an unseemly scandal, as was earlier the great munitions manufacturer, Herr Krupp. The latter gentleman is rumoured to have killed himself after the Kaiser was unable to hush the matter up."

"Now we have descended into gossip!" I grumbled, turning to my window. Outside, twilight was fading as we left Nottingham behind. "If you don't mind, Holmes, I would rather discuss my mission than these German peccadilloes."

"Very well," conceded the detective. However, he was silent for some moments, as though reluctant to broach the next item on his list. "Watson," he continued finally, "the Austrians may ask you about a certain Herr Wolfe, who was invited to Welbeck Abbey but declined to come. Franz Ferdinand had desired to thank Wolfe for an assignment he recently conducted for Vienna in the Balkans."

"Herr Wolfe? I've never heard of him. Do you know the fellow?"

"Quite well, actually. 'Nero Wolfe' is a rather fanciful alias used by my son Scott."

"Scott?" I marvelled. "Surely, the boy was very young for such a mission?"

"He was not yet twenty-one in May, when it began," replied the proud father. "As you know, Mycroft has been grooming Scott for intelligence work ever since his days at Harrow. You may recall that Austria-Hungary and Russia nearly came to blows during the spring, after the Serb and Montenegrin armies invaded Albania, that new country whose creation blocked Serbia from the Adriatic. One of the London Conference's more unwise decisions, in my view."

"I remember all too well," I said. For several weeks, it had appeared the Balkan conflict would plunge all Europe into war. With the Great Powers divided into two armed camps, Austria's and Russia's respective allies were obliged by treaty to support them.

"The Austrian heir-apparent was determined to have peace, despite the clamouring of his generals to crush the Serbs. In order to defuse the crisis, Franz Ferdinand secretly approached Sir Edward Grey[24] to despatch a British envoy to negotiate the Montenegrins' withdrawal from Scutari, the Albanian port they had just taken after a long siege."

"I remember that as well. The Turkish garrison and their Albanian allies held out for months against the Montenegrins. Scutari's fortress surrendered only after its commander was murdered by his traitorous successor."

---

[24] British Foreign Secretary from 1905 to 1916. He served under the Liberal governments of Campbell-Bannerman and Asquith and in Asquith's wartime coalition.

"No doubt," Holmes replied a bit impatiently, "To return to my story, Scott—as the stepson of Count Vukčić—was the obvious choice to serve as envoy. He and Vukčić, escorted by agents of the Austrian *Evidenzbureau*, met with King Nicholas in Scutari and urged him to surrender its fortress to the international naval force outside the harbour. The old king reluctantly acceded to his councillor's assurances. The Montenegrin troops withdrew, and a broader European conflict was successfully averted."

"What a diplomatic triumph for your son!"

"Not so, I fear," my friend responded glumly. "You see, Scott and his stepfather, relying upon Austrian promises, pledged to King Nicholas that he would regain Scutari in the peace settlement. As you recall from the treaty signed in Bucharest, this did not occur. 'Nero Wolfe' feels that he unwittingly affronted his adoptive family's honour. Mycroft may soon discover that his promising new agent's first assignment will also be his last."[25]

"Was the Archduke guilty of bad faith?"

"I daresay not. The Emperor himself cannot predict the machinations of his foreign office, nor had the Austrians the final word in Bucharest. Even so, I shall be interested to learn what Franz Ferdinand may have to say about the matter."

By now, our train was rolling into Worksop. It was a town of moderate size, notable chiefly for mining and malting, and famous in Elizabethan times for growing liquorice. The station at which we arrived was architecturally reminiscent of that age, although on this night it was being decorated to delight another royal visitor. Few other Worksopians were then in evidence, so Holmes and I had no difficulty in securing transportation to the business district. Because we were

---

[25] Nero Wolfe referred to his 1913 mission on behalf of Austria, as well as subsequent adventures in World War I and post-war Yugoslavia, in Rex Stout's *Over My Dead Body* (New York: Bantam Books, 1994 [1940], pp. 10-11, 18-23, and 117-121. Wolfe repaid the Austrians by fighting for Montenegro in the war.

not yet expected at the Abbey, Mycroft had suggested spending the night in the town's newest hotel and making our own way to Welbeck in the morning. Inevitably, his brother had a different plan. Holmes gave an address on Bridge Street to our driver, who soon halted before a decrepit structure named the Old Ship Inn. It appeared to pre-date, if not Queen Elizabeth herself, at least most of her successors.

"I say, Holmes," I called dubiously as he began taking down his luggage, "Do you intend for us to share the tap-room with Captain Billy Bones?"

"Not 'arf, gov'nor," my friend replied, his accent unexpectedly dropping into lower-class vernacular. Quickly, he gestured for me to leave the cab. After requesting its owner to remain, I joined him in the doorway beneath the juttied upper floor.

"I shall be residing here for the duration, Watson," the detective muttered. "While its appearance may be unprepossessing and its comforts minimal, this hostelry possesses a unique feature that will be highly advantageous to our mission. Please address any communications you may send to Bobby Jenkinson, a retired groom or trainer. I have not yet decided which."

"Will I see you at Welbeck in this guise?" I wondered, recalling that Portland kept a renowned stable and had won the Derby for two years running in the 'Eighties.

"Not—as the saying goes—if I see you first!" Holmes smiled. "Seriously, I shall not venture onto the estate without first improving this disguise. At present, it is too like my actual appearance. Now," my friend concluded, "you had best proceed as scheduled to the French Horn Hotel. Our cabbie appears to be becoming restive. Good luck, Doctor! I shall await your first report with interest."

With that, he nodded cordially, and we went our separate ways. Although I spent the remainder of the evening quietly researching Mycroft's notes, inwardly I was simmering with anticipation of the morrow, feeling younger than I had in years.

237

CHAPTER 3

Three Days Among "The Great"

I arose early on Saturday, happy to see that the clear autumn weather still prevailed. After an excellent breakfast in the French Horn's dining room, I hired a dogcart for the drive to Welbeck Abbey. So pleasant was the morning that I alighted as we entered the estate's magnificent park, instructing the driver to take my luggage to the house while I walked the remainder of the way alone. Soon I arrived in a green dell populated by enormous oaks, reminding me that Welbeck's grounds lay within the original boundaries of Sherwood Forest. One ancient specimen—a veritable Methuselah of trees—undoubtedly pre-dated Robin Hood and might have been producing acorns at the Conquest. Sadly, it was all but dead, for the trunk had long ago been pierced by an archway wide enough to accommodate a coach-and-four. I later learned from Portland that this was the famous Greendale Oak, mutilated in the eighteenth century by a predecessor out to win a wager. There was one noble ancestor I should not have cared to claim.

The house, I had read some years ago in *Country Life*, was "a sombre pile, massive and ugly in many styles." It had indeed been founded as an abbey, but in the century after the Dissolutions had been substantially rebuilt by a younger son of Bess of Hardwick. Later, it had fallen to the Bentinck family, whose founder accompanied 'Dutch William' to England in 1688 and thereby gained a dukedom. The present Duke of Portland was the sixth to hold the title. Despite its chequered history, the Abbey was assuredly, as John Evelyn once described it, "a noble but melancholy seate." Its west front, which I came to at the end of a long drive, boasted battled parapets and a great square tower, while the gabled east front rose high above broad terraced lawns that faced a narrow lake. On my left,

I could see two imposing Jacobean erections, one of which (I remembered from the article) housed the stables and a riding school. The other had been remodeled by the fifth duke for a picture gallery; but that aged, eccentric nobleman became preoccupied with constructing tunnels between the Abbey's several buildings and vast, underground rooms. All was left a shambles when the old man died, and I wondered what the present duke had made of it when he inherited Welbeck from his cousin at only twenty-one.

For the moment, however, I was more concerned with announcing my arrival to anyone who might take note of it. Fortunately, my unpaid driver was still waiting, and the household servants were at that moment carrying my bags to whatever fate awaited them. I was kindly advised by Portland's butler that as I had not (as he delicately put it) brought my valet, a footman would be sent to assist with my unpacking and, when I had refreshed myself, convey me to the Duke. His Grace would await me in the Titchfield Library.

Properly refreshed, I was admitted to the library, where I found a grey-mustached, slightly portly gentleman rather like myself, although better tailored. He strode across the ornately shelved and decorated chamber with his hand outstretched.

"I am pleased to welcome you to Welbeck Abbey, Dr. Watson," Portland graciously assured me. "Mr. Holmes—I refer, of course, to Mr. *Mycroft* Holmes—has told me a good deal about you. Having briefly been a soldier in my youth, I am honoured to meet a veteran of Maiwand and a recipient of the Afghan Medal."

"I fear, Your Grace, that I did little to deserve it," I admitted, "aside from getting shot. Rather less than Bobbie, our regimental dog, who also got the medal."[26]

---

[26] Bobbie, a mongrel from Reading and regimental pet, stood with the 66th Berkshires' "Last Eleven" in their heroic last stand against the Afghans. Although injured, he was able to rejoin Dr. Watson and other wounded members of the regiment. On returning to England, Bobbie and other survivors of the 66th received the Afghan War medal personally from Queen

"Yes, I recall Her Majesty's broad smile when she presented it," my host chuckled. "A gallant little fellow. But to return to present day, *your* Mr. Holmes will not be joining us, I understand?"

"No, but he is at hand and can be called if needed." I paused, uncertain how much information the detective would wish me to reveal. "For now, he is residing at an obscure inn in Worksop."

"That was at my suggestion. The Old Ship has . . . peculiar advantages that may be of some use." Portland, who seemed somewhat preoccupied, did not enlighten me as to those advantages. "*Well*, Doctor, I am afraid I shall see little of you before the shooting starts, except at dinner." At his courteous gesture, we left the library and progressed down a long corridor leading to the driveway I had entered. "Our imperial guests arrive tonight from London, and for the next few days Winnie and I shall be showing them the other great houses in the neighbourhood. Our own Bolsover, of course, and Chatsworth. Have you seen Chatsworth?"

"Holmes and I were there on an occasion in the old duke's day." I did not describe for him my last encounter with the Germans: a night in 1901, during the secret alliance negotiations held at Chatsworth, when the two of us had nearly lost our lives.

"Quite a character, old Hartington," laughed the Duke. "I still miss him. His nephew and I shall take Their Highnesses to view the house of Bess of Hardwick, our common ancestor." Here we passed through Welbeck's imposing portal out onto the drive, where a beautiful Lorraine-Dietrich limousine awaited Portland's pleasure. I had heard that His Grace—unusually for a devotee of the track—was also an enthusiastic motorist.

"I am off to Worksop, Dr. Watson, where Gibson, my head gardener, is decorating the station for the Archduke's visit. We're planning an avenue of palms and shrubs, with great pots of

---

Victoria. See: https://www.britishbattles.com/ second-afghan-war/battle-of-maiwand/.

chrysanthemums. You may not know that his Imperial and Royal Highness is a flower fancier."

"I do, actually, and find the fact surprising."

"You will find Franz Ferdinand a surprise in many ways. His public personality, which results largely from the way his wife is treated in Vienna, is very different from the face he shows to those he trusts. The latter is the true measure of the man. Those who know His Highness well (and Winnie and I feel fortunate to count ourselves among them) believe him to be the only man who can transform his uncle's ramshackle realm into a modern state. If Austria-Hungary's nationalities problem can be solved peacefully *within* the empire, it will go a long way towards preventing another European war.

"Forgive me," Portland added, nodding to his chauffeur to open the car door. "I did not intend to lecture. Tomorrow, some good fellows will arrive with whom you will have much in common. Do you know Lord Lovat, Doctor, of South African fame? And my old friend Harry Stonor—a crack shot, Harry. I believe he has a message from a former client to impart." He paused and glanced at me enquiringly. "Anything else before I go?"

"Talking of messages," I suddenly remembered, "Holmes requested that Your Grace recruit a lad from the estate to carry my reports and any instructions he may wish to send. Would that be possible?"

"Of course," the Duke replied a little doubtfully, "if Mr. Holmes believes it would be useful. I'll instruct my head gamekeeper to find a likely boy. We shall be meeting this afternoon to plan the shoot." He raised his stick to me in parting. "Farewell, Dr. Watson, until dinner. I am very glad to have you with us."

I stood bemused as the white limousine moved slowly down the drive. Although Portland could hardly have been friendlier, something in his manner puzzled me. It was as if certain facts had been withheld from me, and I had no understanding why. With an inward sigh, I turned back to the house, wondering—as I seemed so far to be the

241

only guest—whether I should appear for luncheon or have a tray brought to my room. For all my admiration of 'The Great,' it had been years since I spent time in a great house, and seldom ever without Holmes. On my own, would I be ignored by the luminaries ("Who is that man? Why is he here?") who had expected to meet the great detective? Would Franz Ferdinand be as disdainful of a proxy as the young archduchess I had once encountered in Trieste? If so, successfully accomplishing my mission would be difficult indeed. Then I recalled my old friend's precept: "Theorising without data, Watson, is a futile exercise." Comforted somewhat by his words, I regressed to my quarters to await the coming meal.

Happily, my first three days at Welbeck did much to alleviate these foolish qualms. By Monday evening, I felt sufficiently well-grounded to write a full report to Holmes. I did not detail the Abbey's manifold delights, for they would have been of little interest to my friend. I said nothing of its splendid drawing rooms; nor did I describe the maze of tunnels the fifth duke had constructed, or the subterranean ballroom his successor had converted to a portrait gallery. Portland's stables, with thoroughbreds in a hundred stalls, went unrecorded. Of his art collection, which was worthy of a royal palace, I wrote only of Sargent's portraits of the ducal couple: Her Grace lounging languidly against a mantel, His Grace returning from a walk with his two collies. Recalling the detective's tale of Reginald Musgrave, I did mention one item in the curios: the goblet from which Charles I took his last communion on the morning that he died. But Holmes learned nothing of our splendid dinners, presided over by a lady who seemed (despite my assurance to Priscilla) as beautiful as she had been in 1897. For me, these three days were a private taste of "life among The Great." I regretted only that my wife could not be there to share it with me.

Welbeck Abbey, Nov. 24th

My dear Holmes (or Jenkinson):

As you instructed, I asked Portland (who has been very amiable) to find a local boy to carry messages. This afternoon, he sent one by the name of Willy White, who is twelve years old and seems intelligent. His father is an under-gardener, and the family live in Worksop, which will be convenient. Willy promises that if I complete this missive before dinner, it will be delivered by tonight. How this feat will be accomplished I have no idea.

A happy feature of these house-parties, as you know, is that guests are generally left to their own devices until dinner. I have therefore been able to mingle with my fellow hoi polloi while dukes and archdukes go their way. Two new acquaintances are rather more than hoi polloi. Lord Lovat, besides being chief of Clan Fraser, raised a regiment of scouts to fight the Boers and won the DSO. Harry Stonor ("a crack shot," according to our host) is a Groom-in-Waiting and—despite the disparity in spelling—a cousin of our early client Helen Stoner. "Helen," he kindly let me know, "has passed a very happy life, thanks to you and Mr. Holmes." Both Stonor and Lovat will be good men to have in our corner if a crisis comes.

The Opposition politicians are well represented, particularly the Cecils. All recall our many services to "Lord Bellinger," whose nephew Mr. Balfour was gracious enough to praise my careful handling of a certain ticklish case.[27] The only politician who snubbed me was that "most superior person" Lord Curzon, the ex-Viceroy, to whom I was unwise enough to mention my own time in India.

The Germans are a more intriguing study. My relations with them, understandably, are distant, for they are well aware of our

---

[27] Robert Gascoyne-Cecil, 3rd Marquess of Salisbury (1830-1903), who formed three governments between 1885 and 1902, is called by his real name elsewhere in this volume. Arthur Balfour succeeded him as Prime Minister from 1902 to 1905. The case Watson refers to is "The Adventure of the Second Stain," which took place in 1896 and not (as Baring-Gould asserts) in 1886.

association. Baron von Herling regards me with hauteur and suspicion. I generally avoid the Prince of Fürstenberg, whose gushing, mincing personality contrasts oddly with his burly, mustachioed physique. Von Bork—as you warned me—is a hard person to dislike. Even Portland admits "He is a good fellow, for a German": amusing at the dinner table, expert at both chess and billiards, a tireless companion on a ramble, and (ominously!) a first-class shot. His young and pretty wife, one of the few untitled ladies invited to the Abbey (which would not please Priscilla!), is popular as well. As one bejeweled dowager whispered to me last night at dinner, "It is strange to remember that those nice von Borks aren't English!"

The Austrian delegation arrived on Saturday evening, but only today was I able to speak to one of them. The imperial couple have been touring with the Portlands, so I have seen them only from afar at my end of the dinner table. Franz Ferdinand is a man of fifty, somewhat heavy-set and almost as flamboyantly mustached as the Kaiser. His wife is a tall and striking lady in her forties; she exhibits grace and dignity that make a mockery of her supposed ambition. Both seem delighted with everything they see, and from what I have observed the Archduke's fearful reputation must surely be exaggerated.

This afternoon, I had the opportunity to discuss him with the man you had suggested that I cultivate: Colonel Brosch von Aarenau. Brosch had been exempted from the latest motor tour, so I invited him to join me in a walk. The Colonel is not far past forty, young for that rank in Franz Josef's superannuated army. Even in mufti, he bears himself like a born soldier. It was evident that despite having left the Militärkanzlerei, he still holds his former chief in high regard.

Brosch told me of the Archduke's early life: how he contracted tuberculosis and was given up for dead, the Emperor openly more satisfied with his other nephew, Otto, as the heir. "Otto, who later died of syphilis!" the Colonel cried indignantly. "Add to this insult the Hofburg's treatment of the Heir-Apparent's wife. The Choteks are *among the oldest families in Bohemia, but Prince Montenuovo (who merely reflects the wishes of His Apostolic Majesty) affects to find no difference between a high-born countess and a milkmaid! Is it a wonder, Herr Doktor, that Franz Ferdinand's anger sometimes overwhelms him? Truly, the Duchess's influence has done nothing but good. Those who knew His Highness before their marriage say he has become a different man."*

"Even so," I noted, "so volatile a master must have been difficult to serve."

"Fortunately," the Colonel laughed, "I began on the right footing. When I arrived for my interview, I found the Heir-Apparent sitting on the floor, playing with his children. All three were quite small in those days. As I stood stiffly at attention, the younger son, Prince Ernst, toddled up and offered me a toy. His father (you may be sure) was watching closely to see how I would react. After a moment of panic, I knelt down, accepted the gift, and thanked the little fellow. The Archduke smiled and rose to welcome me, and I knew that I had passed the test."

I had hesitated before including this remembrance, knowing my friend's dislike of what he would regard as mawkish sentiment. Of more import to Sherlock Holmes would be Franz Ferdinand's political opinions. Here, too, my companion had provided valuable insight during our ramble, particularly regarding the Heir-Apparent's plans to reorganise the empire. To return to my letter:

In his youth, the Archduke visited the United States, where he discovered the federal model as a possible solution to Austria's nationalities problem. Four years ago, Brosch accompanied Their Highnesses on a state visit to Bucharest. There Franz Ferdinand met a Roumanian named Popovici, the author of a book entitled The United States of Greater Austria. *It proposed dividing the Dual Monarchy into no fewer than fifteen federated states, based as far as* possible on ethnic lines. The Heir-Apparent, says the Colonel, now prefers this plan to his old idea of "Trialism," which would only benefit the Slavs.

I enquired whether the Hungarians would not be likely to oppose the plan, recalling that they looked to the last Habsburg heir-apparent as a champion of the Magyar cause. Brosch assured me that upon that subject, Franz Ferdinand has nothing in common with his cousin Rudolf; indeed, he had talked of reconquering Hungary by the sword if needed. Noting my look of consternation, the Colonel added, "I feel sure that this was but hyperbole. The Archduke is often harsh and hasty in his judgements. At times he can even be unjust, but once he realises his mistake he does not hesitate to put things right."

By then, we had reached our destination, a row of greystone almshouses Portland's duchess had encouraged him to build with his winnings from the track. It was not a site of scenic interest, but we guests had been requested to avoid the woods and fields before tomorrow's shoot. Brosch and I paused for a brief rest, while the Duke's collie (who had accompanied us for exercise in her master's absence) strained at her leash to be away. The Colonel turned to me with a thoughtful countenance.

"You asked me, Herr Doktor, whether I found my master difficult to serve. It was not always easy. He will not abide direct contradiction, but his saving grace is that—unlike every other Habsburg—he wants to know the truth. When one has learned how to be frank with him in an acceptable manner, one can accomplish almost anything. The Archduke's education was broad, not deep, but he possesses an incredible quickness of perception. Even in areas where he has only the most basic knowledge, he instinctively makes the right decision. And when one at last has won his confidence, his trust endures. I was called from my regiment to join His Highness on this journey simply because he wanted my opinion of you Englanders!"

I replied lightly that I hoped we had not disappointed. While he reassured me on that point, Brosch expressed discomfort with those now in his master's retinue. He fears especially that young Count von Straten Ponthoz may be a spy for "Conrad and the military clique." Culling my memory of the notes we had received, I realised that he was referring to General Conrad von Hötzendorf, the army's Chief of Staff. It appears that Conrad was once the Archduke's protégé, but they have fallen out. Franz Ferdinand was rightly furious when Conrad allowed the traitorous Colonel Redl to shoot himself before he could be questioned. Later, during the Balkan Wars, he lost patience with the Chief of Staff's demands for war with Serbia, even if it meant fighting Russia, too. Twice he has dismissed Conrad from his post, but the Emperor promptly reinstated him. It was, Brosch grumbled, only the latest instance of their failure to agree. My companion shook his head and, handing me our charge's leash, walked on at an agitated pace. The collie and I were hard-pressed to keep up. When we returned to the lawn of Welbeck Abbey, the Colonel halted, offering me an apologetic smile. Then he told me gravely:

"I truly believe, Herr Doktor, that Franz Ferdinand is Austria's last hope. The reign of His Apostolic Majesty has been a long decline since 1848. His one idea, the Ausgleich, *simply permits the Magyars to ride rough-shod over everybody else. Now, the Serbs, the Roumanians—even our Italian and our German 'allies'—flock like vultures, conspiring with their compatriots inside our borders while they wait for us to die. Do you know the saying in Vienna: 'The situation is hopeless, but not serious'? We muddle onward with our well-known* Schlamperei.[28] *But the Heir-Apparent sees things clearly, and he has his plans in place. I pray nightly that he will be spared until the sad old man in Schönbrunn Palace joins his wife and son at last."*

---

[28] A peculiarly Austrian term connoting laziness, muddleheadedness, and inefficiency—thus, fully appropriate to describe Franz Josef's empire.

In pursuit of our mission, I asked Brosch whether he considered the Archduke to be in danger. "No man in the empire," he replied, "has more enemies, and it now appears they are beginning to combine against him. Several months ago, the Emperor appointed Franz Ferdinand Inspector-General. It may have been a poisoned gift! Next summer's maneuvers—which the Archduke's new duties require him to attend—will be held in Bosnia. Already, the Bosnian Serb newspapers in Sarajevo are calling for his murder. Yet, General Potiorek, the provincial governor, implores His Highness to make a ceremonial visit to the city—on June 28, the day of Kosovo, when the Serbian Empire fell five hundred years ago. It would be madness! And it is no coincidence, perhaps, that the two old rivals, Conrad and Potiorek, are now as thick as thieves."

Although for security's sake I did not comment on the fact to Holmes, the Colonel's revelations showed that Mycroft's knowledge of the dangers that beset Franz Ferdinand was as accurate as ever. Alas, the suspicion that a plot was being hatched in Sarajevo did not ensure the Archduke's safety for the next few days. I therefore sought my friend's advice regarding how I should proceed, urging him to write a quick reply.

One final conversation on that Monday—and a far more pleasant one—occurred too late to find a place in my report. Having finished the epistle and given it to Willy, with instructions to deliver it to "Mr. Bobby Jenkinson," I had almost two hours remaining before dinner. On impulse, I decided to revisit the underground ballroom which housed the portrait gallery. Leaving the main building, I passed through a long, curving corridor whose walls were covered with framed prints. At a distance, I spied two ladies walking towards me. One I identified as the Duchess of Hohenberg, the other as a younger lady I had heard mentioned as her niece. To my surprise, Her Highness appeared to recognise me as the two drew near. With a quiet word to her companion, she stepped across the hallway, smiling warmly.

"Herr Doktor Watson! I am indeed happy to make your acquaintance. How is your 'friend and colleague' Herr Sherlock Holmes?'"

I bowed deeply. "Quite well, Your Highness, thank you. He regrets very much that he was unable to join us at Welbeck Abbey. I had no idea you realised I was here."

"*Jawohl,*" she laughed. "My husband, too, is well aware of it, although consulting detectives are less likely than our police detectives to fall within his ken. He hopes to meet you when the shooting starts. But I recognised your name at once! Did you know that as a girl, I read aloud your *Study in Scarlet* to my sisters? During the years I served Archduchess Isabella, I always found a way to smuggle in the latest issue of *The Strand*. I read your tales of Mr. Holmes's adventures to my children even now."

"Mr. Holmes and I are honoured, ma'am. May I ask which story is your favourite?"

"Why, 'A Scandal in Bohemia,' of course! Its title references my homeland, and I enjoyed seeing a woman get the better of a man. Little did I imagine, Herr Doktor, when I sat reading that story for the first time, that one day I would marry the King of Bohemia myself!"[29] The Duchess sighed a little wistfully, "There were so many things I did not imagine in *those* days, I fear.

"But now," she added, nodding to her niece to join us, "I must introduce you to this pretty lady. Elisabeth, my dear, here is Dr. John H. Watson, the friend and biographer of Sherlock Holmes. Herr Doktor, my niece, the Countess de Baillet-Latour."

I bowed, if it were possible, more deeply than before. The Countess was well short of thirty and quite lovely. Her face reflected

---

[29] Sadly, here the Duchess was anticipating her husband's eventual accession. As noted elsewhere in this volume, the crown of Bohemia had passed to the House of Habsburg several centuries before.

the same intelligence and kindliness as did her aunt's, and her smile was charming. When I enquired whether she was enjoying her visit, she replied, "Much more so than when we came last year, and I got appendicitis!" Both ladies chortled merrily, and I felt vexed by my inanity. To my relief, the Duchess noticed Baron von Rumerkirch, the Archduke's chamberlain, signalling urgently to her some distance down the corridor.

"Heavens, I must go, Elisabeth! The Portlands promised to show your uncle and me their Lipizzaners before dinner! Herr Doktor, would you mind escorting my niece back to the main house? *Danke*, and my apologies." She hurried away while I was still attempting to say something gallant. The Countess smiled indulgently when I turned back to her.

"Her Highness is a very gracious lady," I opined, in an effort to restore my standing.

"Dear Aunt Sophie is the noblest, kindest woman in the world," her niece responded stoutly. "She is my closest friend. It is tragic how little she and the Heir are really known and understood. So much of what is written of them is untrue! Even your English papers speculate that Uncle Franzi will renounce his oath and declare his wife empress when he takes the throne."

"Is there no prospect of that happening? She is certainly worthy of the title."

"But he swore an oath to God!" the Countess cried. "To Catholics as devout as they and I, breaking such an oath condemns one's soul to Hell. As a Protestant, Herr Doktor, you do not understand; but I assure you that my aunt's presumed ambition to be empress is a myth. For her, it will suffice to end the years of slights and insults, and be honoured simply as the emperor's consort. The title in itself means nothing to her."

I thought it best to change the subject. "Your own title, Countess," I said artfully, "intrigues me. Surely it is not Austrian in origin."

250

"Indeed not, Herr Doktor. My husband is a count of Belgium."

By this time, we had returned to Welbeck Abbey's entrance hall. I prepared, with some regret, to say farewell to my companion, for it was nearly time to change for dinner. Unhappily, we were accosted at that moment by the Prince of Fürstenberg, who occupied us for a quarter-hour with chatter even more inane than mine. We were finally rescued by none other than von Bork, who happened by and smoothly invited the Prince to join him in a game of billiards. From the ironic wink he gave us when the two departed, it was obvious he had performed such services before. Once again, I was left with an unwonted, and unwanted, liking for my friend and country's adversary.

I made my way back to my room. It was on the ground floor of the oldest portion of the Abbey, which I understood was seldom used. No other guest was anywhere in sight. While I failed to understand the reason for my isolation, the chamber itself was comfortable enough, so I did not request another. That night, as I lay abed, it occurred to me that I had learned more of the Archduke and his consort than most of their own subjects were privileged to know. Moreover, what I knew engendered a protective instinct I had not felt towards our other royal "clients," not even Emperor Frederick. For whereas that monarch was already doomed, Franz Ferdinand represented (as Colonel Brosch expressed it) the last remaining hope for Austria. Having failed disastrously in our earlier mission for the House of Habsburg, it seemed that this time Holmes and I had a positive duty to succeed. Not, assuredly, for the sake of "the sad old man in Schönbrunn Palace"; to him we owed very little. Our duty was rather to the far-seeing Heir-Apparent, whose accession might preserve the future of an empire and—even more importantly—the peace of Europe.

251

CHAPTER 4

The Shooting Party[30]

When I awoke the next morning, a letter lay upon my bedside table. I was baffled as to how it had arrived there, for I am not an abnormally sound sleeper, and the long-fallen door into my room had shrieked unbearably each time I opened it. Upon inspecting them, I saw that my two ground-floor windows were secure.

Though the letter's method of delivery remained unknown, its authorship was not in question. I identified the folded sheet (there was no envelope) as a type used by country inns and third-rate London hostelries. It was with no surprise, therefore, that I recognised the hand of Sherlock Holmes. Dated only "Monday night," the text read as follows:

My dear Watson:

Your report, although admirably thorough, was extremely long in coming. I had not expected to wait three days to hear from you. While I recognise that you lacked an early opportunity to observe the imperial couple and their minions, information on Portland's other guests would have been more useful to me yesterday. With the shooting due to start tomorrow, it becomes difficult if not impossible to ensure the safety of His Highness.

Nevertheless, I urge you and Portland to do everything that can be done as soon as possible. Surround Franz Ferdinand with the

---

[30] Coincidentally, Dr. Watson's chapter title duplicates the title of Isabel Colegate's 1980 novel. It, and the 1985 film starring James Mason, perfectly capture the social and diplomatic anxieties that beset the British aristocracy on the eve of World War I. Ms. Colegate's novel may have been based on a real incident, for one of her characters appears below in Watson's account of the Welbeck Abbey shooting party.

guards you have identified (Lovat, Stonor, and Colonel Brosch von
Aarenau), whose reliability we shall have to trust. Keep every
German—particularly von Bork—as far away from him as feasible.
Verify that all those enlisted as beaters and loaders are well known to
the Duke. Whatever protection this plan provides may be illusory, for
I do not expect anyone attending the shoot to attempt the Archduke's
life directly. The likely threat will come from a sharpshooter armed
with a long-range rifle, like the one Adolf Meyer intended to use
against the Empress Elisabeth. (Our Teutonic foes are not noted for
imagination!) Let me remind you that Brosch commands a regiment of
sharpshooters, as did Lovat in South Africa. They must not be
overlooked. Finally, Doctor, in making your arrangements with the
Duke, remember not to implicate the Germans or von Bork
specifically—although Portland, unlike most members of the
aristocracy, may be sharp enough to put two and two together.

I was annoyed by the detective's imputation against Brosch,
who could not be an assassin unless he was also a monster of deceit.
Otherwise, Holmes's plan seemed well-conceived. It was too late,
however, to implement the precautions he desired at once. On arriving
for breakfast, I learned that Portland had departed, making it
impossible to revise his preparations for the morning's shoot. I did
manage to have a private word with Stonor and Lovat while we
helped ourselves from the sideboard. Both readily agreed to serve as
bodyguards. His Lordship, without prompting, identified the Germans
as the major threat. Neither they nor the Austrians appeared
downstairs until we left the house.

Shortly before half-past nine, a cavalcade of automobiles and
shooting brakes[31] drew up outside the Abbey, as the Duke, his head
gamekeeper, and the Archduke with his chamberlain returned from a

---

[31] At this time, a type of horse-drawn wagon used to transport shooting
parties, along with their dogs, guns, ammunition, and dead game. Later, the
term was applied to automobiles suited for the purpose.

reconnaissance. We guests piled into the other conveyances, and the party set off for the shooting-ground. I shared a brake with my two compatriots and those twin pillars of British country life, dogs and horses. Naturally, the dogs enjoyed our excursion more than anyone, keenly anticipating the day that was to come.

Not all my readers may be familiar with the shooting parties held at noble houses. They are less common now than formerly, if only due to the expense involved. Under the supervision of a tribe of gamekeepers, the birds (pheasant, grouse, woodcock, and duck) are bred, hatched, and reared on the estate. On the day of a shoot, the gentlemen attending (or "guns," as they are called) take a designated place beside their "loader" with a pair of shotguns; the man reloads one weapon while the other is in use. Meanwhile, an army of "beaters" (all men from the estate) walk through the adjacent woods and undergrowth, making sufficient noise to rout the birds. They fly over, and the "guns" attempt to bring them down, taking care not to poach into the territory of their neighbours. Dogs are employed to retrieve the fallen game, while ladies who accompany the party stand or sit nearby. At such a shoot as Welbeck Abbey's, hundreds or thousands of pheasants—plus the odd, luckless hare or rabbit—could be slaughtered during each day's sport. To fire at deer, or other beasts too big to be humanely killed by buckshot, was of course bad form. To use the term "humanely" may seem strange, but I heard Portland state his preference that guests miss altogether rather than merely wound a bird.

Regrettably, I was too often in compliance with the first alternative. Though I count myself a fair shot with my service revolver, the recoil (or "kick," as my American friends called it) from a shotgun soon becomes painful to my damaged shoulder. To my chagrin, my prowess declined steadily as the day wore on, even when I adjusted to the borrowed guns. That is not to say we were not treated to remarkable displays of marksmanship. I do not recall that Mr. Balfour killed a single pheasant; but most of the party shot quite well.

Stonor, Lovat, and von Bork were miraculous. As for Franz Ferdinand, his reputation as a rifleman was legendary; he had shot all types of game, from tigers in India to chamois in the Alps. Konopischt, his castle in Bohemia, held among its trophies his three-thousandth stag. Some found this bloodlust a disturbing feature of the Heir-Apparent's personality. Yet, as the event we were attending proved, it was shared by royalty and aristocrats in Britain and across the Continent.

On that morning, either the Archduke's eye was out or Nottinghamshire pheasants flew higher than those to which he was accustomed. Even we "guns" down the line noted His Highness's repressed fury as the birds eluded him; it was the only time at Welbeck I saw him out of temper. Added to his trials was the Prince of Fürstenberg, who prattled on incessantly from the adjacent station. How that gentleman expected to converse above the din I could not fathom. Fortunately, his obnoxiousness offered me an opportunity. During luncheon (served under a marquee behind the shooting-ground), I spoke to Portland. The Duke was obviously worried by his august guest's frustration. We agreed to rearrange the stations, exiling the Prince to join his fellow Germans down the line. Brosch replaced him beside the Heir-Apparent, with Stonor and Lovat both nearby. By grouping all the "crack shots" except von Bork together, this change was highly unfair to the other shooters. The rest of us hardly saw a pheasant for the balance of the day. Even so, the main object was achieved. Relieved of Fürstenberg, Franz Ferdinand shot much better in the afternoon and regained his good humour, quite unaware of the motive behind his improved luck.

That evening after dinner, I was approached by Herr von Bork. We had managed to avoid the bridge tables (a dislike of cards being one point we had in common), and he invited me to try my hand at billiards. Although I had not played often since my games with Thurston, I readily agreed. The German was clearly my superior, but my old skill revived enough to offer a degree of competition. When von Bork paused to chalk his cue, I took the opportunity to thank him for rescuing the Countess de Baillet-Latour and me from the talkative Fürstenberg the day before.

"Bitte sehr!" he replied amiably. "Poor old Fürstenberg! The Prince can be a trial, I must admit. He was quite heartbroken to be removed today from the Imperial and Royal Presence. Am I wrong in thinking, Herr Doktor, that you played a part in that decision? I saw you speaking to His Grace at luncheon."

"The Duke did ask for my opinion," I misleadingly agreed.

"So many famous 'guns' around the Archduke in the afternoon! He was assuredly very well protected. I was surprised not to be invited to serve as a bodyguard myself.

"In fact," von Bork added as I bent to the awkward shot he left for me, "it almost seemed we Germans were being isolated from Franz Ferdinand. If His Grace's wish was to protect his guest, why were we singled out? Austria-Hungary is Germany's good ally; he is her heir-apparent."

"I am sure the Duke intended no affront," I answered, feigning concentration, "save, possibly, to Fürstenberg. It was evident that the Prince was treading on the Archduke's nerves." Contrary to my expectations, I sank the ball before me and moved around the table for another shot. My opponent politely stepped aside.

"Do I sense behind these odd precautions," he demanded quietly, "some unknown, guiding hand? Von Herling and I were extremely disappointed that Herr Holmes did not attend the shoot at Welbeck Abbey. Yet, I cannot help but wonder if he is *somewhere* in the neighborhood."

"Anything is possible," I admitted lightly. My last ball shuddered in the pocket but just failed to drop, leaving von Bork well situated to close out the game. With a smile of resignation, I invited the spy to take his turn.

"Well played, Herr Doktor," he acknowledged afterwards, "but the game is mine. As will be, I think, the one to come."

"This one, perhaps," I replied evenly, replacing my cue in the rack beside the table. "We shall see about the one to come. Good night, Herr von Bork. I wish you pleasant dreams." We exchanged well-mannered bows, and I retired to my room to write my next report to Sherlock Holmes.

It was well past midnight when that report was finished. Weariness soon overcame my resolve to sleep "with one eye open" in case I should be visited again. On awakening, I was not surprised to find a second note. This one was considerably terser:

Watson,

A word in haste, for I must keep a watch tonight. This evening, there appeared at the Old Ship a man I recognised, an Irish vagabond who calls himself O'Roarke. He is an embittered ex-Fenian, not much younger than ourselves. Besides several more unsavoury activities, he acts as a messenger in London between the agent known as "Altamont" and Herr von Bork. Michael O'Roarke was responsible for some bloody work in Ireland, and I have no doubt that if our spy intends to employ a non-German to assassinate Franz Ferdinand, he has at hand a man well-suited to the task. I have it on good authority from a source you know that O'Roarke is an expert marksman with a long-range rifle.

Redouble your precautions, therefore, and let me hear from you as soon as possible.
S.H.

As always, the detective made no reference to his own proceedings, so in this regard his message left me none the wiser. It was again impracticable to comply in full with his instructions. On enquiring for young Willy, I learned he had been sent to join the beaters, one of Portland's regulars having fallen out. This decision had been taken by the head gamekeeper without his master's knowledge.

In consequence, I spent a very nervous day. Before leaving for the shooting-ground, I apprised the Duke of the altered situation. He advised his butler and head gamekeeper to beware of any unknown persons posing as servants, gamekeepers, or the like. We both recognised, however, that an assassin could easily remain anonymous in the retinue of a treacherous visitor. It was the first time in living memory, Portland dourly remarked, that a squire of Welbeck Abbey had reason to distrust his guests.

Thanks to our rearrangement of the stations, the morning shoot went well. Portland had quietly entreated Stonor and Lovat to leave a few birds for others down the line, and Colonel Brosch seemed to restrain himself voluntarily. Only the Archduke blazed away as he had done the day before, and more effectually. Having (at his host's suggestion) changed to a heavier-bore shotgun, he proved himself a truly deadly shot. I, meanwhile, spent more time scanning the wood for riflemen than the sky for pheasants, much to the disgust of my poor loader. My contribution to Welbeck's bag that day was small indeed.

When we returned to the marquee for luncheon, I made my way among the beaters, searching each homely English face for a disguised O'Roarke or Holmes. It was a wasted exercise, for I had never seen the Irishman, and none of the older beaters was tall enough to be my friend. On finding Willy White, I asked him to deliver my report to Jenkinson at once. Unfortunately, the boy's duties did not permit him to comply. Willy promised to leave the moment the head gamekeeper released him, assuring me that he could reach the Old Ship Inn within an hour. I remarked that it had taken me a longer time to walk from Worksop, and in response was cheekily reminded of my age.

Our afternoon was enlivened by an upsetting incident which might well have been more serious. It occurred during the last drive. Just as the flushed birds were appearing overhead, an aged gentleman emerged from the trees and began walking down the line in front of us. He was carrying a placard on which was inscribed the Biblical injunction: "Thou shalt not kill." Oblivious to every outraged shout of warning, he proceeded on his way serenely, bringing our slaughter of the innocents to a ragged halt. I heard the Heir-Apparent's startled enquiry, first to Colonel Brosch in German and then in English to the Duke. Otherwise, we shooters stood dumbfounded, while the lady observers (including both the Duchess of Hohenberg and the Countess de Baillet-Latour) exhibited bewildered sympathy for the old fool. He was taken firmly in hand by two loaders and delivered to Portland, whom he began to address in an indignant bellow. I wandered near enough to hear the end of the diatribe, which involved "universal kinship" and the rights of animals. Franz Ferdinand snorted in derision, while our host ignored the charge that he was "a disgrace to your good lady," a noted champion of birds and beasts. The intruder—a Mr. Cardew, I learned later—was escorted off the premises without further ado. However, his object was accomplished, for His Grace declared the day's shooting at an end.

I walked back to the house with Brosch and Lovat, close behind the imperial and ducal party. Poor Portland was apologising to the Archduke at some length.

"I am really very sorry, Your Imperial and Royal Highness. That fellow Cardew is a well-known crank; I ought to have suspected that he might appear. He did the same thing at Nettleby last month, just before that unfortunate incident in which Lord H_____ shot a beater."

Franz Ferdinand had retained his equanimity throughout the disturbance. "It is of no importance, my dear Portland," he assured the Duke in heavily accented English. "We have such lunatics in Austria as well. I have not decided whether they should be shot for insolence or given a medal for their courage, rather like your British suffragettes." His wife gently chided him for this opinion, and Colonel Brosch shot me an amused glance.

I had noticed both him and Lovat eyeing the nearby trees intently during Cardew's interruption. Obviously, their soldierly instincts were aroused. I had also feared that the diversion might conceal a greater threat, but soon realised that an elderly eccentric would be a most unlikely ally for a paid assassin. If von Bork and his Irishman were indeed the danger, why, I wondered, were they so slow to show their hand?

That night, the Portlands held an informal ball in their vast underground portrait gallery. A hired band played the usual waltzes, plus a bit of ragtime, as the subjects of Van Dyck or Reynolds gazed nostalgically down upon the dancers from their odd pink walls. Besides dancing (badly) with my hostess and the Countess de Baillet-Latour, I was able to converse briefly with the Archduke. He was a different man that evening than on the shooting-ground: affable, easy-going, and courtly to the ladies. When His Highness led out the night's last waltz with Duchess Sophie, their mutual affection and delight in the occasion were apparent to us all.

Von Bork avoided me, both at the ball and during the late-night supper afterwards. At one point, I saw him in close consultation with young Count von Straten Ponthoz and the Prince of Fürstenberg, whose demeanour was more serious and sensible than usual. I later observed the senior German present, Baron von Herling, speaking almost angrily to Portland. Upon returning to my room, I could not divine what these discussions boded. I knew only that the last day of shooting would provide a final opportunity to the assassin. My only course, it seemed, was to remain vigilant and await help from Sherlock Holmes.

CHAPTER 5

An Encounter in the Dark

His help, when it came, came as a rude awakening. Two hours before dawn, a well-remembered voice disturbed my sleeping consciousness, speaking in the same calm tones it once had used in Baker Street.

"My abject apologies, Watson, for intruding at this ungodly hour. I would take it as a great favour if you would rise and dress. I am in need of your professional services."

I sat up groggily and switched on the electric lamp beside my bed. Holmes, still attired as Bobby Jenkinson, reclined in the overstuffed armchair across the room. My friend looked utterly exhausted. His Norfolk jacket's sleeve was torn, and there was a deep cut upon his left forearm, which he had made an ineffectual attempt to bandage with a handkerchief. Pushing back the bedclothes, I got to my feet and went to the nearby wardrobe to retrieve my doctor's bag.

"My dear fellow! What on Earth has happened to you? And *how*," I added in sudden realisation, "have you managed to enter this room three times without my hearing you?"

The detective smirked as I bent to examine his wounded extremity. "As ever, friend Watson, you see but you do not observe. Take a look behind this chair." The chair (I did observe) sat before an alcove adjacent to the elaborate Jacobean mantel surrounding the hearth. In the near-darkness, I saw nothing out of the ordinary in that corner of the room.

"The chair can wait," I told Holmes firmly. "Take off your coat. That arm needs my immediate attention." Setting the ewer and washbasin on the table next to him, I carefully washed, disinfected, and bandaged the gash, removing only enough of the caked blood to permit stitching. My friend endured these painful ministrations stoically, although before the stitching he did request a pause to light his pipe. When I had finished, he murmured "Thank you, Doctor," and with a nod directed me again to search behind the chair.

There I saw an open panel in the alcove's wainscotting. An electric torch lay beside it on the oaken floor. Picking up the torch, I shone it down into the darkness, revealing an old but sound wooden stairway leading to an earthen passage six or seven feet below.

"A tunnel?" I enquired incredulously. "I was aware that the fifth duke had dug like a badger beneath the Abbey's grounds, but no one mentioned this part of the house."

"This tunnel was a much earlier duke's project," Holmes informed me. "During the Civil War, the future Duke of Newcastle employed it to escape to Hamburg after Marston Moor. Portland's mad old cousin extended it to join his own tunnel to the riding school. Where do you suppose the other end emerges, Watson?"

I recalled Portland's reticence and Willy's unexpected speed. "The Old Ship Inn!" I cried, adding, less triumphantly, "and, as usual, I'm the last to know. I suppose the Duke told Mycroft of it when they made their arrangements for our mission."

"Exactly so," my friend confirmed, having come to stand beside me, "which made the Old Ship a perfect base of operations. The tunnel saves twenty minutes on the walk from Worksop, and until an hour ago I had believed it was secure."

"What happened, Holmes?" I gestured to him to take his seat while I began to dress. The detective collapsed into his chair, and I saw for the first time the mien of shock upon his face. For a long moment, he only sat and smoked. Then he answered quietly, "The fact is, Watson, that I have killed a man."

"Good Lord! I presume it was O'Roarke. Did he recognise you?"

"Indeed," Holmes replied, gazing at me curiously. "I must say, old friend, that you seem less appalled than I'd expected. I forget sometimes that you were once a soldier."

"Well, I shall certainly require an explanation. I know nothing of your activities over these past days."

"In that case, we had best descend, for we have a body to dispose of. I am afraid," Holmes added wincingly, slipping his injured arm into its sleeve, "that you must do the digging. As it happens, the Old Ship's landlord keeps shovels in the tunnel." I wondered, though I did not ask, how many other bodies had been buried there.

During our three-mile trek in ill-lit gloom, my friend recounted the events that had led to O'Roarke's death. Holmes had first augmented his "Jenkinson" apparel with a wig and beard of greying russet. He had gone to Welbeck Abbey's stables, bearing a testimonial from Portland, in the guise of a retired horse trainer. There he met the Duke's own trainer and the grooms and jockeys who would later serve as beaters for the shoot. As my friend remarked, our long-ago visit to King's Pyland had stood him in good stead.

"Normally," he laughed, "there is no one more close-mouthed with a stranger than a Nottinghamshire countryman. 'Horsey' men, however, share a fraternity that transcends provincial ties. While you were hobnobbing with 'The Great,' I was touring the estate on horseback, memorising the locations of the 'drives' for each day's shoot. By the end of our last ride on Monday, I was fully informed of the geography.

"The next morning, having delivered my reply to your report, I emerged from the tunnel near the riding school. It was too late to have an impact on the first day's shoot, for I could not reveal my presence to the beaters. Instead, I examined the terrain reserved for the succeeding days, marking the most favourable lines of sight for an assassin. On my way back that afternoon, I passed the first day's shooting-ground and was pleased to note from a nearby hillside that you had effected the precautions suggested in my letter. At dusk, I returned via the tunnel to the Old Ship Inn. There my satisfaction with the day's events abruptly ended."

"O'Roarke arrived," I hazarded, employing my "blinding talent for the obvious."

"Soundly deduced, Watson! He was imbibing in the Old Ship's tap-room when I went down for supper. Having met O'Roarke four times during my negotiations with von Bork, I knew that any scruples he possessed had died in the cause of Irish independence. If he should recognise Bobby Jenkinson as Altamont, one of us would not depart the Old Ship Inn alive.

"Fortunately, whisky is the man's Achilles Heel. He was already well into his cups, trying to elicit news about the shoot from the grooms and jockeys I had ridden with that morning. Hoping to remain unremarked, I took a corner bench. O'Roarke's interrogation was not going well. His hatred of the landed class was on display, and Portland's loyal tenants had little fellow-feeling for an Irishman. I heard one snap, 'The Duke's the best landlord in England, you bloody Mick!' as they abruptly moved away. Unluckily, two of the grooms noticed me. They cried out 'Well met, Mr. Jenkinson!' and stopped to have a word. O'Roarke eyed me suspiciously when he staggered from the room. After escaping my inconvenient friends, I ascertained from the landlord that my foe had gone to bed. Then, having had no word from you, I wrote and left at the Abbey the note that you found yesterday."

I explained the reasons for Willy's delayed delivery of my report, a delay that would have fatal consequences. The next morning, O'Roarke had followed the same procedure as had Holmes the day before. He walked to Welbeck along the same road I had used on my arrival, trailed surreptitiously by Bobby Jenkinson. Either von Bork's instructions or his own enquiries had given the Irishman a clear idea of the terrain. He entered the estate through a break in a stone wall and made directly for the third day's shooting-ground.

"There," continued Holmes, "he chose the precise location from which to shoot the Archduke I had myself earmarked the day before. What I did *not* know, Watson, was that O'Roarke had seen me shadowing him and penetrated my disguise. Late that evening, he also saw young Willy leave my room after delivering your message. He followed the boy into the Old Ship's basement and discovered the tunnel. What still amazes me is that he did not proceed immediately to Welbeck Abbey and inform his German master of my identity as Altamont."

It was possible, of course, that O'Roarke had tried to do exactly that. As I started to report the previous night's ball, we came upon the

Irishman's dead body. He was a wicked-looking fellow, shot cleanly through the forehead but still glaring fiercely above his short, grey beard. A bloody knife and broken lantern lay beside him in the dirt. The corpse had not yet entered rigor mortis; so I closed the eyes, straightened the limbs, and performed other decencies. Then I began to dig while the detective went on talking. Even in the presence of his victim, his voice retained its usual urbanity.

"I had intended to arrive at the Abbey, as Bobby Jenkinson, well before O'Roarke. However, upon entering the tunnel I saw the gleam of his light ahead of me. It was only then that I realised the horrid risk of my exposure. I extinguished my torch, praying that O'Roarke hadn't seen it, and moved quickly and quietly towards him through the dark. Fortunately, the tunnel's course was relatively straight, and I knew it well enough by now to avoid impediments and follow the faint glow ahead of me. Like yourself, Doctor, my Irish foe was slightly lame; so I gained rapidly upon him. By the time he noticed my approach and turned, it was too late to raise his rifle, which in any case he had not loaded. Moreover, I was already covering him with my revolver. With few other options left, O'Roarke set his lantern down and met me with an evil grin.

"'How do, Mister Altamont?' he greeted me. 'Ye *look* like an Irishman in that fine beard, but I never believed ye *were* one, even one from the far side o' the Atlantic. Nor did ye *sound* like one when we drank two nights ago, talkin' to the laddies from the fine, great manor. "Bobby Jenkinson," is it? Or would yer name be *Holmes*, a'tall?'

"When I heard *that*, I must admit that inwardly I panicked, Watson. For a moment, I feared for Willie's safety, but he knew only Bobby Jenkinson. Had O'Roarke somehow found your letters in my room? The real question, of course, was whether von Bork now knew his trusted contact Altamont was an imposter. If that revelation had not occurred already, it simply could not be allowed. The contest between us was no longer 'Michael O'Roarke or Sherlock Holmes'; it had become 'Germany or England.'"

266

"Apparently, the old Fenian saw this conclusion in my face, for with a roar he drew a knife and rushed at me, kicking aside his lantern in the process. With better luck than aim, I shot him dead, but not until he got in a last thrust with the knife. I trust, gentle*man* of the jury, that you'll agree I shot in self-defence and for my country."

I could not answer Holmes immediately, for I was climbing from the grave to catch my breath. "O'Roarke could not have seen von Bork last night," I gasped. "It was long past one before the

Portlands' post-ball supper ended. Had they met afterwards, he could not have been returning to the Abbey at the time that you encountered him. Now, please help me get the poor devil below ground."

"I was under the impression that he was there already," the detective quipped (quite unsuitably, I thought). Together, we buried the dead Irishman, and I extracted a promise that Holmes would inform Mycroft of the shooting and have O'Roarke removed and buried decently. Thankfully, considering my friend's wound and my own weariness, our remaining journey was a short one. Dawn was just breaking when we emerged from the basement tunnel in the Old Ship Inn.

CHAPTER 6

The Last Day's Shoot

In contemplating our next action, Holmes and I could not agree as to how we should proceed. He insisted upon joining me at Welbeck Abbey, whereas I believed that with O'Roarke's demise the threat to Franz Ferdinand had largely been removed.

"No, Watson, you do not know von Bork. The loss of his assassin will certainly be a blow, but he is an adaptable fellow. With another day of shooting yet to come, the Archduke's safety is by no means assured. Our spy's improvisations will be unpredictable, so I had best be on the scene."

"But what if you are recognised?"

"I shall take measures to avoid that possibility." His assurance led us to a discussion of disguises. Bobby Jenkinson, my friend decided, had outlived his usefulness; he was well-known to the beaters and would inevitably attract attention. Holmes rejected the idea of masquerading as my overdue valet, for in our modern age it would require him to appear clean-shaven. Instead, he opted to colour the wig and beard of Jenkinson with lampblack, also shortening the latter. Having brought a grey cloth cap and suit of clothes appropriate for loaders, he elected to fulfill that role for me. I saw numerous objections to this plan, two being the state of his left arm and the fact that the party's other loaders would know him for a stranger. Holmes thought these deficiencies offset by the likelihood that our aristocratic German foes would take less notice of a "peasant." As he reminded me, our time and options were both limited.

So it was back into the tunnel for another trek. We returned to my room in Welbeck Abbey still in time for breakfast. Having refreshed my toilette, I left my friend to cool his heels and made an appearance at the table. Luckily, the Duke came down soon afterwards without his imperial guests. Colonel Brosch was there as well, and I was able to persuade both him and Portland to accompany me to an urgent consultation. Holmes had vetoed my request to invite Harry Stonor and Lord Lovat. "Too many allies," he warned me, "are as dangerous as too few."

On entering my lonely chamber, the Duke shook Holmes gravely by the hand. "I am very glad to see you, sir, but I fear I must report a setback. Last night, Baron von Herder came to me and insisted, quite indignantly, that the German shooters be placed closer to Franz Ferdinand today. He felt they were being intentionally excluded—which," Portland added with an uncertain glance at me, "seemed indeed to be the Doctor's plan. I assumed that Monday's change of shooting stations had come at your direction."

"Quite so, Your Grace. I had reason to suspect a threat that did in fact materialise. Happily, that threat has been averted, but I am not convinced that it will be the last."

"And this threat comes from our faithful allies?" Brosch demanded. I had spent the journey to my part of the Abbey apprising him of our mission and Holmes's involvement in the case. Although the Colonel recalled Duchess Sophie's fondness for my stories, he had been amazed to learn that the detective was not a fictional creation.

My friend confirmed that a member of the German party was undeniably involved. "Then I must add my part to the tale," growled Brosch. "This morning, von Straten Ponthoz asked me to relinquish my stand beside His Imperial and Royal Highness to Herr von Bork, with Prince von Fürstenberg to be nearby. I had supposed that the Archduke sanctioned this request, although why he should subject himself again to Fürstenberg I could not fathom. As I have no official standing, I did not feel able to refuse." Portland gloomily agreed that he as host was in a similar position.

"Then we must take counter-measures to ensure His Highness's continuing protection," Holmes declared. "Who among the British shooters is closest to Franz Ferdinand?"

"Simon—er, that is, Lord Lovat," the Duke replied. "His station is on the other side of Fürstenberg's."

"Then Watson and I must take his place. I am to be the Doctor's loader," he added, holding up his inky wig and beard in explanation.

"His Lordship is the better shot," I noted, with no false modesty.

"True, but you and I are 'in the know' and must be placed to take prompt action."

However, both Portland and I urged that Lovat was not a man to be discarded, so the detective grudgingly agreed that he might be informed and placed nearby. His Grace thereupon suggested that Brosch and I return with him to breakfast, lest our prolonged absence be remarked. "I shall have Hudson, my head-keeper, Mr. Holmes, tell his loaders to take no notice of the new man serving Dr. Watson." I thought privately that Victor, my long-suffering loader of the past two days, would only be relieved!

When we came to the shooting-ground an hour later, the air had turned considerably colder, with the sky a clear, unclouded blue. It was ideal weather to pass a pleasant day among high-flying pheasants, eager dogs, and good companions. Sadly, for Holmes and me there would be little relaxation.

I began by having a quiet word with Lovat, who understood the requirement for the change immediately and moved without protest to my other side. Prince von Fürstenberg spoke to me cordially, clearly delighted by his return to imperial proximity. As for Franz Ferdinand, he grew a bit impatient with the renewed flux but settled into his murderous routine once the shooting started. Von Bork, now my near neighbour, greeted me with an ironic bow. To my relief, he appeared not to notice my new loader before turning his attention to the birds. Holmes went about his business with quiet inefficiency. So far as I knew, my friend had never participated in a shooting party, but naturally he was familiar with all types of firearms. Nevertheless, his wounded arm impeded him, and our mutual disabilities made my rate of fire even slower than before. The genial spy did not neglect to chaff me at the end of the first drive.

"*Gott im Himmel*, Herr Doktor! I did not believe it possible to shoot worse than you did yesterday, but you have surpassed yourself! Did the first loader His Grace assigned to you give up in disgust?" Von Bork grinned at the first loader's successor, who had taken up a cringing crouch in order to mitigate his height. Fortunately, a deferentially touched cap sufficed to end the German's interest.

Over the succeeding drives, it was our adversary's prowess that started to decline. He became ever more distracted, as if uneasily awaiting a delayed event he had expected to occur. When it had not occurred by the time we broke for luncheon, I saw von Bork in agitated consultation with von Herder on their way to the marquee. Abruptly, the spy collared a young beater, handed him what looked like half a crown, and sent him flying to the Abbey. "From now on, Watson," muttered Sherlock Holmes, "we must increase our vigilance to the nth degree."

When the shooting party reconvened, I was not the only one with a new loader. "I know that fellow, Holmes," I whispered when I saw the man now handling the German's guns. It was von Bork's valet, who had appeared and spoken briefly to his master on the evening of our billiards game. Moreover, it had been clear on that occasion that the valet had the size and bearing of a soldier. Now he loaded and passed the weapons flawlessly, and von Bork's rate of fire and accuracy began even to exceed the Archduke's. It became almost a contest between the two of them. Before the afternoon's first drive was over, Portland, Brosch, and several of the other shooters (myself among them) had abandoned their own efforts just to watch.

"Well shot, my dear von Bork!" Franz Ferdinand cried jovially as we moved to our next stations. The German, by now looking a bit ashen-faced, merely bowed agreeably in reply. For myself, I could not help but be a little sickened when I saw the enormity of the slaughter our party had inflicted. So profusely lay the dead or dying pheasants that the dogs ran themselves ragged trying to retrieve them. Welbeck Abbey's was the last such shoot that I attended. My reasons had nothing to do with the dire event that was shortly to unfold. At the time, the lust for destruction proved contagious. No longer willing simply to acclaim their champions, every German, Austrian, and Briton kept up an infernal fusillade that soon would echo across the battlefields of Europe. So overwhelming was the din that I actually forget our mission and the danger threatening its august object. One man, thank God, did not.

In a momentary lull, I heard a gasp behind me. The Duchess of Hohenberg had risen from her chair, pointing in alarm in the direction of her husband. Following her lead, I saw von Bork's loader casually aiming a waist-high shotgun directly at Franz Ferdinand, who was intent upon his shooting perhaps twenty feet away. Von Bork also seemed to be oblivious. Then the Archduke brought down an unusually high-flying bird. Portland and von Bork paused to express their admiration; the spy's henchman began to raise his gun. I glanced despairingly at Holmes, realising we could never move in time to stop him.

"*Ausweichen!* I *must* congratulate His Imperial and Royal Highness!" It was the Prince of Fürstenberg, pushing aside his own loader and blundering towards von Bork's. Sherlock Holmes leapt after him, shoving the aristocrat into the valet at the moment that he fired. I could hear the Prince's startled cry and my friend's groan at the insult to his wounded arm. The lethal pellets, scattered between Portland and Franz Ferdinand, miraculously hit neither one. Instantly, all shooting ceased; and there was a cacophony of outraged enquiries, shamefaced explanations, and profound apologies. Meanwhile, the day's last flight of pheasants passed safely overhead, unmolested by a single shot.

Earlier than usual that night, the surviving members of the Welbeck Abbey shooting party sat down to a well-earned dinner of roast game. I use the term "surviving" because several members of the party had decided, somewhat abruptly, to take an early train to London. Oddly, all of them shared German nationality: Baron von Herder, the von Borks, and the Prince of Fürstenberg. The poor prince was almost weeping with humiliation as he bade his hosts farewell, having been refused an audience to apologize in person to the Habsburg heir-apparent.

As for the spy, he had gamely withstood Portland's solicitous concern ("My *dear* fellow, you're not going?") as Duchess Winnie attempted to console his devastated wife. It was not as if the popular von Borks had suffered a disgrace. Their unlucky valet had stoutly pled his innocence when seized by Lovat, Brosch, and Harry Stonor ("He ran right into me, *meine Herren!*"); and Franz Ferdinand had graciously conceded that his near-assassination had been accidental. In fact, he presented his own gold watch to the Abbey's head gamekeeper, in order to commemorate "three days of the most marvellous shooting I have ever enjoyed."

Even so, before departing Herr von Bork found time to have a word with me. "My heartiest congratulations, Herr Doktor! It seems that, after all, you have won the second round of our billiards match. But the match is not over, *mein Freund*—and you may pass that message on to *Meister* Holmes—whenever he puts in his appearance. Until that time, farewell!" With a respectful heel-click of Teutonic salutation, the German spy was gone.

"He is quite right, you know, Watson," said Sherlock Holmes that night on our own train back to London. "This was purely a defensive victory. We were able to thwart our adversary's plan, save the Heir-Apparent, and protect my Altamont identity. But the real contest is yet to come; nor are its stakes in any way diminished. No less than the peace of Europe and the survival of the British Empire still hang in the balance."

With his arm in a sling, but otherwise in his usual persona, Holmes had emerged from my room soon after dinner. I had earlier seen that he was sent a plate of pheasant. While the Portlands entertained their other guests, we were privately admitted to Franz Ferdinand's apartments, where we found the Archduke and his wife, the Countess de Baillet-Latour, and Colonel Brosch von Aarenau. Duchess Sophie crossed the room to take my friend's hands in her own, smiling at us beatifically.

"Dear Herr Holmes, how can we ever thank you and the Herr Doktor? I *knew* 'the great detective and his Boswell' would not let us down!" The young countess added her own tribute by kissing us both softly on the cheek, which I considered more than ample compensation for my efforts. Franz Ferdinand regarded this display with tolerance, albeit a bit quizzically. He appeared ready to offer us his hand, but the detective forestalled the gesture with a brief and formal bow. Rebuffed, the Archduke likewise took refuge in formality. Fortunately, he instinctively chose the right approach.

"Even before today's incident, Herr Holmes, I had wished to meet you. I understand you are acquainted with the mysterious Herr Wolfe, who recently refused a decoration I had offered him. Please tell him how much I regret that certain promises made during his mission to Scutari could not be fulfilled. I shall attempt to make amends to King Nicholas when I am emperor. I shall make any amends to Herr Wolfe he wishes to propose."

My friend seemed taken aback by this unexpected condescension. "I thank Your Imperial and Royal Highness," he replied, "and I shall certainly pass on your remarks to my—to Herr Wolfe when I return to London."

"*Danke. Und vielen Dank, meine Herren,* for the service you provided me today. Brosch has explained that there was more to this afternoon's comedy than met the eye. It seems the loyalty of our young friend von Straten Ponthoz is in question."

"If Colonel Brosch has issued such a warning, it is not for me to contradict it. If I may add a warning of my own, I would advise Your Highness that it may be well to turn a jaundiced eye upon your empire's German allies."

The Archduke laughed and, rather belatedly, invited us to take a chair. "I was not born yesterday, Herr Holmes, and I have lived my life in the snake pit of my uncle's court. I have long known that Count von Straten Ponthoz is a spy for Conrad—but two may play at that game. As for these Pan-German fellows, be assured that I took your conclusions regarding the death of my dear aunt—when at last they reached me!—far more to heart than did the Emperor. Was that not true, Brosch? When next the German Kaiser visits me (as will happen in the spring), I shall speak to him of today's mischief. I am confident that Wilhelm will put a stop to any further machinations."

My friend, I could see, was not convinced. "If I may raise one more point. . . ?" he began carefully.

"*Natürlich.*"

"The trip to Sarajevo, which Dr. Watson informs me is to take place next summer. Watson and I have personal knowledge of the regime in Belgrade, and of those who are fomenting a Pan-Serb insurgency in Bosnia and Herzegovina. Again, I would urge Your Highness to be extremely cautious. Indeed, I would advise strongly against making such a trip at all."

Franz Ferdinand sighed, exchanging a troubled look with Colonel Brosch. "I assure you, Herr Holmes—as I have assured my loyal Brosch—that I have no wish to go to Sarajevo. It is another nest of vipers, and Bosnia in mid-summer is as hot as Hell itself! But it will be my duty as Inspector-General to observe our summer maneuvers in the province, and I rather think my uncle will insist. No doubt I shall be safe enough. When His Apostolic Majesty visited the town three years ago, every street he travelled on was lined with soldiers."

When the detective still looked dubious, the Archduke added, almost kindly: "Pray do not worry yourselves unduly, gentlemen. I have known for some time now that it is possible I shall be murdered." Franz Ferdinand regarded us serenely with the clear blue eyes he would one day turn on his assassin. He turned to smile at Duchess Sophie as she touched his hand. "Each of us, you know, can die at any time. For a man in my position, there can be no help for it. I can only trust in God."

"In that case, Your Imperial and Royal Highness," murmured Sherlock Holmes, "I can but echo the prayer offered in your empire's anthem: May '*Gott erhalte Franz den Kaiser.*'"

My friend bowed, far more respectfully than he had done on entering the room. The two of us departed Welbeck Abbey, leaving the doomed couple to their fate.

EPILOGUE

The Lamps of Europe

In July of 1914, three weeks after the assassinations, I requested another interview with Mycroft Holmes. Our meeting took place in the Diogenes Club. This time, I had no qualms about visiting the King's advisor.

"What truly occurred at Sarajevo?" I demanded upon entering the Stranger's Room. "And what will happen now? I am sure you know as well as anyone."

"Sit down, Dr. Watson," the senior Holmes advised me, imperturbable as always. He gestured toward the decanter of whisky on the table, which I refused. Settling himself within his vast armchair, he gave me the look my headmaster had reserved for quashing impudent third-formers.

"I fear The Archduke's destiny caught up with him at last," Mycroft replied blandly. "He was a man who had too many enemies, so it was bound to happen in due time. As for what *will* happen, Doctor, I am not a fortune-teller. My sources indicate, however, that Vienna will issue an ultimatum to Belgrade. Any other government would have done so long before. While the death of Franz Ferdinand has engendered nothing but relief inside the Hofburg, Austria-Hungary's ministers and generals *must* use this tragedy as an excuse to crush the Serbs. It being the third confrontation since Bosnia was annexed in 1908, Russia will have no choice but to support her 'little Slavic brothers.' You know what will result as well as I. My prediction is that all Europe will be at war within two weeks."

"Had we made known the attempt at Welbeck Abbey, we might have saved them."

"For the moment, possibly, but at what cost? And for how long? Nothing indicates that the Pan-Germans were involved in this

279

conspiracy. You and Sherlock are aware of the elements in Belgrade that armed and trained the young assassins. There is no doubt in my mind that Austro-Hungarian authorities in Sarajevo were complicit. No attempt was made to round up well-known dissidents; every warning of potential danger was ignored. In a city of over eighty thousand people, security was left to a police force of one hundred twenty men. Even after the initial bomb-throwing, Governor-General Potiorek would not allow his troops to line the streets. Why, I was even told the Archduke's car backed up and stopped in front of the assassin! As you and Sherlock saw at Welbeck Abbey, Franz Ferdinand was a terrific slaughterer of game. I suspect that in the last hour of his life, he learned the feelings of a hunted animal."

Mycroft, when he so desired, could be far colder than his younger brother. "Where *is* Holmes?" I asked him gruffly.

"Still in Chicago, finishing the assignment that is now nearing its fruition. As you may know, its importance at the present moment can hardly be exaggerated. However, my brother will be back in Britain by the time the dominoes begin to fall. I am sure you will be hearing from him." With that banal assurance, I was required to content myself, for Mycroft bade me a succinct farewell.

It occurred to me later that I had been unfairly harsh. Much of my anger resulted from a despairing letter I had received from Colonel Brosch, who confessed that he had "completely lost faith in a divine world. I'm like a wounded animal that wants only to creep into a corner and die there. I pray, Herr Doktor, that you and I will not soon renew our brief acquaintance on the battlefield." Eight weeks later, that fine soldier, and most of his regiment of *Jägers*, lay dead upon the field of Rawa Ruska.

During the Great War, I read a propagandistic piece by Wickham Steed in which the journalist asserted that William II, who had visited Franz Ferdinand at Konopischt earlier in June, presented to him there a plan for breaking up the Habsburg empire. The Arch-duke's sons (barred from the imperial succession by their parents' morganatic marriage) would rule two new states created from its remnants, with the empire's German-speaking provinces passing to Berlin. Based on what I saw at Welbeck Abbey of the murdered couple, I cannot credit they would ever have agreed to this reputed "Pact of Konopischt." Moreover, recent scholarship reveals that despite his constant sabre-rattling, the Kaiser was as horrified as anyone when the catastrophe he had done so much to instigate at last occurred. I am reminded again of our old enemy Bismarck, who warned us forty years ago that William II would become "the nemesis of history." Long before this writing, that prophecy was tragically fulfilled.

It was left to Sherlock Holmes, as always, to say the final word. It was spoken many years beyond the Welbeck Abbey shooting party, almost a decade after my stepson Peter had followed Brosch and countless others into oblivion by dying on the Somme. My beloved wife had died in 1921, a victim of grief, I think, as much as cancer. Four years later, my friend and I spent a few days in Hungary with my old acquaintances the Lónyays: three silver-haired old men and a lady who retained a certain girlishness into her sixties. The former crown princess had survived the suicide (or worse) of her first husband, the loss of her imperial titles, the fall of the empire, its last emperor's failure to reclaim his throne, and a Red revolution. She and her husband were now living in comfortable retirement, although estranged from her erratic daughter. Stéphanie remained charmingly outspoken. She was also still writing her memoirs.

"I believe the time has come," she said, "to tell the truth about Franz Ferdinand and Sophie. They, too, belong among the victims. By daring to defy the Emperor, they paid for their happiness bit by bit, and—finally—with their lives. Oh, I knew the methods! Sarajevo was only possible with the imperial ministers' connivance. Franz Josef knew the dangers very well; he just sat back and watched."

"Indeed," Prince Lónyay murmured placidly, stroking his mustache as he watched the roe deer grazing on his terraced lawn.

"He allowed Prince Montenuovo to make the obloquies a hollow mockery. On the Duchess of Hohenberg's casket were placed the fan and white gloves of a lady-in-waiting. None of the imperial family—nor even the dead couple's children!—were permitted to attend the funeral. Karl, the new heir, did anger his great-uncle by going to the burial. Many of the realm's great families (my own included) were likewise represented. 'Every ass,' I remember Prince Windischgraetz remarking, 'is kicking the dead lion now!'"

"Having met the late Emperor Franz Josef," answered Holmes, "I can easily believe such an account. For all his public image as the benign 'Grandfather of Europe,' he was at heart a bitter and vindictive man.

"You know, Watson," pondered the detective, "it strikes me that over a quarter of a century, the deaths of Frederick III, Rudolf, Alexander Obrenović, and Franz Ferdinand had an unfortunate cumulative effect. Tragic though they were, each at the time seemed but an isolated incident. Yet, each brought the Great Powers one step closer to destroying the world in which you and I passed our best days. I shall not forget the words spoken by Sir Edward Grey on the evening after we brought von Bork to heel. 'The lamps,' he said, 'are going out all over Europe. We shall not see them lit again in our lifetime.'"

So ended our service to "The Crowned Heads of Europe." Our best endeavours had but postponed their fall and preserved our own country from immediate destruction. Yet, that in itself is a good deal. The lamps of Europe may never burn as brightly as on the fateful night Grey spoke those words. So long as the British Empire still endures, they cannot be extinguished altogether.

Annotated Bibliography

Major Sources

Allison, A.R., M.A., editor. *The War Diary of the Emperor Frederick III, 1870-1871.* Reprint edition. New York: Howard Fertig, Inc., 1988 [1926].

      Otto von Bismarck's anxiety to suppress Frederick's war diary was not motivated solely by his reluctance to share credit for German unification. As Crown Prince, the future emperor had foreseen the consequences of Bismarckian "Blood and Iron." He wrote on December 31, 1870: "In this nation of thinkers and philosophers, poets and artists . . . the world will recognize nothing but a people of conquerors and destroyers. . . . Bismarck has made us great and powerful, but he has robbed us of our friends, the sympathies of the world, and—our conscience. . . ." When excerpts from the diary were published in September 1888, the Dowager Empress was delighted; her son cried "Treason!"; and the Iron Chancellor threatened to prosecute the editor, Professor Heinrich Geffcken. The entire diary was not published until 1922, as Frederick III had directed.

Baedeker, Karl (firm). *Austria, Including Hungary, Transylvania, Dalmatia, and Bosnia.* London, Dulau and Co., 1900. Online at Emory University's Internet Archive:
https://archive.org/details/01703017.5423.emory.edu

_____. *Northern Germany: Handbook for Travellers.* London, Dulau and Co., 1886. Online at Emory University's Internet Archive:
https://archive.org/details/northerngermany08firgoog/page/n12/mode/2up.

_____. *Switzerland: and the Adjacent Portions of Italy, Savoy, and Tyrol: Handbook for Travellers.* London: Dulau and Co., 1897. Online at Emory University's Internet Archive:

https://archive.org/details/06105005.5436.emory.edu/page/n9/mode/2 up.

Without the Internet, the travel handbooks published by the German firm of Karl Baedeker must have been indispensable in Holmes's day. They were also indispensable for writing stories that depended as heavily on "place" as these. Following Holmes and Watson through Baedeker to Vienna, Trieste, or Belgrade all but restores Franz Josef's vanished realm to life. Contemporary German and Swiss handbooks are invaluable for touring Frederick III's Charlottenburg or the Cathédrale Saint-Pierre, and for locating von Bergmann's seedy Berlin hideaway or Elisabeth's elegant refuge in Geneva. For writers of historical pastiches, Baedeker's handbooks provide an authenticity that modern guidebooks cannot match.

Case of Emperor Frederick III: Full Official Reports by the German Physicians and by Sir Morell Mackenzie. The Reports of the German Physicians Translated by Henry Schweig, M.D. New York: Edgar S. Werner, 1888). Placed online by Google Books: https://books.google.com/books?id=G2DTAAAAMAAJ&pg=PA12& lpg=PA12&dq= Frederick+III%27s+cancer&source=bl&ots=0MYPfuoCby&sig=Ru6 zCctW2HUHjOPP_7i1iXbXORI&hl=en&sa=X&ved=0ahUKEwjI8d zg2ufNAhVD8CYKHREGAIA4ChDoAQhbMBA#v=onepage&q=Fr ederick%20III's%20cancer&f=false.

Readers interested in the medical aspects of "The Dying Emperor" may find it convenient to read competing accounts of Frederick's treatment in one online source. Ordered by Bismarck and edited by von Bergmann, *The Illness of Emperor Frederick III* appeared on July 11, 1888. Nearly all the German doctors contributed reports, but Mackenzie and Hovell were not invited to participate. Sir Morell's final rebuttal, entitled *The Fatal Illness of Frederick the Noble* (London: Sampson Low, Marston, Searle, & Rivington, 1888), was published before the year was out. Both the British and German treatises were highly polemical. Regarding the critical events of April 12, the versions of Mackenzie and von Bergmann are so irreconcilable that it is obvious at least one of them was lying. Fortunately, we have Watson to set the record straight.

Dedijer, Vladimir. *The Road to Sarajevo.* New York: Simon and Schuster, 1966.

Good background reading for the last three stories in the book. Dedijer is more even-handed than Rebecca West about the Obrenovićs, whom he covers only briefly. In a thorough analysis of Franz Ferdinand's political beliefs, plans to reorganize the empire, and foreign policy, Dedijer is more critical than King and Woolmans, emphasizing the Heir-Apparent's personality defects and "many enemies." The book offers a detailed account of the Sarajevo plot, seen primarily from the Serbian side. While acquitting the Archduke of the charge of warmonger, Dedijer firmly rejects the revisionism of post-World War I historians such as Sidney Bradshaw Fay, concluding that Germany indeed offered Austria-Hungary a "blank check" to settle her problems in the Balkans.

Hamann, Brigitte. *The Reluctant Empress.* Translated from the German by Ruth Hein. Berlin: Ullstein ip, 1986 [1982].

Brigitte Hamann's biography is a useful corrective to the romantic Sisi legend. The life of Elisabeth of Austria was no fairy tale. Betrothed at fifteen to her first cousin (the Habsburgs and Wittelsbachs had intermarried for generations past), the Bavarian princess found herself bound to an automaton, nagged by his domineering mother, and smothered by the protocol of his medieval court. Having done her duty by producing an heir, Elisabeth took refuge in total self-absorption. She wrote bad poetry but became an expert rider. She engaged in flirtations and guarded her reputation as a beauty by refusing to sit for portraits after turning thirty. A republican at heart, the Empress believed her empire had "outlived its usefulness." Her one political success was to wrest equality for Hungary from her besotted, if unfaithful, husband. After Rudolf's death, his mother blamed herself, believing her "tainted" Wittelsbach blood had led her son to madness. Elisabeth's last years were spent in lonely wandering; her quick and painless death was one she might have chosen. Indeed, assassination gave "the beautiful Sisi" a poignant and romantic end, maintaining an illusion that ultimately became more persuasive than the life behind it.

King, Greg and Sue Woolmans. *The Assassination of the Archduke: Sarajevo 1914 and the Romance that Changed the World.* New York: St. Martins Griffin, 2013.

Despite the title, King and Woolmans present a full-scale biography of the Sarajevo victims. They plausibly rehabilitate Franz Ferdinand from the many negative assessments of his character, such as Rebecca West's. There is also material on Duchess Sophie's family, the later lives of the couple's children, and the Hohenberg descendants' efforts to recover Konopischt from the Czech government. As for the assassinations, the authors (following Crown Princess Stéphanie) posit the complicity of Austro-Hungarian authorities who feared the Archduke's reform plans and desired a war with Serbia. While their coverage of political issues is as comprehensive as Dedijer's, King and Woolmans have primarily chronicled a love story that is too often overlooked—one equally tragic, and far less sordid, than the more famous tale of Mayerling.

King, Greg and Penny Wilson. *Twilight of Empire: The Tragedy at Mayerling and the End of the Habsburgs.* New York: St. Martin's Press, 2017.

Greg King returns with a new co-author to retell the tale of Mayerling. Unlike the absurdly cast Hollywood movie (1968), it is an unappetizing saga, for "The Inconvenient Heir-Apparent" ended his life closer to John Malkovich than Omar Sharif. His biographers reach substantially the same verdict on Rudolf as did Sherlock Holmes; they are less inclined than Frederic Morton (see below) to romanticize his life. The same holds true for the famous love affair. Mary Vetsera—mostly overlooked in Watson's narrative—emerges here as a wanton innocent, victimized first by her own mother, then by a lover who never intended to fulfill her foolish dreams. King and Wilson "rake through the coals" of Mayerling in exhaustive, forensic detail. Even though they are convinced that Rudolf was responsible, questions remain; the unwelcome conclusion Holmes presented to Franz

286

Josef is one of several theories mooted. Considering his hidebound father and often absent mother, it is no wonder that an intelligent but unstable prince like Rudolf came to a dire end. Disappointingly for the romantics, *Twilight of Empire* demonstrates that one of history's great romances was sadly overrated.

Pakula, Hannah. *An Uncommon Woman: The Empress Frederick.* New York: Simon and Schuster, 1995.

Sherlock Holmes and the Iron Chancellor made valid points about the Empress Frederick. She was undeniably a woman of rare intelligence and character, but her opportunity to establish a British-style constitutional monarchy in Germany came much too late. Through the whims of fate and her own errors, neither Victoria's husband nor her eldest son was able to fulfill her laudable ambition. Wilhelm's love-hate feelings toward his mother were reciprocated; nor was the fault entirely on his side. Their interactions improved once the Kaiser came to power, but the Dowager Empress's end was not an easy one. Afflicted with cancer of the breast and spine, she died only months after her own mother, having ensured that her and Frederick's archives would survive. Hannah Pakula's biography does full justice to a woman who would have been a superb Queen of England, but who expected too much of the very different country she aspired to rule.

Ponsonby, Sir Frederick, ed. *Letters of the Empress Frederick.* London: Macmillan and Co, Ltd., 1928.

Ponsonby was the son of Queen Victoria's private secretary, Sir Henry Ponsonby, whose wife Mary was an intimate friend and correspondent of the Empress Frederick. Shortly before her death in 1901, the Dowager Empress asked Ponsonby "to take charge of my letters and take them with you back to England" without informing her son, Wilhelm II. Captain Ponsonby locked up the letters in his private home, allowing him to assure German authorities that the late empress's letters had not been housed in the British Archives. Sir Frederick finally published them in reply to the German historian Emil Ludwig, whose 1927 biography of Wihelm contained (he thought) bitter and unjust criticisms of the Kaiser's mother, based on one-sided evidence. The Empress's letters to her mother are perhaps the most revealing, and most of the opinions she expressed to Holmes and Watson are reflected there.

Portland, William Cavendish-Bentinck, 6th Duke. *Men, Women, and Things: Memories of the Duke of Portland, K.G., G.C.V.O.* London: Faber & Faber, Ltd., 1937.

Reading his breezy memoir *Men, Women, and Things* leaves the impression that the Duke of Portland must have been a thoroughly delightful fellow. His Grace exhibits a refreshing sense of humor, an appreciation for beauty of all kinds (particularly the feminine variety), and a taste for acquiring the good things of life that his great wealth allowed him to indulge. Yet, he appears to have been free of snobbery and selfishness. Portland was indeed accounted "the best landlord in the country"; Duchess Winnie shared and encouraged her husband's charitable pursuits. One does wonder how the couple reconciled the relentless slaughter of pheasants at Welbeck Abbey's shooting parties with Her Grace's place as the longest-serving president of Britain's Society for the Protection of Birds. The Portlands must have possessed charm and tact to have attracted as prickly a character as Franz Ferdinand—who once admitted that he regarded anyone he met for the first time as a scoundrel! *Men, Women, and Things'* account of the Archduke's near-assassination is wonderfully discreet. Even writing a quarter-century after the event, the old duke depicted the occasion as a simple accident and revealed nothing of Holmes and Watson's role.

Röhl, John C. G. *Young Wilhelm: The Kaiser's Early Life, 1859-1888.* Cambridge: Cambridge University Press, 1998 [1993].

John Röhl's three-volume, 3,900-page biography of the last Kaiser must surely be the last word on this "nemesis of history." Volume I narrates his parents' dismal failure to make their son the German heir to Britain's constitutional tradition. Quoting Sigmund Freud, Röhl reveals that Wilhelm's withered arm, and baffling preference for soldiery over scholarship, caused his mother to withhold her love. His maternal adoration turned quickly to disdain. Unlike Wilhelm, Crown Prince Frederick was torn between British liberalism urged upon him by Victoria and Prussian autocracy and militarism embodied in his own (seemingly eternal) father. Even prior to falling ill with cancer, the hero of Sedan and Königgrätz was a weary, disillusioned man who had lost his son's respect. The Kaiser's first biographer, Emil Ludwig, concluded that Wilhelm waged "a life-long fight against his innate weakness." Although the Iron Chancellor's wily machinations in "The Dying Emperor" put an end to the family drama, his own expectation of controlling the new Kaiser died within two years. As Röhl concludes in his preface: "Not until it was too late did the Bismarcks . . . realize that the impulsive, cold, egotistical young Hohenzollern Prince . . . posed a danger not only to themselves, but also to the German Reich and the peace of Europe." By then, the nemesis had been unleashed.

Stevenson, R. Scott. *Morell Mackenzie: The Story of a Victorian Tragedy*. New York: Henry Schuman, 1947.

R. Scott Stevenson's biography of Mackenzie was evidently researched many years before its publication date. It includes the reminiscences of T. Mark Hovell, Sir Morell's assistant at Charlottenburg, who died in 1925. Hovell's contribution was substantial. It was he who verified von Bergmann's drunkenness on April 12 and confessed to spiriting away the Emperor's war diaries. He also offered perhaps the fairest verdict on his chief: "Morell Mackenzie was a great man, but he was a bit of a humbug as well." Similarly, Stevenson's tone toward his subject, while sympathetic and respectful, is not uncritical. He notes Sir Morell's stubbornness in resisting the cancer diagnosis even in late March 1888, as well as statistical errors in his refutation of von Bergmann. Conversely, he credits Mackenzie with great kindness to his patients (even paying to send one on a therapeutic sea voyage) and with a self-sacrificing dedication that contributed to his early death. Most woeful was Sir Morell's determination to publish the imprudent memoir that ruined his reputation, despite the warning of his loyal Hovell. Nevertheless, Stevenson is firmly on the British side in the medical dispute; he is especially hard on Felix Semon, whose jealousy led him to collude with the Germans to undermine his former mentor. Stevenson's biography should assist fair-minded laymen in sorting through the polemics and esoteric terminology of the medical reports.

West, Rebecca. *Black Lamb and Grey Falcon: A Journey Through Yugoslavia*. New York: The Penguin Group, 1982 [1940].

Shortly before World War II, the noted British novelist, journalist, socialist, and feminist Rebecca West made three trips to Yugoslavia and subsequently wrote this book, her masterpiece. In part a travelogue, it is more profoundly a meditation on the history, mythology, and culture of a region that Ms. West regarded as "the nexus of European history since the late

Middle Ages." Central to her tale is the Battle of Kosovo (1389), which ended the medieval Serbian Empire and doomed its people to five hundred years of foreign rule. Ms. West writes of that half-millennium with passion that becomes polemical and compassion that makes no pretense of being even-handed. The South Slavs, especially the Serbs, are the heroes of her story; anyone who stands in the way of their unity and freedom (Turks, Austrians, Nazis, even their unworthy rulers like the Obrenovićs) is fair game. Yet, Ms. West's passion is so pure, and her prejudice so frank, that she seldom misleads and invariably fascinates. Who else could write this summation of the Sarajevo murders: "At last the bullets had been coaxed out of the reluctant revolver to the bodies of the eager victims"? South Slavic history is, in any case, a tapestry of murders; the assassination of King Alexander (Karadjordjević) in 1934 was the event that drew Ms. West's attention to the region. It also, as she feared, signaled the failure of the Yugoslavian experiment years before the country fell to Hitler. Rebecca West poignantly dedicated *Black Lamb and Grey Falcon* "to my friends in Yugoslavia, who are now all dead or enslaved." Her book remains a lasting memorial to that lost kingdom, and to one of the most remarkable women the 20th century produced.

Other Works Consulted

Abrams, Robert C., M.D. "Sir James Reid and the Death of Queen Victoria: An Early Model for End-of-Life Care," *The Gerontologist*, Volume 55, Issue 6 (1 December 2015), pp. 943–50. Online at: https://academic.oup.com/gerontologist/article/55/6/943/2605449.

Baring-Gould, W[illiam] S[tuart]. *Sherlock Holmes of Baker Street*. Avenel, NJ: Wings Books, 1995 [1962].

Bob, Ellie. "Old Ship Inn: The oldest pub in Worksop." Our Nottinghamshire: A Community History Website. Online at: http://www.ournottinghamshire.org.uk/page_id__127.aspx?path = 0p31p53p71p.

Brook-Shepherd, Gordon. *Archduke of Sarajevo: The Romance & Tragedy of Franz Ferdinand of Austria.* Boston/Toronto: Little, Brown and Company, 1984.
An older biography by a reliable historian; so far as I know, the only other one in English.

Colgate, Isabel. *The Shooting Party.* Berkeley, California: Counterpoint, 2002 [1980].

Dangerfield, George. *The Strange Death of Liberal England, 1910-1914.* New York: Capricorn Books, 1961 [1935].

Durham, M. Edith. *Twenty Years of Balkan Tangle.* London: George Allen & Unwin Ltd., 1920. Online at Project Gutenberg: http://www.gutenberg.org/cache/epub/19669/pg19669-images.html.

The Esoteric Curiosa: "Meet the Portlands: Willie and Winnie Cavendish-Bentinck, the 6th Duke and Duchess!" (2011) The original article (ca. 1912) was entitled: "The Present Duke and Duchess: a Romantic Attachment." Online at: http://theesotericcuriosa.blogspot.com/2011/03/meet-portlands-willy-winnie-cavendish.html.

Flantzer, Susan. "Assassination of Empress Elisabeth of Austria (1898)." Online at: http://www.unofficialroyalty.com/assassination-of-empress-elisabeth-of-austria-1898/.
Includes information on, and a photograph of, Elisabeth's assassin, Luigi Lucheni.

_____. "Draga Mašin, Queen of Serbia." Online at: http://www.unofficialroyalty.com/draga-masin-queen-of-serbia/\
More on the unhappy lady who, before becoming queen, had at times earned her living as a translator, novelist, and journalist.

Heyman-Marsaw, Wendy. *Memoirs from Mrs. Hudson's Kitchen.* Edited by JoAnn and Mark Alberstat. London: MX Publishing, 2017.

Historic Hotels of the World, Then & Now: "1865: Hôtel Beau Rivage, Geneva." Online at: http://www.historichotelsthenandnow.com/beaurivagegeneva.html.

History Answers. "The Red Archduchess: The Hapsburg Heir Who Murdered an Actress & Defied the Nazis" (2015). Online at: https://www.historyanswers.co.uk/kings-queens/five-child-monarchs-who-changed-history/.
    The further adventures of Erzsi, Archduchess Elisabeth Marie. The article's subtitle only hits the highlights!

Jewison, Glenn and Jörg C. Steiner. "Austro-Hungarian Land Forces 1848-1918, Hujcze, September 6/7, 1914." Online at: http://www.austro-hungarian-army.co.uk/battles/hujcze.htm.
    This military site includes an account of the fate of Colonel Brosch von Aarenau, who died in battle with the Russians in the first days of the war.

Koenig, Marlene Koenig. "Royal Musings: Max Egon & Irma, Prince and Princess zu Fürstenberg." Online at: http://royalmusingsblogspotcom.blogspot.com/2012/01/max-egon-irma-prince-and-princess-zu.html.
    One of the Kaiser's more colorful courtiers. After his imperial master's fall, the Prince lived long enough to finish his days as a Nazi.

LemsfordLHG. "Thomas Mark Hovell, FRCS (1853-1935 [sic])." Online at: http://www.lemsfordhistorynews.co.uk/LFHovells.html.
    The article's text states correctly that Hovell died in 1925. More information on him may be found in Stevenson's biography of Sir Morell Mackenzie.

Longford, Elizabeth. *Queen Victoria: Born to Succeed.* New York: Pyramid Books, 1966.

Manchester, William. *The Arms of Krupp, 1597-1968.* Boston/Toronto: Little, Brown and Company, 1968.

Marcum. David. *Sherlock Holmes and a Quantity of Debt.* London: MX Publishing, 2013.

_____. "The Adventure of the Other Brother" from *The Papers of Sherlock Holmes: Volume One & Volume Two.* London: MX Publishing, 2014.

_____. "The Adventure of the Old Brownstone" in *Holmes Away from Home: Adventures from the Great Hiatus*, Vol. II, 1893-1894. Manchester, NH: Belanger Books, 2016.

Martin, Ralph G. *Jennie: The Life of Lady Randolph Churchill.* New York: New American Library edition, 1970.

Met[eorological] Office of the United Kingdom. Monthly Weather Reports. Online at: https://www.metoffice.gov.uk/research/library-and-archive/archive-hidden-treasures/monthly-weather-reports.

Morton, Frederic. *A Nervous Splendor: Vienna 1888/1889.* Boston/Toronto: Little, Brown and Company, 1979.

_____. *Thunder at Twilight: Vienna, 1913/1914.* New York: Charles Scribner's Sons, 1989.

Nottinghamshire History: Resources for local historians and genealogists. "Country homes: Welbeck Abbey, The seat of the Duke

of Portland." *Country Life*, 19 (1906). Online at:
http://www.nottshistory.org.uk/articles/places_wx.htm.

Ready, Set, Jet Set. "Checking in at the Hotel Beau Rivage, Geneva, Switzerland." Online at:
https://www.readysetjetset.net/travel/checking-in-hotel-beau-rivage-geneva-switzerland.

Redmond, Christopher. *Lives Beyond Baker Street: A Biographical Dictionary of Sherlock Holmes's Contemporaries*. London: MX Publishing, 2016.

Remak, *Sarajevo: The Story of a Political Murder*. New York: Criterion Books, 1959.

John C.G. Röhl. *Wilhelm II: the Kaiser's Personal Monarchy, 1888-1900*. Cambridge: Cambridge University Press, 2004.

_____. *Wilhelm II: Into the Abyss of War and Exile, 1900-1941*. Cambridge: Cambridge University Press, 2008.

Satzinger, Helmut. "Crown Prince Rudolf Hunting in Egypt" (slideshow, 2013). Online at:
https://www.slideshare.net/helmutsatzinger/crown-prince-rudolf.

Silver, Carl E., M.D. "The Case of Emperor Frederick III: A Medical-Political Tragedy." Tempe, AZ: *Emeritus Voices: The Journal of the Emeritus College of A[rizona] S[tate] U]niversity*, 2006. Online at:
https://emerituscollege.asu.edu/sites/default/files/ecdw/EVoice6/frederick.html.

Stout, Rex. *Over My Dead Body*. New York: Bantam Books, 1994 [1940].

Turley, Thomas A. "Chairman of an Aulic Council: The Eighth Duke of Devonshire and British Imperial Defence, 1895-1903." Ph.D. dissertation, Vanderbilt University, 1985.

Vivian, Herbert. *The Servian Tragedy, with Some Impressions of Macedonia* (London: Grant Richards, 1904. Online at: https://babel.hathitrust.org/cgi/pt?id=uc2.ark:/13960/t8gf0qz02&view =1up&seq=9.

Watson, Grieg. "Could Franz Ferdinand Welbeck gun accident have halted WWI?" BBC News. 25 November 2013. Online at: https://www.bbc.com/news/uk-england-nottinghamshire-25008184#:~:text=The%20deaths%20set%20in%20train,halted%20th e%20march%20of%20war.

White, Robert. "Worksop, The Dukery, and Sherwood Forest" (1875). Nottinghamshire History: Resources for local historians and genealogists. Online at: http://www.nottshistory.org.uk/white1875/welbeckp1.htm.

Wilson, Mrs. Flora Northesk. *Belgrade, the White City of Death: Being the History of King Alexander and of Queen Draga.* London: R.A. Everett and Co., Ltd., 1903. Online at: https://www.google.com/books/edition/Belgrade_the_White_City_of_Death/HvUDAAAAYAAJ?hl=en&gbpv=1.

Wyon, Reginald and Gerald Prance. *The Land of the Black Mountain.* London: Methuen & Co., 1903, online at: http://www.hellenicaworld.com/Montenegro/Literature/PranceWyon/e n/TheLandOfTheBlackMountain.html.

CPSIA information can be obtained
at www.ICGtesting.com
Printed in the USA
LVHW030352020721
691685LV00004B/260

9 781787 057715